Her lungs burned, her thigh muscles straining under the burst of adrenaline shooting through her veins.

Two soldiers jumped out of the chopper with their rifles up, and her heart gave a great leap of fear. She almost stopped, but remembered Dec's warning and kept sprinting. The men fired past her, the muzzles of their guns spewing fire in the darkness. The bullets sang as they whizzed past her, some close enough she felt their heat. Was Dec still out there behind her?

Halfway there. Keep running.

One of the soldiers motioned with his arm, waving it toward the ground as she drew closer. *Don't stop! Keep going.* He was yelling something, but she couldn't hear him over the rotors.

His arm kept moving, and as she drew nearer, she saw the urgency on his face, saw his mouth move.

"Get *d-o-o-w-n!*"

Terror froze her. Her heart rang in her ears. Everything morphed into slow motion. Instinctively covering her head with her arms, she dove. A blast exploded behind her, rendering her blind and deaf. She plowed into the ground as sharp and hot objects peppered her arm and back, like she'd been stung by a swarm of angry bees.

Disoriented, terrified, she lurched up onto her knees, saw the soldier from the helicopter running flat out toward her. The wounds burned like hellfire, and something warm was dripping over her skin. Blood. Her blood.

Pushing to her feet, she staggered a step, then fell flat. She scrambled up again, determined not to die out here in the desert when she was so close to safety.

Praise for *Out of Her League*

"Ms. Cross writes well, with smoothness and polish and her ability to create sub plots means that she makes a [stalker] theme refreshing. Go for it—this is a super read."

~Between the Lines WRDF Review

Cover of Darkness

by

Kaylea Cross

Cover of Darkness

Cover Art by *Kim Mendoza*

The Wild Rose Press
PO Box 706
Adams Basin, NY 14410-0706
Visit us at www.thewildrosepress.com

Publishing History
First Crimson Rose Edition, 2010
Print ISBN 1-60154-603-3
Digital ISBN 978-1-60154-603-6

Published in the United States of America

Dedication

To Todd and the weasels. Thanks for your support in helping me realize my dream; I know it isn't always easy. Love you guys.

I would also like to thank Captain Kevin Cmolik of the Royal British Columbia Dragoons, and Bob Mayer, US Army, retired, for their invaluable information during the writing of this book. Any mistakes made are mine.

Chapter One

Day 1, Beirut
Evening

As the platter of deviled eggs passed by, Bryn McAllister's stomach howled in protest beneath her elegant Versace dress. The fruit and croissant she'd snagged on her way to the armored Range Rover that had taken them to the embassy that morning had worn off about six hours ago. But her father had more important things to worry about than interrupting their crammed schedule for lunch. She eyed the plates on the buffet longingly.

"Hungry?"

She glanced to her right and caught the American ambassador's knowing smile. "Starving."

"No doubt your father kept you busy all day without thinking to feed you."

"Yes." Not that she'd expected anything different. It was always like that when he was working. Her father, a constant whirlwind of energy, would never think to eat unless one of his staff brought him something. She should be grateful they had so many dinner functions to attend while she was here for her visit, otherwise she might starve.

The ambassador leaned over, his blue eyes twinkling behind rimless glasses. "Food's probably another forty-five minutes away. Wait here and I'll see if I can sneak us a piece of bread."

"You're a godsend," she whispered back, smiling as he left the table.

As she followed his progress across the dining

1

room, a movement caught her attention, and her gaze halted on a waiter standing in the corner. She would have looked away, but something about the guy's posture didn't feel right.

Stiff against the back wall, dressed in a crisp white uniform, the slightly-built man radiated tension. She watched him for another minute, noting how his gaze darted about him, and how he kept wiping his upper lip across his shoulder. He seemed to be sweating profusely, even though the embassy dining room was quite comfortable, almost cool with the air conditioning. In her halter-neck, peacock-blue silk evening gown and high-heeled sandals, Bryn bordered on the verge of chilly.

Yet the man in the corner appeared to be melting like butter in a hot sauté pan.

Either he had a fever, or he was uneasy about something.

Her instincts went on alert. Then she chided herself for being paranoid. Security was tight, the guards well trained. Ben, her friend and head of her father's security team, had personally checked the place over before leaving. The embassy would have screened the staff working tonight. Armed U.S. Marines were standing at the door. She needed to ramp her suspicions down a few octaves and enjoy the evening.

"Your father always boasted to me about how intelligent and beautiful his daughter was, Bryn, but until I met you tonight I thought he was lying."

Tearing her gaze away from the waiter, she turned to the other American diplomat seated beside her and regained her polite smile. "Thank you for the compliment. It's nice to know my father thinks so highly of me."

Especially since he'd been conspicuously absent throughout most of her life.

The American's plump cheeks, already pink

from his third glass of red wine, glowed even more. His bushy white eyebrows reminded her of two fuzzy caterpillars crawling over his forehead. "You must take after your mother."

Bryn cocked a brow. "Why do you say that?"

"Because no man as hard as Jamul could be credited with making such a breathtaking daughter."

She shared a friendly laugh with him, glancing over to wink at her father directly across the polished mahogany table. A handsome man, he was in his late sixties, his once raven hair liberally peppered with gray, his clean-shaven jaw a little softer than it had been in his youth, but still strong. A tall and imposing figure even at his age, his sharp, black eyes gleamed with the shrewdness he was legendary for. She'd inherited his coloring and keen mind, her mother's looks and easy way with people. The best of both worlds in her gene pool, she liked to think.

"My daughter is a rare flower," her father acknowledged with a raise of his glass.

It was stupid, but Bryn blushed at the public praise.

"Now, if you're done trying to win over my only child, Ambassador, let's get back to the task at hand."

The diplomat gave a long-suffering sigh and shook his head at her. "Your father, he never knows when to relax and enjoy himself. Jamul," he said to her father, "we're having a fine evening here. Good food, expensive wine, your charming daughter to converse with...my advisers and the entire Lebanese interior ministry here enjoying themselves." He gestured to the other men and their female companions seated down the length of the table. "And all you want to do is talk business."

"Perhaps my priorities are different than yours,"

her father suggested.

Her dinner companion gave her an exasperated look. "Has he always been this way?"

Bryn nodded, her smile sharp. "Always."

She'd grown up knowing all about his 'priorities,' and that she and her mother had been at the bottom of his list. That was why her mother had moved home to Baltimore when she was six months pregnant with Bryn. Being a single mother was far easier at home with family around to help than living a lonely existence in the same house with the father of your child.

"Lebanon still has many wounds to heal, as you are aware," her father reminded his guest. "There is much to be done to stabilize our government and the region."

Yes, but would anything ever be enough to bring peace? The Middle East's issues were so complex they were overwhelming. She had the feeling her father had summoned her to Beirut for this summit because of her dual citizenship. As Jamul Daoud's half-Lebanese, half-American daughter, she was the perfect addition to the diplomatic conference. She wouldn't put it past him to use her as a sort of human icebreaker, someone to soften the edges around the conference's intent and serve as a living embodiment of the two cultures.

When it came to manipulating something to his advantage, nothing he did would surprise her. He was as ruthless and determined in his resolve as he was shrewd, which was why he had been appointed to serve in the Lebanese cabinet for the past seventeen years.

Bryn knew deep in her bones that his inviting her to stay with him for a couple of weeks had less to do with seeing her and everything to do with this important summit. In fact, most of her visits with him since adulthood had coincided with diplomatic events. She didn't mind, but it would have been nice to have some time for just the two of them.

The American ambassador returned to his seat with a secretive smile and passed her a roll under the table. She accepted it with a conspiratorial wink and tore off a piece, popped it discreetly into her mouth and listened carefully while one of the ambassadors discussed the positions of the different political factions in and around Beirut and the rest of the war-torn country.

Her father, ever the analytical businessman, saw the necessity in maintaining strong ties with the United States. While many of his countrymen hated America and all it represented, Jamul knew his country needed U.S. assistance to survive. A necessary evil, if you will. She kept silent, missing nothing, and during a lull in the conversation turned part of her attention back to the strangely behaving waiter across the room.

He'd moved next to the window facing the front of the building, and as she watched, he darted an anxious glance down at the street below. When he looked up, their gazes locked for an instant. She could have sworn he froze for a split second, then broke eye contact and hurried into the kitchen, out of view.

Weird, she thought, taking a sip of champagne. Something was bothering that guy. He looked almost frightened. The forerunners of unease prickled up her spine. She was definitely going to keep a close eye on him, and if he kept behaving strangely, she'd quietly say something to one of the security guards. Better to look like an alarmist than sit and do nothing.

Responding to the conversation where necessary, taking it all in, Bryn remained vigilant for the waiter. He reappeared a few minutes later and stayed close to that same window, wiped his perspiring face twice, three times, dark eyes shifting this way and that, avoiding her gaze. She stared directly at him, instinct shrieking at her that something was wrong.

Anti-American sentiment was at an all-time high in the region. Beirut itself had its share of known terror cells and many more that were yet unknown. Security was extremely tight in the city, especially around its government institutions and officials. Her own father lived in his compound-like house with bodyguards and other security personnel. Cameras scanned the grounds, and snipers took shifts protecting the property.

Many groups would love to see Jamul Daoud dead because of his desire to maintain political relations with the U.S. Maybe others would love to see it happen because he'd had a daughter with an American woman.

Another waiter, taller, with a small scar bisecting his chin, came and stood next to the first one, then leaned down to murmur something to him. The tight anxiety on the small man's face melted away, replaced by acute relief. He shuffled away to the kitchen and moments later came back with a covered silver dish.

With what seemed to her like the utmost concentration, he placed it ever so carefully on the buffet table against the far wall, then hurried out of the dining room without looking back. The last piece of him she saw before he disappeared was his sleeve as it wiped across his forehead.

She glanced to either side of her to find out if anyone else had noticed the strange behavior, but everyone seemed engrossed in their own conversations. Maybe she was making too much of it.

She turned her attention back to the second waiter, still positioned by the window. A flare of shock hit her when she realized he was staring back at her. Those dark eyes seemed to burn right through her, brimming with hatred, paralyzing her.

Then he smirked. An evil smirk that sent a cold wave of fear up her spine. He knew she'd been watching them. Still holding her gaze, he drew his finger across his throat in a slow slitting motion, then walked away.

The implication of the gesture chilled her.

She shot to her feet, panic grabbing her. "Somebody stop him!" she cried, and the waiter jolted into a run at her words. Everyone at the table stared up at her in shock. "That waiter, stop him!"

Her father frowned at the unseemly interruption and set his silverware down, his brows lowered. "What—"

The waiter was almost past the guards now.

"That man, get him," she continued, shoving her chair back and almost tripping on the hem of her gown as she pointed impotently after him. Why wasn't anyone *doing* anything? Her alarm must have been obvious, because the others at the table had grown silent, staring at her.

"Security!" With her heart in her throat, she struggled to get past the ambassador, gesturing wildly to the security guards. Why didn't they see her? She was waving and yelling like a crazy woman.

A terrible thought occurred to her. Were they in on it? Was that why no one was doing anything?

Her father dropped his napkin on the table and shot to his feet, his face concerned. "Bryn, what are you doing?"

"Just stop him, quick!" She couldn't afford to wait and explain, so she rushed toward the two Marines standing guard as fast as she could in an evening dress and four-inch heels. They finally noticed her, their posture stiffening at the alarm on her face. God, why was everything happening so slowly?

Her father barked a quick command and they'd just gone out the doors after the waiter when the power went out. Heart pounding in the sudden blackness, Bryn skidded to a stop amidst the gasps of the stunned dinner guests. Shouts and three distinct gunshots rang out from down the hall.

Pandemonium erupted around her.

"Get down! Everybody get down!" More security agents rushed in, yelling instructions.

Bryn hit the floor and crawled under the nearest table, breath heaving in and out. What the hell was going on? Some kind of terrorist plot?

A second later an explosion ripped through the room, shattering glass and sending a wall of orange fire through the air. The force of it threw Bryn backwards and slammed her into the wall. She lay there, winded and disoriented. Her head spun. People screamed and sobbed around her, men shouting in English and Arabic, rushing around. She could barely see in the darkness.

Strong hands grabbed her under the shoulders and yanked her roughly out from under the table. Too weak to protest, she moaned as her rubbery legs gave out and she was dragged across the glass-and-debris-strewn carpet, crying out as jagged shards sliced at her skin. The man helping her was speaking in rapid Arabic. It took her a moment to focus on the words, but when her brain processed them, she realized what he was saying. He had the 'traitor's daughter.' He was not her savior, but her captor.

Well, he had picked the wrong target. She would not go quietly, no matter how dazed she was.

She struggled frantically in his hard grip, managed to land an elbow to his ribs, and he swore. Twisting free, she crawled forward a few feet, her damned dress tangling around her legs. Someone else grabbed her and she flipped onto her back with a cry of rage, lashing out with all her strength, using her high heels as daggers.

Her feet hit nothing but air, and when she tried to gain her equilibrium, a thick arm wrapped around her throat, cutting off her breath. She tried to jerk her head back, but it only bounced off her assailant's chest, so she slammed both fists upward, making solid contact on bone. The instant the pressure around her throat lessened, she fought her way free and lunged forward. Smoke burned her eyes and throat. She coughed and blinked fast, blinded by the dimness and her watering eyes.

Amidst the burning wreckage of the room, people still scrambled around. She couldn't see her father as she weaved toward the sliver of light coming from the broken door that led to the hallway. Where was he? Was he hurt?

Chest heaving, lungs burning with the effort, she crawled over to claw at the heavy wooden door, desperate for some light so she could see in the ruined room. Hands wrenched her backward. Someone hit her hard across the back of the neck and something sharp stabbed into her shoulder. She had only a second to register the burn of the needle before everything went black.

Chapter Two

Day 1, Off the Lebanon coast
Evening

Seated in the officers' mess hall, Navy SEAL Lieutenant Declan McCabe took another sip of his blessedly hot coffee and tried to figure out the last clue to complete his crossword puzzle, enjoying the rare moment of solitude. It felt damned good to have some downtime after spending the past four months in and around Iraq, deep in enemy territory. He and his team had earned this leave coming to them, and everybody was looking forward to going home in the next day or two.

Hard footfalls on the linoleum made him glance up. The approaching Navy captain's face was grim.

"You'd better come see this," he said.

Dec rose, already on alert because of that serious expression. "What's up, sir?"

"CNN's broadcasting a bombing at the embassy in Beirut," the captain replied as he led the way down the hall.

Dec's muscles tightened. Beirut was only miles from where the carrier was patrolling. If a SEAL team was needed, they'd probably get the call.

Entering the media room, his eyes locked on the flat-screen TV anchored to the far wall. The embassy was in flames. The explosion had been big, killing at least three and wounding dozens more. Several terrorist groups were suspected, but none had been positively identified.

Dec ran through the immediate possibilities.

Hezbollah came to mind. So did Hamas, Fatah and Al Qaeda. One report said a Lebanese official had been kidnapped, along with an American civilian.

A hostage extraction like that had SEALs written all over it, and since they were the closest team, he prepared himself for the call. His training had him scanning the footage of the burning wreckage for entry and exit points, places where a sniper might take refuge. He searched the crowd for faces he might recognize, but didn't see anyone familiar.

The captain looked at him over his shoulder. "Guess you boys won't be going stateside yet."

"No sir, guess not." Another mission was about to be dropped into their laps. Dec studied the footage a minute longer, then left to find his team and give them the heads up.

****

Day 1, Syria
Late evening

In his Damascus hotel room, Luke Hutchinson picked up the remote to turn up the volume on the TV and then placed it back on the nightstand next to his loaded Glock. An Al Jazeera anchor outlined the bombing and possible kidnapping at the U.S. Embassy in Beirut.

Dammit, he'd *known* his target had been about to do something big. No one else had considered the threat credible, however.

He bet they were sorry now.

As for the city the attack had happened in... God, he fucking *hated* Beirut. He'd served two long tours in that shit-hole back in the eighties and still considered it the worst deployment he'd been on. He'd seen and done a lot of ugly things in his fifty years, but Beirut had surpassed them all.

He listened dispassionately to the report, taking in the images of people being rescued from the building, their clothes and faces covered in smoke and soot. A high-ranking Lebanese cabinet minister had been at the embassy for a state dinner when the bomb had gone off. Information was sketchy, but so far at least two deaths had been confirmed. One source said the cabinet minister was unaccounted for. Another placed his daughter at the scene, and now missing as well.

Tension spread through his gut. Jamul. He could have been at the embassy for the dinner. And he had a daughter. A half-American daughter who visited him each summer. A perfect target if you were a terrorist who wanted some international attention and a whole lot of ransom money to fund your activities.

Like Farouk Tehrazzi.

His cell phone buzzed against his hip. He stared at the caller ID screen and his stomach squeezed tighter when he recognized his son's number. Even though they'd half-assed patched up their rocky relationship a few months back, Rayne wouldn't be calling at this hour just to say hi. No doubt he'd seen the coverage on CNN and feared his friend was in trouble.

Shit, sometimes he hated being right.

He hit the talk button. "Hey, Rayne."

"Sorry to call so late—"

"I wasn't asleep." No surprise there. He didn't sleep much at the best of times.

"I'm watching CNN right now and there's been a bombing—"

"I know. I'm watching it too."

His son sighed. "Think it might be Bryn? Mom told me she was flying out early this week to visit her dad, and now they're talking about this politician's daughter possibly being kidnapped."

"Yeah. I'll find out what I can, okay? I'll call you when I know something." He didn't have to tell his son he couldn't say where he was, or what he was doing. As a former Marine and son of a Navy SEAL, Rayne had known from an early age there were certain things he could never know about his dad.

"I'd appreciate it. Think there'll be a rescue attempt?"

"SEALs, probably." His own SEAL team had done many a hostage extraction, and he knew American officials would already be scrambling to put a plan together. If they went in, Luke bet he knew who would get the job. One name kept coming up from the SEAL community, a rising star within its ranks: Lieutenant Declan McCabe. "Bet it's in the works right now. I mean, she's an American citizen, daughter of a Lebanese official who happens to be a big U.S. ally. Plus her story's all over CNN."

"Any chance you'll be involved? We're all really worried about her."

A picture of Bryn came up on the screen, and Luke was surprised at how much she resembled her mother. "Just tell your mom and pretty fiancée I'm on it. That's the best I can promise for now." At least his ex-wife hadn't called him to find out what was going on herself. A conversation with Emily always made him feel like he was breathing in broken glass.

He ended the call and stared thoughtfully at the screen, into Bryn's dark eyes. His mind put the pieces of the puzzle together. The group claiming responsibility had strong ties to the man he'd been hunting for the past three years. Radical religious zealots, willing to sacrifice their lives for their faith and take as many Americans as possible with them. Not a good sign for the lovely Miss McAllister or her father.

He picked up the hotel phone and dialed a room number. "Davis, you watching this?"

"Yes, sir. What do you want to do?"

"Meet me in the lobby in ten minutes." He crossed the room to pack, then decided to take a quick, hot shower first. God only knew when he'd be able to have another one. When finished, he toweled off and grabbed his duffel from the closet, tossed in some clothes, fake passports and an extra pistol and loaded magazines. They could pick up the rest of the necessary equipment on the way to the Lebanese border.

Al Jazeera showed a picture of Jamul in Beirut back in the eighties, during the civil war that had torn the country apart. His old friend's and the girl's best hope of rescue lay in a covert black-ops mission. If they were still alive, the current generation of his SEAL brothers would get them out. And that meant he and Lieutenant McCabe would be crossing paths soon.

Luke had information that might be useful to them, and he'd make sure they got it. But for now, Farouk Tehrazzi and his group were somewhere near Beirut, probably on their way to the Syrian border. Luke hoped he and the other CIA operatives would get to them before the SEALs did, or it was likely none of the terrorists would be alive to lead them to Tehrazzi and his handlers.

In Luke's experience, terrorists tended not to go quietly into the night when a Spec Ops team went in after them. With any luck, Tehrazzi would be captured and he'd lead them right up the food chain to the big fish himself. And then they'd put an end to Muqtada al-Sadr's reign of power and help stabilize Iraq's security.

Stepping to the door, Luke tucked his pistol into his waistband, pulled the hem of his t-shirt over it, then picked his duffel up off the floor. He checked through the peephole to ensure the hallway was empty, then disarmed all his custom security devices from the door and slipped them into his pants pocket as he walked out.

Davis was waiting for him in the lobby. He was a former Green Beret, now a seasoned CIA officer and physically perfect for Luke's needs on this job. Average height, medium brown hair, medium brown eyes, medium build. He could have been Middle Eastern, Spanish, Russian, Romanian. People tended not to notice him because of his plain appearance, and that made him a highly effective operative.

Those who dismissed him as harmless missed the razor-sharp intelligence and lethality in his eyes. Luke knew firsthand how wrong they were.

As he approached, Davis raised his brows. "What's up?"

"Hunting season's starting early this year. Let's go."

****

Day 2, Somewhere near the Syrian border
Dawn

"Put the woman in here," Farouk Tehrazzi ordered. Heart full of glee, he watched as two of his men brought their unconscious prisoner out of the battered pickup and carried her down the crumbling steps to the cellar beneath the dilapidated house. He'd dreamed of this day for so long he could hardly believe it was happening.

The plan had gone off exactly as he'd hoped. His superiors would be very pleased with him.

"What about the old man?"

With loathing, Tehrazzi glanced at the unconscious body in the bed of the pickup. The only thing he hated more than Americans were those who claimed to be Muslims and licked the feet of the

15

western infidels like starving dogs. His upper lip curled in a sneer of disdain.

"Throw him down there with the woman, but make sure you chain him on the other side of the room."

The men hauled the second prisoner out and dumped him in the opposite corner, chained his ankle and wrist to a pipe and came back out. Yet as he stared down at the dark-haired daughter, Tehrazzi felt an unwelcome twinge of guilt. Islam discouraged harming innocents. For a moment, standing above her inert form, he saw a vision of the depths of hell and his body writhing in its fiery maw. Suppressing a shiver of unease, he reminded himself she was an American, and the illegitimate daughter of his enemy. Still, he almost felt sorry for her. Her death would not be a kind one.

All those years ago he had watched her from afar, gauging her conduct, disappointed that she behaved with a good amount of decorum. It would have been far easier to hate her for having the moral corruption so common among her peers. Jamul's daughter was not like anyone else, though. She'd even stopped once and held the door for him, despite the load of books she'd carried.

Of course she hadn't known who he was, or that he knew all about her and her father. Still, he remembered the dazzle of her friendly smile when he'd made eye contact with her and thanked her. It irritated him that she'd made him aware of her as a man. That bothered him even more than the guilt squirming in his heart for involving her this way.

But now was not the time for reminiscing. His people were suffering all over the world because of men like Jamul Daoud. Muslim women were being raped, children were being killed or starved in the Palestinian territories, in Iraq, Chechnya and Afghanistan. He had a duty to Allah to rid his land of the Zionist and Christian invaders, and Jamul and his daughter would serve as a symbol of his authority.

Steeling himself against another wave of pity for the woman, Tehrazzi started to close the trap door.

"They'll need water," one of his men observed. "Some food, or they'll be dead before we can get the money."

Tehrazzi paused. Looking him straight in the eye, he deliberately let the door slam shut, sealing the two prisoners in their earthen tomb. "Let them rot." He ignored the men's shocked expressions and climbed back into the truck. What did he care about money? His benefactors kept a steady flow coming to him, ensuring he could buy as many supplies and weapons as he needed. The prisoners' deaths would send a far more powerful message to the authorities than any ransom demand he could make.

For a moment two of his men stood there in indecision, casting hesitant glances at each other and the cellar door. If they thought to disobey him and take the traitors food and water, he would shoot them dead on the spot. He would not tolerate disobedience or insubordination. They must have seen the threat in his eyes, because they scrambled up into the back of their pickup quickly enough.

Tamping down the guilt nipping at his conscience, he climbed into the cab. The driver gunned the engine and pulled away in the growing light, bringing a breeze scented with smoke from cooking fires. As they swept past, villagers peeked nervously out of their curtained windows. A sense of peace washed through him as they cleared the village and started across the open desert. Tehrazzi smiled as the air blew pleasantly over his face, the guilt disappearing.

"Allah-u-akbar," he murmured. *God is great.*

****

Day 2, Syrian village near Lebanese border
Early morning

The buzzing of flies woke her. Bryn fought to open her heavy eyelids, blinked groggily in the trickle of light coming through a crack in the ceiling. Where was she? How had she gotten here?

The gag they'd shoved into her mouth almost choked her. She tried to push it out with her tongue, but it was useless. She was so thirsty, and her lips were so dry they felt like they might split open. When she tried to sit up, her hands and feet wouldn't move. Then she realized why.

They'd bound her hands and feet, her arms behind her, and now they were asleep. She hurt all over. Her muscles felt bruised, and the cuts in her arms stung. Her head pounded dully. When her fingers encountered the thick padding of duct tape around her wrists and the pipe she was secured to, her heart leapt in alarm. Breathing fast through her nose, Bryn cast an urgent look around the dirt-floored room and saw her father tied up in the far corner.

She tried to say his name, but only unintelligible sounds came out. He didn't stir. Was he dead? Hurt so badly he was unable to respond?

Don't panic. You cannot afford to panic, and it won't do you any good. You have to think. Calm down and think.

She fought to regain control of her breathing. Bits of the abduction came back to her. The waiter running out the dining room doors, the terrible roar and force of the explosion, the heat of the fireball it generated. People screaming. Someone dragging her away and then the blow to her neck. The sting of the needle. Her head still throbbed in a dull, sickening pain. Little cuts along her right leg and arm stung where the shards of glass and debris had nicked her in the explosion and when she'd been dragged across the floor.

Who had done this to them? Why? Would they come back and torture them for information? She swallowed, her heart skipping a beat.

The best hope would be for a ransom, because that meant they would be kept alive. For the time being at least. But what if their captors had kidnapped them to prove a point, and they had already served their purpose?

No. Stop it. If they wanted to kill you, you'd already be dead.

Wouldn't she? Her father was an important Lebanese politician. Surely his life was of value to his government, even if hers wasn't. Did anyone even know she was missing?

The breath sawed in and out of her lungs. Cold, clammy sweat filmed her skin in the already stifling room. She was totally helpless this way, tied up without even being able to squirm into a sitting position. The best she could do was pull herself up and struggle to her knees, keeping her head bent to prevent it from hitting the low ceiling. When she glanced above her, she made out a faint line of light coming from what she surmised to be the only point of entry into the cellar-like room. No windows, no doors. No food, no water.

Oh God, no water...

The temperature seemed to increase with every minute, so she guessed the sun must still be climbing. Morning. That meant she'd been unconscious for most of the night. Whatever they'd drugged her with had left her feeling like she had the worst hangover. Her head was fuzzy, tongue dry as sand, the gag making it worse. Just thinking of how thirsty she was launched her into another wave of anxiety.

Again she tried to yell against the gag to wake her father, but he still didn't move. Tears burned her eyes. She was so tired, hot and thirsty. Not to mention terrified.

As the minutes ticked by the air grew thicker, the temperature rising steadily. Bryn sucked in precious oxygen through her nose, gasping and sweating as she knelt on the hard-packed dirt floor.

If it kept getting hotter, in another hour or two she figured this place would be too hot to survive in. She'd know pretty damn quick what her captors had in store for them, because if someone didn't come soon to at least give them water, they'd be dead before sunset.

Chapter Three

Day 2, Beirut
Noon

Lieutenant Declan McCabe and his squad of SEALs jumped out of the idling Black Hawk and hustled across the expanse of asphalt separating them from the building serving as the command center. The heat radiating from the ground was intense, especially in combat boots, battle dress utilities and sixty-odd pounds of gear. A group of U.S. Marines guarding the command center saluted his team smartly as they passed through the entrance and made their way to the second floor.

While the rest of the team waited outside the mahogany double doors, Dec went into the briefing room. His executive officer, Harris, was already seated at the long central table along with other military officials. They all looked up when he entered.

"Lieutenant," the XO acknowledged, and made a quick round of introductions. "And this is Luke Hutchinson, a former SEAL," he finished.

Whoa. So the legendary operative really did exist. Dec nodded at the middle-aged man seated across from him, noting his quiet air of power and the direct stare of those dark eyes. "Sir."

"Luke's fine," he corrected in a Southern accent. "I've been out of the Teams a long time now."

That may be, Dec thought, but the guy didn't look like someone you wanted to mess with, even though he had to be in his fifties.

"Luke's a contractor for the CIA and has firsthand knowledge of our targets," the officer continued. "He did a couple of tours in Beirut—"

Poor bastard, Dec thought. He'd known guys that had served in Beirut in the eighties and they always said what a shit-hole it was. Not much had changed, unfortunately.

"—and knows Jamul Daoud personally. He's also working on breaking up certain Mahdi army and Hezbollah cells you've already been briefed about, and one of them's the group claiming responsibility for this latest bombing and abduction." Harris pushed a file across the desk to him. "You already know about Daoud, but here's the file on his daughter."

Dec opened the manila folder and got his first good look at Bryn—pronounced Brin—McAllister. CNN hadn't done her justice. Exotic, black eyes and long, straight dark hair falling from a sharp widow's peak. Five feet, nine inches, a hundred and forty pounds, no health problems. Social worker; hailed from Baltimore but now lived in Lincoln City, Oregon.

No significant other, no siblings, mother and stepfather lived back east. No criminal record or tattoos, but she had an appendectomy scar on her lower right abdomen and a small mole below her left ear. Masters degree in sociology and a black belt in Karate. Well, well. Wasn't that interesting? She wasn't nearly as helpless as she looked. Too bad it hadn't saved her from the bastards when they'd shanghaied her at the embassy dinner. He'd pay money any day to see a babe in an evening gown kick some terrorist ass.

Dec looked up from the folder. "Any confirmation she's still alive?"

Harris shook his head. "None."

He'd seen a lot since becoming a SEAL, but his

insides still shriveled at the prospect of what could happen to Bryn McAllister. Nothing he hated more than someone capable of harming innocents, especially women and children, to further their own agendas. But if Bryn was still alive—and by the contents of her file he knew she was both intelligent and a fighter, so that put points in her favor—they would find her and get her out.

"We don't see any reason for the hostage-takers to kidnap them and then kill them," a Lebanese intelligence officer with a thick accent added. "If they wanted to kill Daoud, they would have made sure he died in the explosion or assassinated him in the aftermath. Kidnapping him and his daughter points to them wanting something more. We expect they'll contact us soon and demand payment of some sort."

Dec listened as the man outlined the political agenda of the group responsible, found nothing new there. Anger management problems, hated the West, blah, blah. The script was getting old. The extremists recruited young men when they were vulnerable and impressionable, poisoning them with footage of women and children being blown up by coalition forces in Iraq and Afghanistan. They targeted the dispossessed, the ones with bottled-up rage they had no outlet for.

Radicalism was like a cancer, metastasizing around the globe until every country was infected by it. The way Dec saw it, it was his job to help cut out the host tumors before they could spread.

"Any idea where they might be?"

"These past few months, Tehrazzi's been active along the Lebanese-Syrian border," Hutchinson said.

Those dark eyes seemed to bore straight into him, magnetic and forceful. Though Luke looked relaxed enough, Dec was almost humming from the coiled energy in the man's body. He wasn't a hair trigger. A patient, cunning predator. Smart, and lethal to the core. Maybe the things Dec had heard about him just might be true.

That intense gaze held Dec's as Luke continued. "We have contacts reporting the hostages are somewhere in this area." With his forefinger he indicated a mountainous area on a Syrian map near its western border with Lebanon. "There's talk of a possible sighting in a house about ten miles from here. We're waiting for confirmation."

Meaning they were still in the process of buying off an informant willing to spill the beans. When threats of force weren't an option, money usually worked like a dream. Wave enough American greenbacks at the right person, and one tended to get the information they wanted. Money still made the world go 'round, even for terrorists.

"And Tehrazzi," Dec mused, "he's part of the Mahdi army in Iraq? Follower of Muqtada al-Sadr?"

Luke sat back in his chair as he gazed at Dec. "Based in al-Najaf, specifically. We know they're an organization of interest to the Iranians, though their government denies supplying them any weapons or cash, of course. As a Shi'a, he's a natural fit for al-Sadr's group. Because he was born in Lebanon, he's active there, and has his fingers in all sorts of other pies. The 2006 war between Israel and Hezbollah gave him a platform to attract a following of his own."

"So he's funded by Hezbollah as well as the Shi'a militias in Iraq, who could in turn be funded by Tehran."

"Exactly. But Tehrazzi is a maverick. He's motivated as much by power as his religious beliefs, so we can't rule out the possibility he's involved with Sunni groups on some level as well. His family connections in Afghanistan also put him in contact with high-ranking Taliban leaders."

"Any other questions?" Harris rested his elbows on top of a manila folder and regarded Dec calmly.

"No, sir."

"Once we get the intel we're waiting for, you'll be wheels up within the hour."

Dec nodded, adrenaline already circulating through his body. "Aye, aye, sir."

They planned the preliminary operation, determined insertion and extraction points. The SEALs would go in and extract the hostages while Hutchinson and his operatives would go after the tangos.

"Good enough for now," Dec said.

It all looked great on paper, but out there in the field in real time, it meant fuck-all. Any operation, whether hostage rescue or target elimination, never went off as planned. That was why an essential part of his training had been to teach him how to think outside the box, to change on the fly and adapt to the fluidity of battle. Either that, or you and your men died horrible deaths and then your family was told you'd been killed in an unfortunate training accident.

He finished the briefing and went out to tell the rest of the team what the score was. Spencer, the medic, raised a sandy brow at him.

"Let's saddle up, gentlemen. Once we get the word, we're wheels up within the hour."

****

Day 2, Syrian village
Nightfall

The dimming light seeping through the crack around the trap door told her nightfall was approaching. Bryn sagged on her knees against the dirt wall, forcing hot, stale air in and out of her dry lungs. In, out. In, out. She drew on all her mental strength, focused on the words like a mantra. If she thought of anything but her next breath, she would lose what little control she had over her terror.

Her body was almost depleted of moisture. Her skin and clothing, soaked with sweat just a few hours ago, were now dry and stiff with salt from her perspiration. Her tongue was swollen, pressing against the gag and almost choking her as she gasped those wheezing breaths in and out. No one had come for them.

For hours she'd tried to get loose, contorting her body into unimaginable positions to reach the tape holding her limbs prisoner, though she'd only managed to exhaust herself and sweat out more precious water. But she was still alive. Her father had stirred a few times, but was either too hurt or too weak to make any attempt at communication.

Bryn started to shiver, ironic considering she'd almost died of heatstroke that afternoon. And even if she didn't spike a sudden fever that signaled her brain and internal organs were about to shut down from dehydration, she knew she couldn't live much longer in these conditions. If the lack of water didn't kill her overnight, the plummeting temperatures would. Depending on where they were, it could dip below freezing. With no water to help regulate their body temperatures, she and her father could very well end up succumbing to hypothermia.

A hysterical laugh bubbled up her throat. *Hypothermia, after all this.*

She'd never imagined being subjected to this kind of torture, let alone withstanding it. And that's what it was—torture. The mere thought of a glass of water almost maddened her. She was already weak, so weak. Even if someone did get to them in time and free them, would she be able to run for it? Unlikely at this point.

When she spared the energy to look around, the

room blurred. She looked at her father, and sometimes saw two of him lying there in the dirt. Not a good sign. This was an awful death. Far worse than anything she'd imagined. And no one even knew where she was. Her mother would probably never know what happened to her.

Which might be for the best, Bryn reflected tiredly, having long since accepted the possibility that she might not come out of this alive. She hoped someone would lie to her mother, tell her yes, your daughter was in fact killed outright in the explosion. Not only would that put the question of her suffering to rest, it would also explain why there was no body to bury.

She might have cried some more, but there wasn't enough moisture left. Instead she grieved with hot, gritty eyes, trembling in the growing darkness with her father's inert form lying a few short feet away. Her energy sapped, she bowed her head and drifted off into an exhausted sleep.

At first, she thought she'd dreamed the sound of footsteps above. She sat up, shivering in the chilly blackness, straining to hear. The soft footfalls came again, in bursts, as though the person was sneaking up to the trap door, then would stop.

Bryn's heart pounded. Was someone coming to finish them off? In her condition, she couldn't even get to her feet to defend herself. The best she could do was lie on her side and lash out with her bare, bound feet. She drew her trembling legs up, prepared to give one good kick.

The trap door above her creaked open and bright moonlight spilled in, blinding her. The person holding it struggled under its weight, and then it dropped to the ground with a thud. Hissed whispers filled the silent air, but she couldn't make out what was said. A moment later the door opened again, and a hooded silhouette appeared in the opening against the moonlit sky. Frozen with fear, Bryn lay coiled, waiting.

The figure slipped inside the opening and landed lightly. Hidden by shadows, Bryn watched as the figure crept closer, moving in an awkward shuffle.

"Don't be afraid," a woman's voice whispered in Arabic.

Bryn hesitated, a seed of hope blooming inside her. Was she here to help them?

The woman broke into an impassioned speech, and this time Bryn could only pick out bits and pieces. "Allah forgive me, I cannot do more..." She crept closer still, holding something in her hand. Not a knife—it didn't glint in the light. What was it? Bryn peered intently at the object in the woman's outstretched hand. Some sort of jar maybe?

"Water," the woman whispered.

Water! Bryn scrambled to sit, every muscle and joint screaming in protest, ravenous for the liquid. The woman came forward slowly, plucked the filthy gag from between Bryn's lips, and tipped the blessed contents into her parched, swollen mouth. She gulped it greedily, spilling some, and the woman murmured something, passed a sandpapery hand over Bryn's hot cheek as though trying to soothe her. She drained it all, crying out in despair when it was empty.

"I'm sorry, my lamb." The woman's voice was rough with age and regret. "I have only enough left for the man."

"Help us," Bryn croaked through cracked lips, shaking with desperation. Her freedom was right there, through that trap door not ten feet away. It was the middle of the night, and even with a full moon surely she'd be able to find something to cover herself with and escape. "Help us," she pleaded again, stronger this time, tugging on her bound wrists so the woman was sure to see. "Free us." She was too weak to scream it.

"Qamar!" a man's voice snapped from outside. "Enough! They will see us!"

The woman knelt before Bryn and touched her face again, the wrinkled countenance exposed by the silvery light, giving her an ethereal glow, like an angel. She looked kind. The wise, deep-set black eyes delved into Bryn, and her sorrow was evident.

"I cannot, little lamb. My grandson—he will find out, and we will suffer." She turned and shuffled her way across to Bryn's father, finding him sprawled on his stomach.

Bryn watched her remove his gag and carefully spill some water into his mouth. He stirred and coughed, and the woman murmured to him gently, coaxing the life-giving fluid down him.

"Dad, wake up! Help me get her to understand! Untie us," Bryn begged, and the woman came back to her, tipped the remainder of the water into her mouth. She swallowed it all eagerly and tried again to pull on her bonds. "Please."

"May Allah forgive me, I cannot," Qamar repeated, regret heavy in her voice. She spoke more, but Bryn couldn't grasp the words. The roughened fingers began to pull the gag back into place and Bryn fought her, twisting her head back and forth, crying out in denial.

"Be still!" Qamar hissed, giving her a hard shake. "You will get us all killed."

A desperate glance at her father showed him prone, unmoving. He wasn't going to be able to help. Defeated and too weak to do anything more, Bryn drooped against the wall and the gag was shoved back into place. Silent sobs wracked her.

"I will come to you again when I can," Qamar promised, and peeked out of the trap door before reaching a hand up to the man waiting for her. "May Allah protect you."

The heavy door fell shut again, leaving Bryn and her father alone in the blackness.

Chapter Four

Day 3, Beirut
Late Afternoon

"We've got 'em."

Dec and the rest of the team looked across the briefing room at Harris. "Where are they?"

"In a village about fourteen miles from the coast. Our contacts were able to smuggle in some water for them, but they haven't eaten in almost two days, so they'll be dehydrated and weak."

The big man grabbed the map from his desk and set it out on the table while everyone crowded around. Dec went over the logistics of the operation one last time. Once they freed the hostages, they'd have to hump it three miles to the extraction point, where a chopper would meet them. The contingency plan was to head out into the desert mountains to a series of caves and establish a secondary point. Just to be sure, he made them all go over it a third time.

He checked his watch. "Okay, boys. Let's lock and load."

The eight-man team hurried out to gather their gear.

"Spence."

The medic looked back at him questioningly.

"Make sure we bring extra IV bags. No telling what shape they'll be in when we find them."

****

Day 3, Syrian village
Evening

All day Bryn had prayed that Qamar would come back. Through the same exhausting, suffocating cycle of heat and sweat and dehydration, she clung to the hope the woman would return and give them water, maybe untie them this time. But night had fallen, and still no sign of her. The only sound was the whistling of the wind overhead, its high-pitched wail echoing the despair in her heart.

Sometime during the previous night her father had roused for a while. He'd been able to utter a few words, so she knew he wasn't hampered by his gag, but then his speech had become slurred and he'd fallen into unconsciousness. She suspected he must have suffered a head injury, possibly a skull fracture, at least a concussion. Whatever it was, he'd need medical attention.

That is, if the dehydration didn't finish him off first.

She imagined sucking on a lemon drop, but even the thought of the sour taste wasn't enough to squeeze any moisture from her mouth. Still weak and thirsty, she had revived a bit since drinking the water last night.

The room didn't spin when she cared to open her eyes and look around her earthen prison. Her vision wasn't doubled anymore. And at least she was rid of the gag now, the wad of cotton long since drying to the point that she had been able to push it out with her thickened tongue. She was pretty sure she'd sweated out all the water she'd consumed, and she felt feverish. Could have been lack of fluids, or it could have been the dozens of cuts on her right side becoming infected.

She quivered in the chilly darkness, the trap door rattling on its hinges occasionally as the wind howled above it. Sometimes fine streams of sand spilled through the cracks around the edges, showering her in a dusty coating.

In the corner, her father shifted. Hope surged at the even breaths he took. She was comforted from that, closing her eyes to better focus on the reassuring sound.

"Someone will come for us," he rasped.

"The woman said she would come again."

"They will come for us," he repeated, and she wondered who he was talking about, if he had begun to hallucinate.

"Yes," she whispered, not wanting to make things worse by telling him they were going to die if they didn't get more water soon. She was going insane, not being able to do anything. If she got the chance to kill her captors for what they'd done to them, she would act on it. The sheer violence of the hatred rising up in her startled and frightened her.

"You are a very brave woman, Bryn. I am so proud to call you my daughter...and I love you." He groaned a little. "Wish I...had been a better father."

Bryn stared at his shadowy outline, her eyes hot. Praise was so rare from this harsh, remote man, and that last admission must have been very difficult for him. But for him to have said it at all was testament to just how grave their situation was. He must think they were going to die in here too, or he would never have spoken to her that way. A lump formed in her parched throat.

"I love you, too." It hurt to talk. Not that there was anything else she could add.

A heavy silence filled the dusty room, as though they had exchanged their final goodbyes, leaving nothing more to be said. Cold and thirsty and exhausted, Bryn hunkered down, wincing at the pain in her strained shoulders. She lay there and shivered, suffering in silence as the night dragged on, the wind moaning.

Dozing in a fitful sleep, she woke suddenly. Her

head jerked up. A sound from outside, above them, maybe footsteps. Was it Qamar? She shifted into a kneeling position, heard only the wind as it gusted.

"Hear that?" her father whispered, his voice distorted through lips that had to be cracked like hers.

"Yes."

She tensed, every ounce of concentration focused on the area of the trap door. Nothing. More silence met the grating of their shallow breaths. More agonizing minutes ticked by.

Please let it be Qamar with some water.

Over the wind came more footsteps. Running footsteps. And then more of them, as if a group of people were rushing toward them. Her pulse tripped. She was so weak now. Far too weak to defend herself, even if they unchained her.

Fear curled low in her belly, its icy tentacles wrapping around her spine, paralyzing her. Had the terrorists come back for them after all?

****

Dec stood poised above the trap door as the wind blew around him, weapon at the ready. One of his men signaled the door was safe, grabbed the handle and waited.

"Go," Dec ordered.

One man lifted it and Dec and Spencer went in, weapons trained.

Dec hit the floor first and swung around, the green glow of his night vision goggles showing him two bodies, tied up on opposite walls, but no terrorists. The stale, hot air hit him like a fist, smelling of sweat and body odor and fear.

"Clear," he called, and shoved the goggles back, approaching the woman while Spencer went to look after the more seriously wounded father.

"Bryn McAllister?" He crouched down in front of

her.

Her dark eyes were huge in her pale face as she stared up at him like he was an apparition out of a nightmare. Covered in camouflage paint, in his fatigues and the goggles, toting an automatic weapon, he must have looked the part to her. Frozen in place, blinking against the swirling wind, she nodded slowly, throat moving as she swallowed.

"Lieutenant McCabe, U.S. Navy, ma'am. We're here to get you and your father out." All business, he ran his hands over her, checking for injuries. "Are you hurt anywhere?"

She shook her head, so he took his KA-BAR knife from his belt and slit the tape on her ankles, then reached around to do the same to her wrists, noticing her evening gown was encrusted with grime and salt. Anger surged up. The bastards had tied her up like an animal and left her to suffocate in this hellhole without any water or food.

She brought her arms awkwardly in front of her and gasped, moving her stiff wrists and fingers awkwardly.

He gave her some water from his CamelBak. She moaned in relief and started guzzling it. He stopped her.

"Slowly," he cautioned, "or it'll come right back up."

His heart squeezed in sympathy as she sipped desperately at the plastic tube, as though she were afraid he would take it away. He let her drain it, eased her up onto her knees. They had to move.

"What's his status, Spence?" he asked over his shoulder.

"Head injury, sir. I've given him a little water, but we need to get him back to the helo so I can work on him. They both need IV fluids, stat."

"Roger that." He took the clothes Spencer handed him and held them out for Bryn. "Put these on, and then we'll get you out of here." They had a little time, since no tangos had been spotted yet, but that didn't mean some weren't waiting in ambush somewhere close by.

Bryn hesitated for only a second, then took the shirt and pants he offered. He would have turned his back to give her some privacy but she was clearly too weak to dress herself. With quick, efficient movements, he stripped the stiff gown over her head and tugged the shirt down to cover her strapless bra. He then helped her pull the pants over her barely-there panties and rolled the cuffs up so she wouldn't trip over them. After tugging on her socks and a pair of boots, he hauled her to her feet. She swayed and grabbed at his shoulders, trembling with the effort of staying upright.

Another hot ball of rage swept through him at her slim frame shaking against him, weak and critically dehydrated after living in an earthen oven for three days. Part of him hoped the group responsible would try and fight their way out when his team found them, so they could dispatch them all to hell where they belonged.

"Here we go," he told her, and hoisted her up through the trap door, where one of his team members waited to pull her out. He boosted himself up after her and reached down for her father, then moved back while Spencer levered himself from the filthy prison. His lungs expanded in relief at being in the cool, clean air, the wind gusts strong enough to spray dirt and sand into his eyes.

He turned to Bryn, who was swaying on her feet. "She needs some more water."

Three CamelBak tubes instantly appeared in front of her nose. He allowed her to have a few more sips from one of them, and then took her arm. "We'll give you some more when we get you to safety," he promised.

At a nod from him, one of his men slid Jamul onto his shoulders and started off behind the point man. The daughter was shivering, her lips cracked, black eyes bruised-looking and dulled with fatigue.

"Can you walk? We have to move fast, so if you can't keep up on your own, we'll have to carry you."

She blinked, nodded. "I'll try."

"Okay. Let's move out."

Two other men started across the narrow street, gave the all clear for them to follow. He took hold of her upper arm to steady her, began walking through the wind, mindful of her exhaustion. After she stumbled for the second time, he slung his rifle across his chest and hoisted her over his shoulder. Her body stiffened but she didn't struggle, and she was light enough that her weight didn't slow him down much.

From building to building they slunk like ghosts, the cloud-covered moon aiding in their camouflage while the wind whipped sand and dust into the air. Bryn held onto the back of his BDUs, remaining still and quiet as they reached the outskirts of the village. The wind grew to a howling pitch, sand and debris obscuring their vision.

Dec and the team put on goggles to protect their eyes and kept moving toward the open desert, where the helo would extract them two and a half miles to the southeast. He shifted Bryn's weight and leaned forward to keep his balance against the full-fledged sandstorm blowing up around them. The inclement weather was sudden and unexpected, since sandstorm season was usually in the spring. Not that Mother Nature seemed to give a damn, because within a few minutes, visibility dropped by a third.

Another quarter mile out, Dec knew there was no way a helo could get to them in these conditions. He stopped the team behind the relative protection of a sand dune and set Bryn down, handing her over to one of his men for more water, and used the radio to contact the command center. Yelling over the wind, he arranged for the helo to pick them up at the secondary extraction point near the caves in another six hours, by which time the ops center expected the weather to improve enough.

They started out again, this time Spencer carrying Bryn, with Dec on point. It took them nearly two hours to cover four more miles, and by then visibility was almost zero, sand blasting their faces and bodies. Since it was impossible to navigate, let alone breathe, Dec finally called a halt.

Digging their way into the sand, the team made a makeshift shelter and hunkered down to weather the worst of the storm. He caught a glimpse of Bryn trying to help secure the nylon tent and was about to bark an order for someone to protect her from the stinging sand when one of the men took hold of her arm and ushered her inside. Spencer set about starting an IV line in the father's arm, but the old man protested.

"My...daughter first," he said clearly, and so Spence went to work on Bryn.

They'd laid her down in the middle of their makeshift tent, an exhausted, fragile-looking thing surrounded by a wall of special ops soldiers. Despite her lank hair, bruised-looking eyes and cracked lips, she remained striking.

Spencer pushed the IV needle into her vein and she winced, but didn't make a sound. Little nicks covered her arm, probably from flying debris in the explosion at the embassy. Spence checked her over and cleaned her up, dabbing on antibiotic ointment and covering some of the deepest cuts with bandages.

She flinched and gasped when he used a pair of tweezers to dig a sliver of glass out of her, and Dec had to stop himself from stroking a hand over her hair. When the third piece of glass came out she jerked and bit her lip, and he finally reached out to hold her hand, offering what little comfort he could.

As his fingers closed around hers, she looked up into his face with those dark, mysterious eyes and smiled her gratitude, then closed them. Something twisted deep in his chest. He had the sudden urge to pick her up and hold her, promise to never let anyone hurt her again. It was totally bizarre and unprofessional of him to even think it, but he'd never been in this situation before, not in all the time he'd been in the Teams.

He glanced away from her delicate, ashen face to find every member of the team staring at her. The air in their shelter practically hummed with protective male energy. It was good in a way, Dec reflected, so long as it didn't distract anyone from doing their job. It meant they were still capable of sympathy and the desire to protect the innocent, even underneath all their discipline and testosterone.

But Jesus, look at them. Eight badass Navy SEALs sitting around fussing over an injured woman, one sliding a folded blanket under her head and another tucking one around her like they were a bunch of goddamn nursemaids. This op was already one for the books, and it wasn't near over.

They gave her more water, then Spencer took a wet wipe and washed her face and neck. Her long, thick lashes fluttered and she sighed in relief before dropping off into an exhausted sleep.

"You got that lip stuff?" Dec asked Spence.

The medic gave him a funny look but retrieved it from one of his pockets and Dec silently smoothed some on her cracked lips. Jesus, it must have been bad for them in that cellar. She gave a small murmur, barely audible above the wind, but it made something ache deep inside him.

Without a word Spencer went to work on the father, checking his eyes with a penlight for even dilation. "Pupils are slow to respond," he reported, dabbing a piece of gauze over a long cut on his patient's temple. "And he's still disoriented. We'll have to wake him every half-hour to check him, make sure he doesn't slip into a coma."

"Well, it's not like we're going anywhere in this." The good news was, neither were the terrorists. But once the storm eased enough for them to move, they better haul ass to the extraction point before the enemy got moving.

Silent except for the wind keening outside the tent, they waited.

Chapter Five

*Day 4, In the Syrian Desert
Dawn*

Bryn's eyes snapped open. Something had brushed against her hip. In the dimness she stared up at the lieutenant looming over her to hook up another bag of saline to her IV.

With effort, she slowed her racing heart. "Hi," she whispered.

She didn't remember a thing after he'd put the stuff on her dry lips. She'd fallen into a sleep as dreamless as if someone had knocked her unconscious.

He smiled down at her, revealing dimples beneath the camouflage paint. A good looking man, and one she would be eternally grateful to.

"Morning," he answered, studying her. His eyes were an amazing shade of caramel. "How are you feeling?"

"Much better." She felt like she might make it after all.

"The wind's starting to die down a little, so we'll have to move out soon. One last bag of fluids for you—" Her stomach growled ferociously, and he grinned, those fascinating golden-brown eyes lighting up. "—and something to eat first."

The medic—Spencer, she'd heard someone call him—crouched down beside her and checked her pulse, then wrapped a blood pressure cuff around her upper arm and inflated it, a stethoscope in his ears. "Bet you've never eaten an MRE before."

41

He had eyes the color of a summer sky. "I have no idea what that is," she admitted, watching him study the dial on the cuff. "Is it awful?" Her pulse throbbed under the pressure of the Velcro strap.

"Depends," the lieutenant answered. "Do you want to start out with a cracker to see how it settles, or do you want to try the MRE version of beef stew? Or maybe spaghetti with meatballs?" He held out two tan pouches, labeled accordingly.

"Take the stew, ma'am," one of the other men advised. "The spaghetti tastes like hell."

Spencer removed the cuff before she could answer. "One-ten over seventy," he announced in satisfaction. "Your blood volume's way up from last night, blood pressure's normal. You're doing great."

Compared to a few hours ago, she felt fricking fantastic. "Please, call me Bryn." Thirty-one was still too young to be ma'amed. "How's my father? Is he awake?"

"No. His symptoms are getting worse," Spencer told her without mincing words. "He'll need surgery once we evacuate him on the chopper. He'll go straight to a hospital in Beirut."

So he did have a serious head injury. Her stomach clenched. She twisted around towards him. Her father was lying on the other side of the tent, eyes closed, and he looked gray. Her chest constricted. "What about his vitals? Did the fluids help him?"

"They've kept him alive so far, yes."

"Lieutenant—"

"Call me Dec. Short for Declan," he explained when she frowned. "Here, start with this." He fished out a packet from one of the equipment bags, then handed her the backpack-like thing with water in it and something resembling a cracker, which she accepted hungrily.

She wolfed it and two others down, keeping an

anxious eye on her father. "Has he woken up at all?" Even with her limited knowledge of first aid she knew enough to be afraid that he would lapse into a coma. By the look of him right now, he might already be there.

"He woke a couple of times during the night," Dec said. "His speech was a little slurred, but that's to be expected. We'll get you both on that chopper ASAP."

He said it with absolute confidence before heading out into the dying storm. He had a steady, competent air about him, a certain calmness that came from being very sure of himself. Even if she hadn't known his rank she would have figured him to be the leader of the group. Bryn felt perfectly safe, despite being in a tent in the middle of a sandstorm with a bunch of deadly men. She only wished there was something they could do for her father.

After she had eaten, Spencer removed the IV needle from her arm while she looked pointedly elsewhere, lest she bring up her breakfast, and bandaged her before helping her into a sitting position. While everyone else packed their gear and got ready to move she hunkered down next to her father, passed a hand over his hair and down the side of his pallid face. His skin was clammy and cool.

Bryn's heart turned over. What would she do if he didn't make it? They might not have been as close as she would have liked, but he was her father and she loved him. The sight of such a powerful, intelligent man lying there so still and quiet broke her heart.

Someone put a hand on her forehead, and she looked up into Spencer's blue eyes.

"You're still a little warm," he told her, pulling a camouflage jacket over her and doing it up as though she were a child. "I gave you a shot of antibiotics last night, but you'll need more once you get back to

Beirut. Some of the cuts on your arm were pretty deep, might be infected."

She studied the scratches and little holes already scabbing over. It was all surreal. A bomb blast, a kidnapping, nearly dying of dehydration, then rescued by Navy SEALs in the middle of the night. Certainly more exciting than her average day as a social worker, even with the often sad cases she had to deal with.

Dec stepped back inside, pulling off his goggles. "Can't see much out there, but it's better than it was last night. Think you can walk, Miss Mc—"

"Bryn, please, and yes I can walk. Thanks again, all of you, for coming to get us." To her horror, a lump formed in her throat and tears burned her eyes. It was nice to know she was hydrated enough to make tears, but damn it, she would not cry like a helpless female in front of these brave men and look weak.

"Believe me, it was our pleasure," Dec answered.

She forced a small smile and lowered her eyes to the ground, biting her lip to keep from crying as she rolled up her bedding. Spencer took pity on her and patted her shoulder.

"Don't worry about it," he whispered so no one else would hear. "You've been through a lot. Nobody thinks less of you for it."

She nodded. "I'm fine, just tired. Don't worry about me falling to pieces or anything. I'm tougher than I look." She cast an anxious glance over her shoulder at her father.

When she turned back, Spencer grinned as he picked up his rifle. "You single?"

She gave him a startled glance and laughed. "Yeah, why? You want to take me out on a date once this is all over?"

He merely widened his grin and made his way out of the shelter.

Outside, Dec organized the team and gave the signal for two of the members to lift her father on a stretcher. "Okay, lady and gentlemen. Let's move."

****

Day 4, Syrian village
Morning

In disbelief, Tehrazzi stared down into the empty cellar. How had they escaped? Not by themselves, he knew that much.

A molten rage swept through him. His plan was ruined. Not only had they lost the leverage to secure the money, but whoever had freed them—probably American special ops—would be on the hunt for him now.

His throat was so tight he could barely choke the words out. "Who is responsible for this?"

One of his men shifted from one foot to the other. They all avoided his lethal gaze as he raked his eyes over them. With effort he reined in his temper. The anger morphed into an icy rage, far more dangerous. "Find out who did this," he commanded. "Then bring them to me."

Someone in the village had betrayed him, and he had a sickening feeling he knew who. They would pay dearly. It was not something he wanted to do, but he must make an example of them to prevent such actions in the future. Even if the prospect sickened him.

"Post a reward for their capture," he snarled, his fury polluting the air around him like a poisonous cloud. "I want them hunted down like dogs." Alive or dead, he didn't care what condition they were in so long as he got his hands on the traitors.

****

Day 4, Syrian Desert

Afternoon

She'd slowed them down.

Bryn hated knowing that. Still weakened, she tired easily on the shifting sand. She was used to walking on sand—she lived right on the beach back home in Oregon—but she'd never done a forced march through a sandstorm while recovering from heatstroke and dehydration.

Dec didn't seem to be all that concerned about it, or he would have picked her up and thrown her over his wide shoulder like he had the night before. He really did cut a nice figure in his battle gear, she thought.

As though sensing her eyes on him, he turned to look at her over his shoulder, pulling the protective covering away from his face and mouth to yell at her over the ceaseless wind. "Okay?"

Rather than wasting precious energy yelling, she nodded and gave him a thumbs-up. She felt like she weighed a thousand pounds. Even her hair felt like a lead weight at the back of her neck. She'd twisted it into a braid and tucked it into the back of her shirt to stop it from whipping around but it hung there, threatening to pull her head backward.

"We're almost to the cliffs—just another half mile."

Might as well be ten, in this weather. She gave him another thumbs-up and trudged on behind him. The two men carrying her father were second in line behind Dec, Spencer at her back, and the last four bringing up the rear. Her muscles trembled with exhaustion but she refused to quit, refused to complain. These men were risking their lives to help her and her father, and she would keep moving until her legs gave out before adding to their burden. And even then she would keep going. If she had to crawl, so be it.

She pushed on, lungs laboring as she leaned into the wind and forced her feet to move one step at a time. These guys were in amazing condition, but she shouldn't be surprised. Her best friend's dad was a former SEAL, so she knew plenty about what they were capable of. Good and bad.

Nearing the end of her limit, she tripped and went down hard on her knees. Spencer was right there behind her to scoop her up, but she pushed away from him and stumbled on, her legs like jelly. She had to pull her own weight, like everyone else on the team. The wind calmed slightly, the sand thinning in the air as the protective wall of the towering cliffs came into view.

You can do this, she told herself sternly. *Come on, Bryn, just a little farther. Suck it up. One foot in front of the other.*

At last they stood at the base of the cliff.

Dec and the others began to dig out equipment while she collapsed on her butt, and someone handed her more water and a protein bar. She wolfed the bar down and with growing alarm watched them work. She didn't see any caves anywhere, and the men appeared to be pulling out ropes and harnesses—

Wait a minute...after all that, did they expect her to climb up the damn cliff?

One of them started up the rock wall, hammering anchors at regular intervals, threading a rope through them.

She gaped at them in disbelief. They were! They were going to have to scale the frigging cliff!

Bryn swallowed hard, wanting to cry. The thing had to be sixty feet high, at least. She couldn't make it. She didn't have anything left.

"Bryn?"

She swung her head around toward Declan. "Y-yes?" Oh man, how was she going to do this? All she

47

wanted to do was lie in a heap and sleep for a week.

He came over to her, hunkered down at her feet. His topaz gaze studied her carefully. "I don't expect you to climb it."

She sighed in relief, closed her eyes and slumped.

"I can carry you up."

Her eyes flew open in alarm. "What?" Like hell he could. Yeah, he was strong—he'd carried her over his shoulder through the desert last night, hadn't he? But no way could he scale that rock face and handle her added weight.

His eyes crinkled at the corners, like he was trying not to smile. "You'll have your own harness, Bryn. I'm not fricking Superman, you know."

"But—but how will I—" She huffed out a breath. "I've never even been to a climbing gym."

"That's okay. I'm going to be with you the whole way."

What difference was that going to make? Oh, God, this was crazy. She watched as they hooked up her father's stretcher and prepared to ascend with it, one man above him and another below. They moved with amazing speed, and were halfway up before Dec spoke again.

"We have to get up there, Bryn. The cave we need is on the other side in the canyon. This storm is going to blow over any time and we'll be exposed. Remember the people who took you? They're still out there, and by now they've got to know you're missing. They'll be coming after us."

He was right. "Okay."

Dec rigged up her harness, pulled her to the base of the rock and checked the ropes. "We're next in line, so here's how we're going to do this. You're going to place your hands first, then your feet, one move at a time. I'm going to be right behind you, like this." He came up and placed his arms on either side of her, brought his knees up under her thighs so she was practically sitting on his lap.

Oh, God, she thought, the contact zinging through her like lightning. Surprise registered that she could even be aware of him that way under the circumstances. He felt warm and solid and safe. Frozen, she stared at the big hands framing hers. Long fingers, wide palms, clean, short nails. The back of his left hand had a crescent-shaped scar on it, about the size of a quarter. His body dwarfed her, and she was tall for a woman. But what would happen if she slipped? She'd knock him and Spencer off with her.

"I won't let you fall, Bryn."

Swiveling her head around to look at him, she swallowed. The certainty in his voice and the quiet resolve in his eyes gave her hope, but she remained unconvinced. She didn't have a choice, however. "I'll give it my best." It was all she could promise. Now if only her knees would stop wobbling.

"I know you will," he answered, his breath warm against her nape, raising goose bumps on her skin.

Give your head a shake, Bryn. She sucked in a breath, placed her foot in a toehold and strained up to reach for a finger hold. Her legs already felt like lead weights and they hadn't begun the climb yet.

"Good girl," he said, rock-hard thigh muscles tensing beneath her. "Now use your legs to push up. Don't pull with your arms unless you have to, or you'll fatigue your upper body."

My whole body is already fatigued, she thought in exasperation. She obeyed him though, exhaling sharp and fast as she straightened, like she did when throwing a punch in Karate. Discipline, she reminded herself. Discipline was the thing.

She moved cautiously, inching her way up with him surrounding her like a second skin. Beads of sweat popped out on her forehead, her lungs laboring to supply her exhausted body with oxygen. Already her muscles trembled, pushed way beyond their limit.

She growled as her legs strained to propel her upward over one particularly difficult section, summoning all her reserves to lock her knees, but her foot slipped. The scream snagged in her throat as Dec caught her against him and she scrambled for a hold, her heart threatening to explode. Clinging to the rock with her fingernails, before she could stop herself, she measured the distance between her and the ground.

"I've got you," Dec soothed, his voice calm, as though she hadn't almost fallen to her death and taken him with her. She hung there against the cool, grainy rock, panting.

"You're doing great, Bryn." His hands and body pinned her in place. "Just rest a minute, get your breath back. And don't look down."

Too late. She released a shuddering breath, fought to keep calm.

"Thatta girl. Close your eyes for a bit, keep breathing. We're almost there."

Liar. They were maybe halfway up. She sucked in a few lungfuls of air while she laid flat against the cliff, body trembling as she absorbed his warmth, his strength. In the wake of the adrenaline rush, her limbs felt limp. "Sorry," she whispered finally.

"Nothing to be sorry about. Just a little slip." He made it sound as if it happened to him all the time.

Tears of exhaustion and fear burned her eyes. She blinked them back and took a deep, fortifying breath.

"It's okay, Bryn. I've got you."

"She all right?" Spencer called from below.

"I'm fine," she answered, willing herself to believe it. "I'm fine," she repeated to herself. *Now get your ass moving.*

"Better than fine," Dec said in her ear. "Amazing."

If he was trying to distract her from her fear, he was doing a damn good job. A shaky laugh vibrated through her. Who'd have thought she could laugh at a time like this? She took another calming breath and looked up. Three of the other SEALs peered down at them, waiting.

Just a little farther. Dec's with you. You can do this.

Bryn resumed the climb, fingers curling tight, legs struggling to support her weight. But she did it. Inch by inch, foot by foot, she climbed. When they reached the top, she all but collapsed, crawling over the ledge and staying there on her hands and knees. Head bowed, she gasped and trembled. Strong hands lifted her, and she was propped up against Dec's solid chest.

"Here, drink this," he ordered, putting the water pack's plastic tube to her mouth.

Between gasps, she drank the water obediently. Jeez, he wasn't even winded.

He passed a big hand over her back in a comforting gesture. "Hard part's done. Now we let gravity help us down."

Oh God, they still had to get down. She didn't want to think about that right now.

"We'll give you a couple of minutes, but we've got to keep moving. We're way too exposed up here."

From beneath heavy lids she glanced around. They were totally open on all sides on the plateau, no protection anywhere. At least the storm had fizzled out, leaving only a strong breeze. With no airborne sand to obscure it, the sun beat down on them with relentless power, the heat sucking all the life out of her. She took another sip of water, clinging grimly to her resolve.

Declan ruffled her hair affectionately, as though

51

she was his little sister. "Almost over, lady. Then you can sleep until the helo comes in."

The first six members began their descent, taking her father's stretcher with them. Damned amazing guys, all of them. They disappeared from view over the edge, leaving her, Dec and Spencer alone.

Both SEALs seemed tense, gripping their rifles, eyes never still, scanning the horizon for any threat. Neither of them looked the least bit tired. No one would ever have guessed they'd just trekked across the desert through a sandstorm and then scaled a steep rock face. While she felt and must look like the living dead.

It could be worse, she reasoned. She could be lying dead in that cellar right now. What was a descent down a sixty-odd-foot cliff compared to that?

Chapter Six

"You ready?"

Bryn glanced up into Declan's camouflaged face and nodded. She stood to let him hook up her harness, noting again how tall and strong he was. This time, with him so close, self-consciousness crept in. She *so* wanted a shower. She must stink to high heaven, and it was only going to get worse.

Something whizzed past her head, hot against her ear.

"Get down!" He tackled her to the ground. Her heart galloped as she realized what had happened. A bullet. Someone had shot at her!

Dec had her pinned flat beneath him, sheltering her with his body while Spencer lay on his belly, scanning through the scope of his high-powered rifle. "Five of 'em," he reported, calmly pulling the trigger. *Crack.*

Dec spoke quickly into his mic, directing the rest of the team on the ground below them. Rocks dug into her belly and pelvis. Squashed beneath his heavy weight, she dimly heard the rapid transmission while more gunshots cracked through the clear desert air.

"Move, Bryn," he commanded, shoving her in the opposite direction. She crawled as fast as she could away from the edge and toward the far end of the open plateau, heart clattering.

Spencer ran ahead and quickly anchored a rope, tethered his harness and dropped over the side. Dec tugged some gloves on her, hooked her up and swung down behind her.

"Jones got two of them," he reported to Spencer grimly. "Rendezvous at the extraction point at twenty-one hundred." His arms tightened around her as he gripped the rope. "I'm going to get us on the ground fast," he warned her, "so just let the rope slide between your hands and let me do the work, okay?"

"Okay," she whispered, shaking. Had her father made it down all right? Was he still unconscious? "Ulp—" she choked as her body fell backwards, hands automatically grabbing the rope to slow her descent.

"Let go, Bryn," Dec ordered.

Fighting her instincts, she did as he commanded, dropping another ten feet and stopping when he caught her against his body. She squeezed her eyes shut, sent up a prayer, dropped again. And again. And again as they rappelled down the cliff until her feet touched solid earth. She all but crumpled to the ground, then Dec grabbed her and slung her over his shoulder, running for cover behind a cluster of boulders next to what appeared to be the entrance of a cave. He set her down and she collapsed in a heap as he peered around the rocks, rifle at the ready.

"Clear," he said softly.

"Clear," Spencer responded.

Dec turned to her. "You okay?"

She nodded. "Fine." All things considered, anyhow. "How about my father?"

"Yeah. They got him down and hidden when the firefight started."

"But has he woken up? He must be starving—"

"No." Sympathy filled his golden eyes. "He's in a coma, Bryn."

"Is he?" she demanded of Spencer, stomach churning.

The medic nodded. "Since this morning."

Fear and grief welled up inside her. "Why didn't you say something?"

"Because we couldn't afford to have you fall to pieces," Dec said bluntly.

Oh, but they could now? She drew her knees up, dropped her face into her hands. "I wouldn't have," she insisted.

Guilt ripped at her. He'd never been much of a parent to her, but still she figured she owed him something more than this numbness. All she felt was a heavy lump in her chest.

"Come on," Dec said, hauling her up by the hand. She followed him into the dark cave and sat next to him.

Spencer held out another MRE pouch. "Here. Better eat something." When he opened it, the scent of beef stew filled her nose, making her stomach growl. She accepted it dubiously, squeezing some of the cold, gooey contents into her mouth. Trying not to make a face, she swallowed it and waited to see if it would stay down. When it did, she forced herself to take another mouthful. Even if it made her gag, her body needed the calories.

Spencer sat down next to her. "Pretty good, right?"

A wan smile was the best she could manage. After the stew and some water, her body seemed to give out on her. Exhaustion swept over her in an overpowering wave.

"Here," Dec said, pulling out a thin blanket and spreading it over the ground. "Lie down and get some sleep while you can." When she crawled onto it, he placed a water pack under her head as a pillow and covered her with his jacket. "Sorry, it's the best I can do."

She didn't care. Lying down felt like heaven. Hidden from the enemy and guarded by two Navy SEALs, she figured she wasn't going to get any safer for the time being. Her eyes closed and she fell into oblivion.

****

She woke at twilight when Dec shook her shoulder.

"How long have I been asleep?" she asked, head fuzzy.

"About four hours."

That long? It felt like ten minutes. She rubbed her eyes and sat up, staring up at him as he loomed over her.

"I thought you should eat something."

He handed her another pouch. "Spaghetti?" she guessed.

"That's what it says, anyhow." He hunkered down beside her with his own pouch.

She ate in silence, watching his profile as he ate. "Where's Spencer?" she asked finally.

"Outside, guarding the entrance of the cave." His eyes scrutinized her. "You ready to get out of here and go home?"

"God, yes."

"Chopper will be here within the hour. We'll need to—" His expression sharpened, then he turned away from her, covering his earpiece with one hand. "Go ahead, Spence." He listened for a few seconds, eyes glued to the slice of half-light coming from the entrance. "Copy that. I'm on my way." Moving fast, Dec shrugged on his pack, grabbed his weapon.

Bryn's heart gave a leap of fear. The spaghetti gurgled in her stomach in a slimy clump. "What's wrong?"

"We've got company. We're gonna draw them away from the landing zone. I need you to stay here and not move until one of us comes back for you. You understand me, Bryn?"

Her eyes widened. "What—?"

"Do not move, under any circumstances. We'll come back for you once we've cleared the area. Understand?"

So she was supposed to stay alone in a darkening cave with snakes and scorpions and God knows what else until they could come get her? Her heart pounded. "But what if—"

"But nothing," he said sharply. "You stay here. Period. Got it?"

"Y-yes." Something clicked beside her, a sharp metallic sound. She flinched when he grabbed her hand, shoved a pistol into it. "But I don't know how to shoot!"

He frowned. Probably wondering why the hell Jamul Daoud's daughter didn't know how to handle a weapon. Well, if she lived through this, she would rectify that real quick.

"Simple. Just point and pull the trigger. There's no safety on this and there's a round in the chamber. It's only a precaution, Bryn, to make you feel better. You're not going to need it, but I thought you'd feel safer having it. Just make sure you don't shoot us by accident when we come back in."

She held the thing gingerly, as though it was a coiled rattlesnake.

He held her gaze. "Lie low and stay quiet. Won't be long." And with that he hustled out of the cave, leaving her kneeling there with the grip of the pistol ice cold in her shaking hand.

In his absence, the minutes crawled by, her shallow breathing echoing in the emptiness while the remaining daylight faded. Her heartbeat reverberated in her chest, a film of sticky sweat trickling down her back. The sky outside turned to indigo, leaving her in almost complete blackness.

Her muscles cramped from being locked in position for so long and a dull tension headache throbbed in her temples. Claustrophobia intensified as the darkness enveloped her. She closed her eyes to help stave off the fear. Focusing on breathing slowly, Bryn tried to imagine she was at home, in a room where the power had gone off. Nothing to be scared of, it was only the dark. She hadn't been scared of the dark since she was a toddler. But she'd never dreamed of being in a place like this...

No. Don't go there. Focus.

Her ears strained for any sound that might tell her what was going on.

A muffled crack broke the stillness. Her eyes flew open. She held her breath, pulse spiking.

Three cracks, louder this time and in rapid succession. Gunshots. Friend or foe? Her chilly fingers tightened around the pistol grip. Shouts came, faint in the desert air. She couldn't tell whether the words were English or Arabic. What if Dec and Spencer were hurt or killed and no one came back for her? The panic she'd held at bay took hold. Her breath came in and out in quick pants.

More gunfire rattled. Were Dec and Spencer all right? Dec had ordered her to stay put, and she would, because she didn't want to put them in any more danger by distracting them. But they were used to operating with the entire team, and now they were out there by themselves. Would they be okay? Yeah, they were SEALs, but they were mortal. Her gaze fell on Spence's medical pack near the cave entrance. She crept over and picked it up, waiting there in case they needed her. Her eyes scanned through the darkness, every sense on alert.

A flash of movement in the distance grabbed her attention.

There. Moonlight glinting on his blond hair, Spencer darted out into the open, sprinting toward her and the cave. Muscles tensed, she prepared to run, waiting for his signal. All of a sudden he arched backward and threw his arms up, crying out as he fell.

No!

Bryn watched, numb with horror as he tried to drag himself toward her. Even from where she stood she could hear him cursing, his grunts of pain. He rose up on an elbow and lifted his rifle, swinging around to fire off a few rounds, then fell back down and dragged himself a few more feet. Then he collapsed, breathing in sharp, quick bursts.

Where the hell was Dec? Spencer needed help, fast. He was a sitting duck lying out there all alone.

Agonizing seconds ticked by. His primitive growls of pain made the hair on her arms stand up, feral and muffled, like he was doing everything possible to keep from screaming. And still no sign of Dec or any of the other SEALs.

It was up to her to help him. No one else was around. She gathered her courage and her strength, eyes riveted on Spencer's helpless form just a few yards away. Drawing a deep breath, she dropped her pistol and took off fast as she could, intent only on getting Spencer out of harm's way.

He twisted up when he heard her, his rifle aimed right at her chest, then froze, his pained grimace giving way to shock and fury. "No!" he shouted. "Get back, Bryn!"

She ignored him and kept coming, falling to her knees when more gunshots shattered the air. The bullets pinged off the rocks behind her, where she'd been standing a second before. She scrambled to his side, saw the dark jets of blood pumping between his fingers from his thigh in rhythmic spurts, pooling on the sand around him.

"God," she breathed, falling on her knees. "Tell me what to do," she demanded, ripping off her jacket to shove it against the wound. He cried out in agony, body arching up. "Sorry," she quavered, hands unsteady as she applied pressure using her body weight. The jagged end of his broken thighbone met her fingers. Her stomach rolled.

"Get back," he gasped. "Dec's coming. I'm okay."

"Shut up and tell me!" She was terrified someone had a bead on them right now. They needed to slow the bleeding and find cover before they had more bullet wounds to deal with.

"Shit. Fuckers got my femoral artery," he panted, looking down at himself. "Christ."

Her mind raced to remember what little first aid training she had. Stop the bleeding. What could she use to tie around his leg? She didn't even have a hair elastic. Her jacket. Blood kept pumping out of him as she fumbled to get the sleeves tied together above the wound, twisting them as tight as she could with her slippery fingers. The warm, metallic smell of it sickened her, fed the panic welling inside.

Suddenly, Spencer shoved her flat with one arm and reared up to fire another couple of rounds. He dropped down again with a deep growl of agony. In the moonlight he looked washed out. He was losing so much blood.

Bryn grabbed him under the armpits, determined to drag him to safety. She had to get him under cover somewhere and get that bleeding under control, and she had to do it *now*.

He tried to slap her hands away. "Leave me. Run. I'll...be...okay."

"Shut up," she snapped again, beyond the ability to stay calm. He probably had a good eighty pounds on her, and in her weakened state she wasn't sure if she could do it. But she was sure as hell going to try.

Lunging to her feet she hauled him, every muscle in her body straining with the effort. He howled, body arching upward again. She fell backwards, crawled forward and grabbed him a second time. More bullets whizzed past, spraying up sand around them. Somehow, Spencer shot off more rounds and she stumbled onward, an animalistic sound of fear and fury and determination tearing from her throat.

She shifted him a couple of feet, then a few more, picking up momentum as she worked her way to the relative safety of the boulders at the mouth of the cave. The muscles in her legs, back and shoulders screamed, but she moved him.

As soon as they were behind the screen of rock she fell flat on her back, shaking and gasping. Spencer lay still for a moment too, their mingled shallow breaths the only sound. She rolled over and crawled to his side with the medical kit they'd left hidden inside the cave.

He rummaged through it and grabbed the tourniquet, wrapped it around himself and she helped tighten it, both of them covered with his blood. His lungs were heaving now, his hands shaking like leaves in a windstorm. In the thin moonlight he was a sickening shade of gray. He was going into shock.

She gingerly moved his leg and stuffed the first aid kit underneath his knee, blanching when he cried out. Afraid to move him again or jostle the leg in case she made the bleeding worse, she stared down at the tourniquet and pressed a wad of sterile bandages across it. Was it working? The bleeding seemed to have lessened. Unless he'd already lost most of his blood.

"What can I do?" she asked helplessly, stroking the blond hair away from his face. Hot tears stung her eyes. "Can I give you some pain meds?"

"N-no," he snapped, his voice hoarse. "T-too late."

Too late? She wanted to ask him why a little morphine would hurt, under the circumstances, but knew he must have a good reason. "Water, then?"

"Noth-nothing—" he bit out, teeth chattering. "N-need blood."

He did, and fast. And they were certainly not in a position to give him a transfusion. She had to keep him calm, try to get his heart rate to slow before he bled out. "I know it's small comfort, but I'm here. I promise I won't leave you. Just breathe slowly."

He made a growl of acknowledgement, lips clamped together in a mutinous effort to keep from crying out in pain.

"My...wife," he rasped a few moments later, quaking.

She kept firm pressure over the wound, the blood seeping through her fingers. Was she pressing hard enough? Her hands were numb, her own heartbeat throbbing in her palms. "What about your wife, Spence?"

"N-need to...tell her..."

He thought he was going to die. Her teeth sunk into her lower lip. *You will not break down, Bryn.* She owed him that much. "Tell her what?" she whispered.

"L-love...her..."

"Yes, of course you do." He was still agitated, but he didn't have much strength left and she didn't want him using it up talking. It was obvious what he wanted, anyway. He wanted reassurance someone would get the message to his wife if he died. Not if, she reflected bleakly. He knew he was dying.

"I swear to you I will make sure she's told," Bryn vowed.

Spencer's eyes closed, lips compressed, his handsome face contorted with pain. She maintained physical contact with him, speaking softly to keep him with her. At least if he died, he wouldn't die alone. Her fingers stroked his hair. "Dec," she whispered into the darkness. "Where are you?"

Seconds later came the pounding of feet over the

sand, more gunshots, and then Dec came flying around the corner. He took in the scene with a single glance. Larger than life he towered over her, panting. He grabbed her by the front of her shirt with one fist and lifted her off her knees, shook her.

Shocked speechless, she stared up at him.

"What the *fuck* did you think you were doing?" he snarled.

Her eyes widened in fear, and her mouth fell open but no sound came out.

"I told you to stay put!" He whirled around to Spencer, efficiently tightened the tourniquet and ignoring the roar of agony, elevated the wounded leg above his heart to help slow the bleeding.

"Hang in there, buddy. Helo's on its way." Then his eyes cut back to her, slicing through her like a blade. "You ever pull a stunt like that again I'll kick your ass, do you understand me?"

"Dec," Spencer protested weakly.

"Save it." He pushed her away and tended to the wound again. "I heard it all over the radio."

His icy tone was the absolute last straw on her stripped nerves. Irrational though it was, his anger cut her deeply. Helpless to stop them, tears flooded her eyes.

"I'm sorry!" she yelled. "I didn't know where the hell you were, and I was scared he'd bleed to death if I didn't do something." She gave his chest an angry shove with the heel of her hand, managed to knock him back a bit. "So you can stop yelling at me, Lieutenant! I was only trying to help." She dashed away the tears spilling down her cheeks, tried to stop shaking.

A great expulsion of air spoke volumes about his struggle to control his temper. "Bryn."

"What?"

Dec surprised her by hauling her into his lap and wrapping his steely arms around her. He squeezed her tight, absorbing the tremor that wracked her. When he released her as fast as he'd grabbed her, she had no idea how she was supposed to interpret his actions. "I know what you did for him."

She shuddered, confused by the quicksilver change in him.

"I appreciate what you did for Spence, but you almost got yourself killed out there. Then I'd have two casualties to take out instead of one. It was my job to take care of him, not yours, and I was coming for him. The first rule in a SEAL team is to never leave your man."

"Yes, but—"

"Don't talk. Chopper's going to set down in six minutes, and when it does, you're going to run like hell straight toward it. I'll lay down covering fire for you, and then I'll bring Spence out. We'll be right behind you." He pushed her back, took her chin in a warm, bloodstained hand and gazed earnestly into her eyes. Hard fingers gripped her jaw. "No matter what happens, you cannot stop. Do you understand me, Bryn? You can't stop, and you can't look back. Got it?"

Meaning, even if he and Spencer were both cut down, she had to keep going. She swallowed hard. "Got it," she answered shakily. Her hands grasped his shoulders, hard. "But if, um…if we don't make it—"

"We're not going to die, Bryn."

Sure. Whatever. She tried a small smile, felt as though her face would crack with the strain. A tension-filled silence stretched between them in the darkness. She settled beside Spencer and held tight to his cold hand. Calm. That's what he needed. She needed to present the illusion of calm to keep him grounded.

Striving for a steady voice, she attempted a stab

at normalcy, even though it was nuts. "Will you both go back to the States after this?" She wanted to believe Spencer would make it, squeezed his hand and was relieved by the pressure in his grip as he returned the gesture.

Dec laid a hand on his buddy's shoulder. "Spence will be laid up awhile and I'll be on Pro-Dev rotation. What about you? You going home?"

"I guess I will, once I know my father's going to be okay." How could they be having such a calm discussion when they might have only minutes left to live?

He checked his watch, leaned over to take Spencer's pulse. "Hanging in there, pal?"

Spencer let out a weak mutter.

Bryn discreetly leaned forward and put her head next to Dec's. "Will he be okay?" she whispered.

"If I can get him on that chopper in the next ten minutes, yeah. They'll give him a transfusion."

Ten minutes? She passed a hand over Spencer's clammy forehead, sending up a prayer for him.

As the seconds ticked past with Spence's harsh breathing filling the cave, her thoughts drifted to the everyday, mundane things she looked forward to having once she was safe at home.

"I need a shower and a toothbrush," she said to no one in particular.

"Don't we all." Dec sighed as he sat on his haunches, eyes scanning the darkness, ever vigilant. "A big steaming shower—"

"With shower gel."

"With shower gel for you," he allowed, "then a steak dinner and a fresh toothbrush, and a big soft bed to crash in."

She almost moaned, she wanted those things so bad. "What do you say, Spence? That sound good to you?"

"Yeah," he croaked, fingers still wrapped around

hers.

"When we get back," Dec said, "I'll buy us all a steak dinner."

Bryn squeezed the hand she held. "How about that, Spence? You want to take me out for dinner with Dec?"

Spencer bit back a groan and forced a weak smile. Then the distant throb of a rotor broke the silence. They all tensed, listening as it grew louder, then louder still.

"There's our ride," Dec confirmed, as though he was talking about a taxi waiting at the curb. "You're going to run real fast, right?"

She nodded. "Like the wind."

"Then let's go."

And just like that he pushed to his feet, snuck out to the edge of the boulders with his rifle. He looked back at his teammate. "You're gonna be okay, Spence. I'll have you on that bird in no time." He raised his eyes toward the helicopter, waiting, then at some unseen signal he turned to her. "Ready?"

"Yes." With one last squeeze of reassurance, she released Spencer's hand.

"Okay, then. Get going."

Now? She hesitated, fighting the strangest urge to kiss him, to cling to him. What if she never saw him again?

"Bryn. Go, now."

"Be careful," was all she could manage past the lump in her throat before she bolted past him out into the clear. The helo sat there a few hundred yards away, like a great black insect perched on the sand. Dec's rifle fired behind her, covering her desperate dash to safety. Her lungs burned, her thigh muscles straining under the burst of adrenaline shooting through her veins.

Two men jumped out of the chopper with their rifles up, and her heart gave a great leap of fear. She almost stopped, but remembered Dec's warning and kept sprinting. They fired past her, the muzzles of their guns spewing fire in the darkness. The bullets sang as they whizzed past her, some close enough she felt the air distort. Was Dec still out there behind her?

Halfway there. Keep running.

One of the soldiers motioned with his arm, waving it toward the ground as she drew closer. *Don't stop! Keep going.* He was yelling something, but she couldn't hear him over the rotors. What was he saying?

His arm kept moving, and as she drew nearer, she saw the urgency on his face, saw his mouth move.

"Get *d-o—o-w-n!*"

Terror froze her. Her heart rang in her ears. Everything morphed into slow motion. Instinctively covering her head with her arms, she dove. A blast exploded behind her, rendering her blind and deaf. She plowed into the ground as something sharp and hot peppered her arm and back, like she'd been stung by a swarm of angry bees.

Disoriented, terrified, she lurched up onto her knees, saw the soldier from the helicopter running flat out toward her. The wounds burned like hellfire, and something warm was dripping over her skin. Blood. Her blood.

Pushing to her feet, she staggered a step, then fell flat. She scrambled up again, determined not to die out here in the desert when she was so close to safety. Gaining her footing, she started toward the waiting chopper, and finally the soldier grabbed her and yanked her over his shoulder. He covered the remaining distance and clambered inside, flipping her onto her back to check her for injuries.

She cried out as her wounded flesh hit whatever she was lying on, and gazed up into his face. In shock, she stared at the familiar features of her best friend, sure she was hallucinating.

"Rayne?" she blurted. What was he doing here?

The man peering down at her shook his head. "No. Luke."

But he looked just like Rayne, Bryn thought blearily. Her whole body trembled. Rayne's identical twin was saying something to her, his voice urgent, but it sounded like it was coming from the end of a long tunnel. Everything was fuzzy. The burning pain in her back and side and arm eased to a dull throb as she stared blankly at the metal roof. She could still breathe, could still move her fingers and toes. But she was cold now, so cold. And where was Dec?

She winced when someone applied pressure to her side. What had hit her? Another bomb?

More shots fired from close by. The rotors sped up, the whine of the engine rising to a shrill pitch. Her body jerked with uncontrollable shivers. Her jaw clenched, teeth chattering. She was shaking apart, cold to the marrow of her bones. She must be dying.

Someone was lowered next to her. She tried to turn her head, but it was so heavy. Another man came into view, blocking her line of vision. His hands moved fast as he ripped open a sterile pack of needles, a bag of blood clenched between his teeth. As he shifted to work on his patient, Bryn recognized Spencer's pale, pinched face lying next to hers.

He was still alive. She tried to lift a hand as she whispered his name. She didn't see anyone else. Had they gotten her father out on another chopper? Someone placed an oxygen mask over her nose. Then Dec's face appeared above her, and she cried out his name through numb lips.

His expression brimmed with concern as he moved to straddle her legs with his knees. "Where were you hit?"

"S-side." The word distorted because of the oxygen mask.

He took hold of her shirt hem and gave a quick yank, rending it down the side seam. She gasped, but he ignored her and turned her halfway over. More pressure against her side and shoulder, and she winced as the pain burned through her flesh like greedy flames. She had the vague impression of being airborne and wondered if the helicopter had taken off yet.

"Dec," she whispered, focusing on his handsome face above her. His golden eyes stared directly into hers, as if he could hold her there with the force of his gaze alone. His warm fingers wrapped around her icy ones.

"I'm here, sweetheart, I'm holding your hand. Can you feel me?"

She nodded jerkily. "C-cold. So cold."

"It's shock, Bryn. You're in shock." His voice was so calm. "But you're safe now. We'll get you to a hospital."

Maybe she wasn't dying, then. Alive and safe. And Dec was with her. But then her vision blurred and she lost it. "Dec!"

He leaned closer, took her face between his hands. She registered the warmth of his fingers against her skin. "Look at me, Bryn, only at me." The stark command in his voice snapped her eyes to his. "Hang on, sweetheart. Hang on just a little longer, okay?"

"C-cold," she whispered, agonized by the way the shudders hurt her wounds. Burning—like someone had poured acid over her skin.

"I know." He wrapped a heavy blanket around her, rubbed his hands briskly over her uninjured side to warm her. "Better now?"

It helped a little, but the terrible shaking wouldn't let up. "Dec..."

"Just think of being back home in Oregon."

Home. Oh God, she wanted to be home. She nodded, holding on to his strength, to the comforting sound of his voice.

"Think of sitting on the beach watching the sun set over the water..."

She closed her eyes, the lids too heavy to keep open. His voice held her steady, lulled her, kept her calm as she floated away from the pain. Her mind filled with images of rolling waves and crimson-stained sky, and then she slipped under the tide of blackness.

Chapter Seven

Day 5, Hospital
Morning

When Bryn woke the next morning, dozens of wounds throbbed and stung across her back and right shoulder, down her upper arm and along her ribs where the surgeon had removed pieces of shrapnel. They'd come from a rocket propelled grenade, he'd informed her before he'd presented the metal shards to her in a stainless steel dish. Sitting up in her hospital bed, she poked them around with her forefinger, studying them with a kind of detached horror.

She must be living in an alternate reality. Any minute now, she was going to wake up back in her bed on the Oregon coast and hear the waves crashing on the sand. Yet the way her body hurt meant all of this was no nightmare.

So much for wishful thinking.

She closed her eyes and lay back against the thin plastic pillow hospitals used to make their patients extra uncomfortable, and focused on breathing calmly. Her poor father was up in the neurological ward after undergoing emergency surgery to drain the blood from his skull. Even with the pressure removed from around his brain, he hadn't regained consciousness. Though she'd asked repeatedly to see him, the staff had refused to let her upstairs, saying she would be allowed in if he improved or worsened. The surgeon had told her to prepare herself for the worst.

Now Bryn faced the reality, the cold truth. She would probably lose her father. She might be an independent, strong-willed adult, but the prospect of life without him made her feel small and helpless.

Her father had always been so strong, so fiercely intelligent. For as long as she could remember, she'd wanted to make him proud. Of anyone important to her, she saw him the least, yet *his* approval was what she'd wanted more than anything. Without him she felt adrift, like her anchor was gone.

Tears burned her eyes even as she scolded herself. She kept her lids closed and bit her lips together until she could get a grip on her emotions. Crying wasn't going to bring him out of his coma, and he would have hated seeing her sniveling during a crisis.

He would have said death was a part of life, and that it was natural he die before she did. Practical and analytical to the core. Some would say cold, but those people hadn't heard the tenderness in his voice when he'd told her he loved her in their earthen cell. Why had he waited so long to say that to her?

Stop it. At least he said it. At least you have that to hold onto.

Once the fear of the crying jag passed, she opened her eyes and stared down at the metal dish in her hands. The jagged splinters glinted, some of the pieces stained rusty red from her blood. God, she could not believe—

"Hard to believe they dug all that out of your skin, huh?" Spencer asked from his bed beside her. Since the hospital was overcrowded, they'd been roomies since he'd been moved in from recovery. "Pretty amazing."

He sounded like he thought it was cool. Maybe it would be to a SEAL, she didn't know. They were all a little crazy to begin with, so there was no telling how their brains functioned. "I guess so," she allowed. The RPG had been aimed at the helicopter, the staff had heard from Dec, but if she hadn't hit the ground when she did, she'd have taken the shrapnel in the head or neck and probably died.

She sighed. She needed a distraction. Watching the clock, waiting and worrying about her father wasn't going to make the second hand move any faster. She shoved away all thoughts of him and her own discomfort and switched her attention to Spencer, propped up with his left leg in a cast from groin to ankle. "How are you feeling, by the way?"

"Damn lucky to be alive."

"What did the doctors say?"

"Busted femur, artery patched with a Dacron graft. You know."

Yeah, sure, standard stuff. Because this sort of thing happened to people all the time.

In hell.

Bryn searched for a safe topic. "Did you call your wife yet?"

Spencer looked away, made a show of smoothing his blanket. "Nah."

She angled her head toward him, frowning. "How come?" Considering what he'd said after he'd been shot, Bryn had assumed he'd want to talk to her first thing. But maybe the Navy had already contacted her? She was probably on a flight right now to come see him.

He fiddled more with the blanket, his brow furrowing. "Well, thing is, I'm not really sure if she's still my wife or not."

"Why not?"

"The final divorce papers were supposed to be delivered this month. She might already have sent them in to her lawyer, I don't know."

Oh, poor Spencer. "I'm so sorry."

"Yeah, thanks." He lay back against the pillow and closed his eyes. Faint grooves around his mouth hinted he was in more pain than he let on. "She just couldn't take me being in the Teams. I'm away so much and I can never tell her anything about where I've been or where I'm going, and even when I'm home I'm training all the time. It doesn't exactly make for a close, trusting relationship, right?"

She nodded, waited for him to continue. Her heart ached for him.

"It's hard for the women," he said. "A lot of marriages don't work out for guys like us."

No, they didn't. Just look at the awful mess Rayne's mom and dad had gone through. She thought of all the scenarios she encountered as a social worker, ran through the likely causes of divorce, other than what he'd said. He seemed like such a nice guy, she couldn't imagine him hitting his wife, so...

"And were you...I mean did you ever, you know...cheat on her or anything?"

He narrowed his eyes. "Why, because I'm in the Navy and we sailors are supposed to have a girl in every port?"

She held up her hands, flinched and dropped them as her wounds pulled. "Hey, I'm just asking. Didn't mean to offend."

"Christ no, I never cheated on her. Have I been tempted? Sure. Would I ever act on it? No way."

"That's good." She stayed silent, giving him the opportunity to keep talking about it if he wanted. The least she could do was listen.

"I even thought about leaving the Teams, hoping that would make her want to work things out, but..." He let out a ragged sigh. "Truth is, it's probably too late now anyway. We've grown apart too much to fix it, even if she was willing. I don't blame her, really."

He didn't blame her? Well, why the hell not? It took two, didn't it?

No, she told herself. Don't go there. It really

wasn't any of her business. No reason for her to put in her two cents' worth. But dammit, she was outraged on his behalf. If his wife had been through what they had in the last two days, out there in the field with terrorists on their heels, she might have been more understanding.

Watching the SEALs in action was something Bryn was never going to forget. She had half a mind to call Spencer's wife and tell her exactly how close he'd come to dying—to protect a total stranger.

The anger felt good after all the fear she'd suffered. Too good, and she let herself go with it until the hard words crowded in the back of her throat. Riding a wave of outrage, she couldn't stop herself from blurting, "If she married you knowing you were in the Teams, then she should stick by you."

Spencer's smile was weary. "Bryn, you don't know what it's like for her when—"

"Oh, yes I do. My best friend's dad was a SEAL, and you know what? Over twenty years ago he left his family thinking he was doing them a favor, and to this *day* his wife pines over him. Trust me on this, Spencer, she would move heaven and earth to make it work with him. You think your wife has it tough? Maybe. Nobody said it was going to be easy, but she can't just up and quit like that. That's not how it works." She huffed out a furious breath. "So the way I see it, she didn't deserve you anyway. If she's ready to give up, then you're better off without her."

He rubbed a hand over his chest, his expression chagrined. "Well, shit. Tell me how you really feel, why don't you."

She lifted her shoulders. "Sorry. Just saying."

Oh, man, she'd love to get his wife on the phone and tell her off. He could easily have bled out last night. He and the others put their lives on the line every time they went to work, even for training. She was living proof of their skill and bravery. No way would she have survived without them.

As the silence grew and held between them, Bryn regretted shooting her mouth off. Ranting about how his wife didn't deserve him probably wasn't the nicest thing to say, especially not to someone recovering from a serious gunshot wound. The anger drained away as quickly as it had come, leaving her filled with guilt. Oh, hell. Blame it on the Demerol. Now she wanted to crawl over to him and hug him.

"Spencer, I'm sorry. It wasn't my place to say that. I just...you deserve better."

"Nah, it's okay." He cleared his throat, shifted his gaze over to her.

She took the eye contact as a good sign. Maybe he didn't hate her.

"You know," he murmured, "I probably didn't seem thankful at the time, but I appreciate what you did out there. I owe you big time."

Bryn's cheeks heated. She hadn't done it to be heroic. Anyone in her place would have tried to help him. "Don't be silly. I didn't do anything—"

"Except drag his sorry two-hundred-pound ass behind cover while taking enemy fire," Dec interrupted from the doorway, making her heart stutter, "and then stop him from bleeding to death."

Dressed in clean fatigues, face freshly shaven, he strode over between the beds and clasped Spencer's hand. If she'd thought he was hot with stubble and camouflage paint all over his face, now he was heart-stopping. Tall and muscular, his dark hair and brows a startling contrast to his golden eyes.

He grinned down at Spencer before shifting his gaze to her. "Isn't this cozy? Just look at you two."

Self-conscious, she made a face at him. He stood there so clean and fit and strong while she was covered in bandages with only a sponge bath to take her body odor down to a dull roar. She wanted to wash her hair so badly she could have screamed.

"Did you come for something important, or are you here to gloat about how healthy you are?" she asked him.

Dec's eyes lit with amusement. "Not feeling so hot, huh?"

"That's an understatement. I've been blown up twice now in four days. Makes me bitchy."

He smothered a laugh and sat on the bed next to her hip. A glance at his hands showed he wasn't wearing a wedding ring. This close she got a whiff of his soap. Her body temperature went up a couple degrees. "I just checked on your dad. No change yet, but he's holding steady. Thought you'd want to know."

"Thanks." His thoughtfulness made her throat close up and the word came out in a husky rasp.

"I brought you something."

She appreciated his changing the subject. "Yeah?" What had he brought to cheer her up? A chocolate bar maybe? Or a bag of chips? No—an icy cold can of Coke. Oh, God, she'd kill for that right now. Her mouth watered.

Instead, he pulled a piece of paper out of one of the pockets in his camouflage pants and unfolded it, holding it out for her to see.

Bryn stared at the purple crayon drawing of a heart-shaped medal. She glanced up from the paper, glowered at him. "Tell me you're joking."

"What?" he asked, all innocence. "It's a Purple Heart." He pinned it to her hospital gown with a safety pin, the brush of his fingers against her left collarbone making her heart knock against her ribs. She stared at his hands. Powerful yet gentle at the same time. "Took me all morning to find a purple crayon."

"Where's mine?" Spencer demanded.

"Yours is coming," Dec informed him. "But Miss McAllister is a civilian, and she wouldn't have gotten one if I hadn't made one for her." His white, even teeth flashed as he grinned at her, dimples appearing in his lean cheeks. "Wear it with pride, sweetheart. I don't know any other woman half as tough as you. I think you just might have made it through Hell Week, you know that?" His amazing eyes showed something close to affection.

Bryn fingered the paper medal, ridiculously pleased by his compliment. "Nah. Sleep deprivation would've made me ring out after the first night."

"I don't think so, sweetheart." Bending down to smooth the hair from her face, he made her blush even more. She almost leaned into his touch, but managed to hold back at the last second.

He shook his head in wonder, dimples peeping again. "You're something else, Bryn McAllister, you know that?"

And before she knew what he was about, he leaned over her and pressed his mouth to hers.

Bryn stiffened. Heat roared through her with stunning force. His mouth was shockingly soft. He kissed her with a lingering thoroughness, his lips warm and firm but tender. He waited until she'd thawed a little before pulling back to gauge her reaction and hovered there, watching her eyes, then dipped back down for another slow taste.

Her fingers curled helplessly into his t-shirt. Every nerve in her body seemed to go haywire, a pool of lava forming low in her belly. When he finally lifted his head she'd forgotten her own name. She wanted to grab him by his muscled shoulders and kiss him senseless, and he knew it.

To regain control of the situation, she pushed him back and cleared her throat, stomach jumping with nerves. "Are you headed back to your base?"

Did SEALs stay on a base? "Or is it an aircraft carrier?" A nuclear sub, maybe.

"In a couple days, maybe. For now we've got to clean up the rest of that cell we tangled with."

Her heart seemed to stop beating for a second. "Tonight?" She hated the thought of him going back out there, now knowing full well what kind of danger he'd be in.

He held her gaze. "Best time to hunt is at night. That's where we're in our element."

"Yeah, and I'm laid up with a busted leg and a patched artery," Spencer said glumly from beside them.

"True," Dec agreed, "but look who you get to room with."

Spencer sighed and closed his eyes with a smile. "There is that. I still haven't thanked her properly, by the way. You interrupted us before I could finish."

Dec sat back and gestured to her with a sweep of his arm. "Be my guest."

"I can't do it with you watching," Spencer complained. "I'm waiting until you leave."

Dec raised his eyebrows. "Oh? And just what are you going to do to her that you don't want me to see?"

Spencer shrugged. "Some more of what you just did, only better."

A nurse came in and checked his vitals, then adjusted the flow of the IV drip and over his protests added another dose of pain medication.

"It will help you sleep," she insisted, coming around to check Bryn's bandages. "And you, too," she informed her. "You both need it."

"Can you just put a little bit in mine?" Bryn pleaded. She hated feeling woozy, hated throwing up even more. Especially in front of the man who'd just lit her body up like the Fourth of July with one kiss.

"Stuff makes me puke," Spencer grumbled

sleepily.

"Me too," she sympathized, watching with a sinking heart as the nurse gave her a full dose anyway. She didn't want to fall asleep while Dec was still here, and she wanted no part of vomiting in front of him. Already the drug had her eyelids feeling heavy.

The nurse fixed the blankets around her, snorted in amusement when she saw the paper medal pinned to her chest.

"Hey, I earned that," Bryn said, covering it defensively with one hand.

"You sure as hell did," Dec agreed.

The nurse pointed a finger at him. "You've got one minute, Lieutenant, then these two need to rest."

He seemed to fight a smile. "Yes ma'am." Bryn's heart leapt as his long fingers twined around her hand. "You get better, okay?"

"I will." He was going to leave, just like that? After he'd kissed her? Disappointment swamped her, but the morphine was tugging at her, pulling her under.

"I'll get in touch when I get stateside," he whispered, smiling down at her. "If that's okay."

"Okay." She tried not to sound too enthusiastic, but it was hard to tell if she pulled it off with the narcotic floating through her veins. She watched helplessly as he walked to the door. "But I didn't give you my number."

He stopped inside the doorframe to look back, his eyes laughing at her. "I'll find you."

As he disappeared from view, fear for his safety made her panic.

"Dec!" she called, fighting a losing battle with her pain meds.

He stuck his head in the door a moment later, brows raised expectantly.

She opened her mouth, closed it, memorizing his handsome face in case she never saw him again. "Be careful," she managed.

His dimples flashed. "Always."

"And thanks—for everything."

He winked. "Anytime, sweetheart." Then he was gone.

To ease the ache in her chest she sighed heavily and closed her eyes against the sting of tears. It was the medication, she told herself. That was why she felt so weepy and alone. Nothing to do with the fact her father might die and Dec had just left.

"Hey, pretty lady."

She swung her head around to look at Spencer. "Okay, you *so* can't mean me."

"Sure I can. I want to thank you now before I go into hibernation, so lean over, will you?"

"Wha—?"

He grabbed hold of her bed railing and dragged it across the floor until it touched his, then palmed the back of her head in one hand and kissed the breath right out of her.

When he released her, she fell back against the pillow. She hadn't really thought he'd do it. As far as thank-yous went, that was a first for her. There'd been no heat in it on either side, though, just his heartfelt gratitude. Not at all like the volcanic rush of Dec's kiss.

"Well." She tried to think of something appropriate to say, lips tingling from the imprint of his mouth on hers, but she was remembering Dec. "Well."

"Thanks for saving my ass, Bryn," he said, eyes closed. "Never thought I'd say this to a woman, but I'd want you on my team any day."

The compliment warmed her to her toes.

A nurse came in. "Bryn?"

One look at her solemn expression, and all the

blood drained from Bryn's face. Her father. Her muscles tightened. "Is he...?" She couldn't say the words aloud. Shock rendered her jaw and limbs rigid.

"I'm sorry. He's taken a turn for the worse," she said, coming over to inject something into the IV line.

A turn for the worse. Wasn't that something they said to prepare family members when their loved one had already passed away? She swallowed.

"This will counteract the morphine, and then I'll help you into a wheelchair and take you upstairs to see him."

Her heartbeat sped up. What if they hadn't come to her in time? What if she didn't get to say goodbye?

As the nurse went to fetch the wheelchair, she caught sight of Spencer's face—full of sympathy. He muttered something about how he was sorry and that he wished he could go up with her.

So she wouldn't be alone.

Oh God, she really was all alone, wasn't she?

The stitches in her arms and side pulled and throbbed, but the pain didn't register as she eased herself into the wheelchair. The nurse hustled her to the elevator and upstairs to the neurological ward, then down the hall to her father's room.

****

Halfway to the cab waiting at the curb, Dec stopped on the sidewalk and looked over his shoulder as the nurse came running out of the hospital calling his name.

"I'm McCabe," he said, bracing himself for bad news.

The middle-aged woman was out of breath as she reached him. "Petty Officer Spencer sent me after you," she panted with a hand on her chest. "Miss McAllister is going up to see her father. The doctors expect him to pass away any time now."

Christ, poor Bryn. He wiped a hand over his face and let out a hard sigh. She'd been through so much already, but to lose her father this way on top of everything else was beyond cruel. At the very least she shouldn't have to go through it alone, which was no doubt why Spencer had sent the nurse for him.

Damn, he couldn't leave her to face this by herself. He glanced at his watch, grabbed his cell phone and dialed headquarters as he followed the nurse back inside. Once he'd explained what was going on, they promised to send someone from Jamul's staff to come and be with Bryn. He would gladly have stayed as long as she needed him to, but he had to be back at the base in less than three hours.

In the lobby, he ditched the elevator and took the stairs, running the four flights two steps at a time. Someone at the nurses' station directed him down the hall and he stopped outside Jamul's room to peer in the window.

Bryn was in a wheelchair, her right arm bandaged as she bent over her father's inert body, holding his hand, squeezing so tight her knuckles were white. Her pale face was turned toward her father, eyes locked on Jamul's face as though she could will him back to life with the power of her concentration. Her lips moved. Was she speaking to him or was she praying?

His heart ached for her as he stood outside the door, hesitant to intrude on her private goodbye. Maybe it would be best for him to wait out in the hall for a while. He didn't want to disturb her, and if he was still here when she came out, he could try and comfort her.

Not that there was much he could do for her. Even holding her would hurt her because of all her shrapnel wounds. But God, he couldn't stand knowing she was suffering this way.

As he watched, her slim shoulders began to shake, and then her head bowed as she gave way to her grief. Her ravaged face turned away as she pressed it to her father's chest and Dec knew he must be gone. He stepped away to give her more privacy, feeling helpless.

Sure enough, a few minutes later a doctor and two nurses went in and stayed only a few minutes before leaving again. As they passed, Dec heard the word 'morgue.' It was over.

Bryn stayed in the room, probably not wanting to leave him yet. Dec tried to imagine sitting there next to his father's body, knowing that when he left, the staff would come in and take him to the morgue and put him in a refrigerated drawer. The thought made him feel sick. His family meant everything to him.

He walked the hallway a couple of times, watching the clock on the wall. After spending almost an hour that way, he only had a little while left before he had to report for duty. Would it be better to leave before she'd seen him?

No. He couldn't do it. He'd wait as long as he could and if she hadn't come out yet, he'd leave a message of his sympathy with the nurses for her. She might have been alone in that room when her father had died, but at least she would know he'd been there.

Jesus, he'd never felt such a powerful need to comfort anyone. And hell, it had been totally out of character for him to kiss her, but he just couldn't help it.

Another nurse passed him, her rubber-soled shoes squeaking on the linoleum, and went into Jamul's room. Less than a minute later, Bryn emerged through the doors in the wheelchair with the nurse pushing her, and when she saw him her expression froze.

She had to be exhausted and devastated, and she seemed surprised as hell to see him standing there. "Dec," she said, voice rough as sandpaper.

He came to hunker down in front of her, took her icy hands in his. The nurse left them alone. "I'm so sorry."

She nodded and sniffed, gazing down at their joined hands. "Thanks."

Damn, he wanted to hold her so bad. She looked so lost and alone it almost broke his heart. He didn't understand how it had happened so quickly, but over the past few days he'd already grown attached to her. Protective of her.

"At least I got to say goodbye," she whispered. "Not everyone has that chance."

He rubbed his thumbs over the cool skin on the backs of her hands. "Someone from his staff is coming to be with you."

Her obsidian eyes were so full of pain. "You came back."

"Yeah. Spence sent someone after me as I was leaving."

"It was sweet of you. I appreciate it."

Hell, he'd have done anything for her. He respected and admired her. Waiting in a hallway an hour or more was nothing. "I didn't want you to be alone."

Staring at him, her beautiful eyes filled with tears, then she flung her arms around his neck and buried her face in his shoulder. Cursing himself for making her cry, he could feel her pain as she battled for control, and slid his arms around her.

Careful of her bandages, he tucked her in close and stroked her back, giving her what comfort he could. She felt so fragile in his embrace. Too small to carry such a burden on her slender shoulders.

After a minute or so she pushed away and

dragged her hands across her wet face, sucked in a ragged breath. "Sorry. I'm okay now."

"Don't apologize." Unable to stop himself, he framed her face between his hands and wiped her tears away. "What can I do?"

She forced a sad smile. "Nothing. You've done more than enough for me already."

No he hadn't. "Want me to take you downstairs?"

"Sure."

Glad to have something to do, he went around behind her and pushed the wheelchair to the elevator and back to her room.

Spencer turned his head as they came in. "Bryn, I'm so sorry."

"Thanks."

Dec stood beside her and glanced down at her face. Her eyes were staring dully now, from exhaustion and pain and grief. Sleep was probably the only thing that would help her.

Two nurses came in to take over and helped her back into her bed. He still couldn't believe the anguish she must be going through. But he was out of time and couldn't do anything more for her.

He came over to her bed, brushed a hand over her hair.

"You have to go?" An observation, not a question.

He nodded.

She reached up and pressed her hand against his where it lay on her head. "Thanks for coming back. It means a lot to me."

"You're welcome." Ah, hell, he couldn't not kiss her again. This time he bent and pressed his lips to her forehead, wishing he could make it better. Straightening, he looked at Spencer. "You'll take care of her?"

"You know it."

When he turned back to her, Bryn's eyes were glazed. "Try to sleep," he whispered. "I'll get in touch with you as soon as I can."

She nodded almost mechanically, as though she was sinking deeper into grief. "Bye."

When he looked back at her from the doorway, her eyes were closed.

****

Day 5, Near Syria-Lebanon border
Evening

Tehrazzi leaned back into the front seat of the battered pickup as it bumped and rattled over the rough dirt road that led to his childhood village, fighting back the bitter rage that filled his heart. When the intelligence had come in that morning about the traitor, at first he'd refused to accept who had helped the Americans escape. He did not want to believe his blood would commit such a terrible sin.

But the evidence was incontrovertible. They had betrayed him, and now they would pay the ultimate price so that no one would dare cross him again.

In his mind he saw his victim paused in front of the fire crackling in the crude hearth to warm her old bones. Every arthritic joint in her body would be aching and throbbing as they always did this time of day. How many hours had he spent rubbing those gnarled hands to relieve her suffering over the years? But her recent actions had sealed her fate. Did she know he was coming for her? He imagined her weakened heart fluttering against the cage of her ribs like a trapped bird.

Mortal terror did that to a person.

Whispers about the foreign captives' escape had circulated through the local marketplace that morning. He had made certain everyone knew he

87

was searching for those who had betrayed him, and when he found them, their deaths would be brutal. A matter of hours ago he had learned the truth about the betrayal. Now, mere minutes remained before he would mete out his swift and savage retribution. Her betrayal had pushed him into a rage so vast...

He forced a calming breath. She would pray for death before he was finished with her. As would her husband. Even the bond of shared blood would not save them from his wrath.

He thought of the stoning he'd witnessed in Kabul a year after the Taliban had restored law and order to the chaos of Afghanistan in the wake of the Communist defeat. Found guilty of adultery, the man and woman had been wrapped in white cloth, bound hand and foot and buried in the ground up to their waists. Neighbors from the village had carried out the sentence.

The memory of the rocks and stones hitting their bodies was still fresh in his memory. He could still hear the sound of it—each dull thud as the stones smashed into flesh and bone, until the white cloth was soaked crimson with blood. Left alone where they lay, the victims had taken another day to die from their injuries.

He was a hardliner. He believed in upholding the traditional Islamic Shari'a law. Should he stone the traitor to death? Behead her? He pushed away the surge of guilt. She was a woman of strong faith. No matter what crimes she had committed here on Earth, there was a place in heaven for her. After her mortal suffering was finished, Allah would have mercy on her, even if Tehrazzi did not.

As they entered the village, people peered out the windows of their tiny mud-brick huts. Children played in the dusty road, but stopped when they saw them. A few dogs skulked in the lengthening shadows. The truck announced his presence for him, as he was the only one wealthy enough in the region to afford a vehicle. Every man, woman and child in that village knew who he was and why he was here.

He thought of his intended victim. Was her husband still out herding the goats? She couldn't leave without him. She was too old to provide for herself up in the mountains, even if she managed to get that far. It was too late to run now. She had nowhere to hide from him.

Arriving at the last house, the driver pulled up and shut off the engine. A curtain twitched in the tiny window looking out onto the street. She knew he was here. Was she praying for her soul's redemption? He and his bodyguard exited the vehicle. His heart pounded as they approached the door of the only real home he had ever known.

The old woman jumped in her threadbare slippers when he threw the wooden door open. It crashed into the wall with a thud. She cowered in the corner, her knees quivering. His long shadow fell over the rug-covered dirt floor.

A second later, he walked through the doorway. Qamar's wide-eyed gaze traveled up his frame and she dared to look into his face. A burning rage swept over him, bitter on his tongue. The taste of betrayal.

He stood there a moment, gazing at her stricken face. Then his upper lip curled in disdain. "Hello, Grandmother."

She shook at the promise of hell in his eyes.

Chapter Eight

Day 6, Beirut
Afternoon

The funeral passed in a blur.

Ben Sinclair, the head of Bryn's father's security team, stood beside her the whole day, never letting her out of his sight, and she was glad to have him there.

A couple years younger than her, the former Army Ranger was a mountain of strength for her to lean upon, making her feel relatively safe amongst the media and crowd of mourners gathered at the Beirut cemetery. He was the protective brother she'd never had, and though she'd sensed more than a platonic interest on his part lately, for her they could never be more than friends.

With Ben's arm around her waist, Bryn was numb as she watched them lower her father's casket. His body couldn't be in that glossy, wooden box being put into the ground. In life he'd been so powerful and charismatic, he'd seemed to take up an entire room when he entered it. That brightly burning flame couldn't be snuffed out forever.

Raising her eyes to the brilliant azure sky, she persuaded herself that he was watching them and allowed herself to imagine what he would think. He would probably shake his head in disgust at the public display in his memory. But maybe, just maybe he would have been proud of the way she was bearing up.

After the ceremony, Ben settled her in her

father's armor-plated Range Rover and drove her back to the compound that was now hers.

Learning that bit of news at the lawyer's office when the will was read had come as a shock. She hadn't thought her father would leave her something so substantial, since they weren't really that close. She was his only child, though, and since her twenty-first birthday, he'd apparently planned to make her his sole heir. He'd wanted his wealth passed on to his blood, proving how much he trusted her.

At this point, she wasn't sure what she wanted to do with the place. She certainly didn't want to live in Beirut, but selling it would feel like a betrayal of her father's lifelong work. He hadn't struggled up from the depths of poverty for his daughter to sell his dreams after he'd gone, merely because it was simplest for her. If he'd taught her one thing about life, it was that the right path wasn't always the easiest one.

Ben cleared his throat as he drove, his pale green eyes sweeping over her face. "How you doing, sweets? Want to take a break before going back to the house?"

She smiled at his profile. He'd been uncharacteristically quiet for the last two days. "No. I'd better get back."

Her presence was expected, anyhow. The reception was going to be huge, over four hundred people coming. Politicians—supporters and rivals alike—distant family members and friends. Ben had seen to it that security was tight. Everyone was on high alert after the embassy bombing and the kidnappings, him especially.

He was guilt stricken at what had happened to her and her father. She'd tried to convince him it wasn't his fault, but despite her reassurance, Ben carried the burden of her kidnapping and Jamul's death on his broad shoulders, and she was at a loss to relieve him of it. Thank God for him, though. She would never have made it through the past couple of days without him.

When the white stone walls of the compound came into view, Bryn suddenly felt exhausted. The almost-healed stitches in her right arm and ribs pulled every time she took a breath. They didn't hurt so much anymore, just bothered her.

All she wanted was to go upstairs to her room and be alone for a while, but that wasn't going to happen. No, she had to make it through another six or so hours of introductions and forced conversations.

The only thing that kept her from losing her mind was knowing Ben would be right next to her. His presence was the sole calming, soothing influence in her life right now. Whatever happened for the rest of her stay here, he had her back. It was a nice feeling.

That kind of stalwart protectiveness made her think of Dec, but with the major difference that she didn't feel the least bit sisterly toward Dec. It had meant so much to her, knowing he'd come back to be with her when her father died. She hadn't heard from him since, not that she'd expected to, but she hoped he was all right. So far she hadn't been able to find out where he was. For all she knew he could be back in the States already.

Despite the chaos she'd had to deal with, he was on her mind constantly. Lying in bed unable to sleep at night, she couldn't help remembering the feel of his arms around her in the hospital, how amazed she'd been that someone so strong and tough could be so gentle. So okay, it wasn't healthy to obsess about a man she'd probably never see again, but she couldn't get him out of her head.

As Ben parked in front of the stone and stucco

Mediterranean-style mansion, he regarded her, jaw clenching and unclenching as he chewed his cinnamon gum—a habit he'd developed when he'd quit smoking the year he'd made the Rangers.

That was Ben for you. Once he made up his mind to do something he was all steely determination and resolve. With nothing but a pack of Big Red to tide him over, he'd given up the smokes the same day he earned his Ranger tab.

His pale eyes were kind as he looked at her now. "Ready to do this?"

Bryn sighed and summoned her inner strength. She was going to need it. She gripped the door handle. She was her father's daughter, and she would handle this with as much grace and decorum as possible. "Showtime."

People filled the house—a sea of faces she didn't recognize and didn't really care to meet. She had to, though. Her father would have expected her to fulfill her duties as hostess, even under these circumstances. The staff had laid out food on the long dining table. Platters with crispy grapes and juicy watermelon nestled amongst sandwiches and wedges of cheese. Above the aroma of food, the heavy scent of lilies filled the air, nauseating in their sickly sweetness.

Funeral flowers, she thought with a swallow. Funny how scents triggered such powerful memories, in this case her grandmother's open-casket funeral. The perfume saturated the room until she was desperate to escape it.

She sought refuge in her father's library. As she pushed open the solid wooden door, the smells of old leather and pipe tobacco brought a lump to her throat. The mahogany desk, set against the window overlooking the grounds, sat unused; the high-back tufted leather chair empty, never to be occupied again by her father.

She shut the door and stood stiffly at the threshold. The room seemed as cold and lifeless as a tomb without his unending reserve of energy to fill it. Maybe coming here wasn't such a good idea. It hurt to see the hub of her father's home vacant and still. She passed her fingers reverently over the desk's polished surface, as if searching for a connection she hadn't been able to forge while he was alive.

Someone knocked on the door. "Bryn? It's me," called Ben.

Straightening her spine, she cleared her throat and turned around. "Come in."

He did, and assessed her with a long look. "Need a break?"

"I just wanted a minute. I'm okay now. The flowers..."

"Yeah. They reek." He shoved his hands deep into his pockets and rocked back on his heels. Then he snapped his gum, a sure sign something was on his mind. "I wouldn't have bothered you, but someone asked to speak privately with you."

"Who?"

"He said you'd never met but that you'd recognize him."

She couldn't imagine who he was talking about. Still, she had a role to fulfill. "I guess I could. Sure, send him in."

He stuck his head out and gestured for their guest to enter.

When the visitor's face appeared she gasped, a hand flying up to her mouth. Ben stiffened in alarm but stayed where he was, watching her carefully. But she wasn't in any danger.

"Hello Bryn," the man said with the hint of a Louisiana drawl.

Her mouth opened. The resemblance was uncanny. He was a little shorter than his son, his dark hair sprinkled with silver and his eyes chocolate brown instead of greenish-hazel, but otherwise she was staring at her best friend, Rayne Hutchinson, twenty years from now.

She dropped the hand covering her mouth. "You're...are you—?"

"Luke Hutchinson," he said, holding out his hand. Bryn took it politely and shook it. "Rayne's dad."

And her father's old friend. "Were you on the chopper the other night?"

"Yeah."

Whoa. "I knew I saw Rayne in there...but of course it was you—" She broke off, studying him. "I thought you got out of the SEAL Teams years ago."

"Sure did. I run a private security company now. Sometimes I do contract work."

Contract work? Well, that was one way to put it. "So why were you on the chopper?"

"I was going after the cell responsible for kidnapping you and your father when the rescue team was sent in. I asked to go along, to help an old friend and his daughter."

"You look just like Rayne," she breathed, hand on her chest. "Or rather, he looks just like you."

"Yeah, so everyone tells us."

"I've heard so much about you I feel as though I know you already. Which of course I don't, but..." She was so glad to see him here in the midst of all these strangers. He represented a connection to her father and life back home, made her feel less alone and almost safe for the first time in a week. "You knew my father, didn't you?"

Luke nodded. "Met him when I did a tour here back during the civil war. I'm sorry for your loss. He was a good man."

"Thank you. I'm sure you're aware I wasn't that close to him. I only got to spend a couple weeks with him each summer."

"He was proud enough of you, all the same." He indicated the framed pictures of her on the desk and bookshelves. "Knowing Jamul, he followed everything you did your entire life, even if you didn't know about it. Likely preferred it that way."

Maybe. Her father had been a man with little time for emotion. But he had loved her in his own way. A sad smile curved her lips, but she was comforted by Luke's words. Part of her wondered if he was speaking from personal experience. "What are the chances of you meeting my father and then me becoming friends with your son on the other side of the world?"

"Yeah, this planet gets smaller every day."

She missed Rayne and his fiancée. "How is he, by the way? Last I heard he and Christa were still ironing out the wedding details."

"Early May, and they're both doing fine."

It occurred to her he was still standing up. "Please, sit." She gestured to a wingback chair, seated herself in the other. "I was so surprised to see you I forgot my manners."

His smile warmed her. "I'm not easily offended, 'specially not by a beautiful woman who's been through what you have this past week."

Bryn hid her grin. Ah, yes, the infamous Hutchinson charm. Must be genetic.

Luke lowered his well-muscled body into the chair, and she had to admire the physical condition he was still in. As his magnetic gaze met hers, an air of authority and power hummed around him.

Thirty-odd years of covert warfare and intelligence work lay in the confident set of his shoulders and blazed from the depths of his dark chocolate eyes. He was every bit as dangerous as his reputation made him out to be. Yet she knew from his wife and son there was a softer, vulnerable side to him.

Not that he'd want her—or anyone else—to know anything about that. In fact, somewhere beneath that ultra-strong exterior he might be feeling awkward. She'd been privy to more dirt about him than the tabloids printed about Hollywood celebrities.

On the other side of the room, Ben cleared his throat.

She glanced over at him, saw him giving her a "what the hell are you doing" look and realized she'd been staring at Luke like he was some sort of fascinating biological specimen. More interesting, the whole time he hadn't broken her gaze for an instant during a silence even Ben had found awkward. She shook her head ruefully at her lack of grace. "Sorry. I didn't mean to be rude. I must be in shock from meeting you face to face."

Something flickered in Luke's eyes. "It's all right. I expected it."

Bryn faltered, sensing he meant that all the things she'd heard about him must be bad. "I'm really glad you came," she admitted, unable to keep the smile from her face. "It's almost as good as having Rayne or Emily here."

His eyes warmed a fraction. "I'll take that as a compliment."

She leaned forward. "Are you in Beirut for business, or did you come for the funeral?"

"Both." He stretched out his long legs and crossed his ankles, hands resting on his flat abdomen. Most men in their thirties didn't have abs as impressive as those. "I have some important information to share with you, and I wanted Ben to be here when I told you. As head of your father's security team he should know about this, but I also thought you'd be more comfortable with him here."

Unease rippled across her skin. What, was she

97

going to need moral support? "That was thoughtful of you, but unnecessary. I feel perfectly comfortable with you." She hoped he believed her. She would hate him to think she was afraid of him and wanted someone around to protect her just in case.

"What information do you have?" Ben asked with a note of suspicion. Though his posture seemed relaxed, Bryn knew he remained vigilant, his brain whirring constantly. That mind of his never shut off.

Luke flicked him a glance and then settled his gaze back on her. The intensity of his eyes made her stomach tighten and she mentally braced herself for bad news. "The man responsible for the bombing and your kidnapping is Farouk Tehrazzi."

Her lungs constricted at the mention of his name. "Yes, that's what I was told."

"Obviously, he's still out there. And if he wasn't sure before, after today's media coverage, he knows you survived."

Cold spread over her palms to the tips of her fingers. She laced them together and squeezed tightly. "I see."

"I can tell you he won't let that go unanswered."

She stared at him, the words echoing through her head. Her lips felt numb, her muscles stiff with apprehension.

Ben snapped his gum once before speaking up. "Meaning what? He's going to come after her again?" His pale eyes glittered with hostility. "You think I wasn't already aware of the threat?"

Luke raised an eyebrow. "Were you?"

Unable to speak, Bryn held her breath and waited for him to elaborate.

"A message was posted this morning on their social media."

This guy had his own social media sites? What a wonderful world cyberspace had created. Scumoftheearth.com.

Luke continued speaking to Ben. "If you're up to your job, you'll be aware that Tehrazzi has issued a fifty-thousand-dollar reward for her."

She gasped, eyes flaring wide. "What?" She glared at Ben. "Did you know about this? Why didn't you tell me?"

His shoulder muscles were taut against the fabric of his dress shirt. "What agency are you working for?" he said to Luke.

"The usual one. Under contract." His lips curved in a humorless smile. "You could call me somewhat of a...Tehrazzi expert."

Bryn's mouth went dry. *Oh, Jesus.*

"In that case, do you know where he is?" Ben demanded.

Luke arched a brow. "More or less. My point is, he's as relentless as he is dangerous, and this threat to her safety is to be taken seriously. She needs protection twenty-four-seven until she's back home, and even then it wouldn't hurt to have a detail keep an eye on her until the cell is destroyed."

Ben swore and started barking orders to his security team over his radio.

Oh God. This couldn't be happening. Not on top of everything else. No, no...she wanted this to be over. She wanted her life back—the life of independent Bryn McAllister who lived on the beach and fought for the children in her caseload.

"Bryn?"

She blinked up at Luke, who was watching her intently.

"Do you understand what I'm saying?"

"Y-yes," she stammered. She had a bounty on her head. Depending on how popular the terrorist's social media sites were, she could have a whole lynch mob after her. Her chest tightened.

Ben set his radio down on the desk, resolve stamped all over his face. "It's going to be okay,

Bryn," he reassured her, his eyes on hers. "You're safe here. I'm making sure of that."

She nodded, unable to think of a single thing to say, suddenly wishing Dec were there to guard her. Then a horrifying thought occurred to her. What if someone had already infiltrated security and was here in the house?

Luke must have known what she was thinking because he laid his hand atop hers and said, "I'm gonna work with Ben on this and make sure we've got everything covered. Nothing will happen to you."

Again, she nodded, only this time she swore the joints in her neck creaked.

Ben uttered another curse. "I'm going to fix her a stiff drink and take her up to her room."

"No," she protested, coming out of her stupor. "I don't need it. I want to know—"

"Let's go," he commanded, gripping her uninjured elbow.

Digging in her heels, she lowered her voice to a stern whisper. "Ben, stop treating me like a two-year-old." She tugged her arm away but he kept dragging her along.

"You're coming with me," he growled, and she smelled the cinnamon gum he was chomping on in agitation. "You're tired, and I don't want you keeling over on me. I need you to lie down for a while, and after Hutchinson and I have discussed this, I will personally brief you, okay?"

Why even bother posing it as a question? She knew Ben, knew it was futile to argue with him when he had that determination about him. He would carry her over his shoulder if he had to, so what choice did she have? She heaved an irritated sigh and glanced back at Luke, heart beating fast. "I want to know everything."

"Of course. I'll be in touch."

With as much dignity as possible, she allowed

Ben to escort her from the library, murmuring her excuses to her guests, hating their expressions of sympathy. No doubt they thought she was overcome with grief and had to seek out her bed like some nineteenth-century female in a fit of vapors.

She ground her teeth together, scanning each face in the crowd. If anyone tried to grab her this time, she'd make them regret it. But nothing tripped her radar.

Ben took her straight up the stairs and into her room, strode across to the window and pulled down the blinds, even sitting her down on the canopied bed before pinning her with a hard look. "You stay put until I come and get you."

His words triggered the memory of Dec saying almost that exact thing to her before all hell had broken loose in the desert.

"No buts, Bryn." His face was stern, hands on his lean hips. "You don't set foot outside this room until Hutchinson or I come get you. Understood?"

Suppressing a shiver, she wrapped her arms around her waist and gave him a baleful look. "Yes." She wasn't an idiot. She understood the danger she was in.

At least, she thought she did.

Her compliance drained some of the tension from his shoulders. "Thank you. I'll post someone outside, and I'll handle this as quickly as I can." He shut the door behind him.

Alone in the spreading silence, she glanced around her. Her king-sized bed stretched beneath her in luxurious splendor. Its blue and cream French toile dressings and bedspread matched the draperies framing the tall picture window that overlooked the rose garden, as well as the thick Persian rug anchoring her bed and antique armoire.

She'd been so excited about this room when she'd chosen its theme and furnishings. It had always seemed like a hotel suite when she'd come here on vacation. Now, despite its feminine elegance, it seemed as much a prison as that filthy hole Dec had pulled her out of.

Chapter Nine

Day 7, Beirut
Noon

Dec stared hard across the hotel dining room table at Luke Hutchinson and folded his arms across his chest. "No."

"That's it? Just no?"

"All right. How about no way in *hell*?"

The corner of Luke's mouth lifted in the ghost of a smile. "I need her, whether you're in or not."

Dec scowled. "Hell."

Signing up for a covert op with the CIA was one thing—it was another to involve a civilian, and a female at that. "You guys must be desperate to even dream this shit up."

"Yep."

"And you must have pulled some pretty big strings to get me assigned for this."

Luke's shoulders lifted in a negligent shrug. "I know some people."

Yeah, he sure as hell did. Wouldn't surprise Dec if the guy played golf with the Deputy Director of the CIA and the head brass at SOCOM. The legendary Luke Hutchinson evidently pulled strings like a marionette master.

Dec sighed and rubbed a hand over his face. "Bryn is still recovering from her injuries. And her father's funeral. She's not up to this, even if she did have the training."

"Don't underestimate her."

"Oh, trust me, I'm not." Dec took a sip of his

beer, sizing the guy up. How can you tell if someone has served time in special ops? Watch how they position themselves in a room.

He and Luke had both instinctively headed for the table at the rear corner, and were now sitting with their backs to the wall to maintain clear lines of visibility, even though they were in a relatively safe environment. Their kind of training never went away.

Bryn did not belong in that world. "I was in the field with her for two days, remember? She's no quitter, I'll give her that, and she's got guts. But this is way beyond her capabilities."

Luke gave an easy shrug, leaned his chair against the wall. "I don't think it is. And that's for her to decide anyway."

"The hell it is." Dec pinned him with a stern glare. "I've worked with female operatives before, but never in the field during a military op. And Bryn McAllister is not an operative."

"She doesn't need to be. Her black belt is a plus, and we'll give her a crash course on the rest of what she needs."

Whatever the real reason Luke needed Bryn for this, Dec figured it had to be damn good. Not that Luke was going to tell him what it was. CIA officers worked with their contractors on a need-to-know basis, and Luke obviously didn't think he needed to know. "So why me?"

"Because she trusts you. You were the one who rescued her, guarded her until the extraction took place, held her hand when she was wounded and made the effort to go see her in the hospital afterwards. You even came back to make sure she wasn't alone when her father died. So that makes you her hero. She's already psychologically attached to you."

Christ, Dec didn't like this at all. If that was

true, it sure as hell didn't help that he'd kissed her and told her he would look her up when he got home. Luke probably didn't know about that part, but Dec was already way too attached to her.

So how the hell could he take this assignment? His objectivity was shot to shit when it came to Bryn McAllister. With her as the team's principal, they all had to maintain professional distance from her emotionally, or people would make bad judgment calls and start getting killed.

As he mulled over that happy thought, Luke regarded him with those miss-nothing eyes. "If you're worried about your objectivity, don't be."

Dec couldn't help the flush creeping up his neck.

"I don't require the same rigid SOP you're used to on this mission. That being said, I expect you to be a professional."

Meaning even though he suspected Dec had some level of feelings for Bryn, so long as he kept them to himself and did his job, he was welcome on Luke's team. Dec didn't find it all that reassuring.

"That's the other reason I wanted you, Lieutenant. I know she's going to be more than just another principal to you. The way I see it, that will only make you more motivated to do your job." He leaned his well-muscled weight into his chair, linked his hands behind his head.

His posture made him seem deceptively relaxed, though Dec knew better. Any hint of danger, and he'd be off that chair quicker than a coiled rattlesnake.

"You're a SEAL. I trust your capabilities and your discipline. Your service record glowed so much it damn near hurt my eyes. And we've both got personal reasons for wanting Bryn safe, so really, I'm as compromised as you are. She'll trust me, but you'll make it that much easier."

What personal reasons did Luke have? "How do

you know she'll trust you?"

"She's a friend of the family. She knows me."

No she didn't. Dec bet less than a handful of people really did. The guy looked as cool as ice. And how could they even be discussing this?

The idea of putting Bryn in harm's way after all she'd been through was wrong. Asking her to hunt down a dangerous, high-profile link in the Islamic extremist terror network made his protective instincts come blazing to the surface. "And what makes you so damn sure she'll listen to you, anyway?"

Luke's deep brown eyes met his, devoid of emotion. "I'm a pretty convincing guy."

What the hell was that supposed to mean? What did the manipulative bastard have up his sleeve that would make Bryn even consider taking this on? He didn't like the possibilities.

"So are you in, or are you out?"

Guy didn't give an inch. Those eyes of his could win millions at a poker table. Unreadable eyes, the kind that belonged to someone who could kill without flinching, without remorse. Did his own eyes look like that? If they didn't already, they would if he stayed in the game long enough.

Not a comforting prospect, but he wasn't going to sit back and abandon Bryn. "If she swallows your bullshit and says yes, then I'm in."

"Good. I'm making you my 2IC."

Dec preferred being in charge, but he could tolerate being second in command with a guy like Hutchinson. So long as he did everything in his power to keep Bryn safe.

Dec followed him out of the lobby to the rental car and watched as Luke methodically checked for booby traps or explosives before getting in and starting the engine. They drove in silence to Daoud's compound in the heart of the city.

Beirut must have been beautiful once. Modern architecture nestled against ancient buildings under the hot sun. Palm trees dotted the streets lined with cafés and shops displaying an array of exotic items, signs written in a mixture of Arabic, French and English. A cultural jewel in the Middle East, once bustling with tourism and commerce.

But now the signs of war were everywhere, from the collapsed buildings and bullet-riddled exteriors to the increasingly impoverished and disenchanted citizens.

Bryn's father had lived in luxury, sealed off from the decay and shells that had destroyed much of the city during the decades of civil war and the most recent clash between Hamas and Israel.

Pulling up to the gated compound, Dec noted with approval how tight the security was. Luke showed some ID to the guard at the main gate, and the little Renault whined its way up the drive to the modern, gleaming, two-story, white stucco house. At the grand entrance, a butler led them inside.

They found Bryn outside in the courtyard next to the sparkling turquoise pool. Wearing a black string bikini, she was smoothing sun block onto her limbs, careful of the angry purple scars on her arms. The stitches must have only just come out and the marks looked damn sore.

All the blood seemed to flood out of Dec's brain at the sight of her in that skimpy bathing suit, showing off the sleek lines of her back and hips. A radio next to her played American music and with her back to them, she didn't hear them approach.

"Miss Bryn," the butler announced.

She swung her head around, shading her eyes with one hand. More healing scars covered her inner arm and upper chest, down her ribs on the right side. But that bikini. Damn he was glad he wore shades.

107

"Some gentlemen here to see you."

Bryn stood up, flipping her straight dark hair off her shoulders so it spilled down her back. The breath backed up in his lungs and for a moment he let himself stare at her. Her body was lightly tanned, lean and beautifully toned, with long legs, high firm breasts and a flat stomach. A jewel glinted in her pierced navel.

Well, that hadn't been in her file, he thought as he struggled to drag his eyes up to her face.

"Hello," she called, squinting against the sun's glare as she pulled a modest wrap over herself.

Too bad, since he preferred her without it, but probably a good thing. She must not be able to see them, or she would have recognized him.

He flicked a glance at Luke, who watched her silently. Obviously their visit was a surprise, which pissed him off even more. She'd just buried her father yesterday, and now they were here—or rather, Luke was here—to spring this on her. Tamping down his irritation, he stepped past Luke out of the shadows and into the sunlight.

"Hey, Bryn."

Delight lit her features. "Dec! I can't believe it! How are you?"

She came right up to him with that same radiant smile and wrapped her slender arms around his neck to hug him. The suppleness of her firm body pressing against him was sweet torture. The scent of her coconut sun block and sun-warmed hair rose around him, stirring him up.

Distance, he reminded himself, but he returned the brief embrace gently, unable to keep from smiling down at her when she pulled back to look at him.

"I'm glad you're okay. I was worried. I tried to find out where you were, but no one would tell me anything."

After all she'd gone through, she'd been worrying about *him*? She was so sweet. "I'm fine," he assured her. "How are you holding up?"

The light in her eyes dimmed a little. "Good. Big turnout at the funeral, and I heard lots of interesting stories from some of his acquaintances. He was a good man."

"Yes, he was," Luke said from behind him.

Bryn peered around his shoulder as the older man came into view, surprise on her face.

Instinctively he stepped closer to her, noting how still she'd gone as she stared at Luke.

"Luke, hi."

Satisfied she wasn't afraid, Dec backed up a step or two to give her some breathing room. Luke flicked him an amused glance, telling Dec his protective gesture had not gone unnoticed.

A furrow creased her brow. "Is something wrong? I mean, I assume you didn't come by just to say hello. Did you?"

"Got something I wanted to talk to you about," Luke said evasively. "Can we sit down somewhere?"

"Sure, at the table over there." She gestured to the teak furniture under a pergola dripping with grapevines.

She knew something was up, Dec would bet on it from her rigid posture. He could practically hear her brain humming as it puzzled out what was going on here.

Dec chose a seat opposite her and met her worried glance with a smile, taking off his shades. "You look pretty good for someone who got hit with an RPG not much more than a week ago."

The quirk of her lips was nervous, a little forced. "Thanks. My stitches just came out this morning."

"They sore?" *Of course they're sore, dumbass. Look at them, for crying out loud.*

She lifted her shoulders. "A little. I've healed up

pretty well, though."

"I'm glad." He glanced over at Luke, who seemed in no particular hurry to end the awkward conversation.

Bryn looked at him, too. "Ben talked to me about everything last night. Is something more going on?"

"Nothing more on that front."

"What front?" Dec asked.

"Tehrazzi putting a reward out for her capture."

Dec's jaw tightened and he glanced at Bryn, expecting to find fear in her eyes, but saw only acceptance. In that instant, any doubts he'd had about coming on board vanished. She needed someone to watch her back. He had the time, and the means. He wasn't budging.

Arms folded across his chest, he waited for Luke to get down to business.

Bryn faced him suddenly, the intensity in her dark eyes slicing through him. Then her gaze whipped back to Luke. "So what can I do for you?"

"Need a favor."

What a bunch of bullshit. Dec barely withheld the comment. He knew exactly how this was going to play out. Luke was going to use the guilt thing, telling Bryn she had a chance to get the guy responsible for her dad's death and her suffering.

I'm an old family friend, you know you can trust me. And Dec and I put our asses on the line to get you out of harm's way. So you owe it to yourself, your father, us and your country to take this job.

There was a lot about how CIA operatives worked that Dec didn't know, but this was a real eye-opener. And it seriously pissed him off.

"Oh," Bryn was saying. "What kind of favor?"

Good. At least she sounded wary.

"An important one," said Luke.

Oh, Christ, here we go.

Luke set a photo on the table in front of her. "Do

you recognize him?"

She studied it with a thoughtful frown, then shook her head. "No. Should I?"

"Farouk Tehrazzi."

Her eyes snapped back to the picture. "*He's* the one who planned the bombing and kidnapped us?"

Dec understood her surprise. Tehrazzi didn't look like your average Islamic terrorist. Nothing about him looked remotely Middle Eastern, except maybe his full beard, but that was light brown. With his fair skin and moss-green eyes, he looked more like a Maine fisherman or lumberjack than an Islamic militant.

That was the thing about the war against these extremists—people back in suburban USA could be living right next to a sleeper cell member, and have no clue they were greeting a would-be suicide bomber when they waved over the fence at their neighbor while cutting the lawn. The stereotype of a terrorist being a Middle Eastern-looking man with a crazy gleam in his eye couldn't be further from the truth. Many were college educated—lawyers, doctors, PhDs. You just never knew who you had to watch for.

Luke pushed harder. "You sure he doesn't look familiar?"

"I'm sure. Why?"

Luke dropped another photo on top of it. "Because he went to Harvard the same time you did."

Her eyebrows shot up. "He did? I don't recognize him, but it's a big school."

"He's a couple years older than you. Graduated the year after you did with a master's degree in political science."

Her expression tightened. "So are you saying he knew about me back then? That he's been trying to get to me this whole time?"

Luke regarded her solemnly. "Tehrazzi was born and raised in Lebanon, and when he was in his teens he caught the eye of a wealthy Syrian businessman named Masood. Masood took him under his wing and sent him to the States to earn a degree. During his studies, Tehrazzi continued to be involved with the Hezbollah movement that was gaining strength in Lebanon. Yeah, he knew who you were, but your father was the real prize he was after. He hated that your father advocated for a relationship between his government and the U.S. It was dumb luck for him that you were here for the political summit when he executed the plot." He shifted forward and gazed at her in earnest. "As to why I'm here today... I need your help to bring him in."

Her mouth fell open. "Me? What could I do?"

Luke didn't look the least bit guilty—and he should have—as he laid on the burden of responsibility. "You've escaped him. That means he's going to want you real bad."

Dec watched her absorb the whole thing silently, but didn't have a clue as to what was going on in her head. He kept waiting for her to laugh in Luke's face. He wanted her to say no. He telepathically begged her to outright refuse, tell Luke he was crazy.

"But I'm not qualified. I don't have the training," she protested in confusion.

Dec silently applauded her. Yeah, that was one of the major strikes against her and this whole gig.

"Surely you can find someone better suited to—"

"I've already told you, Bryn," Luke interrupted. "He *will* be coming after you again. It's only a matter of time. He's already put a bounty on your head."

She paled at the reminder and took a moment to collect herself. "So you're saying what? That you'll protect me if I'll help you?"

"You're going to need protection either way, but

if you come on board with me I can help provide that. Tehrazzi is well trained and elusive as hell. Bottom line? I can make him go away that much faster if I have you."

Her expression oozed incredulity. "And what makes you so sure you can guarantee something like that?"

Dec arched a wry brow at Luke. He'd like to hear this too.

The former SEAL ignored him. "Because your presence will give Tehrazzi...incentive to come out of hiding."

Bryn didn't miss a beat. "You think he'll resurface if you use me as bait."

Dec searched her face for any flicker of expression, but none came. So far he was impressed by her backbone, but a bit alarmed that she'd listened to this much without blowing the whole thing off. Did she realize how dangerous it would be?

He didn't want her within a hundred miles of a terrorist, let alone trying to lure the kingpin straight to her. That's the only reason he'd agreed to take this job. If she was going to do this, then he was going to be there to keep her safe.

Luke gave a wry smile. "You speak some Arabic, you look like a native and you have a strong motivation to want this guy taken out of the picture. You don't need a lot of training to do this. All I need is for you to get his attention so we can draw him out of hiding, and we'll take care of the rest."

"But because I represent a personal failure for him, your chances of bagging him are much greater if you dangle me in front of him."

She was like a bulldog, wouldn't let Luke wiggle out of admitting the truth. Dec admired that.

"In a manner of speaking, yes."

She considered it all, chewing on her lip.

Say no, damn it. Come on, Bryn, you're a smart

girl.

Instead, she aimed a glower at him. "And why are you here for this meeting?"

"Because I needed another operator," Luke answered for him. "And I prefer to work with SEALs when I can because they're disciplined and I know how they work. Specifically, I want McCabe because he's the best they've got, plus I know he'll do whatever it takes to keep you safe."

Her dark eyes softened as she stared at Dec, but she said nothing.

Which was good, because Dec couldn't come up with anything to say either. Besides telling her not to even think about doing this.

Then Luke pulled a manila folder out of his briefcase and slid it across the table toward her. Like a man coming up with a trump card.

Alarm bells sounded in Dec's head. "What's in there?" he demanded, afraid he already knew, and damn sure he didn't want Bryn seeing it.

She reached for it anyway, giving Luke a sideways glance.

Dec grabbed her wrist. "Don't open it, Bryn." He leveled a glare at Luke. "What's this?"

Luke ignored him, watching Bryn. The bastard must have known curiosity would get the better of her.

She pulled her hand from his and went to open it.

"Damn it, no," Dec said, snagging her hand again. It was soft, slender in his. He shook his head at her. "You don't need to see whatever's in there."

She didn't flinch. "I'm a social worker, Dec. I can handle it."

"No—"

She used a quick wrist break and got loose, taking him off guard and giving him a pointed reminder of her martial arts training. Bracing

114

himself, he watched her flip the file open. She sucked in a quick, soft breath, her eyes filled with horror.

Dec angled his head. A photo of a decapitated woman dressed in a Burqa. A burning rage filled his gut that Bryn was seeing this. He glared at Luke.

"My God, it's Qamar," she whispered.

Luke measured her reaction closely, ignoring Dec's anger. "Tehrazzi tortured some villagers and found out she and her husband brought you water. After several hours of torture, that's how he repaid her." He flipped the page to the next photo. "And her husband."

She flinched at the hideous new image of the old man's decapitated body.

"They were his adopted grandparents."

"Dear God." Her fingers hesitated on the awful photograph, then started to shuffle to the next one.

"Jesus, that's enough," Dec said, slamming the folder shut and tossing it to Luke in disgust. But it was too late. Bryn's eyes were already brimming with a lethal rage.

Luke pressed his advantage. "So will you help us?"

She turned her head and sought his gaze. "Dec?"

His answer was instant and heartfelt. "Go home, Bryn. You've been through enough. Go home and sit on the beach and watch the sunset, breathe in the fresh air. Be safe and warm."

She held his gaze, probing his eyes for something. What, he wasn't sure. Then she turned back to Luke. "If I agree, what kind of protection will I have?"

"Dec's in if you are. You'll have the two of us and the rest of my handpicked team. Maybe some of your father's security team, if I like what I see."

"And you honestly think I'm your best chance of nailing this guy?"

He gave her a meaningful look. "Would I be here otherwise?"

Bryn studied him. "Emily always said you were the one she'd want watching her back if she were in trouble."

Some turbulent emotion flickered in Luke's dark eyes before he masked it with a stiff smile. "She'd know all about that, wouldn't she?"

A subtle undercurrent of tension simmered between the two of them. What was that about?

Bryn nodded. "I guess she would, but that's still how she feels. And since I trust her and your son, I guess in a roundabout way I trust you too. But I'd feel a damn sight better with Dec there."

Dec was glad she trusted him and had faith in his abilities, but he still couldn't believe she was giving this serious consideration. *Come on, you don't want to do this. The guy sliced the heads off dear old gram and gramps. You need to go home, get back to your life and put all this whacked shit behind you.*

She regarded them both for a moment more, then nodded. "Okay. If you think I'm what it's going to take to nail him, then I'm in."

Dec couldn't believe his ears and had to clench his fists to keep from dragging them through his hair in frustration. He wanted to grab her, shake some sense into her. Didn't she understand the danger she'd be in? The danger she would inadvertently put them all in? She would make them that much more vulnerable because men were innately programmed to protect women. And she was no ordinary woman.

If she was in danger or hurt, they would wind up taking stupid risks to save her because of basic instinct, let alone that Dec already felt something for her. And that wasn't a good thing if he was going to have to protect her on this assignment.

Mission accomplished, Luke squeezed her hand.

"Thank you."

Chapter Ten

Day 8, Beirut
Morning

Dec wasn't really into surprises. In his choice of vocation, they were never a good thing. But when he walked into the training room at the compound next morning, he got a big one.

Bryn, hair wound in a long braid and dressed in a ji, was full-out sparring with someone. While he stood at the door pulling off his shades, incredulous, she let loose with a series of impressive kicks and punches at her opponent. Whoever he was, he was quick, but even so the dude barely managed to block a rather vicious kick to the kidney.

Bryn danced back, gathering for another attack when the guy went after her, forcing her to dodge and duck his blows. Dec's shout of anger at her partner's lack of restraint stuck in his throat as he watched her defend herself. She blocked two kicks and a combination of punches before moving in for a jab, only to be thrown over her partner's hip.

She landed hard on the tatami and rolled to her feet, right back into the action. When the guy threw her again, she hit the mat and tried to roll out of it, but Dec knew she was hurting. She was slow to get to her feet, bent over, her lips pressed together in a bloodless line. Her eyes, however, burned with steely determination.

He shouldn't have been surprised that instead of calling a halt she went right back into her fighting stance. Her sparring partner, his back to Dec, lunged toward her.

Dec's patience came to an abrupt end. "That's enough!"

His voice boomed through the room, and both fighters stopped and whipped around. His boots thudded on the hardwood as he stalked toward them, ready to tear the man's head off his shoulders for hurting Bryn.

"Dec," she panted. Her hand came up to press against her right side, and she winced. "What are you doing here?"

Her partner came up and steadied her with an arm around her back.

"What the *hell* are you doing?" Dec aimed a lethal glare at the big son of a bitch, then studied her. She was far too pale for his liking. "Don't you think it's a little soon for this kind of workout?"

Her chin came up. "I have a black—"

"I know what you've got," he snapped. The man standing next to her had him by an inch or two and ten pounds of muscle, give or take. Something possessive snaked through him as his gaze locked onto that brawny arm wrapped around Bryn. Some foreign part of him felt like growling.

"Dec, this is Ben Sinclair," she said, breaking the tense silence. "Ben, Dec McCabe. He's the SEAL that got...Dad and me out." Her eyes clouded at the mention of her father.

"A SEAL," Sinclair said, tightening his hold on Bryn. "Wow. I'm honahed." His south Boston accent didn't disguise the animosity behind the words.

Dec disliked him on sight. "You're the head of security?"

Sinclair's pale green eyes stared straight back at him, a mocking light in their glacial depths. "You did your homework."

Dec ground his back teeth together, tried for diplomacy. Ben Sinclair was a thirty-one-year-old

119

former Army Ranger who had done covert ops and hostage extraction. For the past four years he'd been Jamul Daoud's head of security. Two years younger than Dec, he'd done more time in the Middle East than Dec had completed in the military.

Whatever. He didn't care if the asshole was best friends with the director of JSOC. His primary concern on this op was Bryn. Period. *He* was in charge of her safety, no matter what Sinclair thought, and in his mind the former Ranger already had two strikes against him. A: Sinclair hadn't pulled his punches while he sparred with Bryn; and, B: Dec fucking hated the proprietary way Sinclair handled her.

If he was being honest, he hated it even more that she allowed it.

He told himself it didn't matter. Even if Bryn and the security chief had a thing going, that wasn't going to change how this op went down. He'd signed on to look out for Bryn, and that's what was going to happen. While he reminded himself of this, he couldn't help staring a few holes in Sinclair's perfect, movie-star face.

As though Sinclair knew what was going on in his head, his mouth lifted in the ghost of a smile. "How's ya back, sweets?" he asked, turning to Bryn as though Dec wasn't standing there glowering at him.

He slid his arm up toward her shoulders, pressing his hand into her muscles, earning a moan of pleasure from her. "Why don't you get showered up and then I'll work out some of these knots for you?" The rolling cadence of his Southie accent removed most of the R's.

She glanced uncertainly at Dec. "Okay. You guys gonna call a truce so I can leave you alone together? I've seen enough blood spilled to last me a lifetime, thanks."

Dec forced a smile. "Nah, we're cool. Go ahead." He waited until she'd closed the door behind her before addressing Sinclair. "So you're a bodyguard, a martial arts expert *and* a massage therapist."

Sinclair's eyes glinted. "Whatever the situation calls for. I'm highly adaptable."

The bastard had balls, Dec'd give him that. "So why don't you explain to me what the hell you were thinking, going at her so hard?"

"I've known her for years now, McCabe. I think I know what she can handle and what she can't."

"And yet you don't care that she just had her stitches removed and has a long list of healing muscle tissue?"

"You mean her right deltoid, triceps, vastus lateralis, serratus anterior and pec major?"

Dec's eyes narrowed at the punk, surprised at how hostile he felt. He was not going to lower himself and go after him. No matter how good it would feel.

Sinclair raised his eyebrows in feigned astonishment. "Didn't you read the part in my file that said I was a medic, too?"

Okay. Fuck polite. "Yeah, I saw that. I also read the part that said you didn't pick up on the threat at the embassy the day the bomb went off, killing five people and resulting in Bryn and Jamul's kidnapping. Which was when my team had to find and extract them," he couldn't resist adding.

Sinclair's eyes frosted. "Fuck you. If you're so worried about her, then why the hell are you putting her in the middle of this shit with Tehrazzi?"

"I'm not," he said tightly. "I tried to talk her out of it. If I had my way she'd be back in Lincoln City right now with a security detail watching her."

"So why'd you sign on, then?"

"Because she's dead set on going through with this and I don't trust the CIA to keep her alive."

Sinclair's posture lost its aggressive edge. "You and me both."

A heartbeat passed. "Well, then, I guess we're on the same side after all."

"Yeah." The younger man sighed, his shoulders relaxing as he ran a hand through his dark hair, short in back and a little longer in front. "Look, Bryn's an amazing girl. I trained her for her black belt, with a lot of other CQB thrown in. She can handle herself."

Close quarter battle skills were handy if you got assaulted in a nightclub, or in an alley someplace. Cold comfort against the terrorist network they were after, seeing as any contact would most likely involve automatic weapons or an RPG, so hand-to-hand wasn't going to help much. Sinclair had to know that. "As far as I'm concerned, our job is to keep her from needing to use any of her fighting skills. You feel me?"

"Hell, yeah." Sinclair strode away, grabbed a towel off a bench and wiped his face. "She really is good. See for yourself."

"I plan to."

When Sinclair turned his broad back on him and sauntered out, Dec felt his molars grinding together. So much for friendly introductions. They didn't have time for arrogance and hostility between team members, so Sinclair better quit that shit ASAP. And so, Dec realized, had he.

He wasn't used to anyone questioning his authority, let alone confronting him with outright defiance. Reality check time. This wasn't going to be a standard military op. The guys he'd be working with were private contractors, trained in the military but no longer forced to abide by its strict rules of rank and regulations. He wasn't worried, though. Luke Hutchinson might have a reputation as a scary-ass bastard, but he was a professional. No way would he jeopardize the mission by inviting someone on the team he didn't have absolute confidence in.

That said, Dec was going to make damn sure everyone on the team knew their place. Starting with Bryn.

****

Dec was waiting for Bryn when she came out of the change room, and from his expression, his initial impression of Ben had not been a good one. Understandable, she thought, summoning up a friendly smile to lighten his mood. Ben could be a giant pain in the ass sometimes.

"So what's the plan for today?" she asked brightly.

Dec ran a cursory glance over her, then focused on her eyes. The jolt of awareness she felt was so sharp it made her breath hitch.

"You don't seem any worse for wear."

She gave herself a mental shake. "I feel great. Stitch marks are a little sore in spots, but that's all." Actually, she'd loved being able to let loose for a while, even if she didn't have her usual strength and stamina yet. But she wasn't going to admit that when Dec had that disapproval on his face.

He studied her for the longest time, making her want to squirm. She clenched her fingers tight into her palms to keep from fidgeting. Was this some kind of test? See who would look away first—eye-contact chicken? Well, he'd have a long wait on that one. She raised her brows in silent challenge.

He didn't exactly smile, but his eyes warmed a fraction. "I think maybe we need to set some things straight."

"Okay." This ought to be enlightening.

"I want to clarify your role in this mission."

"I'm going along as human bait for a terrorist with a hard-on for me because he wants to prove to the world—"

"Because he wants you *dead*, Bryn," Dec interjected flatly. "Plain and simple. We're all infidels to him. And you're worse, because you're a woman, *and* the half-American daughter of a U.S. political ally." He angled his head, frowned. "Do you get that? Do you understand the kind of hatred I'm talking about?"

"Yeah, I've got it." It was all she thought about sometimes, especially late at night when she woke up sweating and gasping as though she was suffocating back in that god-awful cellar. "My background is in psych and sociology, Dec, so I understand just fine. I'm actually quite intelligent," she added with a good deal of bite.

"Yeah, but there's book smarts, and then there's street smarts. You've got the book smarts covered—"

Her back went up. "I'm a hell of a lot tougher than you think I am." And he should know that. Hadn't she dragged her tired and wounded ass across the desert without complaining?

Dec sighed, his expression almost disappointed. It should have pissed her off, but instead she felt insecure, as though some part of her was desperate for his approval.

"You're mentally tough, and you're no quitter, but you're not on this op to prove any of that to anyone. The street smarts, Bryn, are where I come in. Me and the rest of the team. Got that? Any training we do with you in terms of hand-to-hand or firearms is only as a self-defense last resort. Meaning, you only get to use them if the rest of us are dead, because that's the only time you'll need to use them." He raised his brows exactly as she'd done. "Got it?"

His mention of them dying took some of the

starch out of her backbone, and she swallowed past the sudden tightness in her throat at the thought of any of them coming to harm, especially for her sake. "Got it."

"So then you'll understand why this Charlie's-Angel-meets-Bruce Lee thing I saw ten minutes ago won't be necessary from here on out."

For some reason, his words stung. On some level, she'd expected to impress the hell out of him. Come on, even a Navy SEAL would have to respect a girl sparring like that while she was still healing, right?

"And," he went on, as though lecturing a truculent four-year-old, "I expect you to do as you're told, when you're told. No questions, no exceptions. Ever."

She blinked up at him, wondering if she was really hearing this. Was this the same man who had kissed her in the hospital? The same one who had smiled at her with admiration and tenderness? Because that's not who she was staring back at right now. No, this was Declan McCabe, professional warrior. Remote, all business. Hard. As if that kiss had never happened and she didn't mean any more to him than the next person he came across.

"Bryn? Tell me what I want to hear."

"Yes. Got it." Okay, so she was just another assignment for him, she realized, hating the lick of pain blooming in her chest. While they worked together, their relationship would have to be purely professional. Period.

She wasn't stupid. She knew he was only doing his job the best he knew how. And maintaining his distance from her would make that easier for him. Probably would increase her chances of living through this, too, and she was all for that. But was it too much to ask for him to be nice to her? If he wouldn't allow himself to revert to the tender,

125

flirtatious Dec she'd known in the hospital, he could at least be civil.

Wow. Wasn't that a stunner to realize how attached to him she'd become in such a short time? Transference, she decided. Had to be. He'd saved her life, after all. No wonder she went all gooey over him. But as far as he was concerned, that train had reached its final destination. And if she knew what was good for her, she'd get on board with that theory.

Okay, onward and upward. "So...does this mean we're still friends?" she asked, giving him a hopeful grin calculated to make him into a human being again.

"I'm not here to be your friend, Bryn."

Whoa. Must have lost his sense of humor somewhere since the last time she'd seen him. "You know what I think?" she ventured, determined to break past this harsh side of him and push away the hurt his cool manner stabbed her with. "I think Ben put you in this mood."

A frown formed over the bridge of his nose. "I'm not in a mood. I never get in moods."

Uh huh. "No, I understand, believe me. Ben does that to me, too, sometimes. But don't worry, you'll like Rhys much better. He keeps Ben in line when no one else can."

"Rhys?"

"Yeah, you know, Ben's twin brother?"

Dec stared. "His twin?"

Bryn stifled a laugh. "Uh-huh. Fraternal. He's coming in tonight, didn't Luke tell you?"

Dec's smile was stiff. "No. No he didn't."

****

Ben liked that Dec's eyes were always moving as he ushered Bryn toward the Range Rover and into the back seat. So far at least, the guy seemed to be taking Bryn's protection seriously, which put points in his favor because she was going to need all the help she could get.

Ben had tried everything to persuade her to change her mind about taking on this op. He'd ranted. He'd pleaded. He'd tried logic. He'd threatened—something he used only as a last resort with Bryn, because she was likely to let him have it between the eyes.

Nothing had worked. She was as stubborn as her old man. Once that chin of hers stuck out, forget about changing her mind. So now the only thing left was to cope with her decision and work with the others to keep her safe.

He was already well on his way to developing an ulcer. Popped Tums like they were candy, and kept a roll in his pants pocket at all times, along with his gum.

Dec stared at him through the Range Rover's open back door. "We got a different set of wheels? Something that doesn't scream 'Very rich, important people inside, please shoot at us.'"

"Not unless you want to drive her yourself in the two-seater Mercedes." He couldn't help but smile at the other man's grunt of annoyance. "This baby might not blend in with the local traffic, but it's armor plated and reinforced. And it's comfy too, right Bryn?"

"Very," she agreed, buckling her seatbelt as Dec slid in beside her.

Driving toward the gates, Ben angled a glance at him in the rearview mirror. "You mind if we pick my brother up at the airport after her doctor's appointment?"

"So long as we don't have any security issues along the way, I don't have a problem with that."

Ben sighed. "Ever the optimist."

Though to be truthful, he was a little more edgy than usual this morning. He'd never had to protect anyone who had a bounty on them from a sophisticated terrorist cell. And Bryn was kinda hard to miss, even with his cherished Red Sox cap covering her hair and dark glasses shading her eyes. Her baggy shorts and t-shirt might be nondescript, but a person would have to be blind not to notice the body beneath them.

Blind, and dead from the neck down.

At least the sleeves were long enough to cover the scars on her arm, because they were a dead giveaway to anyone targeting her.

To help keep her calm Ben chatted with her along the way, but every time she tried to draw SEAL-boy into the conversation, Dec answered with a grunted word or two, pointedly shooting the effort down. Jeez, the guy was an uptight bastard, he thought, pulling up in front of the medical building before Dec propelled Bryn inside with a hand wrapped around her arm. Dec's unyielding attitude reminded him of his twin, Rhys.

He needed another Tums. Christ, he was strung tight as a trip wire and they hadn't started the op yet. If he didn't keep a tight lid on himself, not only would he piss off Bryn, who didn't like being told what to do and hated men being possessive of her, but he'd be off the team. Off the team meant he'd have no choice but to sit on the sidelines and hope the others would keep her safe.

To hell with that. The only way he was leaving this team was if he stopped breathing.

Keeping the engine running, he noted who came and went, the cars entering and leaving the parking lot, but nothing tweaked his radar. It was so damn hot he was sweating like a hooker in church. Beads of perspiration rolled down his temples and soaked his chest and armpits. He was glad Bryn didn't complain about any of this, just did as she was told without whining. He was so damn proud of her.

Had he been here to see her, her father would have been, too.

Ben pulled in a deep breath of hot air to ease the pressure building in his chest. God, look at her, taking on this op after everything else. Her whole right side was peppered with scars, and although they would fade from purple and red to a silvery white, they'd never disappear. He'd been working vitamin E oil into them and forcing vitamin C down her, but damn, he hated that she was hurting more than she let on.

That was Bryn for you though. Stubborn to the core. But what about the scars he couldn't see, the ones that worried him most—the psychological ones?

It was all his fault. The guilt ate at him. He should have found some way to prevent what had gone down at the embassy. He should have sensed something was up. He'd been back at the compound checking the security cameras when the bomb had exploded. Christ, the memory made his heart clench. By then, there was nothing he could have done. But as head of Daoud security he should have seen it coming, should have been there to get everything secured in the aftermath.

If he'd succeeded, she and Jamul might not have been abducted. Bryn wouldn't have suffered in that hellhole, wouldn't have been wounded. And Jamul wouldn't have died.

He'd been a mess the whole time she'd been missing, hadn't eaten, had hardly slept. And when the call had finally come that she was safe in the hospital, he'd broken a dozen traffic laws getting to her as fast as he could. Since then she hadn't been sleeping for shit. When she did, she left her bathroom light on and cracked the door open so she wouldn't be alone in the dark.

The whole time he'd known her, Bryn preferred to sleep in complete darkness. But now she was too afraid to close her eyes, was afraid to be alone in the dark because she'd been out there in the desert for two days in a godforsaken hole in the ground without food or water.

Bryn didn't blame him for any of it, though. She'd made that perfectly clear when he'd picked her up at the hospital. The sight of her lying so still and fragile in that bed, covered with shrapnel wounds after watching her father die had nearly broken his heart. Then, despite her stitches and bandages, she'd crawled into his lap and held on like she was afraid someone would tear her from his arms.

He'd savored every precious second of it. She wanted the world to think she could handle everything on her own, that she didn't need anyone's help, but Ben knew her better.

In there somewhere was the woman whose eyes went dreamy when she saw anyone holding a baby, the woman who had clung to him in the hospital while her world fell apart. She *did* need someone, wanted someone, and Ben would love to be the guy she chose. He was beginning to lose hope she'd ever look at him that way.

Her absolving him of blame didn't matter, though. He couldn't get over it. He'd failed to protect them once, at the cost of her father's life, and he'd made a vow to himself to die before letting anything happen to Bryn.

Christ, just the idea of her being in danger from Tehrazzi made him half-crazy. Where she was concerned he'd always had a protective streak, but now he hated letting her out of his sight.

Yeah, Hutchinson was a legend in the Spec Ops world, and he was up there with the intelligence crowd too, but Ben wasn't going to hand Bryn's life over to him without being there. So far, McCabe seemed competent enough. Maybe Bryn was a little too attached to the newcomer for Ben's liking, but at least the SEAL distrusted Hutchinson and his CIA handlers enough to sign up for the job.

When Dec and Bryn returned, he pulled away from the curb and joined the flow of traffic in downtown Beirut. "So?"

"I'm good to go," Bryn announced. "Clean bill of health."

"We need to hit a drugstore for the sleeping pills your doctor just prescribed you," Dec reminded her.

In the rearview, Ben caught the way Bryn's jaw tightened.

"No," she said with tired patience, "I told you, I don't need or want them."

"We should get them in case—"

"*No. I. Don't. Want* them."

The anger in her tone was so rare, SEAL-boy must have managed to irritate the shit out of her in the four short hours they'd spent together this morning. For some reason, Ben felt like grinning.

"Now, now, children," he chided. "Let's play nice."

He stopped for a red light behind a rattling diesel truck, a low-grade tension filling their vehicle. In the passenger side-mirror he saw a silver car weaving its way through the lanes of traffic. The light turned green and Ben waited impatiently while the smoking diesel started rolling with a grinding of gears, its balding tires inching forward slowly enough to make the most patient driver want to drive up its tailpipe.

Another glance in the mirror showed the silver vehicle closer still, near enough for him to be able to make out the two occupants: twenty-ish males, Middle Eastern. They seemed to be looking back at him.

His instincts lit up and his hand tightened on

the steering wheel. The damned truck was still taking its sweet time, and the only other options were to slip into the middle lane—a fine choice if you wanted to end up boxed in by bad guys and get shot to death—or drive onto the crowded sidewalk and run over a shitload of innocent people.

"Silver car?" Dec asked, his eyes pinned to the side-mirror.

"Yeah." His fingers gripped the wheel as he considered his shitty options. He'd have to risk it and force them into the center lane.

Dec's voice broke his concentration. "You need to—"

"I got it," he said tightly, resenting that the guy would tell him how to do his job. He hadn't become Jamul Daoud's head of security by being an idiot.

The truck in front finally shifted into second gear, and Ben waited for those precious inches he needed, then wrenched the wheel and nosed them into the center lane, nearly taking the bumper off a taxi. While the pissed-off driver flung up a hand and leaned on his horn, Ben hit the gas.

Behind them, the silver car's tires squealed as the driver gunned it, cutting into the center lane and accelerating.

"Hang on," Ben said grimly, catching sight of Bryn's worried face and Dec's hand as it flashed out and yanked up hard on her shoulder belt.

****

"Keep your head down," Dec commanded, shoving hard on the back of her neck.

Bryn's cheek hit the seat, her seatbelt digging across her chest as the Rover's engine roared and the vehicle leapt forward, then lurched sideways and back again as they dodged the traffic.

She closed her eyes and focused on breathing,

taking comfort in Dec's warm weight pressed on top of her torso as Ben zigzagged away from whoever was following them. Above the metallic taste of fear in her mouth, she smelled the leather seat beneath her and Dec's warm, clean scent.

Her mind raced. Had someone really recognized their vehicle? Or her? Dec's million precautions didn't seem so annoying anymore.

The Rover's tires screeched as Ben took the corner at breakneck speed, and through the cacophony of blaring horns she swallowed a squeal of fright. Their back end fishtailed, then righted, Dec's grip tightening on a fistful of her shirt. Was he getting ready to haul her out and make a run for it if they crashed?

Her fingers curled into his sleeve as she lifted her gaze to his face, finding him staring intently out the rear window. Above the noise of the engine came a distinct cracking sound.

"Shit," he muttered.

Shit what? She lifted her head in a flare of panic.

"Stay down," he snapped, exerting more pressure on her nape.

Something pinged off the Rover. Christ, were they being *shot* at? "Dec—" she croaked.

"We're fine," he said above her, his hold on her unrelenting. "We've got armor plating and bullet-resistant glass."

"Hang on, guys. Just another few turns," Ben said while Dec's weight kept her in place as the Rover skidded around a sharp left.

Her seatbelt snapped tight across her body as Ben slammed on the brakes, throwing her forward. Dec crashed into the back of the front seat with a grunt then flung himself back on top of her as the vehicle turned another corner and zoomed ahead.

"You okay, Irish?" Ben asked.

"Yeah. I'm good." Dec shifted into his original position against her. "Just lose 'em."

"Roger that."

Belatedly Bryn realized Dec must have taken off his seatbelt to shield her with his body. She choked back a cry of protest and squeezed his forearm, the muscles solid under her clammy fingers. As his thumb moved against the side of her neck in a gesture of reassurance, she wanted to cry.

The Rover's engine hummed as Ben maintained their speed, then revved as they took another curve and accelerated, their unimpeded route and speed suggesting they'd finally hit the freeway. Above her, Dec's body relaxed, but when she risked a glance up at his face, his gaze was still fixed out the back window. Had they lost whoever had shot at them?

"Got the plate number?" Ben asked.

"Yeah."

Another few minutes ticked by until Dec eased his weight off her and helped her sit up. Heart racing, she could only stare out the windshield and savor that she wasn't bleeding from a bullet wound or burning to death in a fiery car wreck.

When Ben asked if she was okay, she met his gaze in the rearview mirror and forced her creaky neck to move up and down. Swallowing the lump stuck in her dry throat, it dawned on her that her fingers were wrapped around something. Glancing down, she found Dec's hand clutched in hers. Since he wasn't pulling away, she didn't let go.

"Well," Ben announced to no one in particular a few moments later. "Guess my brother's gonna have to find his own ride back from the airport."

Chapter Eleven

When Luke entered the dining room that evening, the first things he noticed were the dark circles under Bryn's eyes, and her rigid posture. Not surprising considering the reports he'd received about the car chase and shooting that afternoon, but not good signs, as he'd already been questioning her mental ability to take part in this op.

Everything he knew about her said she was strong and resilient, but she'd need every ounce of backbone she possessed. And whatever he personally thought about taking her along didn't mean shit. If they were going to nail Tehrazzi, they needed her. Period.

She poked at her salad and kept glancing at her father's place at the head of the table. Out of respect for him they'd left the chair empty, but it was probably worse for her to see it unoccupied. Clearly she had to make herself swallow the bite of greens on her fork, almost gagging as she forced it down.

"Hey, boss," Ben said around a mouthful of lamb. "Got any news?"

"That source of yours pan out yet?" Dec asked.

Luke slid into his chair and placed his napkin across his lap. "He did. Word is Tehrazzi's headed to Damascus. No better place for a terrorist to do a little fundraising. Except maybe Baghdad."

Bryn stiffened. "Damascus?"

"Tehrazzi's got backing from all sorts of sponsors," Dec explained. "Wealthy businessmen, Hezbollah, Hamas, Shiite militias in Iraq. Maybe even state backing from Iran."

Hell, knowing Tehrazzi, it was likely. They just hadn't been able to prove it yet.

One of the household staff came to the doorway. "Excuse the interruption, but there is a phone call for you, Miss Bryn."

"You can't leave yet," a deep voice called from the doorway, and everyone turned toward it.

"Rhys!" Bryn cried, jumping to her feet and heading for the dark-haired man who stood there grinning at her.

"Hey, little girl." The former Delta operator caught her up in a hug.

"I'm not little." But even on tiptoe she could barely reach high enough to wrap her arms around his neck. "And I'm three years older than you."

He set her down. "No. Are you really?"

"Please, like you don't have everything about me memorized, right down to my social security number and bra size."

He held up a wide palm in defense, navy-blue eyes laughing. "Strictly for professional reasons." Then he gathered her tight against him and spoke against the top of her head. "I'm real sorry about your dad."

"Thanks."

She led him to the table, where he shook hands with Luke and Dec and scrubbed a hand over his twin's hair on his way to his seat. "Hey, little bro."

"Hey, dickhead."

Rhys swatted the side of Ben's head. "Watch your mouth in front of Bryn."

Ben rolled his eyes. "Yeah, because she's never heard me call you that before."

Stretching his long frame into his chair, Rhys helped himself to the food on the table. "I hear I missed out on some excitement today."

The happy light in Bryn's eyes snuffed out. "Yeah. It sure was...exciting."

"Well, don't worry about a thing. All four of us will take care of you until this thing is over." His voice held grim determination.

As Bryn excused herself to take the phone call, Luke helped himself to a warm roll, his mind humming. "Dec, I need to know if Bryn's ready or not. This can't wait much longer."

"As ready as she's gonna be. We've gone over self-defense, CQB, firearms, some anti-surveillance. She's got the basics down."

"Where's her head at?"

"She'll manage. She's very..."

"Stubborn," Ben finished for him, setting down his fork and popping in a piece of gum. "That's the word you're looking for."

Dec grinned. "She is a little headstrong, yeah."

"She won't let you down," said Rhys. "She's smart, and as loyal as they come. She'll do what she has to, and would rather drop dead from exhaustion than quit. Keep that in mind."

"We will," Dec said. "Her safety's paramount, even more than bagging Tehrazzi."

Chewing on rice pilaf studded with stewed dates and scented with cinnamon, Luke saw the twins' grudging appreciation, but then Ben leaned forward and rested his elbows on the table. "Tell me again why you need her so badly for this op?"

Luke fielded that one. "Because Tehrazzi wants her."

Ben snapped his gum. "Uh-huh." The muscles in his arms tightened, aggression showing in the narrowing of his eyes. "So what, we tour her through town a little, let everyone see her and wait for the fish to start jumping? Like this afternoon?"

"Sort of."

Rhys folded his arms. "You really think Tehrazzi'll jump?"

"Trust me, he'll jump."

Rhys's black brows shot upward. "Because that's what his psych eval says, or are you his biographer?"

A cold smile spread across Luke's face. "Something like that."

"Look," Dec said. "None of us like that Bryn's going into harm's way. But that's where we come in. If we do our job right, she'll never be at serious risk. Let's tie this up and get her the hell home safely."

"Sorry about that," Bryn said, returning from the library. She looked at Luke. "That was your wife on the phone."

The comment threw him. He did his damndest to hide any reaction, but the mention of Emily jarred him inside. He hated that anything could affect him in such a way while he was working. He forced the mouthful he'd been chewing down a throat suddenly gone too tight. "Ex-wife."

"Right." Bryn's gaze dropped to her plate as she sat down. "Sorry."

He waved away her concern. "She was probably worried about you."

"Yes, until I told her you were staying here." When he didn't reply, she set about cutting a piece of meat. "I said I'd hired you to look out for me until I went home, and she was relieved."

"That's good." The last thing he needed was Emily knowing Bryn was working for him. The less anyone knew about what was really going on, the better for all of them.

Bryn slanted a glance across the table at him. "She said to say hi."

Something painful expanded in his chest. Something that burned like hope. So he squashed it, out of habit. "Did she?"

"Yeah, and that I couldn't be in better hands."

He met her level stare with a bland one. "Nice to know she thinks of me that way." They both knew what a load of shit that was. If Bryn was tight with his son, and if she and Emily were close enough that his ex would call here to check on her, then Bryn must know exactly what kind of man he was.

And what kind he wasn't.

He tossed back the rest of his water. "When everyone's finished dinner, we'll check our supplies while McCabe and I get our rides set up. We'll leave for Damascus at oh-four-hundred."

Bryn pushed to her feet. "Think I'll...run up and take a bath. See you guys in the morning."

With her exit Luke headed into the library to go over some maps, debating Bryn's connection with his ex-wife and son and the added weight that placed on his shoulders.

And he thought of Tehrazzi, still at large six years after the hunt for him had begun. Probably out there riding one of his beloved horses right now. In all the time he'd been tracking him, one constant had remained in Tehrazzi's life—his horses. He loved them more than anything else, maybe even more than the God in whose name he waged jihad.

Sighing, Luke was reminded of how desperate he was in order to try this. If anything happened to Bryn while she was under his care, he could kiss his fledgling, sorry-assed relationship with his son goodbye, and Emily...well, she might finally wind up hating him. But he couldn't see any other way to get the job done.

Was he sure Tehrazzi would bite if Bryn was the bait? Damn right he was. He knew him better than anyone else.

You should, the derisive voice in his head pointed out. *You trained the son of a bitch in the first place.*

****

Curled up in her bed with a Jane Austen novel,

139

Kaylea Cross

Bryn relaxed amid the rumbling of masculine voices drifting up from the lower floor. Having the military men in the house—special ops soldiers at that—she didn't worry for a second that she wasn't safe. It amazed her that four alpha males could function together without fistfights and bloodshed.

Not that there was any doubt as to who was the alpha of this pack. Luke's dominance was unquestionable.

At least Ben and Dec seemed to have settled whatever differences they'd had and were acting like buddies now. Earlier they had sat around the table discussing the latest information on the men who'd come after them this afternoon.

After passing on the license plate to the local law enforcement, within an hour they had received a call saying two men had been arrested. Not only had they neglected to ditch their car, but they'd parked it right in front of the apartment where its owner lived and had gone inside.

The police reported the men had seen the reward posted on the web for her capture. They'd followed the Range Rover to the doctor's office and chased after them in the hopes of shooting out a tire so they could ambush the vehicle and snatch her.

Stupid, yes, but still a threat. Amateur criminals could be equally as dangerous as seasoned ones, especially to innocent bystanders. No matter how she viewed it, she was a marked woman, and it wasn't a matter of if, but when, she would be targeted again. Odds were her pursuers couldn't all be incompetent.

Despite the criminals' ineptitude today, Tehrazzi had almost gotten her. Again.

He wants you dead, Bryn...

Dec's voice pierced her thoughts. Back at the compound after the car chase, he'd hustled her out of the Rover straight into the living room, where he'd

140

settled her on a sofa with a throw blanket. He'd been so sweet with her, like at the hospital. And though she'd have loved to crawl onto his lap and burrow into his chest, she'd kept that impulse to herself, afraid he would have distanced himself from her again.

A communal laugh came from below and she sighed wistfully. If it had been old times, with just her and the Sinclair twins, she would have been down there playing cards or Monopoly with them. But for some reason, Dec and Luke made her feel like an outsider, even though she technically now owned this place.

That empty dining chair at the head of the table haunted her. Closing her eyes, she allowed herself to grieve for her father, for what their relationship could have been. After his funeral she'd found boxes and albums in his study, full of pictures of her from infancy to adulthood. Luke had been right in his observation about her father. She'd cried because even though he'd been half a world away, he'd taken the trouble to follow her life.

At first she'd wondered why he'd hidden that part of himself, but after some pondering had decided he hadn't wanted to appear weak. Plus, had he shown the kind of affection and attention she'd craved, he might have inadvertently placed her in jeopardy long before the bombing at the embassy and their kidnapping.

She'd also found pictures of her father with Luke, during the civil war back in the eighties. Luke looked so much like his son, it was uncanny. No wonder Emily had a hard time when Rayne was around.

It was ironic. Here Bryn was, well on her way to falling in love with a SEAL, despite it being a disaster waiting to happen. And Luke was downstairs right now, planning the mission, logistics, strategy, resources at their disposal and a million other things she didn't have a clue about.

She had no worries about them taking care of her. During her visits here with her father, Ben and Rhys had been like her personal Secret Service detail, and they would now raise that to a whole new level.

As for Dec, she knew he hated her being involved, and because he was the only one to have seen her in action in the field, she had to wonder what he really thought of her. Maybe he was convinced she was going to get them all killed.

She put a hand to her throat. God, what if she did something wrong and they got shot or blown up because of her? What if they were maimed or killed because she'd been stupid and stubborn enough to sign on for this op? She'd rather die than be the cause of any more deaths.

Footsteps along the hall caught her attention. She jerked the forgotten paperback off her lap, fumbling to open the pages as someone knocked at her door.

At her invitation the door cracked open, revealing Dec's silhouette backlit by the wall sconces in the hall. "Hey."

She drew her knees to her chest, pulse picking up. "Hey."

"Can I come in?"

"Sure." She scooted further against the headboard to make room for him, and he sat at the foot of her bed. This close the scent of his soap teased her, making her wish she could bury her face in the curve of his neck just to breathe him in.

His gaze was thoughtful. "How you doing?"

"Good. I'm good. You?"

He smiled, revealing that sexy pair of dimples. "Don't worry about me. I'm tougher than I look."

Eyeing the width of his shoulders, she smiled

back. "You look plenty tough to me."

He hesitated, and she realized he was making an attempt to be more human with her. His guard was lowered, his posture relaxed. "You need anything?"

"No thanks. Was just reading a bit. You know, help take my mind off...everything." She was exhausted, but maybe insomnia was for the best. More than once she'd woken out of a dead sleep drenched in sweat, terrified she was still in that damned cellar.

"Is it working?"

"Nah."

He studied her a moment. "You know, if I could make all this go away, I would."

She leaned back into her pillow. "Maybe we could chat for a while."

"Sure. What about?"

"Anything except...all this." Maybe now would be a good time to let her curiosity about him get the better of her. "You have a family back home?"

His tawny eyes met hers, their unusual color more arresting thanks to the thick black lashes framing them. "Parents, and a brother and sister. In Montana."

So he wasn't married. Thank God. Now she didn't need to feel guilty about poaching when she daydreamed about him. She did envy him, though. She'd always wanted siblings. "Are you close?"

"Yeah. You?"

"Mother and step-father live in Baltimore. But I'm guessing you already knew that." When his eyes lit with amusement, she knew she was right. "It was in my file, huh?"

"Yeah."

"What else was in there?"

He moved his broad shoulders in a negligent shrug. "Your background, education, identification

143

marks—"

"Such as?"

"I know you had your appendix out."

Oh. "Anything else?"

His eyes laughed at her. "Why? You afraid I know some dirt you don't want anyone to find out about?"

"No dirt here," she assured him. "It's just weird that you knew all about me before we met and I still don't know anything about you."

"Made our job easier when we came in to get you."

How much would he reveal about himself if she kept questioning him? Some level of secrecy had to be maintained, she supposed. It would make him that much more effective at his job. And of course there was the issue of him keeping a professional distance between them. She didn't want to have *that* conversation with him again.

"Luke told me you were a friend of his family. That true?" His question surprised her.

What a tidy way for Luke to sidestep all the complications of their shared connections. "His son's my best friend in the world, and I'm pretty close to Luke's ex-wife."

"Bet that bugs the hell out of him."

"I bet it does too. They all get along okay—I mean, they're civil to each other and everything. And the guys took a stab at burying the hatchet this past spring, so it's better than it was. It wasn't easy for any of them with Luke's line of work, which you can well imagine." Which was why it was so, so stupid for her to even daydream of being with Dec. She *knew* what sort of misery could come from that. What was wrong with her?

"Yeah, a lot of marriages don't work out under that kind of stress. It would take some special kind of woman to hang in there for the long haul with one of us."

She kept to herself that she figured she could handle it. "But sometimes it's not the wife who wants out. And even when they part ways, it doesn't mean they don't still love each other."

His gaze sharpened. "Meaning Luke was the one to leave?"

It wasn't her place to fill Dec in on Luke's private history. "Let's just say Emily would give up everything to be with him. In a heartbeat. I think he feels the same way, but he's either too stubborn or paranoid to let it happen."

"Stubborn, huh. I know a few people too stubborn to know what's good for them."

Despite herself, she snickered. His answering smile almost melted her bone marrow.

"What about the twins? Where'd you meet them?"

"At a restaurant in Boston. I was working at this Greek place one weekend in college for some extra money when they came in with some of their military buddies." She'd been dancing, and they'd stuffed her costume bra and belt full of money. On the sly she'd paid for Ben and Rhys's dinners, and after her show they'd invited her to join them.

"Ah."

"Did you know they grew up in foster care?" She was babbling, couldn't seem to stop. "Their mother was a crack addict in Southie, had them living out of a car. Social Services took them in when they were ten and they went through hell until the Sinclairs adopted them at fourteen." She swept a stray lock of hair from her face. "That's how I ended up choosing to be a social worker. No child I was involved with was going to get tossed around like they did."

Actually, she'd probably been a caretaker all her life. Being raised by a single mother, Bryn had always been very protective of her. "Anyway, we kept in touch while I went through grad school and after they left the military, I mentioned to my father that they might be interested in doing private security. One thing led to another, and here we are."

Dec nodded. "So with your job, it's the kids you're in it for?"

"I can't stand knowing kids are out there suffering all sorts of abuse, especially when it comes from the people who are supposed to love and protect them. If I find out about it, I do everything in my power to take that child away to a safe and loving environment." She cocked her head. "What about you?"

"What about me?"

She lifted a shoulder. Hopefully she was coming across as casual and not scaring him off. "What did you do before becoming a SEAL?"

"Earned my engineering degree with the Navy two years before I entered BUD/S."

"An engineer? What kind?"

"Civil. I learned how to make bridges, and then in the Navy I learned how to blow them up. Turns out blowing them up's way more fun. Who knew?"

So he wasn't just an elite soldier with a pretty face. He had a mind every bit as formidable as his tactical skills, which made him even more irresistible to her. Though to be honest, if she hadn't seen him in action in the field she would never have believed him to be lethal. He came across as so calm and kind, she had trouble reconciling what she saw in him to what she'd witnessed out in the desert.

She wanted to understand what made him tick. "So why did you decide to be a SEAL?"

"9/11, same as a lot of people. I got real pissed off and decided to do something about it. The SEALs seemed the obvious choice, since we're deployed to hot zones all over the world. Lucky for me, I was good at it. I thrived on the challenge."

"Challenge? I know what they do to you guys. You call being tortured and living day and night in freezing cold water with no sleep a *challenge?*"

His dimples materialized. "Loved it. See, the trick is to not quit. That's all that got me through the training, and why other guys rang out. Sheer willpower. Most trainees are in great physical shape, but the mentally tough ones are the guys who finish. You stop thinking about how bad it is and just do it."

He laid his left palm on the mattress, the crescent-shaped scar on the back of his hand reminding her of when he'd framed her body with his against that sheer rock face. "If you let yourself think about being cold and wet and tired for days on end, you'll never make it because your brain's telling you you can't endure it. So you shut everything out except what you're doing at any given moment and get through it one task at a time."

She eyed him like he was nuts and he laughed.

"When you think about it, they have to train us the way they do. They need guys who are motivated, mentally tough and won't give up on themselves or their teammates. Pretty simple, really."

If she looked awed by that speech, she couldn't help it. He was heroic down to his core and he didn't seem to realize it.

"Anyway, that's why I signed up."

"How long are you planning to stay in?"

"Not sure. Another few years, unless something changes."

Like the number of limbs or his vital status. "And then what? Private contracting?" Part of her hoped he would say something that would turn her off getting involved with him, to make it easier to get him out of her head.

"Maybe some, but..." He gave a faraway smile. "My older brother and I built this log house in Montana. My kid sister decorated it. We have this

147

pipedream of turning the place into an adventure ranch."

"Like hiking, horseback riding?"

"Yeah. Rock climbing, kayaking, rappelling—"

"God forbid you forget the rappelling." After her rappelling experience on that Syrian cliff, she wouldn't be trying that again any time soon.

"Absolutely. So yeah, that kind of thing. What about you? What do you like to do?"

"Camp, hike, kayak. Love to swim. Teach dance classes. Other than that, I'm kind of an outdoorsy type."

As his expression turned thoughtful, it occurred to her they'd just discovered they had more shared interests than they'd imagined. Would have been easier to find out they had nothing in common. She fought back the yawn that had been forming, hoped she concealed it well enough.

He still noticed, of course. Nothing got past him. "Better get some sleep while you can. We've got a long day ahead of us."

"Okay. Thanks for talking with me. It helped." Venturing a glance at him, she found him looking back at her with warmth in his eyes, same as when he'd kissed her in the hospital. Her poor, stupid heart fluttered. God, she was in big trouble.

"Yeah. About tomorrow," he began. "I wanted to tell you...look, you don't have to do this. It's not too late. You can still walk away and no one will think less of you for it."

Wouldn't they? She'd been given this opportunity to help collar the man responsible for the bombing, the kidnapping, Qamar's murder and her father's death, preventing him from hurting any more innocent people. If she had died and her father was in her place, wouldn't he have done whatever he could to bring Tehrazzi to justice?

Absolutely. So how could she not do the same for

him? She owed him that much, to show courage and resolve and push past her fear and insecurities. No way would she let him down.

"Don't do this out of revenge, Bryn," Dec said quietly. "Even if we get Tehrazzi, it won't bring your father back."

The words hit her in the heart like an arrow. "I know that. But I still have to do it."

He stared at her. "For who? Him? Or you?"

"For all of us."

He looked away, and she wished he hadn't. It felt too much like he was shutting her out.

"Just say you'll help me. I'm scared enough about what's going to happen without having you mad at me."

His head came back around to face her. "You know I will, if that's your decision. And I'm not mad."

"But you think it's a really bad idea, right?"

"Doesn't matter what I think."

"Yes, it does. To me it does."

He sighed. "Do me a favor then, okay? Sleep on it. Think it over again—"

Think it over? That's all she'd been doing.

"—and remember what happened today. Because if you go ahead, that's the kind of danger you'll be putting yourself in until it's over."

Yes, and the rest of them with her. She nodded, toying with the toile coverlet. "I understand."

"So you'll think about it?"

"Yes."

He seemed relieved, and reached into his back pocket to pull out a plastic pharmacy vial. "I picked these up for you just in case." The sleeping pills she hadn't wanted rattled in the bottle. "You want to take one now?"

Rather than riling her, his thoughtfulness touched her deeply. She accepted the bottle from

149

him, the brush of his hand against her palm sizzling up her arm. He looked so capable, the muscles of his chest and shoulders stretching his t-shirt. She remembered how that steely strength had pressed against her as he shielded her with his body in the back of the Range Rover.

But no, she couldn't think like that right now. Her hand tightened around the vial. "Will you promise me something too?"

"What?"

She struggled with putting her feelings into words. "If I do this, I want your word that you won't take any stupid risks because of...me."

His eyes were steady as he looked at her, looked *into* her. "Don't you worry about me."

She grabbed his hand, squeezed it. "No, please. Swear to me."

He returned the pressure, gazing down at their entwined fingers. "Risks come with the territory, and that's why there're people like me out fighting the bad guys. I've signed up for this whether you join us or not, and I can take care of myself. But if you come along, then I'm going to take care of you too." He released her hand and stood, the mattress shifting as his weight lifted.

Right then, it was all she could do to remain where she was and not wrap herself around him, partly to ease the guilt nagging at her, partly for reassurance that she was doing the right thing. But she knew he would never tell her that.

"So," he said, tucking his hands in his back pockets, his biceps exposed under his sleeves, "you want to take one of those things?" He indicated the pills in her hand with a jerk of his chin. "I can get you some water."

"No thanks. But I'll keep them on the nightstand, just in case."

"Okay. Sleep tight, then."

"You too."

After he'd left, she pressed a hand against the center of her chest and let out a slow breath, her whole body aching for him. Not for sex, though that would have been so good, but merely to hold him. To be able to reach out and touch him in the darkness and know that he was beside her.

God, she was nuts for letting herself think of him like that. Weren't Luke and Emily reason enough to get the idea of a relationship with Dec out of her head for good? Yet try as she might, she couldn't let it go. She craved him with a yearning so deep it scared the hell out of her.

Setting her prescription on the table beside her, she wondered what her chances were of getting to sleep without a sleeping pill, and figured they were slim. Too bad she was too damned stubborn to take one.

****

Syrian Desert
Night

The mare's black mane streamed out behind her like a banner as she transitioned from a canter into a gallop. The coarse hair whipped at Tehrazzi's face as he crouched over her neck, urging her onward with only the pressure of his knees. Her muscles coiled beneath her skin in a fluid rush, setting his heart pounding as they soared over the desert, hooves pounding the sun-baked earth. A triumphant laugh of joy escaped him.

Nothing was so glorious as this, nothing so perfect as the communion of horse and rider as they merged into a single being. Heaven must feel like this. Perhaps Allah would grant him many horses like this one when the time came for him to make his final sacrifice.

He let the mare run until she showed signs of fatigue, then slowed to a trot and finally a walk while her sides heaved in and out. He leaned low against her and murmured praise of her performance, one hand releasing the reins to pat the sweat-covered coat. Ghaliya was a beautiful animal, his favorite of all his horses, given to him by a Saudi prince who funded his activities.

Of all the Arabs, the Saudis bred magnificent animals. Even Osama bin Laden, himself of the Kingdom, had been a fine horseman. Though a Sunni, Tehrazzi considered him a great leader in the global jihad they were engaged in. They had ridden together on several occasions, the last time when he had been invited to visit the revered leader in the border mountains of Pakistan.

Ghaliya tossed her great head and blew out a snort, her wide-spaced, intelligent eyes scanning the ground as she picked her way through a dry wash toward the makeshift stable his men had built at the entrance of a cave.

Tehrazzi dismounted and led her to her stall himself, removing the bridle and bit with care before brushing her coat with a curry brush. Even untied, the mare stood still for him and seemed to sigh in enjoyment, bringing a smile to his lips as he stroked the sweat and grime from her glistening ebony body.

He disliked anyone else touching her. Everyone knew not to go near her unless ordered to do so, and only by him. He and Ghaliya had a bond that went far beyond the comprehension of the company he kept, and he would let nothing taint that sacred connection.

Easing his hands over her chest and legs, he noticed she was favoring her right foreleg. Closer inspection revealed a small slice in the frog of her hoof. He spoke gently to her as he prodded it, made soothing noises when she butted his shoulder with her velvet nose.

"Be easy," he told her, rubbing the stiff tendons in her ankle, and was rewarded with a warm puff of air from her nostrils against his hair, and then her lips as they nibbled at his bearded cheek. He laughed again and pushed her head away, rising to complete his grooming. When he was done, he stepped back and let her out.

Standing in the doorway of her canvas-draped stall, he smiled as she lowered herself with a mighty groan and rolled against the still-warm earth. She reminded him of a child frolicking in the snow.

"She is beautiful."

Over his shoulder, Youssef was standing in the shadow of the tent. The young aide's turban was filthy, stained with sweat, the patches of bare skin on his upper cheeks above the bushy beard he'd grown glowing with a bad sunburn. "Yes. She gives me great joy."

Youssef's eyes turned sly. "And I have brought you news that will give you even greater pleasure."

Tehrazzi glanced back at Ghaliya, who had risen to her feet and was shaking off the dust like a wet dog. "Tell me."

"Our sources have confirmed that Masood has been talking with the Americans responsible for the woman. He invites you to attend a meeting tomorrow night."

Tehrazzi sucked in a breath, the blood surging in his veins. "Where?"

"At his private club in Damascus."

Rank hatred filled his heart. "Have our contact accept our host's invitation."

Then, God willing, the Syrian and Daoud's daughter would meet Allah's final judgment.

Chapter Twelve

Day 9, Beirut

Luke loaded the last of their gear into the rental car and shut the trunk, then rounded the side to ride shotgun next to McCabe, already behind the wheel with the engine running. Bryn was in the backseat between Ben and Rhys, making a valiant attempt at keeping her eyes open in the pearly, pre-dawn light. She was exhausted, but hadn't complained once, which he was thankful for.

God save him from whining. Worse than fingernails scraping over a chalkboard.

For his part, McCabe maintained a quiet presence in the driver's seat, glancing in the rearview every so often at Bryn. He was probably cataloguing the shadows under her eyes and all the scars and bruises tracking down her right arm. Luke knew they marked the whole right side of her body.

Impatient to get going, he wondered what he and Davis would discover at the meeting with their Iraqi informant in Damascus later today. Davis was already on his way there in his own car. Luke would meet up with him after they all checked into the hotel.

The use of informants was a necessary evil in this business. The trick was to never trust anyone, and after the years he'd put into intelligence work, it was second nature to be suspicious. People like his Iraqi informant were loyal while the cash was coming in, and the pressure from the other side wasn't high enough to outweigh their involvement with Americans.

They still weren't moving. "What're we waiting for?" Luke asked.

Dec nodded pointedly at Luke's right shoulder. "Seatbelt."

Eyeing him with amusement, Luke fastened it with a smirk, then lifted his brows at the 2IC, who grinned and shifted the car into gear. He wasn't sure exactly what he'd expected from the SEAL, but this calm, cool, collected routine was a welcome relief on his crowded mind. He liked the guy already. McCabe went about his business in a composed, methodical way.

McCabe didn't miss anything, filing away every detail in a mind Luke was willing to bet was every bit as sharp as his own. Dec's body language and carriage made it plain he was not to be messed with.

Beneath that deceptively relaxed exterior, Luke recognized the lethal soldier inside. As SEALs, both he and Dec had seen and done things most people could never imagine, let alone experience. To his way of thinking, that made them closer than most brothers. Only difference was, Dec wasn't nearly as hard as Luke was.

Yet. Give him enough years in the Teams, and he'd wind up the same. Luke almost felt sorry for him.

He was damned glad to have Dec to back him up, and even more glad that the twins were here to help protect Bryn throughout this operation. Besides being concerned about her emotional strength to take this on, he was almost as worried about Ben. Ben's feelings for Bryn ran deep, probably deeper than he let on. If anything happened to her on Ben's watch, he would never get over it.

Luke scratched his stubbled chin as he considered the implications of Ben's attachment to Bryn. He understood the why of it. She was steady, strong, loyal and smart. Not to mention there wasn't a straight male on the planet who wouldn't find her attractive. She was easy to be around, didn't do the drama thing or act like a diva, as some in her position of wealth would. No, she'd gone out of her way to make it on her own, a constant source of irritation for her father.

Jamul had secretly admired the hell out of her, living alone on the Oregon coast and scrapping it out in the trenches as a social worker, but he'd gladly have provided her with every comfort she could ever want.

No way that was going to happen, though. Bryn was way too independent and stubborn to take handouts from anyone. Luke couldn't help but admire the hell out of her for that.

No wonder Ben worshipped Bryn from afar. But if she knew how Ben felt about her, she didn't show it. Man, that had to hurt a guy's ego. Talk about a shriveler.

That's why Luke preferred to stay unattached. Life was a hell of a lot easier when you didn't run around with your heart on your sleeve, begging someone to stomp on it. Not that he had a heart anymore. He'd given it away more than thirty years ago to his ex-wife. What remained in the middle of his chest was merely the pump that kept him alive, bothered less and less by twinges of emotion.

Behind him, Bryn failed to smother a jaw-cracking yawn. Her fourth in as many minutes.

"Go ahead and grab some shut-eye if you want," Dec said to her. "We're all impressed enough with you. You don't have to keep trying so hard."

She flashed him a shy smile and if Luke wasn't mistaken, her cheeks flushed. Interesting. McCabe was already attached to Bryn on a personal level. If she was into him, that would add another wrinkle for Luke to worry about, and it might cause friction between McCabe and Ben.

Right on cue, Ben wrapped a brawny arm around her shoulders and urged her head down against him.

Wonderful. His background check showed Ben could be a bit of a hothead, and feeling territorial over Bryn with the second-in-command was not going to be a party. Maintaining his hold on her, Ben stared out the window, appearing completely at ease. Which was total bullshit.

Luke had seen the bottle of Tums on the bathroom vanity, and he was willing to bet they weren't there because Ben liked the taste. He was quietly freaking over Bryn's involvement, and maybe her interest in McCabe.

Keeping his thoughts to himself, Luke sipped the travel mug full of coffee and analyzed this cozy love triangle, still in its infancy. He stole a glance at Rhys in the rearview mirror, his big frame folded in the back seat, watching the scenery pass out his window.

He was quiet, methodical and controlled. His superiors in Delta said he never got rattled, could always be counted on when things got tough. The rock of his team.

Luke could almost hear the guy's brain humming from the front seat. Sometimes quiet was a blessing. Keeping your mouth shut and your eyes open was the best way to stay alive in this business. It had saved his own ass more than a handful of times.

Maybe Rhys's calm would rub off on his brother and ease Ben's anxieties about Bryn. They'd worked well together so far. Rhys throttled Ben back, and Ben in turn fired him up.

Luke would have to see how it went. If Ben couldn't keep it together, he and Rhys were going to have to knock his ass back in line.

****

By the time they reached Damascus and checked into their hotel, Bryn looked ready to drop. Dec convinced her to grab some more sleep while the twins headed out for a recon op. Luke was out with Davis, who'd come from Baghdad to meet with their informant.

Bryn's skin seemed pale to the point of translucency, dark circles beneath her obsidian eyes. So beautiful, though. Strong and valiant, yet vulnerable at the same time. He wanted to gather her close and hold her, stroke her long, shiny hair until she drifted off. Her dark eyes tracked him, uncertainty in their depths.

Dec hunkered down in front of her, and the catch in her breath when he took her hands made him look up into her face. The flare of heat in her gaze made his belly clench.

"You're exhausted. At least try to rest," he said, trying to distract his body from the hunger he sensed in her. His hand twitched, wanting to touch more of her.

"Okay."

Her lashes were so long they touched the base of her eyebrows, and formed thick crescents over her cheeks when she closed her eyes. A heavy sigh escaped her, as though she carried the weight of the world on her slender shoulders. He wanted to crawl in beside her so bad he forced himself to release her and take a step back. Then another. And another.

He made himself comfortable on the other bed, glanced over at her and found her fast asleep already, her full lips parted. It had taken an act of will to not pull her close and kiss her lingering sadness away last night. He sure wished she had more to smile about.

And that she was thousands of miles away from the nearest terrorist.

When his cell vibrated he grabbed it. The screen showed a text message from Luke. He'd made contact with his informant, Fahdi. Some sort of meeting was going to happen tonight between Tehrazzi and Masood.

Dec shut the phone, hoping like hell Bryn wouldn't need to be involved in whatever they had to do tonight. Truth be told, he wasn't sure he could maintain his professional distance if she was in danger. If he let his control slip when things got critical, someone could pay for his mistake with their life.

To distract himself, he set about working on one of the radio transmitters they'd be using. Before long Luke strode in, setting a new map onto the bed. "Meeting's tonight at a club downtown. Twenty-one hundred."

Dec set aside the transmitter. "Your informant's sure Tehrazzi's going to be there?"

"Him and a few of his deputies."

"And how the hell are we going to get in? Security will be tight. We setting up a diversion?"

"Yep." Luke gestured with a jerk of his head. "With Bryn."

She'd stirred at Luke's entrance, and now her head snapped up from the pillow. "Me?"

"Forget it." Dec's voice was clipped, cold as the glare he aimed at Luke. "Tehrazzi would recognize her in a second, and there's no way—"

"The only way we could get in on such short notice without raising too much suspicion is if we provided the...entertainment."

Bryn swallowed. "Entertainment?"

Dec's eyes flared. "What, you want to parade her in there and offer her up as a prize to the host?"

"All we need to do is provide enough of a

distraction so you can plant the tags and get the intel. Then we leave."

Dec folded his arms across his chest. "By asking her to pose as a whore."

Luke ignored him. "Setting off explosives isn't going to get the job done tonight, Lieutenant. And I'm not asking her to be a whore." His keen gaze sought hers. "Think you could put on a performance tonight?"

"What sort of performance?" Dec demanded.

"Belly dance," Luke answered.

"Belly dance?" Dec's eyebrows flew upward as he cranked his head around to stare at her. "You belly dance?"

She tucked a lock of hair behind her ear. "Ah, yeah. I teach classes back home."

The idea of her dancing that way was insanely hot. "Think you can pull it off?" Belly dancers were not exactly respected in Middle Eastern culture. If she did this, she would practically be begging to be propositioned. Could she go through with it, knowing Tehrazzi was there, watching her? The idea of that slimeball's eyes stripping her naked made his stomach turn.

"We'd have to cover your scars somehow," Luke mused. "With the right costume and makeup, Tehrazzi might not recognize you."

She chewed her bottom lip.

"I wouldn't have suggested it unless I thought it was feasible."

"If he did recognize me, what do you think he'd do?" she asked.

"He'd know it was a trap," Dec answered. "He might be a sorry piece of shit, but he's not stupid. If he sees her, he'll try to kill her. And even if he doesn't, our cover's blown and he'll go to ground. We may never get another shot at him."

Luke grunted. "Got a better suggestion?"

Dec's silence answered for him.

"Will you guys be inside with me?" Bryn asked.

Luke nodded. "At least one of us will be with you the entire time, to make sure no one but the highest bidder gets to...sample your talents."

"What?" she quavered.

"Christ," Dec muttered, dragging his hands through his hair.

"It's all an illusion, Bryn. All you have to do is dance, and once Dec gets everything in position and gives the all clear, I hustle you out the back exit to the car."

"And you think I'll be safe?"

"You'll be safe," Luke promised.

She regarded Dec.

"You know what I think," he said.

"Well?" Luke prompted. "Are you up for this? Just one show, and then maybe you'll be finished your part of this."

She let out a breath. "Okay. I'll do it."

Dec bit back a curse and Luke looked at him. "So, which one of us is gonna take her shopping?"

****

The nightclub was located in the heart of Damascus. Modern architecture warred with the minarets of ancient mosques, the call to prayer drowned by the traffic and thumping techno music. That must chafe the radical jihadists' asses, Bryn thought as she stared out the bullet-resistant window of the limousine.

She fought down the jitters in the pit of her stomach, wiped her hands on the robe covering her from head to ankle.

She'd performed at restaurants before, filling in for dancer friends. But they'd been family restaurants full of children. Now Luke was asking her to perform for a group of men known to fund and engage in terrorist activities. The kind of dance he had in mind wouldn't be her normal routine of flitting from table to table, making the coins on her skirt jingle for a delighted child or a couple celebrating a romantic evening.

No, this would have to be sexually charged, something men would expect from a prostitute. A woman seducing a lover. She cringed.

Beside her and also in disguise, Luke was silent. She'd have given anything to have Dec beside her instead. Luke made her feel safe, but Dec would have given her an extra dose of courage. After all, she was dancing for him tonight.

She'd decided that would see her through the humiliation of every man in the room placing bids to see who would be the lucky one to spend the night with her. She had to be a siren, calling to her lover, and she had to make it believable. The only way to do that was to think of Dec while she performed.

The limo pulled up beside a glitzy nightclub. She rubbed a hand over her bubbling stomach.

"Ready?" Luke asked.

She nodded. Although she wanted no part of this, she didn't blame him for suggesting it. After all, she'd agreed to help them get Tehrazzi. If things went as planned tonight, her role in the mission would be over and she would be on her way home. Luke was Rayne's dad, Emily's beloved ex-husband. He wouldn't do anything to deliberately put her in harm's way, right?

Yes he would.

Deep down, Bryn knew Luke would do whatever he had to in order to snare Tehrazzi. Including offering her up like a human sacrifice, family ties be damned.

When he let her out of the vehicle she stepped onto the curb in her high-heeled sandals, careful to keep her eyes downcast and the lower part of her face covered. Modesty was in the script tonight, a little something to pique the men's interest. Something to add to her mystique.

With a firm hand on her elbow Luke led her through the crowd, into the throng of expensive Italian suits and the cloying scents of cologne and tobacco smoke. She felt light-headed all of a sudden.

"Keep breathing," Luke murmured for her ears only. "You're safe, I swear it. I've got half the team in here waiting for us. Ben's here, too."

"Where's Dec?"

"Doing his job."

That didn't ease the anxiety. This was just like those dreams you had when you were naked on stage and everyone was staring at you. Except this time, she would be *almost* naked and there really *was* going to be a crowd of men staring at her. Perspiration gathered under her arms.

Luke ushered her into a back room where two beefy security types eyed her with interest. A nasally Arab voice came from behind her, and she turned to face a middle-aged, heavy-set man with a goatee and balding pate, dressed in a dark suit with a blue pinstripe shirt. Heavy gold rings adorned each hand and a gold chain nestled in the furry thatch of chest hair where the shirt lay open. He reminded her of a Mafioso gone bad.

"Mr. Masood," Luke greeted him in Arabic, clasping the man's shoulders and exchanging the customary greeting of kissing each cheek.

"Welcome. My sources tell me I am about to experience pleasure like no other."

"Yes. My niece, Yasminah." He indicated Bryn with a sweep of his hand.

The Syrian reached out a pudgy hand and grasped her chin, forcing her to meet his eyes. She resisted the impulse to jerk away from his touch, the overpowering cologne doing little to disguise his body odor.

"Very beautiful."

Bryn struggled to find her voice and recite the practiced line. With just the right amount of coyness, she looked at him through lowered lashes. "I hope you will be pleased with me." To her own ears her voice sounded husky, and she attributed it to her dry throat.

Masood's lips curved, and her skin crawled at the lust burning in his eyes. "Of that I have no doubt, little flower."

As he released her chin and dismissed her with a wave of his hand she forced her knees to stop trembling. Retreating to the shadows, she closed her eyes and conjured up an image of Dec.

You're doing this for Dec. Just imagine him watching you. Tell him everything you feel for him when you dance.

"Yasminah."

Her head jerked up at Luke's voice.

"They're waiting for you."

Show time. Her stomach did a back flip. *Suck it up, lady. You've got a job to do.* Raising her chin, she inhaled a steadying breath and went to take the stage.

****

Somewhere in Damascus

Tehrazzi folded his arms across his chest and leaned in the doorway, backlit by the hall light. The prisoner's harsh breathing pleased him. He could smell the man's terror as he sat bound to the chair, the whites of his eyes showing all around the irises.

He held the frightened gaze. "You know what I will do to you if you have lied to me?"

The man shook his head in a frantic motion. "I have not, I swear it—"

Tehrazzi nodded to his bodyguard, who unsheathed a jeweled dagger from its scabbard with a hissing sound as steel slid against steel.

"I am telling the truth!" the prisoner shrieked, jerking away from the blade as it pressed against his throat. A trickle of blood spilled down his neck, staining the sweaty collar of his white dress shirt.

"And you say this tape will prove Masood is setting me up?" Tehrazzi asked.

The prisoner had his eyes shut, was shaking so hard the wooden legs of the chair squeaked against the floor. "Yes, yes!"

Tehrazzi crossed to the table next to him and played the recording. By the time it finished, his blood was boiling. The Americans were planning to trap him tonight. All because of Masood.

The pain was sharp and terrible. Much worse than he would have expected.

Traitor. How could he have admired such a man? To think he'd once idolized him as mentor and benefactor. In the end, their twenty-year friendship mattered no more to Masood than the no-doubt lucrative business deal the Americans had offered him. Handing him over to the infidels for *money.* An unforgivable sin. One he would pay the ultimate price for.

His vision blurred as the rage took hold. The betrayal tasted bitter on his tongue.

He looked over his shoulder at the prisoner, whose eyes held a tremulous hope now that his veracity had been confirmed.

"Loyalty is a rare thing in today's society. I will spare your life." The man sagged in his seat with a quiet sob. Tehrazzi pinned him with merciless eyes. "But I cannot risk you playing one side against the other, as your boss has done."

The man went rigid.

For a moment he almost changed his mind. This man had told him the truth. No. His suffering was necessary to prevent others from turning against him. "As I cannot ensure you will hold your tongue, I will have to take more…severe measures." After tonight, no one would dare cross him again.

Steeling his heart, he nodded to his guard.

Assoud grasped the prisoner's chin, blade ready. "Open wide."

The man jerked his head away, eyes wide with horror. "No," he begged, "please, I swear I will not—"

"When you're finished," Tehrazzi said to Assoud, "we will go take care of this latest problem." He walked out without glancing back, agonized screams following him into the darkness.

Chapter Thirteen

On the street, a few doors down from the club, Dec heard the hush fall over the place and his guts clenched. Any moment now, Bryn would be starting her performance. She didn't need to do it, either, because security hadn't been as air tight as they'd expected and he'd already planted the bugs. But hauling her away before she'd done her show would tip everyone off that something was up.

As the music floated down the alley to him, every cell in his body demanded he barge in there and hustle her away to the car. He hated the idea of any man leering at her while she was onstage wearing next to nothing.

He imagined her dancing, her body gyrating in her skimpy costume. He'd seen the damn thing earlier when she and Luke had returned from shopping, so he had a vivid image of the gold-beaded bikini. And now a roomful of men with sex on their minds were ogling her. A growl of frustration locked in his throat.

A few minutes ticked by, his muscles tightening to the point of pain. Christ, he hated this whole thing. He'd rather have taken on the entire club with his team than put Bryn through this. She had to be scared, even with Luke and Ben in there.

The music changed from a pounding rhythm of drums to a slow, sensual beat. His feet shifted in agitation as he stood there, watching for the all-clear signal. He wished they'd stationed him in the club with her. At least he would have been able to see for himself whether she was okay or not.

But of course, that was why he was standing out in the fucking alley all by himself, wasn't it? He didn't think straight when it came to Bryn, and Luke knew it. The only reason he was on this mission was because of the white-knight complex he had developed toward her. Add the instability of the sexual attraction between them, and it equaled an explosion waiting to happen.

Footsteps had him swinging his head around. They grew louder as they approached to his left on the sidewalk. Dec's fingers tightened on the Glock concealed inside his jacket.

Pressing close against the brick wall, he peered out at the main street. Ben came into view, hands smoothing his necktie as he passed under a streetlamp. The all-clear signal.

With a breath of relief, Dec made his way to the sidewalk and turned the corner just as Ben disappeared into the club. Keeping with the plan, he took up his position close to the fire exit while Ben pushed through the crowd to get close to Bryn.

But when Dec moved into place with his back to the wall, he caught sight of her out on the stage and his spine jerked. His field of vision narrowed until she was the only thing in it. The crowd in front of him seemed to vanish, the room closing in.

The erotic throb of the drums echoed in his empty head, the sight of her hypnotizing him. He forgot about staying alert for Tehrazzi and his lieutenants, or the man who funded their operations. Everything in him was riveted on Bryn.

Luke had wanted a diversion, and that's sure as hell what she was.

She glowed under the lights, the golden bra pushing her breasts high, the low-slung skirt leaving her toned midriff bare. As she undulated, the jewels dangling from her navel glinted, drawing his eyes to her abs, rippling with her movements. Bangles decorated her arms, her hair trailing halfway down her sleek back in a dark waterfall as she twirled on the balls of her bare feet. She moved in a graceful rhythm, her hips dipping and circling in blatant invitation, the beaded fringe on her skirt swaying.

Her eyes, outlined with heavy makeup, paralyzed him with their sultry heat. In a trance, he watched her lift her arms above her head, her hips gliding up on one side and down on the other in a move worthy of the highest-paid stripper, then she threw her head back as her entire body shimmied and every piece of jewelry and bead on her quivered, like...

Jesus, almost like she was having an orgasm. The jolt of lust that surged through him made his head spin. Were his eyes bleeding?

Dear Christ in Heaven, she was the sexiest thing he'd ever seen in his life.

His jaw nearly fell open when she followed that amazing move by sinking to her knees and then to her back, her legs tucked underneath her at an impossible angle. From that position she somehow lifted her torso off the floor without using her arms and did some more of those mind-melting undulations, abs rolling, her arms and hands making snakelike motions in the air above her.

She had every man in the room mesmerized. She was sex personified, a woman writhing in abandonment beneath her lover. Dec could barely breathe.

When the performance ended and the music faded, the audience fell into an awed silence, then erupted into a cacophony of applause and yells.

Jerked back to reality, Dec stood by the exit while Luke escorted her into the back room with a heavy-set Arab man. His eyes cut around the club, settling on Ben in the opposite corner, who was watching him with rigid features.

Dec's pulse thudded. Something wasn't right. He thrust his chin towards Ben. *What's going on?*

Ben lifted four fingers.

Shit. Only one man was supposed to be back there with them—that heavy-set guy was supposed to have won the bidding war for Bryn. And now she had four men with her, expecting her to...

A primitive, dominant rage roiled through him. If anyone laid a hand on her, he'd...

He'd what? He was on the other side of the damn building.

He took a deep breath, forced it out, then another. Through the haze of anger he maintained his gaze on Ben, who straightened his tie and started toward the door that led to the back room. Dec moved through the crowd after him, Glock in his grip.

****

Bryn's heart pounded as the hoots and applause filled the room. The spotlights shut off, leaving her breathing out a sigh of relief. It was over. She'd done it, despite her wobbly knees and tense muscles.

Almost done. Her eyes swept over the crowd as she left the stage. She didn't see Dec, but Luke appeared at the stairs, and she grabbed the hand he offered. His firm grip calmed her.

"Great job, lady," he said, handing her a robe to cover with. "Ready for the rest?"

"Yeah." She just wanted it done, the sooner the better. "Is he waiting for me?"

"In the back."

She geared up for the next part of her act, keeping her eyes downcast as she trailed behind him. He made her feel completely safe despite the circumstances. Masood was waiting next to Ben at the door. The Syrian's dark eyes gleamed when he saw her. She shivered. *You can do this. It's only pretend, and Luke won't let anything happen to you.*

She forced what she hoped was a seductive smile at the Syrian and let her eyes stray to Ben. He nodded to her, and she could almost hear his words. *It's all right, sweets. I got your back.* She sent him a silent thank you with her eyes and gripped Luke's hand tighter. He squeezed back.

Masood preceded them into his office, his bald spot gleaming in the recessed lights in the ceiling. His shirt had sweaty spots between his shoulder blades and under his arms. She hoped she wouldn't have to touch him much.

"A few of my associates wished to meet you, little flower," he said.

What? She smothered a gasp when she saw the four middle-aged men seated around a table, watching her. She fought not to glance at Luke. This wasn't supposed to happen. It was only supposed to be her and Luke and Masood back here.

Luke's calm expression never faltered. Okay, he'd already adapted to the situation. Now it was her turn.

She refocused on her role. "Of course," she murmured in Arabic, even though her heart was racing.

Masood took her from Luke, brought her over to meet the others. The hand he splayed over the base of her spine was lower than she was comfortable with, and damp against her skin above the low-slung skirt. He rubbed her there, fingers caressing.

She gritted her teeth. What did she expect? He thought she was a whore he'd paid for. Bryn clenched her jaw as he showed her off like a prized mare to his friends, struggling to stay in character. A secretive glance, the hint of a smile. Seductive yet mysterious, a little bit shy. From the hungry glint in Masood's eyes, she figured she was doing a decent job of it. But this meek and subservient routine was not for her.

He took her chin in his fingers, and she gazed up at him through her lashes while trying not to shudder at the lust on his face. "Would you like something to drink?"

"If... If it would not be too much trouble."

One corner of his mouth went up. "Some champagne?"

"Lovely."

He trailed a hand down her bare arm. "Yes, you are."

She resisted the urge to wipe his touch away when he went to the bar. Luke was talking with the others in rapid Arabic, laughing and seeming completely at ease with his new companions.

Lucky him. He got to be one of the boys while she played courtesan to a sweaty stranger.

Masood returned with her drink. He draped an arm across her shoulders. "Shall we go get better acquainted?"

Ew. "I would like that." She barely refrained from grabbing his meaty wrist and throwing him to the floor on his ass. The image empowered her.

He sat in a leather chair behind a massive mahogany desk and patted his lap. "Sit with me."

She froze an instant. Her stomach turned but she slid into his lap anyway, and went rigid as she felt the erection prodding her backside. Her eyes cut over to Luke. *Get me out of here*, she willed him, but he didn't even glance her way.

Bryn braced her hands against the Syrian's damp shirt, revolted by the cloying scent of his cologne that tried to mask his offensive body odor. A thick thatch of hair erupted from his collar. She stared at the heavy gold chain tangled in it. *Relax, Bryn. Act the part. It'll be over soon.*

Not near soon enough.

She forced her muscles to relax, met his hungry gaze.

"You are beautiful," he murmured, trailing a hand over her hair so the back of it brushed against her breast.

Her belly tightened to the point of pain.

The hand slid down her back and settled on her hip, squeezed her butt.

Her head came up, and she tried not to glare. He smiled, must have taken the action for interest because he gripped her hair in a fist and planted his lips on hers in a wet, passionate kiss. She jerked her head back. His smile widened. "Shy little flower. Shall we go somewhere more private?"

Oh God... She cast a desperate glance at Luke. *Get me the hell out of here, now.* He didn't acknowledge her predicament, but she'd bet he was aware of every single thing going on in the room. How much longer was she going to have to suffer this? Masood had grown impatient, was sliding his slimy mouth down her neck toward her breasts. She shuddered, wanting to kick his ass. "I—"

The back door burst open. She jumped. Masood jerked and swiveled his chair about.

Bryn froze. A man stood in the doorway holding a shotgun. She raised her terrified gaze to his face. A scar bisected his chin.

The waiter from the embassy. The one who'd gestured slitting her throat.

Terror snaked through her.

"T-Tehrazzi," Masood blurted, body rigid beneath her.

As if on cue, he appeared in the doorway.

Oh shit. Her heart slammed. His green eyes burned as he stared back at her with recognition.

The scarred man next to him raised the shotgun. *No!*

Her hands flattened against Masood's shoulders

as her muscles gathered to shove away. She saw Luke erupt from his chair and take a lunging step toward her.

Too far away.

Her head swung back around.

In slow motion, the gun barrel came up. Glinted in the light. Two black holes stared out of the muzzle. Pointed at her.

Masood shrieked. Raised his arms over his face.

No! She threw her hands up to shield herself as the shot exploded.

****

Dec stayed where he was as Ben approached the bouncer, said something to him. The man laughed and stood there chatting. Everything was okay so far, or Ben would have alerted him otherwise. Now they had to wait and see which of the four men got to take Bryn home with him.

He glanced around, his gaze sweeping over the crowd. Still no sign of Tehrazzi. Just as well. The tracking devices were planted. If he didn't show, they would find him soon enough.

Turning his head, he spared a glance at Ben. His body language was tense, his face grim. When his hand moved toward his belt where he had hidden a sidearm, Dec began making his way over to him.

Ben turned to him, his eyes brimming with shock and horror. His mouth moved in an unmistakable F-bomb.

As his blood pressure nosedived, Dec *knew*. Somehow Tehrazzi was already in that room with Bryn.

"Christ," he breathed, sprinting into action.

Two shots rang out from the back room.

The place went silent, then chaos erupted.

Heart in his throat, Dec muscled his way

174

through the throng, weapon up. Ben and the bouncer had already plowed through the door.

His fear for Bryn made sweat break out on his forehead. Nearly there, but it was like trying to swim upstream through a merciless current as the crowd pushed and jostled, dragging him backward with them in their panic to escape.

Elbowing people out of his way, he finally made it to the back room only to find it empty, except for a pool of blood soaking the carpet beneath the desk. Crimson spatters covered the wall. The warm, metallic smell of it hit him. His heart careened in his chest. *Please, God, don't let it be Bryn's.*

With his pistol gripped between his hands, he crept along the wall and ducked his head through another doorway, checking the adjoining bathroom. More smears of blood. Above the hand dryer, a window stood open. Bloody handprints stained the sill. He edged closer. A fragment of gold cloth hung from the frame, its beaded, bloodstained fringe glinting under the fluorescent light.

All the air rushed out of his lungs. "Bryn!"

****

"Go, go, go!" Ben yelled in her ear, shoving her down the darkened alley.

Bryn ran headlong in her bare feet as fast as her skirt would let her, heart thundering in her ears. Tehrazzi and his men were out there behind her, gunning for her. Terror gave her feet wings.

Ben's shoes pounded behind her, so close his rapid breathing fanned the back of her neck. The heel of his hand pressed into her spine. As they neared another alley he shoved her sideways into it, and she slammed into a wall before righting herself and pressing against it, gasping. The brick felt cool and rough against her bare back.

"Run," he snapped, eyes scanning the darkness the way they'd come, pistol in hand. "I'll catch up." When she didn't move, he turned those pale green eyes on her. "I said go. *Now*."

She obeyed, sprinting on wobbly legs. At the far end of the alley, voices floated toward her. Angry male voices, speaking Arabic. She skidded to a stop, heard Ben's feet behind her and darted to the right. The alley snaked left, then right. Dead end ahead.

She spun around. Backtracked to a side alley she'd passed and ducked down it. Her breath sawed in and out. She followed the twisting labyrinth, fear pushing her on. A stitch burned in her side but she kept going until she reached another turn.

Here she stopped, bent over at the waist to suck in air, legs trembling. Silence. No voices, no footsteps. Had she lost Ben? She had no idea where she was. All the buildings looked the same. A whimper caught in her throat. What if Ben and Luke never found her? The scent of blood rose up to her nostrils, making her stomach lurch. She'd been sitting on Masood's lap when the scarred man had blown a hole in his chest, barely missing her. She shuddered at the memory.

Soon she had her breath back, but she was still alone. A few parked cars lined the alley, a cat slunk past out of view. Something rustled along the gutter. A rat maybe. She shivered.

Wait—something else. She strained to hear it again. There. Voices. To her right. Speaking Arabic? She didn't plan to hang around and find out. She spun on her bare heel. A muffled shout, then the thud of running feet reached her ears.

She ran and ran, soles slapping against the ground, but the footsteps advanced. A sob caught in her chest. She rounded another corner and came out on a street. Frozen, she blinked in the light, lost and terrified. Another shout behind her. She took off.

Breath straining in and out, she sprinted down the block, slowing as she approached another alley. Glancing behind her, she saw nothing, stood there shaking before pivoting forward again.

And smacked straight into a tall, hard male body. Strong hands grabbed her shoulders and whirled her around the corner into the dark.

She screamed and instinctively drove her fist upward, but her attacker blocked it, using his weight to pin her against the wall. Squashed flat, she couldn't gain enough breath to scream, and thrashed in his grip.

"Bryn. Bryn!"

She stopped fighting. The faint glow of a streetlight around the corner gave her enough light to see. Trembling from head to foot, she looked up into a pair of golden-brown eyes. "Dec," she cried, crumpling against him.

"Are you hurt?" he asked, stepping back to run his hands over her. "You're covered in blood."

"Not mine," she wheezed, willing her heart to slow down. "Masood's. He's dead. Tehrazzi's bodyguard shot him. Luke went after him."

"I know. Look, there's a car waiting for us just down the street. Only two more blocks, then we're home free."

She nodded, so overjoyed to see him she felt like crying. "Okay."

He took her hand and led her toward the street, checking left and right, gun in his free hand. Bryn strode beside him, watching his every move. They were in a rough area of town. Figures lurked in doorways and windows, watching.

Partway down the first block, they heard it at the same time—someone behind them approaching at a run.

We aren't going to make it.

Instantly Dec grabbed her and pushed her into a

darkened doorway, shoved his gun in his waistband and lifted her leg to wrap it around his hip. She gasped, grabbing his leather jacket to steady herself, staring up into his shadowed eyes. What was he doing?

They waited, listening, their bodies pressed so closely together she could feel his chest move as he breathed. His body heat warmed her, his fresh scent enveloping her. A minute ticked by. Two. He didn't ease up from her. She quivered against him, part fear, part arousal, and his body responded.

She held her breath at the feel of his erection against her lower belly and stared into his face, their gazes locking.

A muted voice floated through the darkness. "A woman...dressed in a dance costume. Did you see her running this way?" Arabic. A muttered reply followed, then the footsteps resumed. Closer with each passing second. What were they going to do? She tightened her fingers on Dec's shoulders.

"Bryn?"

She swallowed, afraid even though he was protecting her with his body. "What?"

"Go with this, okay?"

He didn't give her a chance to reply, just took her face in his hands and leaned down to cover her mouth with his. She gasped, and he took advantage by angling his head, sliding his tongue along her lower lip before stealing inside.

A shockwave of heat flashed through her. Her fingers clenched as she arched upward, a moan of confusion escaping as he explored her mouth with devastating skill. Shouldn't they be running? His mouth was so warm, and he was so good her eyelids fluttered down.

A thumb swept over her cheekbone. His other hand trailed down her throat and over her shoulder, sparking electricity in its wake. She made a murmur of protest, not understanding how she could be responding to him under the circumstances.

The treads on the sidewalk grew louder, but he continued to kiss and caress her as though they were about to fall onto a bed somewhere, as though they weren't in mortal danger. She shook in his embrace, torn between wanting him and the fear they would be shot dead any second.

When his hand slid down over the curve of her breast, she gasped into his mouth, eyes flying wide as those footfalls grew louder and louder while her body trembled under his touch.

"Shh," he murmured against her lips. "Kiss me back."

Footsteps echoed. Their pursuer was almost on top of them now.

Dec's thumb grazed her nipple, and her concentration splintered. Battling the drugging sensations, she swallowed a moan, straining against him as he kissed her and wedged his thigh between hers, pressing right where she throbbed and burned.

Surely this was carrying pretense a little too far? she thought wildly. They were about to be killed, and he was all over her. She pushed against his sternum.

But Dec continued to seduce her with his mouth, a deep groan of satisfaction rumbling from his chest as though he wanted to yank her skirt up and take her right there in the doorway.

Which was exactly what he wanted their tail to think. Anyone on the run wouldn't be getting busy in a back alley, would they?

Her heart slammed against her ribs as she kissed him back, distracted, flinching at each measured footfall behind them.

When the paces slowed to a stop, Bryn jerked her head from his grasp but Dec held her fast, kissing her so deeply that all that came out was a

179

throaty moan. Every muscle in her body wound tight as a wire. She hung in his grip like a living statue, unresponsive. A beat passed, then another, and finally whoever was looking for them continued past them.

Dec finally released her mouth, hovered a breath away. And waited. Minutes elapsed.

She sagged in his arms. He lifted his head, still checking whether the man was coming back. He was so beautiful, she thought in despair as she gazed up at him. Was this as close as she would get to having him? An act played out in a shadowed doorway?

She closed her eyes and tried to calm her swirling emotions, focusing on the strength of his body, his heat seeping into her. His clean, spicy fragrance filled her lungs. Relief made her legs weak. The one wrapped around him fell from his hip.

He straightened, gazed down into her eyes. "You okay?"

She nodded, then looked away.

"Sorry. Had to make it believable."

"It's okay." She wished he hadn't apologized.

When he stepped back, she fought the urge to cling to him. "We'll give it another minute before we get out of here." Then he surprised her by threading his hands in her hair and kissing her softly, twice, three times. The sweet contact spiraled to the pit of her stomach. He lifted his head, grabbed her arm. "Let's move."

She followed, not knowing what to think, what to feel anymore.

****

No one said a word all the way back to the hotel. Ben and Dec escorted her upstairs to her room and checked inside before letting her in. Bryn was barely inside the door before Ben left, leaving her alone with Dec.

He stared at her a moment, then made a show of taking off his jacket and draping it over a chair. "Go ahead and have a shower," he said. "You'll feel better."

Too unnerved to think straight, she went into the bathroom and confronted her reflection in the mirror above the sink. The costume was torn and covered with rusty bloodstains, her face pale but for the slutty makeup smeared under her eyes, hair mussed and tangled. Her lips were swollen from Dec's kisses. She squeezed her eyes shut.

Then she peeled off the ruined garments, set the shower as hot as she could tolerate and stepped under the pounding spray. After scrubbing herself, she washed her hair and killed the water, wrapped herself in a towel and dried her hair. After brushing it smooth she cleaned her teeth before pulling on a robe hanging on the back of the door. When she emerged in a cloud of steam, Dec was sitting in a wingchair.

He stood, gaze sweeping over her. Fighting the urge to fidget under his scrutiny, she reminded herself that while she didn't look her best, she looked a hell of a lot better than she had before the shower. But what was he thinking right now? Why had he kissed her like that after the threat was gone?

"How do you feel?" he asked.

"Better."

His amber gaze ran over her once more. "You look beat. I should let you get some sleep. Need anything before I go?"

He was leaving? She'd assumed he was going to stay the night with her, even if only for security reasons. Disappointment filled her. Even if he didn't want to be with her in an intimate way, she would have felt much better with him sleeping beside her.

Just so she could feel the warmth of his body and hear his breathing in the night.

He studied her in concern. "Maybe Ben should stay with you. You've been through a lot."

"No, that's okay." What she meant was, she didn't want Ben. But for some reason she was too chicken to say it. Something about the way Dec held himself made her sure he would turn her down. She didn't think she could take that kind of humiliation on top of everything that had happened tonight. Ducking her head, she bit down on her lower lip.

He sighed and came toward her, opening his arms, and she melted right into them, pressing her face into the hollow of his throat to inhale his scent. A shudder ripped through her. He made a murmur of reassurance, running a hand through her hair. It felt like heaven.

He kissed the top of her head and tucked her under his stubbled chin, strands of her hair snagging on his whiskers. Sudden tears burned her eyes, and she let out a ragged breath. She could stay like this forever. He made her feel so safe.

Under the muscles across his chest she could hear his heart beating, a steady, calming throb. He was so strong, so protective of her. She lifted her face. Something in his eyes made her heart stutter. His gaze was impossibly tender.

"What?" she whispered.

He shook his head, eyes moving over her face as though he was memorizing every detail.

"Dec?"

He relented with a sigh. "I saw a piece of your costume caught in the bathroom window. A blood trail all over the floor and handprints on the windowsill. I didn't know if you'd been hit." His arms pulled her in tighter. "I thought he'd taken you again."

Her skin went cold. "It was close." Squeezing her

eyes shut, she laid her head on his shoulder and savored the strength surrounding her. "Tehrazzi recognized me the second he appeared in that room."

"You sure?"

"Yes. I think he knew I'd be there, bet he thought he could get me and Masood at the same time. He came out of nowhere with a bodyguard and that gun, and without a word, that guy blew a hole right through Masood's chest." And when she'd leapt up with a scream locked in her throat, the bodyguard had lunged at her. "When I saw him coming at me, Ben took him down, then hauled me into the bathroom and shoved me through the window. Luke went after Tehrazzi."

How had Tehrazzi known she would be at the club? He couldn't have, unless someone in the team's circle had blabbed.

It pissed her off and scared the hell out of her at the same time. She could have been killed.

A growl vibrated through Dec's chest. "We might have a leak somewhere."

"Know any good plumbers?"

"I'm pretty handy at fixing leaks. Luke is, too." His cheek pressed against hers. "God, I *hate* that you're caught up in this."

"I volunteered for it."

"Don't remind me. I'm still kicking my own ass for letting you."

"Are you kidding? It's not your fault. Luke had me nailed in so many ways, even without you there. He knew it before he asked me, too, because of my connections with his family and his ties to my father. He only wanted you along because he knew I'd be more comfortable with you on the team."

He nuzzled the crown of her head. "You know what your problem is?"

"I'm too damn stubborn?"

"That too, but you're too smart for your own

goddamn good."

A smile pulled at her lips. "Third in my class at Harvard."

"Yeah, I read it in your file." His hands wandered over her spine, sending licks of heat in their wake. "Speaking of which, there was no reference to you being a belly dancer. Glad I didn't know that ahead of time, because it would have messed me up. As it is I can't stop thinking about how you looked out on that dance floor."

"You saw me?" She hadn't realized he'd been in the building with her.

"Oh, yeah. And now I can't get the picture of you out of my head."

Her breath caught in her throat. She raised her head to look at him. "What did you think?"

"Please," he said with a laugh, stroking the side of her face. "Every man in that room was drooling all over themselves."

But she didn't care about any other men. "I want to know what *you* thought."

He met her eyes. "Like you have to ask."

She stared back, unwilling to let him squirm out of answering.

Something flared in his eyes. "You were the sexiest thing I've ever seen in my life."

Her lips curved. The throb low in her belly began to pulse. "I'm glad. Because I was imagining I was dancing for you." She swallowed, having made herself completely vulnerable to him.

His whiskey-colored eyes flared. The stark hunger in the made her breath catch. "God, don't say things like that to me."

"Why not?"

"Because it makes me want things I can't have."

Why was he so dead set against taking her to bed? It wasn't like she expected a marriage proposal from him afterward. "Why can't you have them?"

His expression became shuttered. "You know why."

She'd spooked him. *Don't go*, she cried silently. She needed him. Her hands tightened around him in protest, her gaze falling to his lips.

His gaze dropped to her mouth, too, his hands moving up to sift through her hair, as though he couldn't help himself. "Ah, hell," he muttered, and bent to brush his lips over hers.

Bryn sighed and went up on tiptoe to kiss him back, sliding one palm around his nape and opening her mouth to him. He groaned and pulled her closer, deepening the kiss as the urgency roared through her. Then he slowed and she strained to get closer.

The stroke of his tongue over hers made the blood pound in her head and between her legs. Her heart seemed to swell in her chest as she reveled in the feel and the taste of him, that leashed hunger and power.

His hands trailed down to grasp her hips, making them both moan as she rocked into his erection. He slid one hand up to glide against the curve of her breast, fingers caressing through the terrycloth.

She arched, giving him better access and demanding more. When her head fell back, he followed with his mouth, pressing hot kisses over her jaw to her throat. His tongue swept gently over the tender spot beneath her ear. She gasped. He sucked at her sensitive skin. She grabbed hold of his shoulders, let her hands coast over his muscled chest and hard abs.

Against her neck, he sucked in a breath, stilling as he waited for her touch.

More. She needed more. Her palm slid across his waistband, then lower, until she was stroking the length of his erection.

He pushed his hips against her hand, his lips

losing their languorous rhythm against her throat. With a strangled groan, he covered her mouth with his, tongue plunging inside. Bryn urged him on, squeezing his erection in a firm grip. He shuddered.

More. She didn't care if they made it to the bed. Standing up right here was good enough.

Her whole body throbbed with the need for release. One tug, she thought, willing his hand to move to where the robe gaped between her breasts. One tug and she'd be naked, and maybe then he wouldn't stop.

Dec suddenly broke the kiss and pulled away.

Confused, shaken, she reeled back and looked up at him, breath unsteady.

He was so gorgeous, his eyes all lit up, sexual heat pouring off him. But he backed up a step. "Bryn," he began, his voice deep and all gravel. "I have to go. Lock the door behind me."

"Wha—?"

"The door," he rumbled, heading for it without looking at her. "Make sure you lock it."

Rooted to the floor, she stared after him. Her body wept in protest. She couldn't bring herself to call him back, no matter how much she ached inside. Her pride, though tattered, was all she had left to keep her standing.

Dec paused at the door, then glanced at her over his shoulder. She saw the need and regret there. "Ben's next door if you need anything. I'll see you in the morning." Then he stepped into the hallway.

Standing there alone in her robe, suddenly cold without his warmth, Bryn felt like crying.

"Bryn." His harsh voice was muffled through the panels. "The door. Lock it, *now.*"

She went over and threw the deadbolt, leaned her forehead against it, body and soul crying out for him.

Then, in a whisper so soft she thought she might

have imagined it, he said, "I'm sorry. Sleep tight."

Chapter Fourteen

When his cell phone rang later that night, Ben set the razor down next to the sink and checked the time. 23:20 meant he'd been prettying himself up for a hell of a lot longer than he'd thought. Used to take him ten minutes from start to finish, but since he'd grown the goatee a couple days ago to help disguise his features, it took way longer to shave around it rather than scrape the whole deal off.

Wiping off the remnants of shaving cream with a towel, he answered. "Yeah."

"Hey," Dec said.

"Hey." Why the hell was he calling? He'd expected McCabe to be tangled in the sheets with Bryn by now. That's why it felt like he had a hot coal buried in his belly. Even the handful of Tums he'd downed hadn't helped any. "What's up, my man?"

"I'm going over some intel with the boss here. Wondered if you could check on Bryn, maybe stay with her. She was pretty spooked."

Yeah, well, no shit. She'd had someone's heart and lungs blown apart all over her.

"She shouldn't be alone tonight," Dec finished.

Ben's mouth went dry. *Holy shit.* They wanted him to stay the night in Bryn's room. He could just imagine what kind of shape she was in right now, reliving that moment when Masood's chest had exploded while she'd been in his lap.

He ran a hand through his damp hair. "Yeah, no problem."

"Thanks. I'll call you if we hear anything."

"Sure." Disconnecting, Ben gazed down at his

phone. Why the hell had Irish left her alone if he knew how scared she was? From what Ben had seen, Bryn was more than willing to accept comfort from the SEAL.

Had he left because he didn't trust himself? Yeah, Ben could guess how that scenario played out. And yet Dec had walked away, then called him for help. He blew out a breath.

This was dangerous ground for him. Jesus, he wanted to be the one she needed. Just once, he wanted her to look at him the way she did Irish, to take the solace he wanted to give her. He wanted to open his arms and have her walk into them with something more than friendship, to let him comfort her with his body. God, he would give anything for that chance.

Inhaling deeply, he picked up the hotel phone and dialed Bryn's room. She answered, her voice fragile. Something squeezed in his chest as he imagined her wrapped in a robe or blanket, huddled amongst the bedding all alone in the room next door.

"Hey, it's me," he said. "I thought maybe you could use some company."

"Oh, I'm...fine."

Sure you are, sweet thing. "It's been a hell of a day, honey. How about I come over for a little while? At least you'll be able to sleep if you know I'm there."

She hesitated, then said, "Okay, if you don't mind."

Mind? Hell no, he didn't mind. Even if he was the dumbest shit in the universe for setting himself up for this kind of torture. "I'll be over in a sec."

Stuffing some clothes and ammo into a duffel, he slid his cell into his jeans pocket and tucked his Glock into the waistband. Checking the peephole, he went out into the hall, keeping his back to the wall as he hustled to Bryn's room and knocked. When she opened the door and stepped back to let him in, his lungs constricted.

Her feet were bare, the tips of her painted pink toenails curling into the carpet as she stood there in the oversized hotel robe. Her dark hair spilled down her back, the ends curling as though she'd let them dry naturally. Without makeup she looked terribly young and vulnerable, her dark eyes wide in her pale face.

"Hi," she whispered.

"Hi." He shut the door behind him, maintaining his grip on the deadbolt to keep from reaching for her. She looked so sad and lost, it was all he could do not to wrap her in his arms and carry her to the wide bed. He swallowed. "Rough night, huh?"

Her arms, dwarfed by the robe rolled up at the wrists, wrapped around her waist. "Yeah."

How the hell had Dec left her when she looked like that? "You hungry? I could grab us something."

"No, I couldn't eat right now. I'm tired, but I'm too strung out to sleep."

"Understandable."

"Maybe we could watch a movie or something."

God, he wanted to hold her so badly. Every cell in his body screamed at him to. "Sure. Whatever you want." He *so* meant that. Whatever she needed from him, he was more than willing to give.

As she climbed into the bed, he caught a glimpse of her sleek, muscled calves and thighs. The tension in his muscles worsened. A smile touched her lips as she glanced over her shoulder at him, still frozen by the door. "I'm glad you came, Ben. You were right. I don't want to be alone right now."

"Good. Glad I could help." He felt almost light-headed with the need to go to her. Instead, he dropped his duffel next to the wingback chair and settled into it.

She stared at him. "You can sit on the bed with me."

His guts knotted. "Thanks, but I'm good." And he *was* going to be good—Boy Scout good.

As she switched on the TV for some channel surfing, he hated the awkward silence stretching between them. He should say something to her. Probe a little, then let her open up and unload all the tangled emotions bottled inside. Instead, he watched her profile as she settled on a channel.

Ben winced as one of the actors was shot. Hands curling around the arms of the chair, he studied her reaction as more bullets flew, tearing apart human flesh and bone. She hugged her knees to her chest, her beautiful face haunted. One of the actors screamed as a round hit him, and she flinched.

Ah, shit. She so shouldn't be watching this. "Bryn."

Her eyes glistened with unshed tears. "There was nothing else on," she whispered. Her gaze was full of torment. "How can men kill each other like that, Ben? Like life is nothing to them. Like tonight." The bewilderment in her grief-stricken voice stabbed at him. She'd gotten another glimpse of his world, and he was damn sorry for it.

Good intentions be damned, he couldn't stand to see her suffering. He got up and crossed the room, set his weapon on the nightstand.

The bed dipped beneath his weight as he took the remote from her, flipping it to an Iraqi news network before pulling her into his arms. She went willingly, huddling against his chest like a child, grabbing fistfuls of his t-shirt and pressing her cheek into his shoulder.

Goddamn, it felt so right as he hauled her up and cradled her in his lap. When her shoulders shook in a silent sob, he closed his eyes and pressed his face into her silky hair, breathing in her soapy scent.

"S-sorry," she choked against the tears.

"Don't be. Go ahead and let go."

"Oh, B-Ben..."

"Shh. It's all right, I've got you." He kept his voice low, soothing, letting her cry as he swept a hand down her back, memorizing the imprint of her body against his. Her tears soaked the front of his shirt while the sobs turned to hiccups, then exhausted little sighs that left her limp against his chest.

She stirred but didn't pull away, and for that he was pathetically grateful.

"God, Ben, I'm so scared for all of you."

His hand paused in its motion against her hair.

"I keep thinking about how fragile life is. And you, and your brother, and Dec and Luke out there going after people like Tehrazzi..." She shuddered.

He blew out a breath, not knowing what to say to ease her mind. Their lives weren't pretty, and for someone unused to that kind of violence... "We're good, Bryn. We've all been trained by the best programs in the world."

"I know, but you're only flesh and blood." She sat up and wiped her hands across her cheeks. "I don't know why I thought I could handle it."

"Handle what?" He bit back a protest when she moved away to lean against her pillow. "Tell me."

"Everything." She sighed, staring down at her fingers as they twisted the comforter. "This mission. Setting up Tehrazzi." She hesitated. "And...Dec."

For a moment he couldn't get his breath, like she'd socked him in the diaphragm. "What about Dec?"

She shrugged. "I know he's an operator. I knew that going in, and I still thought I could deal with it. But after tonight, all I can think about is him, or you, or anyone else on the team getting killed."

She must have seen something in his face, because her eyes and smile turned sad. "God, Ben, I didn't know being in love could hurt so much."

Yeah, he could relate.

"Sometimes I wish...that I'd fallen in love with you instead."

His fists clenched so hard his fingers went numb. "Why do you say that?" By some miracle his voice stayed steady.

"Because I don't think he'll ever feel the same way about me."

Well if the dumb fuck didn't, then he didn't deserve her.

"Like tonight. He kissed me in that alley, he kissed me in this room, then left. Even after what happened tonight, he left me." She buried her fingers in her hair. "I'm so confused."

Gathering up the last of his pride, Ben found himself coming to McCabe's defense. "It's because of the job, Bryn. He's a SEAL, and SEALs don't take their responsibilities lightly. And on this op, you're his responsibility."

"I know, but...oh, hell, that's enough. I'm sorry for dragging you into my pity party."

"Don't apologize. It's been a bitch of a day for us all." And his had been topped off by having his heart carved out with a dull knife. He rubbed a hand over his sternum as though this could cure the persistent ache and the heartburn beneath it.

Bryn caught his fingers, laced them through her own and squeezed tight. "I'm sorry, Ben." Her eyes were wet. "I wish I felt differently."

"Nothing to be sorry about." She couldn't help her emotions, couldn't change them no matter how much he wanted her to.

"Will you still stay with me?"

The uncertainty in her face pissed him off. "I can't believe you'd wonder about that. Of course I'm staying with you."

Her relieved smile tugged at his aching heart.

"Thanks. And will you stay on the bed with me? If it's too selfish of me—"

"If that's what you want, you know I will." Hell, he'd still do anything for her, no matter what her feelings for him.

She snuggled down under the covers, hand linked in his. He turned off the TV and stretched out beside her on top of the sheet. "Want me to leave the lamp on?"

She shook her head. "So long as you're here, I don't need it."

Ah, fuck, that one hurt too. "Flatterer." His fingers found the switch.

A sleepy smile touched her lips. "Just remember that the next time you're pissed at me."

"I'll try. And you let me know if things don't work out with you and Irish, okay?"

Her fingers tightened around his. "In a heartbeat."

He lay next to her in the darkness, listening to her breathing and savoring the warmth of her hand in his.

****

Day 10, Damascus

Tehrazzi's hands trembled as he raised his cup of early morning tea to his lips. Even though he'd called off the search for Daoud's daughter, he hadn't been able to calm down completely.

He'd accomplished his primary goal but failed to capitalize on the opportunity that came with it. The knowledge pricked at his skin like a barb.

When he'd seen her in the back room of Masood's club, he'd thought he was imagining her sitting on the Syrian's lap like a whore. But she'd recognized him. Her eyes had given her away. The instant her gaze fell upon him they'd widened in terror.

If he'd known about her being there, she would have died too. Except she'd leapt off Masood, after Tehrazzi's bodyguard had fired the killing shot and then dragged Tehrazzi out the back exit before he could go after her. The American protecting her had wasted no time in getting her out of there, and despite Tehrazzi and three of his men looking for her, she had slipped through his fingers.

How had he not known about her performing at Masood's club? She could not have been there by accident. But who would have put her there? And why, except to draw him there? Only one plausible explanation came to mind. Unease rippled over his skin.

His teacher.

It was the only thing that made sense. His teacher knew him, must have known he wanted to find her and fix his mistake. One of his men had reported seeing a man matching his description in the room with the daughter. Tehrazzi had been too focused on her to notice him.

For him and Daoud's daughter to be there tonight, someone had to have sought out his teacher to tell him about the meeting tonight.

His suspicious gaze traveled around the humble room he and his followers occupied. The others ate and spoke quietly to one another, oblivious of his mounting anger. He recalled the other betrayals that had come before this. His grandmother. Masood. Would one of his men think they could manipulate him this way?

"I cannot help but think we have a traitor here amongst us," he said in a low voice. They all fell silent and looked at him. He scanned their faces for any signs of guilt or nervousness. "If I learn that one of you has betrayed me to the Americans..." He sucked in a breath, let them feel the resolve in his steely gaze. "I will make you beg for death."

Leaving them all staring at him, he rose from the circle and went to another room where he laid out a prayer mat. Facing Mecca, he knelt upon it, clearing his mind of the image of his teacher's face and the fear from his chest that the man who created him might be hunting him.

He breathed in and out slowly, cleansing his body of all toxic thoughts. When he was in the proper state to address Allah, he bent and laid his forehead against the mat in reverence and prayed that Allah would continue to bless him with his mercy.

Most of all, he prayed that Allah would protect him from his teacher.

****

Dec lay in the darkness on the hotel bed, staring at nothing. It wouldn't have mattered what he was looking at, because all he could see was the devastation in Bryn's eyes when he'd pulled away in the middle of fondling her breast while his tongue had been shoved in her mouth.

She'd felt so incredible in his arms, he'd been desperate to tear her robe off just to get his hands on her naked skin. And that hand squeezing his cock. He'd sworn his eyes had rolled back in his head.

God, if this situation was half-assed normal, he'd be wrapped around her naked body right now. Instead, he was pissed off at himself and sexually frustrated, stewing in a room down the hall while his CIA handler slept in the next bed. He couldn't decide if he was feeling sorry for himself or if he just wanted to kick his own ass.

He was torn in two. On the one hand, he had his high moral code of conduct to contend with. The professional, do-the-job-properly-the-first-time part. On the other hand, he was attached to Bryn in ways that made it impossible for him to maintain his distance from her.

Knowing she wanted him every bit as much as he wanted her was damn near killing him. Never mind that dance he'd witnessed. God, the image of her in that golden costume was permanently burned into the backs of his eyelids.

He'd dated lots of women, had thought he'd loved one or two of them, but what he felt for Bryn eclipsed all of that. This emotion was so deep and primal it bordered on obsessive. He wanted to take her away from the world, keep her all to himself. It shocked the living shit out of him.

In another life, they might have met under different circumstances and gotten to know each other by dating like everyone else did. But so far, their relationship had the makings of a soap opera. Everything was too intense, too conflicted.

Dec wanted normality with her. To make her laugh—she needed to laugh more. He would love to make her smile every day. Make her feel good.

He wanted to be able to take her to dinner, feed her while candlelight played over her smooth skin. Wanted to watch movies with her, take her for long walks and kiss her on the beach, romance her until she couldn't see straight and then burn up the sheets together with amazing sex. Anything but the situation they were in now, trying to keep her alive while they hunted one of the most dangerous terrorists on the planet.

It was a wonder his head hadn't exploded yet.

He needed this mission to be over. He needed to rejoin his team, assume the leadership role he was most comfortable in, and not have to worry he was on the verge of sabotaging his career by wanting something he shouldn't. You didn't screw with the principal, literally or figuratively. Not unless you wanted a dishonorable discharge and a glass of hemlock to wash it down with.

The cell phone on the table between the beds buzzed, and Luke came out of a dead sleep to answer it in less than a second. Dec rolled onto his back and exhaled, gathering himself as he listened to Luke's responses. Marching orders, no doubt. Not happy news, anyway, since it was after two in the morning.

Luke set the phone down. "We're going to Baghdad."

Baghdad. Hooray. "All of us?"

"Yeah."

Who'd have thought he'd be back in that hellhole so soon? And now Bryn would be there with them. "When?"

"Bird's coming at oh-five-hundred. Have the others meet us in the lobby at quarter to."

Swinging his legs over the side of his bed, Dec welcomed the adrenaline flow, grateful for the way it cleared his head. This was what he needed, what he'd been trained for. Purpose. Movement.

Maybe now he could get Bryn out of his mind for ten minutes.

Chapter Fifteen

Day 10, Baghdad
Morning

Baghdad in September was pretty much what Bryn had expected: dry, flat, and hot enough to rival the interior of a car baking in the sun. She was miserable, but tried not to let it show.

Things with Dec were strained. He'd barely spared her a glance all morning. Things with Ben weren't much better, but at least he was making an effort to stay friends. She felt bad about hurting him, but what else could she have done? It would have been much worse to give him false hopes. She loved him, but not the way he wanted her to.

Nope. That aching, heart-squeezing love was for the man who couldn't, or wouldn't, meet her eyes after things had gone too far between them last night. Studying his profile across the helo's vibrating deck as it landed, her chest hurt even more.

Next to her, Rhys nudged her. "Forgot to give you this." He held out a chocolate glazed doughnut.

Her mood improved a bit. "Thanks."

Okay, she reasoned, chewing on the deep-fried treat. So she'd been shot down last night. But even if Dec *had* walked away and was doing everything he could to avoid her now, at least she knew he'd been as revved up as she had. Bryn did the tally sheet in her head.

He wanted her.

She wanted him.

She was falling in love with him. Might already

be there.

He...liked her a lot.

Well, at least they had the wanting part down.

Things could be worse. It could have been totally one-sided on her part. That would damn near have killed her. At least she could hope things would work out between them after this was finished.

For now, though, they all had a job to do. She was a member of a team—the weak link, mind you, but still a member—and she had to put her emotions aside. No way was she going to make things awkward.

Dec wouldn't either. He was much too professional to let something as pesky as personal feelings get in the way. She had the feeling he was giving her a cooling-out period. Once they landed in Baghdad, he'd act like nothing had happened between them. And he'd probably keep acting that way until it was over.

So fine. She could handle it. Plus, she didn't want him to know how deeply she was into him. If the idea of having sex with her spooked him, her falling in love with him would freak him the hell out.

After the chopper dropped them off at the airstrip, they unloaded their gear and headed to the terminal where an Iraqi man in khakis and a white golf shirt waited for them. Maybe in his late twenties, he had a short black beard and wavy hair, a gold chain nestling beneath his collar. He smiled in welcome, revealing white teeth that overlapped slightly at the front, and went forward to shake Luke's hand.

"This is Fahdi," Luke announced. "He's our civilian contact here in Baghdad—anything we need, he's our man. Right?"

"You got it," Fahdi responded in near-perfect English, shaking hands with the others. When he caught sight of her, his eyes widened a fraction and he hesitated before offering his hand.

"I'm Bryn," she said, shaking it firmly. She detested weak handshakes.

His eyes were like liquid espresso as he studied her, his lashes so long and thick they belonged on a fawn. "Hello, Miss Bryn."

Luke clapped him on the back. "Bryn's our secret weapon."

He released her hand. "Weapon? You are a soldier?"

"No, I—"

"She's the woman who's going to make Tehrazzi sit up and pay attention."

Fahdi's head whipped toward Luke. "You are tugging on my foot."

Luke grinned. "No, I'm not pulling your leg. And it's up to you and the rest of us to make sure she stays safe."

The younger man glanced at her again, this time with trepidation. Was he afraid for her? Or was he horrified by the idea of having to work with and protect a woman?

"You got our ride ready?"

Fahdi seemed to shake himself, then grabbed a couple of bags and headed toward a black Suburban. When everything was loaded, Dec handed Bryn up and she scrambled into the back seat. As she'd expected, he was acting as though he'd never avoided her. Whatever helped him sleep at night, she thought with a sigh.

No one said much on the ten-minute trip to the operations center in the middle of the city. Bryn stared out her window into the dusty streets as people carried their wares to and from the local market.

Women cloaked in robes and headscarves carried out their daily chores, children trailing behind them. On the dashboard was a photo of Fahdi standing with a woman who barely came up to his shoulders, holding an infant in her arms, four dark-eyed kids clustered about them.

It must be tough to raise a family in Baghdad with the threat of bombings every time you went to buy food, worrying that your children could be caught up in a firefight while they played outside. She didn't envy Fahdi or his wife.

"Home sweet home," Ben said, wrapping a steadying arm across her shoulders as they pulled up to a compound lined with barbed wire fences and gatehouses, uniformed Marines standing with their M-16s at the ready. Bryn couldn't help the way her heart knocked against her ribs and forced her muscles to relax. Too late to back down now.

In a courtyard in front of an imposing cinder-block building, they piled out of the truck. Pasting on a brave smile, she followed Dec into the gloom of their temporary barracks. The instant she crossed the threshold a wave of cool air hit her. Air conditioning. Bless them.

The twins were already unpacking their gear into footlockers at the end of the metal beds lining the longest wall. The adjoining room appeared to be a bathroom, with one toilet, a urinal and a cramped, not-so-clean shower.

"You can sleep against the end wall," Dec told her, pointing to the far bed, and she was glad when he chose the bed next to hers. "We'll get you a curtain so you can have a little privacy."

"Thanks. Do you snore?"

"Don't think so. Why?"

"Because Ben does, so you can borrow some of my earplugs."

"Hey," Ben protested. "I do not."

Luke strode in. "Everyone settled?" He dropped a duffel on the bunk nearest the door, set his hands on his hips. "Just like summer camp, huh?"

Sure. The kind where arts and crafts were followed by anti-terrorism classes.

"I thought we'd get a head start, meet the rest of the team we'll be working with at the TOC."

More acronyms.

"Tactical operations center," Dec translated.

"You up to it Bryn, or—"

"I'm good." The last thing she wanted was to make them think they had to handle her with kid gloves.

Outside, the heat hit her like a slap, sucking the air from her lungs. She trailed after everyone to the Suburban Fahdi already had running, the lone female in the midst of these armed, elite soldiers. Man, she was so in over her head.

The TOC was a concrete building three floors high, heavily guarded. Each room was crammed with desks, their surfaces littered with computers and electronic devices. People in uniforms came in and out in a constant tide of motion, speaking on headsets or cell phones. Bryn felt totally out of place and instinctively planted herself beside Dec.

Luke appeared a moment later with a gorgeous Arabic man. "This is Ali. He'll be helping us in the field when we need backup, and is pretty handy with digging up information on bad guys operating in Iraq."

Ali shook everyone's hand, hesitating and flushing when he got to Bryn. His smile was warm and genuine. She liked him instantly.

"Rhys?" A titian-haired Caucasian woman stood in the doorway, her brown eyes wide with surprise.

Rhys chuckled in delight and went forward to grab the newcomer in a one-armed hug. "I'll be damned," he chuckled. "What the hell are you doing here?"

"I got a promotion," she said, beaming up at him.

"You call an assignment in Baghdad a promotion?"

Her ironic smile was radiant. "Go figure."

"Guys, this is Samarra Wallace. We've worked together in Europe." He gestured to his twin. "This is my brother, Ben."

Sam studied him as she shook his hand. "Ah, the prodigal son. You're taller than I thought you'd be."

"Huh. Funny, you're shorter than I thought you'd be. The way my brother talked about you I thought for sure you'd be at least seven feet tall."

"Sorry to disappoint. Nice hat, by the way."

Ben tilted his head. "You a Sox fan?"

"Born and bred."

"Sam's our communications expert," Luke added.

Her smile widened when she looked at Bryn. "I'm very glad to meet you. I've heard a lot about you."

"Oh. Good things, right?"

"Absolutely."

"Well, don't believe everything you hear," Ben cautioned. "She's a pain in the ass, just like the rest of us."

"I'll keep that in mind." As Sam raised an elegant brow, Bryn caught Ben's interest in the newcomer. His eyes flicked down to her left hand. Checking for a wedding ring?

"You'll be working mostly with the twins here," Luke told Sam. "Ben is our electronics wizard, so he can help you work on coms for our ops. Rhys'll help out when necessary, otherwise he and Ali will be with the rest of us on logistics and security. And depending on what's happening, you can keep Bryn company."

"I'd like that."

"Me too," Bryn said. "It's been a while since I've

had any girl talk."

Luke checked his watch. "Think you could feed her while the boys and I go out for some recon?"

Within ten minutes, Sam had assembled an amazing array of treats in a private office. "You *do* eat junk food, don't you?"

"Damn right I do." Bryn accepted the plate of salad loaded with fresh fruit, eying the donuts for later.

"I heard Lieutenant McCabe and his team came in for you and your father."

"Yes, thank God. It was surreal."

"I can imagine." Sam forked up a bite of strawberry. "I bet you were surprised to be asked to join Luke's team."

"Yeah. But my father would have done it for me." And she would not let him down.

"I think you're very brave."

Bryn pushed a spinach leaf around her plate. "I don't know if brave's the right adjective. Pigheaded, maybe. But what about you? You're a contractor working for the CIA in Baghdad. Who's the brave one?"

"Nah. I'm just a techie, not an operator. I wouldn't last ten minutes out in the field." She looked up, met Bryn's gaze. "I hear you were amazing out there."

"Who'd you hear that from?"

"Luke, who heard it from McCabe." She cocked her head. "You seem surprised."

Bryn cleared her throat and unwrapped her Snickers bar. "It's hard to tell what Dec's thinking." A flush crept up her cheeks. "About me and all of…this."

Sam's smile was understanding. "You really like him, huh."

A deep sigh escaped her.

"It's okay, you know. It's not like you've broken

some social taboo or anything. And who could blame you? I mean, look at the guy." She set down her fork and dabbed at her mouth with a napkin. "When Luke briefed us, I asked him how he got the lieutenant to sign up. Apparently he only agreed to come on the op to take care of you."

What? Bryn set her unwrapped chocolate bar down. "Luke said that?"

Sam frowned. "I thought you knew."

"No. Oh God, I didn't." The wave of guilt went straight to her heart and lodged there, throbbing. Why would he do that? He didn't owe her anything.

Sam touched her hand. "I didn't mean to upset you."

"No, I just...I don't want him to put himself in danger for my sake." Dammit, she'd begged him not to take risks for her, and it turns out she was the reason he'd come along in the first place?

Sam set her hands on the table, palms down, and stood. "Come on. We're getting out of here. Let's go back to my place for a glass of wine without the risk of contamination from the testosterone floating around this place. And the curious ears."

She tugged Bryn to her feet like they were long-lost friends. Being around Sam felt as comforting as sliding on a pair of cozy slippers. "Let's bounce. You can tell me all about Rhys's sexy brother on the way."

She was beginning to think Sam was a godsend. For a while she might even be able to forget she was in Baghdad to lure Farouk Tehrazzi out of hiding and that Dec was risking his life for her.

****

Funny how he'd forgotten what the stares felt like. Dec had already done three tours in Iraq, spent most of one in and around Baghdad, but driving through the streets in the front of a Humvee with his teammates, the weight of those hostile stares hit him with an unease that made the back of his neck prickle. Hands tightening on his automatic weapon, he catalogued the houses in the upper-scale neighborhood, the resentment and suspicion on the faces they passed.

Not that he blamed them. Since Saddam had been overthrown, their country had been plunged into chaos. Every murder and suicide bombing created more hatred, more young men willing to kill and be killed. Like the two men they were after now.

Through Fahdi, Luke had used them to penetrate one of the enemy militias. In the past twelve hours, something big had started brewing. The team had to bring them in and find out what they knew about Tehrazzi's whereabouts and plans. Depending on intel, the op would go down tonight or tomorrow night.

"That's the place up there," Luke said as he drove. "Third one on the right with the iron gate and the high wall."

Dec scanned the house for ways to get in and out. "How many people living here?"

"Six," said Ali from the back seat. "The father's an invalid, stays on the first floor. His wife sleeps upstairs, as do their four sons."

"Who are our guys?" Rhys asked.

"The eldest two. Eighteen and twenty-one. The younger ones are fifteen and eleven."

Great. So when they charged in during the middle of the night to grab their suspects, they would have to deal with a hysterical woman, an invalid and two freaked-out kids.

Again, Dec wondered about Fahdi. He was on the CIA's payroll, and Luke had taken him on as an informant a couple months ago. Luke knew his stuff, so Dec wasn't particularly worried about being set

207

up by the Iraqi. Somewhere in the midst of all this, Luke would have someone watching Fahdi to make sure he stayed on track. Davis, maybe. But money was a powerful motivator. So was fear.

Dec figured his loyalty could go either way under the right circumstances, and Fahdi didn't owe them anything. They weren't his countrymen, or Shi'a—or even brothers in Islam. Maybe the money was simply too good to pass up?

An explosion rocked their vehicle.

"Jesus and Allah," Fahdi gasped, grabbing his chest as Luke slammed on the brakes.

Dec gripped the dash with one hand as his head snapped forward. In front of them, about half a klick down the road, a plume of smoke rose into the air. Heart pumping like a jackhammer, he craned his neck out the window. Swore. "Looks like a suicide bomber just detonated in the outdoor market."

"Jesus," Ben muttered.

People ran, waving their arms, screaming. The traffic ground to a standstill.

Fahdi leaned forward so his head came between the front seats. "Any...casualties?" he asked in a near whisper, eyes glued to the carnage.

Dec shot him a questioning look. The Iraqi had gone pale. Surely he'd seen this before?

Fahdi swallowed. "My wife... She was going to the market...with my daughter and the baby."

Dec exchanged a glance with Luke. Shit. No wonder Fahdi's face was pasty with fear. "We'd better go help."

Luke sighed. "Roger that." His phone rang. "Yeah," he answered, listened for a minute. Then his eyes shot up to stare out the windshield. "Okay, don't move. We'll come to you." He disconnected. "Davis is pinned under some debris."

"How bad?"

"Bad enough he can't get out himself." He

208

shoved a pistol into his waistband. "Ali, go get Bryn at Sam's and take her back to the barracks while we take care of this."

"Why," Dec asked, alarm prickling over him. "Davis find something about Tehrazzi?" Because if Bryn was in danger, he wanted her to have more protection than Ali could give her.

"'S all good," Luke said, opening his door. "Let's move."

Rhys grabbed their first aid kit and they piled out of the truck. Fahdi was on his cell phone, trying to reach his wife.

Dec waded through the crowd, mouth tight at the burning wreckage of the car that had detonated the explosives, creating as many pieces of shrapnel as possible. A crude but effective method to inflict the most harm and terrorize the civilian population. But then, there were a lot of ways to die in Baghdad.

When they finally returned to their barracks, Ali met them at the door. "She's inside," he said. Dec found Bryn reading on her bunk. She sat up as they filed in, and her welcoming smile warmed him.

Then she noticed the bloodstains on his BDUs. He'd tried to clean most of it off before coming inside, but the way her smile disappeared told him he was still a mess. Tough to keep clean moving dead and mutilated bodies, though.

Her eyes were worried. "Are you all right?"

"Yeah."

"What happened?"

Dec avoided her gaze. "Suicide bomber."

"Was that the bang I heard an hour ago?"

"Yeah. Davis got cut up a bit, but he's okay." His back was going to hurt like a bitch for a while, though. The beam they'd pried off him had left one hell of a mark. "We dug him and some of the other wounded out."

"That's why you've got blood all over you." She

wrapped her arms around her waist.

He wanted to hug her, but didn't dare. *Yeah, Bryn. Baghdad's not a nice place. People get blown up here every day. And I hate that you're sitting here in the middle of it.* There was nothing he could say to make her feel any safer at the moment. He felt bad about that.

At least Fahdi's wife and two small children were safe. They'd been at home when the bombing happened. Other women and children hadn't been so fortunate.

He didn't want to think about that anymore. "Sam take good care of you?"

Bryn seemed to understand why he'd changed the subject. "Sam took amazing care of me." She glanced at Luke. "She's awesome."

"Yeah," Luke responded, tossing his armored vest onto his bunk. "She's a sweetheart. We're lucky to have her, too. Her boss back in Langley didn't want to let her go."

Bryn brushed at her pants. "So besides the...incident, how did it go out there?" She faltered when no one answered right away. "I'm not supposed to ask?"

"Don't worry about it," Dec said, removing his body armor. They were all on a need to know basis, except Luke. He was the only one who knew all the details of what was going on during this op. Yet even he didn't know everything in the big picture. That was the luxury of a Deputy Director back at CIA headquarters in Virginia. "We were just doing some recon, getting the lay of the land so far as Tehrazzi's connections in Baghdad go."

"Well. You're all back safe, so that's all I care about."

She amazed him. Even after what had happened last night in Damascus, she was still handling everything well. He'd never met a stronger woman.

He just hoped she had the stamina to keep it up until the job was done.

The others headed back to the TOC while Dec grabbed a quick shower and then hit the computers to find out if they had any new intel. He'd volunteered to stay behind and watch Bryn because he didn't want Ali to do it. The control freak in him was on board with the possessive male programmed to protect her himself.

After passing on a couple of tidbits to Luke, he went back into the room to check on Bryn to see if she needed anything. It probably wasn't the best idea that they were alone together after last night in her hotel room, but he had enough sense to maintain distance from her.

He appreciated that she hadn't pressed him about what had happened. Most other women would have at least tried to pry an explanation out of him, yet she had handled herself with remarkable maturity—something he probably shouldn't have been surprised about, although she had to be confused about the mixed messages he'd been sending her. Shit, he was confused enough for both of them.

If he'd been working this case as a civilian, his conscience wouldn't have been so torn up. But he was an active-duty SEAL, and he couldn't let his feelings for Bryn get in the way. So far he'd allowed his attraction to her to compromise him to the point that he'd not only kissed her, but would have loved to get her naked in that hotel bed.

Bryn knew it. Hell, she *wanted* it, which made it harder for him to do the right thing and maintain the boundary—blurred as it was—between them.

He found her sound asleep on her bunk, the paperback dangling from her hand. Stopping in the doorway, he let his eyes sweep over her face and the pool of dark hair spreading across her pillow. Sleep was the best thing for her right now. He had no idea how she'd coped with all that had happened without having a breakdown. She was a total sweetheart, and he would never have guessed someone so feminine and gentle could be so incredibly tough.

She was everything he'd ever wanted in a woman and more, and that made it so much harder to keep his growing feelings to himself. When this whole thing finished, he could see himself getting serious with her. She was so alone now, and he wanted to make her feel secure. He had a big, close-knit family back home. They'd take her in and love her to pieces.

Bryn stirred in her sleep. Her brows twitched, her expression seeming troubled.

He had a feeling she wasn't having a nice dream.

Her hand jerked on the paperback. Her breathing quickened. Then her eyes flew open and she sat up with a gasp, scanning the room fearfully. When she saw him, she relaxed, but drew in an unsteady breath and swabbed at her face. A sheen of perspiration dampened her skin.

Ah, baby. "You okay?"

"Fine." She dropped her gaze, wiped at the sweat on her upper lip.

He crossed the room and hunkered down in front of her. "Nightmare?"

She nodded and bent to retrieve her book without looking at him, rattled, but trying not to let it show.

He knew about waking up with his heart slamming against his ribs because of a flashback. When she shoved her fingers against her eyes with a tired sigh, he couldn't stop himself from passing a hand over her hair. "Lie back down."

She hesitated a moment, then did as he said, watching him.

"What was it about?"

She lowered her eyes. "It was...when Masood was shot. I was sitting in his lap." Her fingers pulled at the edge of her blanket. "I heard the gun go off, felt the bullet hit...and the blood spattering. I wasn't sure if I..."

Ah, hell. "If you'd been hit."

"Yes." A shiver rippled over her. Then another. And another, until she was shaking.

Dec couldn't stand to see her hurting. He wanted to hold her, make her feel safe, but he'd confused her enough already, so he shouldn't touch her. But damn, she looked so fragile and alone. The least he could do was offer her comfort in a platonic way.

"Scoot over," he said, ignoring the flare of surprise in her dark eyes as he stretched out beside her and laid a hand on her back. She immediately tucked in close and rested her cheek over his heart. He clenched his jaw. He wanted to wrap around her so badly, but couldn't let himself. "Better?"

"Yes." She sighed, the heat of her breath penetrating his shirt.

He held himself back, managed not to slide his arms around her. To soothe her, he ran his fingers through her long hair. The dream was probably still vivid in her mind. He decided to give her a different image to focus on. "Close your eyes and pretend with me," he whispered.

Her lids dropped. "Pretend what?"

"That you're in the loft of a log house in the foothills of the Rocky mountains."

The corners of her mouth turned up. "In Montana?"

He grinned. "Maybe. I'm there to guard you. You're warm and safe, no one else around for miles. It's dark, and there's a storm outside, so you can hear the wind against the windows and the rain

213

pounding on the roof." He toyed with the ends of her hair. "There's a fire burning in the fireplace beside the bed, tucked under the eaves." Over the past week he'd imagined making love to her there more times than he could count. "Can you see it?"

"Mmm, yes."

"Imagine you're cuddled up in the bed under a down quilt, listening to the rain and the crackle of the fire. You're exhausted from hiking all day through the forest and swimming in the lake. Your eyelids are heavy, your muscles are tired. All sleepy and warm." He waited a breath, tortured by the heat of her body. "You there?"

"*So* there."

"Good. Stay there and just breathe. Listen to the storm outside and know you're safe, wrapped up in that bed. Relax your muscles, let your mind go blank. Feel the warmth of the fire on your face."

He slammed his imagination shut as it put him naked in that bed with her and focused on slowing his own breathing. He kept his touch on her hair gentle, lulling her back to sleep as the minutes drifted past. Her breaths deepened. Her muscles relaxed. He could almost hear the rain on the roof.

When he was sure she was sleeping, he eased himself away from her and climbed off the bed. Before he could change his mind and crawl back in with her, he made himself leave the room.

****

Baghdad
Evening

Tehrazzi watched the live feed coming from the informant's house from a camera hidden in the front entrance ceiling. Preparing to leave for their interview, Fahdi tugged on his shoes and then stood to hug his wife. "Don't worry," he told her with a reassuring smile. "I'll be very careful."

Wise of him under the circumstances, Tehrazzi thought.

The woman wrapped her arms around her waist. "The Americans will protect us?"

Oh, yes, they would certainly try. *If* they knew about the forthcoming meeting, which they did not. Tehrazzi had made sure of that.

"They will. I'll be back late. See you in the morning." He walked out into the dusty street, and Tehrazzi lost the video, but maintained audio with the electronic bug secretly implanted in Fahdi's watch. The GPS chip beacon blinked on the screen in front of Tehrazzi as Fahdi turned west and headed toward the setting sun.

Tehrazzi imagined the tickle of the breeze on his skin and the aroma of cooking meat wafting through the air. He'd walked the same route many times at this time of day.

The sounds of the traffic thinned out as Fahdi advanced deeper into the city. After crossing the river and winding his way through the tangle of streets and alleys, he turned again, heading away from the water toward their appointed meeting place in the crowded Shi'a neighborhoods, where more security cameras picked him up.

As the informant neared his destination, Tehrazzi's blood hummed with anticipation. Were Fahdi's palms damp? Did his heart beat faster with each approaching step? He had to feel the eyes on him as he moved, and suspect some unseen presence was following him. As if hearing his thoughts, Fahdi touched the pendant hanging from his neck and muttered a prayer.

Tehrazzi wondered again how trustworthy this contact was. If money could buy his loyalty for the Americans, then it should be easy enough for

Tehrazzi to buy his loyalty back. But how much did he know?

This game Fahdi had involved himself in was dangerous enough without knowing everyone's dirty secrets. He would be wise to turn a blind eye to everything and simply be the messenger he was being paid to be. But perhaps Fahdi could do more for their Muslim brothers and sisters suffering under this terrible occupation.

"Move in," Tehrazzi transmitted to his bodyguard.

"With pleasure," Assoud responded.

Fahdi picked up his pace when footsteps sounded behind him, and Tehrazzi knew why. Sunni death squads prowled the area at night. Fahdi must know anyone could have followed him here. And sometimes, those you thought were friends were more dangerous than your known enemies.

On screen, Assoud closed in and laid a heavy hand on Fahdi's shoulder.

Fahdi whirled around. "Jesus and Allah," he breathed, recognizing Assoud. He placed a trembling hand over his heart. "I am unarmed, as always." He handed over the paper bag containing the required money.

Assoud stared hard at him then systematically frisked him, stepping back only when he found no weapons. "You're early."

Three more of Tehrazzi's men stepped out of the shadows, menacing with their silence and rifles. Fahdi swallowed and glanced between the newcomers and Assoud.

"The woman. Is she here?"

Fahdi nodded. "They brought her this morning."

Yes, right after they escaped me in Damascus. Tehrazzi zoomed in.

Assoud grunted. The thin scar on his chin stretched as he smiled. "You know what happened to the Syrian and his informant last night?" His hand idly stroked the jeweled hilt of a dagger sheathed at his hip, reminding Fahdi that Masood had been assassinated, and his spy had returned without a tongue, courtesy of that very same knife.

"Y-yes."

"You would not do anything to deserve such a fate, would you?"

"No." He took a step back.

"Your family would be very glad to hear you say that."

Fahdi paled. "You swore," he croaked. "You swore you would not hurt them if I helped you."

Tehrazzi was unmoved by the fear in his voice.

With a jerk of his head, Assoud called the other three men forward, and gripped Fahdi's arms to propel him toward the steel door of the third building down the street. Another camera followed their progress. Fahdi struggled for a moment, but the attempt was useless. He was trapped, and had nowhere to run if he did manage to break free.

"My employer is most anxious to meet you," Assoud said.

"T-Tehrazzi?"

"Keep your mouth shut."

On screen, Fahdi's Adam's apple bobbed as he struggled to swallow his terror. Tehrazzi knew what he was seeing in front of him. The shadowed building he occupied lay ahead, its beige concrete walls bleak. Most men who saw the inside of it never came out again.

Despite the informant's resistance, Assoud muscled him toward his fate.

"I-I only work with the Americans to provide money for my family."

Exactly. And thus he would do anything to save his loved ones. Anything Tehrazzi wanted.

Assoud shoved him. "If you walk out of here

alive, know that you are being watched wherever you go. No place is safe for you to hide from us."

"Bring him to me now," Tehrazzi commanded, growing impatient with the way Assoud toyed with his victim. Timing here was critical, as he had an important meeting to attend in Najaf that evening.

He had no doubt the interview with this Iraqi civilian would be quick. Within a few minutes of the bodyguard's questioning, they would know exactly where Fahdi's loyalties lay and how best to exploit them.

Chapter Sixteen

Day 11, Baghdad

When Luke came out of the office early next morning, Bryn was waiting for him, munching on a banana. The furrow in her brow told him she had something on her mind.

She tossed her hair back. "Does Tehrazzi know I'm here?"

Luke took a sip of his steaming coffee. They'd been so goddamn close to getting him in Damascus. He'd been stunned to see Tehrazzi in the club doorway with his bodyguard. The closest he'd come to him in six years, and Luke had failed to get him. It drove him nuts. "Yes, as of last night."

He couldn't tell her any more, though. Fahdi had made brief contact to say he'd delivered the message to Tehrazzi, then hung up. Odd, since he was usually a gregarious sort.

The plan was to clear up a thing or two about one of his team members. Davis and Ali were out there now, sniffing around for more information. In case Bryn was right and Tehrazzi had known she was going to be at the club in Damascus, he wasn't taking any chances.

Davis and Rhys had both reported Sam acting suspiciously. Little things. Nervous behavior. And she was friends with Fahdi and his wife. Luke doubted it meant anything important, but he wasn't willing to risk not following up on it. Besides, he had one other person on his radar as well. Both of them were being watched carefully.

Bryn pitched the peel into the garbage and folded her arms. "And what does that mean for me?"

"Nothing, yet."

She blew out a frustrated breath. "I'm not a machine, you know. I have feelings, nerve endings. I don't want to sit around waiting like a staked goat for Tehrazzi to come and get me. So what am I supposed to do? Sit inside twiddling my thumbs? Is it safe for me to go outside at all?"

He shrugged, though secretly he was impressed by her grit. "As safe as you going anywhere in Baghdad." If someone as observant and paranoid as Davis could get caught up in a suicide bombing, then anyone could.

"I did agree to come along for the ride," she allowed. "And while I understand your need for secrecy, I would appreciate you letting me know where I stand in terms of your current plans for Tehrazzi."

He tried not to let his amusement show, admiring the way she stood up to him. Few people attempted it. "That was a polite way of asking me what the hell I'm doing."

He had her. He could tell she was fighting back a smile.

He put a hand on her shoulder. "Nothing's changed. As long as you're covered by one of us, you can come and go as you please. Stay with Sam if you want. Hell, go shopping. Tehrazzi's not in the city, or we'd have found out about it. For now, we wait."

Until they discovered whether they had a mole, or located Tehrazzi. Which might not be comforting, but at least he'd given her an honest answer. He didn't have any firm plans for her yet.

"Okay." She studied him. "By the way, I have a business proposition for you."

He cocked an eyebrow. "What kind of proposition?"

"I know you're thinking of starting your own contracting firm."

"I am."

"And you know I've inherited my father's estate."

His attention sharpened. "Yeah."

"Thing is, I'm not sure what to do with it. I don't intend to live in Beirut, but I don't want to sell, or rent it out to someone I don't know and trust."

"So what are you telling me?"

"I wondered if you might be interested in renting the place from me to use it as your headquarters. I mean, Beirut is a pretty good place for a guy like you to set up, don't you think?"

"You've obviously given this some thought."

"Well, since you're Rayne's dad and Emily's ex and a friend of my father's, it feels right to ask you. I think he would have approved."

No wonder she got along so well with Rayne and Emily. She had spunk in spades. He smiled, a genuine eye-crinkling, teeth-flashing smile. A rarity, these days. "I'll think about it."

****

That evening Bryn lay on her bunk staring up at the ceiling. Dec and Luke were in the next room going over some new intel, and the twins were with Sam and Fahdi somewhere in the city. Ali was out on an expedition, prowling for information. That Davis guy had come in for a private meeting with Luke. Everyone had a purpose here but her.

She'd spent most of the day with Sam, helping her out with mundane tasks. Bryn wondered if Ben had noticed Sam's sidelong glances. Probably. When it came to female interest, Ben was a human radar.

Bryn sighed. If she didn't find something to do soon, she was going to go crazy.

She found Dec and Luke in the nerve center, bent over some maps, three computer screens glowing. Dec straightened to look at her, and that damned flutter went off again in her belly.

"Hey."

She blew out a breath, silently scolding herself for her reaction. "Can I help with anything?"

The two men looked at each other.

"Filing? Sorting?" She felt stupid. She'd done worse than intrude on them, she was an annoyance. She wanted to shrink into herself. She hated having nothing to contribute.

Resigning herself to an evening climbing the walls, she pivoted on her heel. A cell phone rang and after a short pause, Luke spoke to Dec.

"Ali's got a lockdown on Tehrazzi."

Bryn froze in the doorway. Her heart bumped hard. Would Luke use her now?

His face was relaxed, but his eyes were intense as he listened to whatever Ali said. "Roger that," he replied. "I'll contact you once we're airborne. Rendezvous at the insertion point."

Disconnecting, he said to Dec, "Helo's meeting us at the airfield in twenty minutes. This intel is perishable, might not last more than a couple of hours." Then he studied her thoughtfully.

Her stomach clenched.

"What are we gonna do with you?"

She didn't know.

"You can't stay here without someone to guard you. You'll have to come with us."

Her eyes widened, shot to Dec. His jaw was taut. "I—"

"If Tehrazzi's not in the village we're going to, he's somewhere close by," Luke said. "If he finds out you're there..."

He might come out of hiding. "You want me to go into the village with you?"

"If necessary, yes."

Her heart rate doubled. "But I'm not—"

"If you have to go in, I'll go with you."

She glanced at Dec.

"Up to you," he said. "No one's going to force you if you're not comfortable with it."

Meaning he wished she'd say no. She might have, but going along could mean finishing this off tonight. If it worked, she could be on her way home tomorrow. And her father's death would be avenged.

She was tempted.

"Think about it during the flight," Luke coaxed. "If you decide not to go in, you can stay on the chopper after we insert, and then one of the guys can pick you up at the airfield. But right now we've got to move."

"Okay."

Dec pulled an armored vest over her and donned his web gear, then from the gun lockers collected two pistols, ammunition and a rifle. As her brain finally figured out that they were going downrange, her whole system buzzed with nervous energy.

In the Hummer she found herself speeding through the darkened streets, Dec on his radio to Sam and the twins. At the airfield a helicopter awaited them, rotors turning. Dec helped her aboard, settling her into her seat and fixing her up with a helmet and earphones. Within seconds they were loaded and airborne, the ground falling away beneath them until the lights of Baghdad twinkled below.

Over the radio Luke and Dec planned the mission with the backup team at the TOC. Trained to be calm and capable under pressure, Dec smeared camo paint on his face and throat, the backs of his hands.

The men synchronized their watches, discussing things with too many abbreviations and acronyms for her to grasp more than the basics, which was probably a good thing. The helo banked to the left, the desert below a darkening landscape of shadows, a sea of sand illuminated by the thin crescent moon.

"Well," Luke said, "you coming or not?"

Bryn chewed her lip. Tehrazzi didn't know they were coming. They had the element of surprise on their side. Dec and Luke would protect her. Besides, if Tehrazzi was where the intel said he was, she wouldn't even have to go to the village.

Do it, Bryn. Get the job done and you can go home.

She swallowed the lump in her throat. "Yes."

Through the earphones Dec started briefing her. "Luke can take point, and you can stay back with me. It won't take that long to hike in and out—way less than you did with me in Syria."

Oh yeah, she felt *so* much better about this. Where was an airsick bag when she needed one? She didn't know the first thing about the kind of mission they were supposed to execute. What if she did something wrong? Blew their cover, slowed them down? She twisted her chilled fingers together.

She flinched when Dec took her by the shoulder and pulled her toward him, his warm fingers smoothing something cool and moist on her face. Cammying her up, so her fair skin wouldn't give them away. She shivered, realized she'd clamped her hand around his hard forearm, and closed her eyes.

"You're going to have to touch down," Luke said to the pilot. "She won't be able to fast-rope in."

"Roger that."

Oh, God. She was already compromising their safety, wasn't she?

"Bryn, look at me."

Her eyes swung up to Dec's face, his golden eyes emphasized by the dark greasepaint.

"This'll be a piece of cake. You'll see."

224

He always tried so hard to convince her she wasn't a burden. "Okay."

A few minutes later the rotors whined and the helo slowed for descent. Dec and Luke checked their gear one last time, and then Dec placed a different helmet on her head, secured the strap under her chin and pulled something over her eyes. "Night-vision goggles. Wait 'til you tell your friends."

Yeah. If she lived through this, it would definitely be a cool story.

His hand landed on her shoulder again, his touch solid, lending her courage. "When we set down, keep your head low and jump out, then run until I stop you. Luke will be in front, and Ali will be waiting for us."

She nodded, making the too-large helmet bob, eyes adjusting to the goggles that lit the pitch-black landscape with a weird green glow. Luke maneuvered to the doorway, rifle in hand, and as soon as the wheels bumped against the ground, he was gone.

Bryn leapt out and took off after him as fast as she could in her crouch. Her hair whipped around where it emerged from under the helmet, the wash from the rotors creating a miniature sandstorm that beat against her clothes.

At a run, she followed Luke to a dune, the pulse of the helicopter growing fainter. When he went to his knees, Bryn felt a hand on her back, Dec right behind her. He placed a finger to his lips and motioned for her to get down. Trying her best to breathe slowly and quietly, she dropped onto her belly and held still while the two men took their bearings and assessed the situation. Without a two-way radio, she couldn't hear their communications.

"Clear," Luke confirmed.

"Clear," Dec echoed.

Letting out a relieved breath, she awaited

further instruction. Where was Ali?

Dec hunkered next to her. "Okay?"

She nodded, afraid to speak.

"Follow Luke, but stay back a little ways. Keep quiet unless there's an emergency. I'll be right behind you."

She nodded again, realized she'd grabbed his hand and let go abruptly. When Luke got to his feet she stayed a few steps back and copied his every move like a mime, careful to place her feet in his prints in the sand. Paranoia overwhelmed her brain, forming images of landmines and trip wires. Her heart drummed against her chest like a crazy metronome.

Their feet swished through the sand as they moved, quickly now, her vision fixed on the back of Luke's head as it turned this way and that, scanning the horizon, weapon always poised. Unarmed as she was, if they did run into trouble she wouldn't be any help unless she found rocks small enough for her to throw. She clamped her teeth together to stem the burst of hysterical laughter.

Suck it up, Bryn. One foot in front of the other. Pay attention.

They hiked across the desert for what seemed like a long time—long enough for blisters to form where the backs od her heels and baby toes rubbed against the insides of her boots.

Coming to a rise, Luke slowed his pace, signaled for her to stop and crawled forward over the crest on his forearms. Dec came up beside her and laid a hand on her back, in reassurance or command, she wasn't sure. After a few seconds, Luke disappeared from view. Dec's hand pressed against her shoulder blades, keeping her still.

Every fiber of her being tuned to the man next to her, the warmth of his body imbued with the scent of soap and musk that was all Dec. As impossible as it seemed, a sense of calm stole over her.

They stayed like that for a few minutes longer, Dec's hand warm against her spine. The instant his body tensed, she whipped her head around to look at him.

"Copy that," he murmured into his mic, peering down at her through his goggles. "Ali's confirmed the target's in the house. Luke's going to order a drone strike and paint the target with a laser while we stay here for cover support."

House? Out here? She glanced up at the sky. Were drones flying around up there? Unreal. She'd seen stuff like this on CNN, but never dreamed she'd experience it firsthand. Now that she had a front row seat, she would rather have passed on the opportunity.

"I'm going to creep a little further to keep an eye on things, but you can stay here if you want," he added in a whisper.

Oh. He meant she might feel better not witnessing the explosion, human lives being lost. How many people were in that house, anyway? And how did Luke know if they were all terrorists or not?

He couldn't know, and maybe he didn't care. So long as Tehrazzi was killed, collateral damage was justified. Could he be that cold-blooded? So callous? Yes, he really could. The blood drained from her face.

"Bryn? What do you want to do?"

Some tiny part of her, a part that shamed her, wanted to watch the warhead go off and know Tehrazzi was being blown to bits. But mostly the idea of watching and knowing someone was dying shriveled her insides. Especially when innocent people might be involved.

"Any civilians in there?"

Dec went dead still. "No. Look, maybe you should—"

"I'll come with you." She didn't want to be left by herself, so she'd go with him and shut her eyes, pray with everything she had that no innocent blood would be shed.

He hesitated. "I'd rather you didn't." It wasn't a command, though.

He didn't want her seeing it. How did he cope with this part of his job? "I'm coming."

She shadowed him to the crest of the hill, where the village came into view, a cluster of five or six mud houses in the middle of the desert. She had to wonder what the lives of these villagers were like, what sort of existence they eked out in such a barren, lonely place.

They waited in absolute silence for Luke to apprise them of the situation. When the report came Dec whispered, "Affirm," into his mic. "Air strike inbound." He indicated the house furthest to the left.

Rather than cowering from what was going to happen, as she wanted to, an alarming excitement bubbled up inside her. Ashamed, she stared at the dimly lit windows of the target house and reminded herself that other people might be in there too. "Tehrazzi's really inside?"

"Yeah. When I tell you, get your head down and keep your eyes shut or you'll toast your retinas."

The alien emotion intensified, roaring through her in a frightening rush of vengeance and glee. The man responsible for her father's death and all her suffering was about to meet his demise. Her hands shook as she scanned through the built-in high-powered binoculars. *Gotcha, you bastard.*

Dec glanced at her, then confirmed into his mic that there was no additional activity. He pulled a map out of his vest pocket and double-checked the coordinates with Luke. "Stay here," he ordered her. "I'm going to go a little further and make sure we haven't been spotted. Don't move until I come back."

She froze in place as he crept forward and disappeared from view. Left alone on the cool sand, she lay there, afraid to move, her pulse beating a frantic tattoo.

Then voices broke the stillness, barely detectible.

Heart lodged in her throat, Bryn swiveled her head. Two shadowy figures had appeared in the distance. A young girl led a donkey by its halter, chattering to a child perched on its swaying back. What in God's name were they doing out alone at night? They headed down the dirt road straight toward the house where Tehrazzi was apparently holed up.

Every muscle in her body went rigid with denial. "Oh no…"

Had Dec heard the kids? Did he know they were in danger? Could he alert the children before the air strike?

Not if he hadn't seen them.

What should she do? She was too afraid to yell out in case someone started shooting, but no way could she sit back and let those children suffer. The breath shot in and out of her nose as she counted backward from ten, praying Dec would do something so she wouldn't have to.

Ten, nine, eight…

The little boy laughed. Bryn squeezed her eyes shut.

Four, three, two…

No Dec.

One.

Bryn took off running. Her thigh muscles bunched as she scrambled down the rise, breath coming in jerky gasps. The ill-fitting helmet jiggled up and down, obscuring her vision, so she yanked at the chinstrap and shoved the thing off her head. And kept running. She *had* to get there before the air strike. Had to save the kids.

"Bryn!"

Ignoring Dec's shout, she sprinted hard, fueled by adrenaline. Bouncing off rocks and boulders, she reached the road and scrambled to her feet, breath sawing in and out of her lungs in sobs. She could not let innocent children be caught up in this.

"Bryn, no!"

She ignored him. The children weren't stopping. She opened her mouth and screamed the Arabic word for stop. It came out in a high-pitched wail, and both children jerked around to face her in fear. "Stop! Go back!" she yelled, waving her arms in a frantic effort to get them to move. "Run!"

But rather than scurry away from her as she'd intended, the girl yanked on the donkey's halter and hurried toward the house, probably terrified of the apparition screaming at them in the middle of the desert.

"Go back!" she yelled again, slipping into English.

The girl kept going.

Something heavy slammed into Bryn's back, tumbling her into the dirt. Dec, shielding her with his body, the air strike moments away. He pressed her down, begging her to stay still, but she couldn't give up. Pinned beneath him, she raised her head and stared helplessly at the children.

She was too late. As if in slow motion, the toddler atop the donkey looked back at her, shadowed eyes wide as he advanced unknowingly toward his death. The image burned its way into her brain.

"*No!*" She couldn't bear this. Couldn't live with it.

A quiet hiss reached her.

"Head down! Close your eyes!"

She struggled in Dec's grip. Then the missile hit

the building and exploded, the pulse of light blinding her. Dec tried to cover her eyes but the blast wave knocked him off her and slammed them into a rock. He cushioned the blow for her, but the air around them burned like a blowtorch as debris flew.

Her lungs felt scorched, her face singed as she struggled to her hands and knees, fighting hysteria, the concussion of the blast driving the breath from her. The house was nothing more than a pile of burning rubble. She couldn't see the children. Where were they? Maybe they'd been far enough away from the explosion. Maybe they were still alive. She had to find them.

Her legs wobbled under her as she staggered to her feet. Dec was rolling to his hands and knees as she passed him at a jerky run toward the wreckage. Dec pounded over the sand behind her, coming up fast, closer and closer.

She found a new burst of speed. Her heart and lungs screamed in protest as she forced her body to its limit, eyes fixed on the carnage before her. Gasping from the prolonged exertion, she stumbled to a halt where the children should have been. Kneeling, she began digging with single-minded intent, heedless of the sharp timber and rock slicing her hands and arms.

"Come on, come *on!*" She grunted, hefting a chunk of wall out of the way. In the gap she'd opened, a foot appeared. Small. Unmoving. The little boy.

Stricken, she sat immobile for a split second, mind refusing to acknowledge what was right in front of her eyes. A wail of grief tore from her throat and she clawed at the surrounding rubble, exposing more of the crushed body.

Hard hands closed around her shoulders, dragging her up and away. She struck out mindlessly, screaming as she lashed out with a solid elbow to the throat. The hands released her immediately and she fell to the ground, scrambling back to the young body.

Someone grabbed her again, tighter this time, around her ribs. Almost cutting off her air.

"Bryn. Bryn!" Dec.

She fought him like a madwoman. "Let me *go!*" she screeched, landing another blow to his face, but he blocked it, swearing. He tried to snatch her again, missed. Back on her knees she went, tearing at the rocks covering the little legs. If she could just free him, maybe it wasn't too late. They could take him on the helicopter to a hospital.

Someone else grabbed hold of her, far less gently. Spinning to throw a punch, she came face to face with Luke. Illuminated by the ghastly orange light of the flames, the look in his eyes should have scared the hell out of her, but she was beyond reason.

He shook her once, hard, making her head snap back. "Get out of here, *now.*" He shoved her toward Dec.

With a cry of outrage, she lashed out at Luke with the side of her hand. Quick as lightning he whipped her arm up and behind her, held it there on the point of pain, where he could snap the bones with one twist of his wrist. His expression was unyielding. "Don't make me hurt you, Bryn."

"You bastard," she wept, struggling futilely. "Let me get him out at least!"

"No. You're going to turn around and get your ass on that incoming chopper, and you're going to do it now."

"Bryn, come on," Dec urged. "Come with me."

"I can't just leave him here! Don't you understand?" Their callous indifference was unbelievable.

"There's nothing you can do," Luke said tightly,

hauling her toward Dec.

"I won't leave him like that." She twisted hard, a wrenching pain in her elbow as she resisted Luke, not caring if she dislocated her arm.

Suddenly his hands clamped on either side of her neck in a pressure lock. She squeaked and tried to break it, but he'd moved in too close and she didn't have any leverage. Within seconds her vision went hazy, and she went down.

****

Dec leapt toward her as she fell. "Jesus," he exclaimed, catching her dead weight an instant before she hit the ground. He hauled her into his arms and shot Luke a glare. "What the hell—"

"She lost it," he said with a shrug, starting for the rendezvous point without a backwards glance. "I didn't hurt her. She'll come to in a minute."

For Christ's sake, he could have broken her neck. Or strangled her. Bryn hung limply in his arms, face streaked with grime and tears. Ali was gaping at them with his mouth open, backing away to give him room to move her. Shifting her carefully onto his shoulder, Dec hustled them down the road into a clearing to await the helo.

"Bryn? Baby, can you hear me?" He set her on the ground and took her face in his hands, reassured by the steady throb of her carotid pulse in the hollow beneath her ear.

"She'll be fine," Luke said.

Dec aimed a lethal glare at him. "Don't fucking touch her again, do you hear me? I could have handled it without hurting her."

Luke stopped in the midst of reloading his rifle, gazing back at him with unnerving, icy eyes. "Yeah, I saw how well you were handling it."

Dec looked away, feeling dirty. Would he end up

like Luke if he stayed in the Teams long enough? Only to wake up one day and not recognize the man staring back at him in the mirror?

The thump of the inbound helo's rotors saved him from thinking about it anymore. When it touched down he lifted Bryn to one of the crewmembers and climbed aboard, pulling her inert form into the cradle of his lap. When Ali and Luke swung in beside them, she moaned and stirred, eyes flickering beneath her closed lids.

"We're on the helo," he told her, keeping his voice low and soothing. "Just a while longer. We're going to land near the closest city and get you to a hotel."

Her lashes fluttered, then she was looking up at him with dark, confused eyes.

"Hi," he said. "You feeling okay?"

She winced. "My neck hurts."

"Yeah. Getting knocked unconscious will do that to you." His fingers moved to massage the knotted muscles where a bruise was already forming. He sent another dark glance at Luke, who was manning the doorway as they flew over the target to reconnoiter. They made another pass when he commanded it.

"Clean-up crew's on its way," the pilot informed them. "They'll get DNA to ID the tangos."

Bryn stiffened in his arms, and he knew she'd just remembered the kid buried in the wreckage. Dec didn't know what to say so he simply held her, willing her to take what comfort she could from him.

They flew to a point outside of Najaf, then used a borrowed pickup to drive to a small hotel. Bryn remained silent throughout the hour-long journey, staring stonily ahead through the windshield, holding herself rigid between him and Ali.

He wet a spare t-shirt with some water and scrubbed most of the camo paint from her face, as gently as possible, but she still wouldn't look at him. Maybe she thought he was a murderer now. The idea hit him square in the gut.

When he helped her down from the truck at the hotel her legs buckled. He and Ali held her up between them, trying to draw as little attention to them as possible as they crossed the darkened parking lot. They waited in the back stairwell until Luke came to give them their room keys, and pretty much carried her up the stairs to her room. Dec went in with her while Luke disappeared down the hallway to their shared room.

Ali took off after him and the door shut behind them with a thud. Pushing away, Bryn headed to the bathroom, but not before he saw her slim shoulders quaking with silent sobs.

"Bryn—"

She shook her head. "I need to…be alone," she quavered. "Please."

And so he stood there like an idiot while she locked herself in the bathroom to cry her heart out.

God, he hated this. Hated that she'd gotten involved in the first place, and that she'd had to witness the awful things she'd seen today. There was nothing he could say or do to erase them. The least he could do was let her grieve in private. He dragged his hands over his hair, down his face.

With a heavy heart, he made sure her door was securely locked and went to his own room. As he entered Luke grunted in greeting, cell phone in hand. The hiss of the shower running made him assume Ali was in the bathroom. "Clean-up team got the samples. They're at the lab now. Damage was too bad to confirm whether Tehrazzi was in there."

Yeah, well, when a Hellfire missile hit a mud building, there usually wasn't much left afterward.

"Don't think we got him, though. I took a shot at someone on horseback leaving the scene. Might have winged him. We'll find out soon enough."

Horseback? Why the hell would Tehrazzi be on a horse? He stalked over to the sink and grabbed a washcloth, ran the faucet and scrubbed at his paint. Luke tossed him a bottle of Head and Shoulders—he'd be damned if he'd say thank you—and Dec squeezed some onto the washcloth without a word. As always, the camo came off like magic. For good measure he splashed handfuls of cold water on his face, wondering what in hell to do about Bryn.

Shit, she was going to be so traumatized, PTSD was going to seem like a picnic. He knew those kids' deaths had ripped a hole in her soul. His wasn't feeling good at the moment either. He'd never been responsible for a child's death. God, he felt like puking. He dried his face, Luke watching him in the mirror.

The older man leaned back in his chair, laced his hands behind his head. "So, how's our girl doing?"

Dec rinsed the sink out. "She's locked herself in the bathroom."

A beat passed. "Better not leave her alone too long. She's probably damn sore."

He gave Luke a scowl via the mirror. "Ya think?"

The other man ignored him, went to pick up the remote from the nightstand and started flipping through the channels. He decided on a news program and settled back against the headboard, crossing his ankles and looking for all the world like the most relaxed guy on the planet. Without taking his eyes off the TV, he asked, "So, you gonna leave her in there by herself?"

"She said she wanted to be alone."

"Bad idea."

"Really." He'd love to tell the guy what he could do with his unsolicited opinion.

"Yeah. Leaving her alone right now is a piss-poor idea. Gives her too much time to think." More flip-flip with the remote.

Yeah, well, after today any chances he had with her were pretty much over, so what did it matter? And even though he longed to go to her, he couldn't cross that line until this mission was over.

He'd already come close a few times, so he damn well couldn't be trusted alone with her. His rational brain would shut down, rendering him a mass of primitive male instinct, dying to comfort her any way she'd let him. And he knew she would let him.

Luke sighed. "Look, McCabe, this is off the record. I'm not worried about you compromising our mission because of the way you feel about her."

"I don't—"

He held up a hand. "Save it, son. I wasn't born yesterday, and my eyesight is just fine, even if I am an old turd. So here it is, Lieutenant. You want her, you better get your ass in there within the next two minutes, or it'll be too late."

Dec could hardly believe his ears.

"Yeah, I'm getting fucking soft in my old age. Just go already," he continued, checking the cell phone on the nightstand. "Trust me, you'll regret it for the rest of your life if you don't."

Dec had no idea what that cryptic comment meant, but understood the wisdom behind it. Even if the sight of him turned her stomach right now, she shouldn't have to deal with the aftermath alone. "Don't wait up."

Luke's lips curved, but his eyes were fixed on the TV. "Get your ass out of here."

Chapter Seventeen

A few minutes after Dec left, Ali emerged from
the bathroom and mumbled something about going
out for a while. As the door shut behind him, Luke
sighed and flopped against the pillow, suddenly tired
to the bone. The day's operation was just one in a
long line of missions he'd undertaken in the name of
duty, but in some ways it felt like the one that would
seal his fate in hell.

On the backs of his closed lids, he could see
Bryn's face as she took off after those kids, her
expression when she'd crawled through the rubble to
dig like a desperate animal for the small foot poking
out from the debris.

He thought of Tehrazzi. Tried to figure out what
he would do now. Right after the warhead had
exploded, some sixth sense had made Luke double
back to the edge of the village. Through his NVGs
he'd seen the outline of someone galloping away on
horseback.

Without a doubt, Tehrazzi. He'd taken a shot
even though the rider was well out of range, and
thought he might have clipped one of them—
Tehrazzi or the horse—but then he'd heard the
yelling over his radio and had to run interference
with Bryn to get everyone on the helo before anyone
unfriendly came looking for them.

In his mind he replayed the moment he'd fired
his weapon, staring through the scope at Tehrazzi's
fleeing back. He could have sworn the horse
stumbled an instant after he'd pulled the trigger.
Yeah, he might have hit it. Talk about putting a

hitch in your giddy-up. Tehrazzi would lose it if anything happened to his horse.

He'd have to wait and find out if anything came of it. He hadn't been able to see much when the chopper had taken a quick pass. Maybe the clean-up team would find something.

With a sigh, he rubbed his gritty eyes. Kids' deaths were always the hardest to take. And if it was bad for him, a hardened shell of a man, he didn't want to think about what Bryn was feeling. As a social worker, any contact with kids would compromise her to a certain extent, but to see two blown to hell in front of her...

Shit, he'd have spared her that, if he could have. He only wished he could have gotten to her sooner, knocked her out before the missile hit. Hell, he wished she hadn't been there at all now.

Didn't matter at this point. Besides, he'd tried to make amends by sending McCabe after her. God knew she'd need a warm body right about now to hold onto. As he recalled his warning to Dec about regretting his actions, that familiar pain started up in his chest. A splitting sensation, like someone was using a rib-spreader on him.

Nothing to be done for it, and he'd sure as shit tried everything to make it go away. Booze, women, meds, war. Nothing worked, and he only ended up feeling worse for his efforts. So he'd quit all that years and years ago. Way he figured, the searing ache was his punishment, richly deserved.

After all, he'd been the one to walk away from Emily.

Of all the things he regretted in his life, that was the one that towered above all the others—the Empire State Building in a subdivision of two-story houses. In over twenty-five years, not a single day had passed without him wishing he could undo that single unforgivable act.

That day his wife had startled him at the sink and he'd turned on her with that hunting knife, pinning her against the refrigerator with the blade pressed against her throat. He'd jerked back at the terror and the horror in her eyes. Then he'd thrown the weapon across the room to bury itself deep into the wall and she'd shrunk from him, like she expected him to come back and finish her off.

But instead of staying and trying to somehow work it out, he'd taken off. Packed his bag and climbed like a zombie into his truck, leaving her screaming and begging him to stay. When he'd taken one last look in his rearview mirror, she'd collapsed in a heap on the driveway, sobbing. God, the memory of it still made him sick with despair and self-loathing.

At the time, he'd told himself he was doing the right thing. It was safer for her and their son if he went away, let them build a new life for themselves. He couldn't be trusted around them, was too highly strung to function as a husband and father. No telling when he'd snap, but he would one day, and he sure as hell didn't want to be around his family when it happened.

Even now, all these years later, he'd rather swallow a bullet and blow the back of his head off than hurt them. Since he'd been out of the Navy, he'd managed to dull that lethal edge somewhat, insulate that part of him that was a trip wire waiting for a trigger. But he didn't delude himself that he was normal. After all he'd seen and done, there was no chance of that. He was, and would always be, a killer.

And even though he knew and hated that, some sick part of him held out hope for Emily and him. He smirked bitterly. Jesus, he was a selfish bastard even to wish for that. She had to be the most forgiving human being on the planet, because by some miracle she still loved him, though he didn't understand it. And on the rare occasions they spoke on the phone, he was careful not to say anything that might give her false hope, after all the years of hurt and separation between them.

Christ, what a life he'd carved out for himself. It seemed no matter where he went, he left a trail of destruction in his wake, a walking natural disaster. He really had to scale it back, he thought, reverting to the day's operation. Maybe it was time to take his business to the next level, establish a permanent site stateside, hire a crew he trusted. He was getting too damn old for this shit.

On that happy thought he let himself slide into a doze, his pistol resting beside him on the nightstand. When his cell rang his eyes snapped open and he came fully and instantly awake, checking the call display, expecting news about the forensics.

The displayed number froze him as if he'd been tasered. His heart rate tripled like he was sprinting, his mouth dry as sand.

Emily.

As he sat there like a shell-shocked idiot and stared at the phone, it rang and rang. Two more rings and it would divert to voicemail. Yeah, he should just let it go. Talking to her right now would be like pouring gasoline over himself and lighting a match.

Whatever she was calling about couldn't be good, since she only made contact when someone had died. Or, like the last time, because their son had been shot.

Knowing it was the wrong thing to do, with an unsteady hand he picked up the phone open and put it to his ear. "Hello." He braced himself for her voice, the wave of pain it sent through his chest.

"Luke, hi," she said in her Charleston accent.

"It's Emily."

Yeah, like he wouldn't know that voice even in a coma. "Hi, Em. You okay?" He wondered who had died this time.

"I'm fine, thanks. I just... Well, I was actually wondering about Bryn, and I thought you might know how she is."

"She's okay." Hopefully Dec was with her, taking care of her right now. For some reason he needed to keep talking to Emily, to unload some of the weight from his shoulders. "We had to take her with us on an op today."

"Oh. Everything...go all right?" He caught the hesitation as she sent out the gentle probe.

"No, actually." He couldn't say more, but it eased him to tell her that much.

"I'm so sorry, Luke. Is everyone okay?"

"Pretty much."

Silence stretched over the line. "How about... How about you?"

God, she broke his heart with her kindness, she really did. Finally, and without knowing why, he said, "I'm tired, Em."

She gave a murmur of sympathy that made him feel like a shit for burdening her with his baggage. "You've been out there for so long now, you must be tired. You're not getting any younger, you know."

He uttered a quiet laugh. "Tell me. I was just thinking about that."

"You gonna retire?" The hopeful tone had caution bells clanging in his head.

"Not in the normal sense." No, there would never be a normal anything for him again. "I was thinking of getting out of the field, though. Maybe open up a permanent facility back home, hang out my shingle. After I take a vacation. I think I need a vacation." Why the hell was he telling her this? Like he was putting out feelers—

"I think you should, Luke. It's time you had a life again."

With me. He heard the words as clearly as if she'd spoken them.

His guts clenched. Oh, shit, this was like trying to maneuver through a minefield. Time to employ some escape and evasion tactics. "Yeah. Listen, I'll get Bryn to call you, okay?"

He could almost imagine her closing her eyes and biting her lip in disappointment.

Finally, she spoke again. "Is she really okay?"

"She will be."

"Are you—I mean, do you think you should go and see—"

"She's not alone, if that's what you're wondering."

"Okay. Ah, that's...good." He could almost hear the gears turning in her head. "Who's with her?"

One side of his mouth lifted in a grin. Emily was gonna love this. "One of my guys." Her protest had him biting back a chuckle. "Don't worry, it's good. I wouldn't have sent him to her if I didn't approve."

She made a throttled sound. "Luke—"

"Trust me, she's in good hands."

"Is it Declan?"

He shouldn't have been surprised. Bryn must have told her about him. "Yeah."

Emily's laughter flowed over him like cool, clean water. "My God, I can't believe you're playing cupid!"

He flinched. "Oh, hey, let's not take it that far. I have to maintain the reputation of a heartless asshole."

"Yeah, well, you know that won't wash with me."

He'd set himself up for that one. She was tenacious, if nothing else—almost as bad as him, when she set her mind on something.

"So, you coming home soon?"

His only real home had been with her. "Maybe

after this job, for a bit." *Nope, don't ask. You don't want to know, so don't*— "Why?" God, he was a sucker for punishment.

"Oh, nothing. Just thought if you were coming back and hanging up a shingle, maybe we could..."

She wouldn't—

"...go for dinner sometime."

Luke exhaled the breath he'd been holding. For God's sake, even after all he'd put her through, even though he knew she expected him to shut her down, she'd reached out to him. Christ, his eyes were stinging. "Em, I—" His phone beeped, and he jerked it away to check the call waiting number. The TOC. "Oh, dammit...Em, I'm sorry, but I have to take this."

"O-okay," she stammered, and he hated hurting her yet again, even in that small way.

Then he surprised himself by saying, "I'll call you later if I can, all right?" Could be days, though. Or never.

"Sure, of course." She sounded unconvinced. "Take care of yourself, Luke."

"You too, Em. Bye." He connected to the next call, willing his heart to stop pounding, wrestling his brain into work mode. "Hutchinson." As the voice on the other end spoke, he found himself tensing again. "You sure? Okay. Yeah. Got it." Hanging up, he stretched out on the bed, blew out a breath and contemplated his options.

He'd suspected it. Had even planned some contingencies in case he was proved right. Man, he hated being right sometimes. Nothing to do now but deal with the situation.

Someone on his team had turned to the dark side. And Luke would mete out his own brand of justice.

****

When Dec knocked on Bryn's door, she didn't answer. After calling her name and waiting a few seconds, he figured she must still be in the bathroom and used her extra key. The shower was running behind the closed door. How long had she been in there now? Long enough to have a good cry.

"Bryn?"

No answer.

He knocked. "Bryn, it's Dec. You okay in there?"

"F-fine."

She didn't sound fine, but he'd give her some more time. Four minutes passed, then five, and still the water ran. "Bryn, say something."

"I'm f-fine," she repeated.

More time passed, and with each minute, his tension levels increased until his gut was tied in knots. "All right, that's it. I'm coming in," he warned, and jimmied the lock free. A cloud of steam hit him, thick and humid as it wafted from behind the shower curtain. She didn't say a word, didn't give the slightest indication she was aware he'd intruded on her privacy. "Bryn, tell me you're okay at least."

"I'm ok-kay."

The hell she was. He covered the four steps to the bathtub and gripped the edge of the plastic curtain. When she made no objection he grew really worried and pulled it aside to peek in.

She was huddled in the tub, fully clothed, directly under the spray of scalding water. Her dark eyes were haunted as she gazed up at him, arms wrapped around herself, shaking, her hair plastered to her skull. "I'm fine. J-just cold."

Something twisted in his chest, as though a giant fist had reached in and squeezed his heart. "Baby," he whispered. Unlacing his boots, he tossed them aside and climbed in beside her, fully clothed, squeezing against the wall to pull her into his arms.

She burrowed into him like a frightened child waking from a nightmare. Only she hadn't been dreaming.

Heart aching for her, he held her tight, her shivers wracking him. The water beat down on them and he bent over her, sheltering her from the full brunt. Her fingers curled into his wet shirt. Her face pressed against the base of his throat, warm breath washing over his sensitized skin. He stroked one hand down her hair and the length of her spine, marveling at how perfectly she fit against him.

She calmed, her breathing becoming slow and even, the convulsive shudders subsiding. Then she sighed and leaned her weight against him as though content to remain in his arms under the cooling flow of water. His body, however, was raging hot. If he didn't put some distance between them soon, he wasn't sure he could hold back.

"Better now? Want me to order us some food while you get out of these wet clothes?"

"Thanks."

"Okay."

But she didn't move. In fact, she didn't seem in a hurry to go anywhere. She turned her face into his neck and nuzzled him, setting every nerve ending on fire. Her lips touched a kiss under his ear, making his growing erection jerk. Not good.

He set her away from him, surging to his feet and grabbing a towel to drape around her. "I'll let you dry yourself off," he blurted, snagging another towel for himself, stripping off his soaked t-shirt and tossing it in the sink on his way out. When he shut the door behind him, he leaned against it and took a deep breath, scrubbed a hand over his face.

God. Another second in there with her and it would have been too late. As it was, his hand was shaking as he picked up the phone and dialed room service.

He rubbed the towel over his hair, peeled off his pants and underwear, then wrapped the towel around his waist, flopping down on the bed while he waited to place his order. Bryn wasn't thinking straight right now, he reminded himself. She needed soothing, to feel safe and protected, and she needed sleep. Shoving her down onto the mattress and getting inside her as deep as he could get wasn't going to help matters.

Maybe something light to eat, fruit and cheese and bread or something, to settle her stomach and help her unwind. He'd have to check out some of the more serious cuts and scrapes she'd suffered, too. Maybe rub her neck for a while. Then he'd tuck the covers around her and stay while she slept, so she wouldn't be alone—just in case she had nightmares. He knew how much of a bitch flashbacks could be.

Still on hold, he turned his head at the sound of the bathroom door opening, and the air sucked right out of his lungs. Bryn stood backlit in the doorway, stark naked, every gorgeous line of her body silhouetted in eye-popping relief.

Her black gaze stroked over him like a caress, bold and possessive as she crossed the room toward him in a movement he could only describe as a prowl. His cock leapt to urgent attention.

A voice came on the other end of the line, but Dec didn't hear a thing besides the roaring in his ears. He dropped the receiver into the cradle with a clack, his heart thudding against his ribs.

Oh, shit. He was so screwed.

****

She'd shocked him, she thought with satisfaction. Good. She liked that he was the one to be off balance for once. And it was high time they did something about the sexual energy between them.

247

Almost giddy with feminine power and anticipation, she stalked toward him. As he dropped the phone into place and sat up, his expression hovered between alert and wary.

Yes. Be afraid, Declan. Be very afraid.

She was going to eat him alive.

Pulse hammering, she flicked her damp hair over her shoulder, holding his gaze as she tossed a handful of condoms onto the coverlet. He opened his mouth as if to protest, and she cocked an eyebrow at him, daring him to chicken out.

Coming close enough that her thighs brushed his knees, she placed a hand on either side of his towel-clad hips and leaned down to press her breasts against his chest. His heart beat fast against her as she rubbed against him, a feline move of enjoyment.

Her hardened nipples slid over his bare chest. A gasp escaped as sensation rocketed through her, his eyes molten as he stared back at her. She bent her head and with exquisite precision, covered his mouth with hers.

He pulled back. "Bryn..."

She caressed him, hands roving over the taut muscles of his chest, back and shoulders. His bright gaze held an unnerving mix of lust and anger. He hadn't touched her yet, his hands remaining clenched on his lap, but the tension pulsed from him in waves. The air in the room crackled with it.

He made no move to push her away, so she kissed him again, licking and nibbling his mouth as the ache in her lower body intensified to a relentless throb. She rubbed her tongue against his, teasing, coaxing, then let her hands drift down his chest and belly to the erection straining against the towel. She stroked him, thrilling at the intake of his breath, then squeezed him through the thin terry cloth.

He snatched her hand and she stopped, pulling back. His eyes burned into hers, a muscle jumping in his jaw. Breathless, she stared down at him, waiting.

"No," he rasped. "Not like this."

"Not like what?"

His hands moved up to grasp her shoulders, holding her away from him. "Not when you're hurting and jacked up on adrenaline."

Pain spiked her chest. He had no right to analyze her. Emotions rolled through her. Anger, grief, longing, despair.

Need.

She pulled in a deep breath, fighting the urge to wrestle him to the sheets and ride him until she wore off some of the frantic energy battering her. She couldn't stop this, would die if she did.

"Bryn..."

She leaned down and kissed him some more, willing him to unlock everything bottled inside her. Her lips trailed over his jaw, down his neck, nibbling where the base of his throat joined his shoulder. He tilted his head back, one hand fisting in her hair to hold her there. A groan escaped him. "Baby, this is such a bad idea. You're not thinking straight."

The hell she wasn't. She *needed* him.

She pushed him backward. He didn't fight her, lying on his back with his hands tangled in her hair. Her fingers caressed him, her tongue flicking as she moved lower, over the plane of his stomach, dipping into his navel.

The muscles under her mouth went rigid and she rubbed her breasts against him, shivering while her hands slid over his hips, unknotting the towel with unsteady fingers. His cock sprang free, thick and swollen against his abdomen. She licked her lips and stroked him, dying to taste him, to make him writhe and come in her mouth. Rubbing her cheek against the hot length of him, she let him see it in her eyes.

"Christ," he breathed, fingers clenching in her

hair.

Here was her power, she thought, kissing the swollen tip, licking at him, slow and torturous. He hissed out a breath. When her mouth closed around him and sucked gently, his hips came off the bed and he gave a throttled groan. *Yes.* This was what she wanted. Control, power. She moved faster, thrilled by the way he gasped and closed his eyes, neck arching.

So beautiful, and all hers.

"Stop," he hissed through clenched teeth.

No way. Instead she slowed. His eyes speared her, predatory, almost dangerous. She sucked harder on him, her tongue flicking at the tender spot under the taut head.

"*Stop.*" The hands in her hair jerked her backward.

Bryn released him and stared at his heaving chest, into his glowing eyes, burning like banked coals as they seared her. Aroused as hell, and a little angry.

Dec reached over and grabbed a condom, tearing open the packet and covering himself. Then he reached for her, hauling her up until she straddled his hips, her hair swinging forward around them like a dark curtain. He pushed it back with gentle, unsteady fingers.

"I want to be inside you," he said, rising to kiss her as he dragged her down to meet him. She went willingly, pouring everything she had into it, sliding the damp glow between her legs against his throbbing erection. They both moaned.

Bryn broke the kiss and sat up, holding him to her, maintaining eye contact. He shuddered as she sank down upon him, and she tipped her head back with a sigh as she took him deep inside. His fingers clamped on her hips as she started moving in an undulating rhythm that made him swear and rear up to grab her, his mouth closing over her nipple. Whimpering at the tender suction, she held him fast and picked up speed.

Almost as if he sensed her backing off from the pleasure, he eased away, hands digging into her hips to hold her still. Panting, they stared at each other in a battle of wills.

Well, he might be stronger, but he couldn't prevent her from using her internal muscles. As she clenched around the solid presence filling her, his jaw tightened, eyes flaring.

Unwilling to stop, she pushed him. Squeeze, release. Squeeze, release, in a relentless, secret massage.

"Careful," he warned, voice rough with arousal. "You're playing with fire."

Her abdomen fluttered. If she hadn't been so turned on, if she hadn't trusted him so much, the intensity on his face would have scared her. But she wanted him too badly to listen to the whisper of doubt in her head. She'd come this far, and she wasn't going to give up. The aggressive energy swirling between them only heightened her urgency.

The anger rose up, bitterness and despair driving her to torment him. "Stop me then, Dec," she taunted, aware that she was baiting a caged tiger but unable to stop herself. "Go ahead, I dare you."

Something flickered in his eyes, then he flipped her beneath him, pinning her hands flat against the mattress with his own. Unease seeped through the haze of her arousal as she lay helpless beneath him. Though she trusted him, something about being held down right now triggered alarm.

"One sided doesn't work for me," he said in a low voice. "I want you with me." Holding her gaze, he eased his hips back and shifted his weight higher, then thrust forward.

Lightning sparked deep inside. She gasped and

shut her eyes, something hot and soft and vulnerable quaking in her chest. "No." She tried to ease herself from under him.

He ignored her, pressed her deeper into the mattress. Through her closed lids, she could feel his gaze burning her face, and turned her head aside.

This wasn't what she wanted. She wanted to be on top, to focus everything on him, to make him go crazy. She didn't want to feel anything but that. The rest was too close to the surface: the vulnerability, the anger, the passion and the tenderness, the grief.

A knot of swirling emotion clogged her throat, the pressure tearing through her chest until she wanted to scream and claw at him in punishment. Her eyes sprang open.

But Dec moved again, stroking over a wellspring of sensation inside her, all the while gauging her reaction with those piercing eyes. Her body arched beneath him, stiffening as she resisted. "Dec, no—" Tears stung her eyes. She blinked them away. "Let go. Let go of me!" Her voice broke and she bit down hard on her lower lip.

Dec bent and kissed each eyelid, then her mouth. When she dared open her eyes, his gaze was understanding, full of a mixture of hunger and tenderness that made her heart quake. This was so much deeper than anything she'd felt before. The enormity of it frightened her. Her body instinctively struggled, like an animal in a trap.

He held her there firmly, his grip somehow both gentle and commanding while he nibbled at her mouth, her jaw, the vulnerable place where her pulse fluttered beneath her ear.

As the sharp edge of fear ebbed in the wake of his tenderness, she trembled. He was so deep inside her she could feel every heartbeat as it pulsed through him. When he teased his way into her mouth, the glide of his tongue against hers made her moan, her body quivering even as it rebelled against what he was making her feel.

"Gently," he whispered against her lips. "Stop fighting me."

She shook her head, growing frantic. "Dec—"

"You change your mind?"

She stilled. "N-no."

"Then shh." His hips rocked again, igniting that spark low in her belly. She moaned and contracted her muscles around his length, her fingers squeezing his, then trailing around his back in desperation when he released them.

He nuzzled her throat. "Yeah, hold onto me..." As he thrust again, he slid one hand between them to touch her swollen clit. She grabbed onto his shoulders and jerked in his arms.

"Ah...God," he breathed, his fingers licking over her in a slow caress. A breathless moan escaped her and she bowed up hard. "You're so beautiful."

The pleasure spiraled tighter and tighter under his clever fingers, his cock caressing a place inside— it was almost unbearable. Her hips lifted into him, her nails digging into his shoulders as her body took over.

So good, she thought with a sob. Nothing had ever felt so good. She couldn't get enough of him, couldn't stop. She tightened around him, moaning, straining...almost there...

"Please," she whimpered, uncaring that he'd reduced her to begging. He was so strong, yet so gentle with her.

His rhythm never faltered as he bent his head and murmured against her ear. "Shhh...you're right there, baby. Take it." His fingertips continued stroking, the orgasm building and building inside until tears trickled from her closed lids.

He kissed them away as she fought to keep from sobbing in his arms, hanging on the edge, subconsciously afraid to let go in case she shattered into a thousand pieces.

"Don't stop, sweetheart," he crooned, moving faster. "Let me feel you come. Oh, God...Bryn..."

She arched up and pulsed around him, crying out his name, screaming inside. It went on and on, an earthquake shaking her as he suddenly pounded into her and flung his head back, a deep groan wrenching out of him as he let go with a shudder.

Dec sank down on top of her and buried his face in her neck. She locked her arms around him and held on as though he was an anchor in the middle of a hurricane. Her body absorbed his weight, the torrent of volatility draining away in the silence like water down a drain. All too soon, he tried to move away.

"No," she protested, holding fast, battling the last of her tears.

"Shhh." His arms slid beneath her as he rolled them over. "I just don't want to crush you."

He tugged the covers over her as she lay sprawled across his chest. A languorous peace stole through her as he stroked her hair and neck with his warm hands, his body wrapping her in a cozy cocoon. Hiccupping sobs shook her as he soothed her, exhaustion rolling over her like a wave. As her lids drooped, he shifted, easing out from under her.

Her head came up, relaxing only when he lifted his hand to her damp face.

"Better now?"

She lowered her gaze.

"Hey, no hiding. Look at me."

After a moment, she sniffed and raised her eyes to his.

"You okay?"

She closed her eyes with a sigh, chest aching. "I'm sorry I—"

He tilted her chin with a finger, forcing her eyes

open. "Nothing to be sorry for, so don't apologize. I loved every second of it. I just wish it could have been under different circumstances."

Yeah. Her, too. At least he wasn't shutting her out. A tremulous smile curved her lips, words crowding her throat but she forced them down, struggling to pin down what she felt, afraid of scaring him off, more afraid of not telling him. "Dec, I—"

He trailed a finger across her collarbone. "You have the most amazing skin. I've never felt anything so soft. I could touch you for hours."

His words heated her up all over again. She could hardly believe he was staying so intimate with her. She'd been afraid he would retreat into his shell and leave once they'd finished. Earlier in the bathroom, she'd prepared herself for that. But he was still here, treating her like a lover, as if he really cared about her.

"I love the way you touch me." He made her feel desirable and feminine. Cherished.

She reached out to cup his cheek and he stilled, eyes darkening as she pressed her parted lips against his. Even with the hunger building between them the kiss stayed tender and he let her control it, followed every movement and caress of her tongue. She wound her arms around his shoulders and pressed close to him, sighing at how his arms cradled her.

She'd never felt like this about anyone. Even the best of her boyfriends had bored her within a few months. What would Dec be like in the real world? Would he unwind in front of the TV, watching sports? Or would he hike or go rock climbing? She pictured him with her in Oregon, sprawled on her couch overlooking the rolling ocean, relaxing with a bottle of beer.

It probably wasn't healthy to leap into the

future like that, even in her fantasies, but the image was so vivid. She'd come in from the beach and kick off her sandy shoes, return his easy smile of greeting and crawl atop him so she could give him a proper hello.

She had to stop thinking like that. She was setting herself up for heartbreak.

His cell phone rang. Just like that the spell was broken. She released him. Every awful detail of the air strike came back to her.

God, those poor children...

He met her eyes as he responded to the caller. "Yeah." He listened, his expression unreadable, but a fine tension took hold of his shoulders. "Understood."

Out of politeness, she tried not to eavesdrop, and went into the bathroom to dress. A picture of the little bodies buried in the rubble flashed through her mind. Guilt and sadness beat at her. She took several deep breaths, forced the geyser of emotion deep inside where she wouldn't have to deal with it. She couldn't face it yet, didn't want to.

When she came out of the bathroom, Dec was still sitting on the bed. "Was that Luke?"

He set his phone down. "Looks like Tehrazzi made it out."

Her heart stuttered. "Are they sure?"

"Yeah. Fahdi's meeting with a contact tonight to see if he can find out where he's gone." His eyes were solemn.

So those innocent children and whoever else had been in the house had died...for nothing? Her throat spasmed.

How had Tehrazzi known about the air strike? Unless they'd been mistaken and he wasn't in the house at all, had maybe been tipped off by someone. Or... She raised horrified eyes to Dec. "Do you think he heard me yelling at the girl? Is that why he—"

"Don't go there, Bryn."

"But what if he did? What if it's my fault?" she whispered, voice cracking. She'd failed to save the children *and* helped Tehrazzi escape.

"It wasn't your fault. Don't ever think that, baby."

The endearment made her eyes sting. Knowing he cared and that he wanted to ease her suffering took what was left of her to pieces. She lifted a trembling hand against her mouth.

Dec's eyes softened. "Come here."

"Can't. I'll fall apart...we don't have time."

"We've got time," he replied, advancing toward her, ignoring how she backed away. Before her shoulders bumped into the wall he caught her hand and tugged her back to the bed. "Come lie down with me."

"No," she moaned, fighting the tears. "I don't want to cry anymore. I'm sick of crying...doesn't do any good anyway."

Those strong arms drew her down to the bed until her head rested in the cradle of his shoulder and her body pressed full length against his. "We're not going back to Baghdad until morning. It's just you and me here, Bryn. It's okay if you let go. I'll hold you together."

The words unlocked her shaking throat so she could breathe again. How did he stay so calm and in control? Was he so used to seeing innocent bystanders die? Or was he holding all that in? She maintained her control, glad to have him wrapped around her. Lying safe in his arms, the last thing she remembered before her eyes closed was his rough whisper against her ear.

"It's going to be okay, baby."

Chapter Eighteen

Day 12, Iraqi Desert
Morning

No one said a word to Tehrazzi as they trudged over the rugged terrain. Most of his traveling companions were young, unseasoned trainees, their faces etched with strain and exhaustion. Their weakness irritated him beyond bearing.

Only one of his lieutenants had survived yesterday's air strike, and he was being carried on a litter, his head bound and his back covered with deep burns. He kept slipping in and out of consciousness, which was probably a blessing.

When he came to, his agonized cries made Tehrazzi's skin crawl. Every time the breeze picked up, the stench of burned flesh rose, choking him. Several men had stumbled to the side of the trail to be sick.

Tehrazzi's ears buzzed as loud as a swarm of flies in his skull. His vision was blurry, and his feet had trouble picking over the rocks, slow and uncoordinated. Sometimes he weaved and had to stop, panting and sweating as he fought to keep from throwing up in the dirt.

But at least he was alive. For a few minutes after the explosion he hadn't been sure.

He glanced back for Ghaliya, being led by a youngster behind him. He hadn't trusted himself to stay in the saddle, and if he led her himself he feared tangling her feet with his awkward gait, so no matter how much he disliked handing her off, she was safer with someone else.

A wave of gratitude overcame him. She had saved him. If not for her, he would have been in the house with the others when the missile had hit, instead of in the humble stable he had found to shelter her at the edge of the village. It was a miracle she hadn't gone mad from the force of the explosion.

When he'd picked himself up and screamed her name over the ringing in his ears, she'd been standing beside him and bumped him with her muzzle. The relief had sent him to his knees again. Outside, when he'd seen the crater where the house had been, he'd clambered up onto her back and allowed her to gallop off, carrying him to safety.

Yet he'd sensed someone watching. Tracking him. Hunting him.

He'd been aware of a prickling at the base of his neck. Acting on instinct, he'd slumped forward over her mane just as the bullet whined past, grazing her shoulder. Ghaliya had whinnied but kept going, and soon they had gained refuge in the foothills and met with his followers.

Still, the uneasiness would not leave him, a low-grade hum in his gut, despite his attempts to push it out of his consciousness. He feared his suspicion was true—that his teacher had found him at last.

With determination he put it from his mind and meditated, thanking Allah for His grace and protection. He allowed himself to drift as he placed one foot in front of the other, ignoring the burn in his muscles and the strain on his heart and lungs during the climb into the hills. When they reached the Iranian border, they would be safe. For now, they had to find temporary shelter and make contact with their source in Baghdad.

A shout from behind him made him whip around, and he had to grab his head to stop it spinning. Opening his eyes, he waited until his vision cleared and saw a group of his men gathered around Ghaliya, arguing amongst themselves.

The mare's head jerked up at their sharp, careless gesturing, her ears back, eyes wide at their angry voices. Bright blood stained her glossy coat where her flesh wound had reopened on her shoulder. Someone was probing at it in an attempt to stop the bleeding.

A growl of rage vibrated up his throat. The man closest to him backed away with a fearful expression as he started toward the group.

Ghaliya pulled on the tether holding her, a neigh of fear splitting the air. Others grabbed it to hold her still and she balked, rear hooves scrambling over the ground.

"Stop!" he commanded, vision blurring from anger and the concussion.

As one they turned to him, and as his fury registered, they released Ghaliya's red halter and leapt back, making her shy up.

If those imbeciles didn't stay still, he'd—

Ghaliya stumbled as her rear hoof slipped on a stone. Tehrazzi's heart lodged in his throat. The youngster in charge of her lunged forward in an attempt to grab the lead rope, and his magnificent horse rose on her hind legs, pawing at the air with her forelegs. Front hooves slicing through the air, her injured back leg buckled, and she tipped sideways toward the cliff.

"No!" Paralyzed, he could only stare as his worst fear came true.

His vision tunneled.

Ghaliya squealed and tried to right herself, her wide eyes staring straight at him as she toppled over the edge.

Stricken, stomach heaving, Tehrazzi sprinted to the spot where she'd fallen and peered down. *Allah, please let her be all right.* Over the roar in his ears came her agonized screams and bile rose in his throat. Her black body thrashed weakly in a wadi partway down, her broken forelegs flopping uselessly as she tried to stand.

Without realizing he'd moved, he found himself scrambling down the steep wall past some of the others. They froze at his guttural cry of grief as he raced to Ghaliya's side.

On level ground, he approached her slowly, speaking to her in a soothing voice though tears streamed down his face. The whites of the mare's eyes showed as he came nearer, ears pricked forward at his crooning tone. As that gentle, agonized gaze settled on his, he saw the mute plea in them and sobbed as his heart broke.

Falling to his knees beside her, he stroked her quivering neck, fiery pain burning in his chest as she attempted to butt his shoulder with her nose. Quaking with shock and anguish, he unsheathed the jeweled dagger from his belt, careful to keep her from seeing it.

He passed his hand over the fine slope of her forehead and nose, her panting breaths and whinnies tearing at him. Gathering a breath, he brought the knife up and sliced through her throat with a hard, clean swipe. Her head snapped up, her body jerking as she stared at him in stunned surprise, her blood gushing from the mortal wound.

He held her heavy head in his lap while her lifeblood soaked through his clothing into the sand beneath them, her trusting eyes fixed on his as she died. When she breathed no more, Tehrazzi tilted his tear-stained face to the sky and screamed to the heavens.

As her blood congealed around him, his rage and hatred condensed in his soul. His teacher would pay for this. Him and Daoud's daughter.

By Allah, I will make them all pay.

****

Day 12, Baghdad

A little after nine that morning, Ben leaned back in his chair at the computer terminal and stretched his arms over his head. A mighty yawn worked its way up his throat and cracked his jaw, making his eyes water. After the night's work they'd put in, he wanted a hot shower and a bed, in that order and nothing else.

What a goat-fuck the op had been. Not only had they missed Tehrazzi, but watching those kids die had to have leveled Bryn. He hoped to hell Irish was taking good care of her, and that he'd finally ditched his rigid code of conduct in order to give her the comfort she must need right now. Jesus, Ben thought. Who the hell would have ever guessed he'd wish for *that*? The idea didn't hurt so much now, though. Not since he'd met Sam.

His phone rang, and he was surprised to see Sam's number displayed. Earlier that morning he'd offered to see her home from the TOC, but she'd waved him off with a good-natured reply and taken a cab. He picked up. "Hey, sweets. Miss me already?"

"Ben, someone's been into my place."

He sat bolt upright at the alarm in her voice. "What? Are you all right?"

"Yes, but someone broke in this morning around five. They've been into my computer and took some personal mail."

Ben was silent a moment. "They take anything else?"

She huffed out an irritated breath. "I know it doesn't sound like a big deal, but my gut says differently."

Okay. "Why's that?"

"They took a letter from Neveah, and opened my email file with her name on it."

Why would they bother unless they meant to use it for something? Sam's cousin meant everything to her. If someone had been looking for a way to gain leverage with Sam, they'd done their homework.

"I also found a transmitter in my smoke detector—"

"*What?*" What kind of crazy bullshit was this?

"—so I figure there have to be more. Could you come over?" She'd dropped her voice to a whisper.

Yeah, because that'll help if someone's listening in.

"Damn straight. We're on our way."

He and Rhys drove straight over and went through her suite room by room. While Rhys stayed with her, Ben headed to security to review the hotel's CCTV tapes. He returned and told them a dark-haired man of medium build was seen entering her room at about oh-four-fifty that morning, but the images weren't clear enough to ID him.

Sam's face was pale as flour at the news. She handed him the dime-sized transmitter she'd found in her smoke detector.

Suspicion took root in his gut as he sat down at her laptop to look at her emails. With a few keystrokes, he entered her password and found an email from her cousin saying she was flying to Kabul in three days. So, Neveah was off to save the world again with Doctors Without Borders. Imagine completing medical school and residency only to pack up and leave all creature comforts behind to fly to the ass end of the world and put yourself in the middle of a moonscape war zone.

Ben closed the file and turned his head to look at Sam. "Got anything else you want to tell me?"

She swallowed and broke eye contact, which made the acid churn in his stomach. "I've—I've been followed."

Ben raised a brow. "Is that right. When?"

"I don't have any hard evidence, but I feel someone behind me sometimes when I'm out."

For God's sake... "How long has this been happening?"

"A week or two now."

"And you only thought to tell someone about it now?"

She fidgeted. "After this morning, I realized it's not just my imagination playing tricks on me."

Yeah, and wasn't that a damn shame? "Any reason I don't know about that might explain why someone has taken such an interest in you?"

Her posture and expression radiated nervousness. "No."

Christ, he hoped she was telling the truth about that.

He analyzed this new intel. Who the hell was it he'd seen on that video? Not anyone from the Najaf op, because they'd only arrived in Baghdad two hours ago. That left Fahdi and Davis, but why in hell would they have broken in to Sam's place? Besides, it could easily have been a stranger. American contractors had plenty of enemies in Baghdad.

Whoever it was, someone had been watching her carefully enough to be certain she hadn't returned home last night. Which meant someone was keeping a very close eye on her.

The question was, why? Either she had information someone wanted, or she was hiding something and they were trying to find it.

His brother was still checking around the apartment for other bugs. "Find anything yet, Rhys?"

"Negative," Rhys called from the bedroom.

The whole place was immaculately clean.

Everything was in its place, and then some. The woman was a manic organizer. No wonder she'd noticed her cousin's letter was missing. Ben scanned the room with a critical eye, trying to decide where he'd plant a bug.

He got up and walked to a framed picture hanging on the wall above her couch, and carefully pulled a corner of it away from the wall. He almost missed it. Craning his neck, he peered closer. There. Something green and metallic. A micro-transmitter. Bingo. He grabbed it between his thumb and forefinger and pried it loose. "This look familiar?"

She shook her head. "It's not one of mine."

Her defensive answer made the nape of his neck prickle, and reminded him that she built and hid things like these for a living. "I didn't say it was. I just meant it looks the same as the one you already found."

"Oh. Yeah, it's the same."

What did they have on her to warrant bugging her place? He eyed the cordless phone extension on her desk. "You check that thing?"

"No, I didn't want to touch anything else until you got here."

He opened up the handset and sure enough, found one in there, too. Were there more? Might be cameras here as well, he thought, glancing around at the possible hiding places. "Any other spots you can suggest?" She should know. She'd bugged plenty of rooms in her tenure with the CIA.

"No. You guys seem to have it covered."

Did the CIA have her under surveillance? Luke was the obvious answer because he had the highest security clearance and knew things the rest of them didn't, but it could have been any of the handlers at the office. Or was it someone with terrorism or extortion on their mind? Hard to believe any CIA operative would be so sloppy as to leave evidence of their presence.

Unless they wanted her to know they were keeping tabs on her. They might if they suspected she had something they wanted.

Ben thought of the possible culprits in their cozy little group. Fahdi had been acting weird for the past day or two, curt and withdrawn, and he was friends with Sam. If Luke had noticed the change in behavior, he hadn't said anything, but Ben doubted Fahdi would have the guts or the know how to do this in the first place.

Davis, maybe. He was a cool customer. Always skulking about, never socializing with anyone. More of a loner than Rhys, if that was possible. But what reason would Luke have for wanting Sam tagged? The whole thing made Ben damned uneasy.

At any rate, it was safer for her to return to the TOC until they knew what was going on. "Let's get you out of here and get some answers." Maybe while they were at it, Ben would get some of his own.

On the way out, Rhys stopped in front of a picture of Sam and Neveah hanging on the fridge. They were in the desert with a pair of camels, the pyramids rising behind them in the distance, other tourists captured in the frame with them. A frown creased his forehead as he squinted at the thing.

Ben frowned at him. "Problem?"

"Cairo," she said to Rhys, coming up behind him. "We met there in May, after the op you and I worked in Paris. Why?"

Ben squinted at the photo too. What the hell was his brother looking at? Rhys knew Neveah, and yeah, she was a knockout, but it wasn't like his twin to gawk at a woman like that. Did he see something Ben didn't?

Rhys continued to study the photo as if he was memorizing it. "How is she, anyway?"

"Good," Sam said.

Enough, already. "Let's go," Ben prompted.

They took her back to the TOC in the Suburban, Ben's shoulder bumping against hers until he draped his arm around her to cushion her. He escorted her inside, sat her down and offered to stay with her. Reassuring him she was fine, she buried herself in work for the next hour until Rhys returned with Luke and Fahdi.

Luke came straight over to her, and with Ben following for extra security, took her to an empty room so they could talk alone. Watching from the other side of the plate glass window separating them, she spoke while Luke stood there with his arms folded. Ben detected nothing in his boss's expression or body language that betrayed surprise, but he was a legend for a reason.

The one-sided conversation continued for another minute while Luke's eyes remained steady on Sam. His expression remained unreadable. Finally, Luke cocked his head, and Ben lip-read his response. "Only one way to find out, isn't there?"

What the hell did that mean? Find out what? Ben tried to puzzle everything together. Whatever it was, Luke had just given her the go ahead for something.

The door opened and Sam forced a smile as she and Luke came out.

"Everything all right?" Ben asked. She looked even more nervous than she had back at her place.

"Yes, fine."

Tell me another one, sweets. Ben followed them to another door and waited outside. Sam emerged a few minutes later, and passing him to round the corner, ran smack into Fahdi.

"Sorry, Miss Sam," he blurted, reaching out to steady her.

"It's okay. I'm fine."

Fahdi brushed a hand over his shirt as though

smoothing wrinkles and reached for the gold chain caught on his collar. Sam beat him to it, closing her fingers around the pendant to settle it into the v of his open collar.

Fahdi grinned down at his good luck charm. "Thank you." His espresso eyes regarded her with warmth.

"No problem." Her voice was a mere thread of a sound. As she stepped aside to let him pass, she met Ben's hard stare and forced another smile.

Shooting Luke a questioning glance as she walked away, Ben had a really bad feeling something big was going down.

****

Two hours later, Dec sauntered into their barracks in Baghdad and nodded to Ali, seated on his bunk reading a Sports Illustrated. "Got time to drive us to a meeting?"

Ali swung his legs over the side of his bunk. "Sure. Where to?"

"Gotta head over to the TOC and meet with Luke."

"Okay." He snagged the keys to the Humvee and headed for the door.

Dec withheld a weary sigh. After the night they'd had in the desert, he'd been hoping for another few hours' downtime, mostly for Bryn's sake. But they'd come closer than ever to getting Tehrazzi last night, so they had to follow up while the trail was hot.

He glanced down the row of bunks to hers, where she lay on her side watching him. "Tired?"

"A little."

Damn, he shouldn't leave her alone, even just to go to the TOC. If he were Bryn, he wouldn't want to be left alone either. Whenever he closed his eyes, he saw her stricken expression as she'd tried in vain to rescue those children.

Mind made up, he pivoted and headed for the door, throwing it open. As he exited, his first breath of air hit his lungs like a blast furnace. Beads of sweat popped out on his skin, the midday sun beating down on his head through his wide-brimmed hat.

As he came around the side of the building, he scanned for the Suburban and saw it parked along the perimeter fence next to the heavily guarded gate. The Humvee was in front of it, boxing it in. Fahdi must have left it there after his meeting with a contact last night.

"Ali, wait. Bryn's coming with us, so we'll need the Suburban."

Ali turned around and caught the keys Dec tossed at him. "Sure, no problem. I'll just move the Hummer. Be right back." He hustled across the baking asphalt to the vehicles.

Christ it was hot, Dec thought, heading back into the blessed coolness of the barracks and paused at a window. Helluva nice kid, Dec thought as he watched Ali.

Out on the street, a boy passed by with his mother, his curious gaze fastened on Ali's uniform. The boy smiled and gave him a thumbs-up. Ali grinned and returned the gesture. Dec could only hope the boy would grow up to defend his country as Ali had, rather than destroy it.

Ali was one of the lucky ones. Dec had read his file. A couple of years ago Ali had nearly participated in a suicide mission. An imam had recruited him through a local madrassa for a radical militia. The leaders filled him so full of hate for Americans and all things western he'd actually prayed for God to let him blow himself up so he could kill as many of them as possible.

His father, a policeman, had somehow found out what Ali was involved with and begged him not to go through with it. Whether or not the plea had registered with his son was not mentioned in the file, but next morning, the father went to work and never came back. He was gunned down outside the police station by the leader of the same militia Ali had trained with.

After that, Ali decided blowing himself up would only perpetuate the cycle of violence. At that moment, he'd chosen to be part of the solution for his people instead of part of the problem. Which was why he was now working for Luke. Dec admired the hell out of the kid for trying to make a difference.

Turning away from the window when Ali climbed into the Humvee, Dec grabbed his duffel and packed an extra pistol and some ammo. If anything happened on their trip to the TOC, he wanted to be prepared. Adding some bottles of water, he glanced up at Bryn, who was covering her hair with a headscarf.

"It's five hundred degrees out there," she complained, "and I have to boil inside a robe while you guys can run around in t-shirts."

"But you look so hot in it," he teased.

She glared at him. "That's because I *am* hot." Then she laughed. "Idiot."

"Ready?" he asked.

"Y—"

The roar of an explosion shattered the air.

The blast rocked the building, lifted them off their feet, the concussion blowing out the windows. Glass sprayed. Dec threw his body over Bryn, tumbling her to the floor and holding her there underneath him. When the earth settled, he scrambled up, shoving Bryn back down, barking at her to stay put.

"Everyone okay?" he panted.

Rhys and Ben came running around the corner from the back office. "Yeah." Their faces were tight as they grabbed their rifles and followed him to the door. People were shouting and screaming, and as Dec burst outside, the carnage brought him up short so fast the twins plowed into him.

"Jesus Christ," he breathed at the ball of flame and smoke billowing from a crater beside the perimeter fence. Fortunately, because the explosion had occurred closer to the road than the barracks, the damage within the compound seemed minimal.

Beyond it, windows all along the street had been blown out, shards of glass littering the ground. Several buildings were pockmarked with shrapnel holes. Blackened vehicles lay in twisted disarray.

Rhys pushed past him like a battering ram through the demolished gatehouse into the gawking crowd. Grabbing an Iraqi soldier, he demanded in Arabic, "What happened? Did you see anything?"

The man pointed with a shaking hand. "The Humvee. It just...exploded."

"Christ...Ali," Dec muttered, skin crawling at the devastation in front of him. If they hadn't needed the bigger Suburban so Bryn could accompany them, they'd have climbed into the Hummer. If not for her...shit, they'd be charred corpses right now.

Ben and Rhys wore the same expression he knew must be displayed on his own. They'd escaped death by an eyelash, but Ali...poor bastard. Dec prayed he hadn't known what hit him, told himself that he wouldn't have felt anything.

Sirens wailed nearer, shaking him out of his stupor. The three of them waded into the fray, helping to secure the area while the ambulance and fire crews dealt with the wounded and the flames. When he could do no more, he returned to Bryn, found her huddled against the wall.

"Car bomb," he confirmed in response to her

271

questioning gaze. "Someone rigged the Hummer."

She gasped, one hand flying to her mouth. "Oh, God, was Ali—"

"Yeah."

Her eyes closed.

His cell vibrated. "McCabe."

Luke's voice was sharp. "What the hell's happening over there? I can see the smoke from here."

Dec told him.

"EOD team there yet?"

"Negative. First responders are still cleaning up."

"Okay. Lie low and I'll make my way to you. Meanwhile, find out what they uncover. I'll contact Ali's family."

"Roger that." At least he wouldn't have to deliver that news. But where was he going to stash Bryn while they puzzled this thing out? They should get her out of the country as soon as possible.

No way could he stomach her being in jeopardy again, and until this mission was finished, she was a major Achilles heel. With their team's security compromised, it wasn't safe for her to remain with them. "What do you want me to do with Bryn?"

"Take her to Fahdi's place. Hala will keep her company."

He hesitated. "With no one to guard her?"

"It'll only be a couple hours, but move her now. And see if you can get hold of Sam."

He didn't like it. Didn't like it at all. Maybe she could go to Sam's instead. "Roger that." He dialed Sam's number and waited, disconnected and dialed again. "Shit. Sam's not picking up."

He put the phone away and held out a hand to Bryn, pulled her up. Staying here wasn't an option until they made it secure, and maybe not even then. Whoever had planted that bomb had already gotten into the perimeter once. Unless they found out who was responsible, it could happen again. "Come on, let's go."

"Where?" she asked in an unsteady voice.

"Fahdi's. You can stay with his wife until I find out what the hell's going on."

****

As Dec hustled Bryn past the wreckage on the street, the horror of it seeped into her, slipping past the barrier of her shock. People lay scattered on the ground, bleeding and crying and twitching. She recoiled from their torn and burned flesh, the stench sickening her over the scorched metal and acrid smoke. Her head spun as they passed the carcass of the blown-up vehicle.

That could have been her. Could have been all of them. Dear God, they would be dead right now if not for Ali. Her throat tightened. *Poor, sweet Ali.*

"Don't fall apart on me now," Dec muttered, gripping her arm.

His words hit her like a slap. "I won't."

Trailing after his long strides, her legs hampered by her robe, she wished for the thousandth time she'd chosen not to come on this mission. What had she been thinking? Dec had been right about her. She wasn't cut out for this, couldn't take this bombardment of danger and death.

While he weaved in and out of the crowd milling around, the smoke curling into the air, she grabbed hold of his hand. He tightened his fingers around hers, his acknowledgement of her need for reassurance staving off the panic as they meandered through the neighborhoods to Fahdi's house. He didn't say another word to her until Fahdi's wife answered the door, welcoming them with wide eyes.

He ushered her inside, eyes scanning the place.

"You should be safe here," he said, pressing his cell into her hand, but his expression was grim.

He probably didn't want to let her out of his sight after the bombing, but she understood he had to secure the area and find out who was responsible. He'd already explained that the phone was preprogrammed with various numbers where she could reach him, and that they would be using it to keep tabs on her via the GPS chip.

Not that they'd need to with her here, but it made her feel better to have it. Then his hand came up to cup her cheek, and she leaned into it, wanting to hug him so badly it was all she could do to hold back.

"I'll come for you as soon as I can, okay? But if you need me before then, call." He wrapped her up in his arms for a moment and kissed her once.

Her heart weighed heavy as he walked away, disappearing from view. She wanted to call him back, beg him not to leave her. What if another bomb went off at the compound? Fahdi's wife spoke softly to her in Arabic, of which she only caught some, then put a tentative hand on her shoulder and led her inside.

Bryn's heart kept racing, her mind caught in the fiery wreckage of the Humvee. She took a couple deep breaths as she followed Hala into the room at the rear of the house and stood staring over the courtyard with its fountain and palm trees.

Roses bloomed in a rainbow of color, their cupped heads nodding in the breeze carrying their sweet scent. A wind chime tinkled from the frond of a palm tree. For a moment Bryn felt disoriented. The peaceful oasis came as a shock. Beyond the concrete wall, the plume of black smoke roiled up into the sky.

Someone tugged at her robe and she looked down. Karima, Fahdi and Hala's five-year-old daughter, was staring up at her. Bryn forced a smile. "Salaam."

Full of empathy, the little girl's hazel eyes seemed way too old in her young face. One tiny hand reached up and wrapped around her fingers in an offer of comfort.

Touched by the child's intuitive kindness, Bryn sank to her knees and pressed a kiss to the smooth forehead. "Thank you, little one," she whispered.

With a pleased smile, the girl towed her to a different room and showed Bryn her dolls.

The afternoon passed quickly, and by the time Bryn had helped her hostess prepare dinner amid a mixture of gestures and halting Arabic, the sun had set. After they ate, she helped Hala bathe the baby and get the others ready for bed. Bryn loved every second she spent with the children. They reminded her of the good things in life. And what was important. These children were the future of Iraq. She prayed they would have a peaceful place to live soon.

Later, when Hala handed her the baby wrapped in a fuzzy blue blanket, her heart squeezed. She sat in a chair and snuggled him close. The sweet scent of him made her ache.

Singing softly, she rocked him, nuzzling his downy black hair with her nose. He made a murmur of contentment and yawned hugely, his long lashes resting against his smooth cheeks as he slept in her arms. So innocent. Precious.

Bryn closed her eyes and breathed him in, savoring the warm weight of his little body tucked so trustingly against her. She wanted this someday. Someday soon. She wondered if Dec wanted kids, too.

Hala stood watching from the doorway, a smile wreathing her face, as if she'd known holding the baby was exactly what Bryn needed. Stealing one last snuggle, she placed the baby in his crib and the two of them went to sit in front of the television. When the news anchor reported on the explosion at the compound, Hala hurried to change the channel.

After a while, she went into the kitchen and returned with some hot tea. Grateful for her kindness, Bryn wished she was completely fluent in Arabic so they could talk properly. She approved of her mothering skills, especially of how clearly she adored her children. As they drank, Hala kept glancing at the clock on the wall. Was she wondering where her husband was?

Bryn searched her vocabulary. "He is probably helping the men at the…" She didn't know the word for explosion. "Fire."

Hala looked down at her teacup, tension taking hold of her frame.

"I'm sure he's fine," Bryn added to reassure her.

When Hala lifted her gaze, it was filled with sympathy and…trepidation.

"What is it?"

The other woman pressed her lips together.

"Hala?" She risked putting her hand on Hala's wrist. It trembled. "What is it?" Her chest tightened.

Her hostess's hazel eyes clouded with tears. "You should not be here," she began in a hoarse whisper.

Bryn's skin prickled.

"My husband," she said, wringing her hands, her voice stronger this time. Her gaze traveled to the window overlooking the garden, where a smudge of smoke from the bombing stained the twilit sky, then reverted to Bryn.

The fear and shame in that gaze hit Bryn like a fist.

"He is… You are in danger here."

As her brain processed what the woman was saying, Bryn's stomach plummeted. The blood drained from her face and her mind shrieked with denial. *Fahdi. Oh God, not Fahdi...*

Hala's shoulders jerked as she began to cry. "You should never have come here."

Chapter Nineteen

*Day 12: Baghdad
Evening*

"I still can't reach Sam," Ben said to him. "You heard anything from her yet?"

Dec shook his head. "Nothing."

"Rhys is out sniffing around, but she wasn't at her place when I went by." He rubbed the back of his neck. "It's not like her to drop out of contact like this. Think she's okay?"

"Let's hope so." Dec didn't like it either. Not a damn bit. There were too many unknowns right now, and Sam falling off the radar wasn't easing the tension in his gut. And now Bryn was at Fahdi's, with no one to protect her. He'd hated leaving her there, but he hadn't had a choice.

Nearby Luke was talking with the head of the Explosives Ordnance Disposal team, examining something in his hand. His expression went black.

"Uh-oh," Ben said under his breath. "This ain't gonna be good."

No shit, Dec thought as Luke stalked over to them and dumped a chunk of metal into Dec's palm.

He studied it, gearing up for bad news. "Nice fuse."

Next Luke handed him a timing mechanism. "Iranian. Could have been planted on the Hummer by anyone, but it had to be someone we know, and who would have sympathetic ties to Tehran?"

"A Shi'a," he reasoned.

Luke kept gazing at him.

Dec's heart and lungs constricted as he connected the dots. *Shit...*

"Fahdi." Ben confirmed.

"Oh, Jesus," Dec moaned, breaking out in a clammy sweat. "What are we gonna do about Bryn?"

"Nothing. Leave her where she is for now."

"Are you fucking nuts? If we're right about Fahdi, he could turn her over to Tehrazzi, or kill her himself."

"Fahdi's not going to do anything to her. Tehrazzi wants her for his bodyguard to kill in front of him, so if Fahdi's working for him, he won't touch her. Right now, Bryn's our best hope of finding out whether he planted the bomb, or if he's our mole. Let's wait and see what she can dig up."

Dec's heart was in his throat as a terrible realization hit him. Jesus. Luke had suspected Fahdi all along. That's why he'd ordered him to take her to Fahdi's. "You son of a bitch. You sent her there as bait, didn't you? You had me put her there even though you knew she'd be without protection."

Luke didn't answer.

"What the hell's *wrong* with you? She's a civilian—"

"She's a *member* of this *team*. She signed on for this—I'm not asking her to do anything she didn't agree to."

"Fuck that!" Dec fought to get hold of his temper, drilled him with a dark glare. "We have to at least contact her, make sure she's all right."

Luke's eyes hardened. "If she knows we suspect Fahdi, she won't stay long enough to find out what we need to know, will she? Hala and Fahdi aren't going to hurt her."

"We can't just leave her there." His stomach was in knots. He wanted to get her out of there, right now.

His new cell rang. He snatched it, stared with a

tripping heart at the display. "*Bryn.*"

"Fahdi did it," she blurted. "Fahdi planted the bomb. His wife just told me—"

"Shit." He mouthed the information to Luke. "Where are you?" His heart was pounding at the thought of her in that house, in a bomber's house.

"Running down the street. I snuck out so I could call you," she panted. "Hala probably knows I'll warn you. What if she tells Fahdi?"

"It's okay, Bryn." He had to calm her, keep her coherent and focused. "You need to get out of there now. Find some cover, somewhere you can drop out of sight. We'll come find you, track the GPS chip in the phone."

"That's not your call to make," Luke said.

Dec thrust the phone at him. "Then *you* tell her we're leaving her there." His muscles were coiled like springs, ready to snap.

Luke's lips thinned, but he didn't argue further. He was probably beating himself up for trusting Fahdi, for not seeing through the guy sooner. Probably still hoped Bryn could ferret out more inside info that would help him nail the bastard. Well, that was Luke's problem. Damned if Dec was leaving her there as bait for another second if he could help it.

"Does she know where Fahdi is?" Luke demanded.

Dec put the phone to his ear and relayed the question, then shook his head. "If Hala has any clue, she's not saying."

Luke looked at Ben. "Lock onto Fahdi. We're bringing him in."

Forget Fahdi. "Bryn first," Dec snapped, then more softly to Bryn, "Keep moving, baby. Make sure you're not being followed. And stay on the line with me, okay?"

"O-okay." Her breath hitched.

Christ, he hadn't meant to scare her even more, but he had a real bad feeling. No doubt Fahdi knew by now that his attempt to assassinate them had failed, and there was Bryn, the perfect target, awaiting him at home. Why the hell had Dec let Luke go ahead with this?

He dashed outside, Luke and Ben on his tail. His frantic gaze fell on an army vehicle parked at the curb. He tore over. Leaving Luke to pull the Iraqi soldier out of the front seat, he and Ben did a quick once over to check for explosives before climbing inside. He put the phone to his ear. "Bryn, you hidden yet?"

"No, I can't see anything to—Where are you?"

Her fear hit him hard. "We're on our way." His fingers tightened around the phone as Luke gunned it. "How long, Ben?"

"Barring roadblocks, about seven minutes."

He kept talking to her as the minutes ticked past, linking to her with his voice, trying to keep her level as she slipped away from Fahdi's house into the darkening neighborhood, alone. Goddamn Fahdi. He'd actually liked the son of a bitch. Why would he do something so despicable? Had to be the money. He couldn't wait to get the bastard, and could tell Luke was itching to as well.

"Three more blocks," Ben said.

"Any minute, Bryn." Then, on the other end of the line, he heard the screech of tires, Bryn's sharply indrawn breath.

"Oh, God, Dec!" she yelled, making the hair on his arms stand up. "Two men. They saw me. They're coming after me." He made out her running footsteps as she fled for her life.

He barked her name, muscles tight as a steel cable. She screamed. A clatter followed, as though she'd dropped the phone.

"Bryn!" he roared, desperate for her response.

281

No answer, just grunts and her desperate cries as she struggled against whoever had her. "Jesus Christ," he said hoarsely, "they've got her."

****

Bryn broke free of the meaty arms wrapped around her, a scream trapped in her throat. Her heart thundered in her ears as she lunged away, but someone else caught a fistful of her robe and wrenched her backward. Whirling on him, she landed a punch to his face, barely registering the pain in her hand, and flung herself backward with all her strength.

They would not take her.

Not this time.

More hands grabbed at her.

Heels planted, she turned. Kicked one guy's feet out. Damned robe kept tangling around her legs. Turned again.

Another man coming at her. She crouched in her fighting stance.

Punch.

Wheeling around, she drove up with her elbow toward his throat. Missed.

Spin. Block left. Block low.

Punch.

A fist glanced off her ribs. She sucked in a breath.

Punch. She threw him over her hip, screaming her rage at him.

The man flew to the pavement with a grunt. She turned to face the other.

Come on, you bastard.

She aimed high. Kicked. Caught him in the shoulder. *Keep moving.*

Punch.

He staggered back with a curse.

Panting, she broke free again and took off down the street, weaving in case they drew a gun so she'd be harder to hit. Where the hell was Dec with her backup? Footsteps thundered behind her, getting closer. Closer. A sob caught in her throat. Tiring fast.

A heavy weight hit her between the shoulder blades and she went crashing down. If they captured her they would torture or kill her. She could *not* let them take her.

Fight, Bryn. Struggling out from under his sweaty weight, she choked when he locked a damp, hairy forearm under her throat. As he squeezed, her vision dimmed.

****

A block away, Dec gripped the door handle as Luke pushed the vehicle to breakneck speed, hurtling down the street and around the last corner. There was Bryn, in the shadows fighting off two men, battling her way out of a headlock.

"Fuck!" Dec snarled, body coiled tight. As Luke careened to a stop, Dec and Ben exploded out of the vehicle and took off at a sprint.

Bryn fought loose from one of her attackers, landing an elbow to the groin and scrambling away, but the other man snagged her ankle and hauled her toward the waiting car, pistol in hand. Dec raised his Glock, but didn't have a clear shot.

Swearing, he ran on, oblivious to the bullet ripping past his head. They must be under orders to kidnap her without harming her, but if she kept fighting, they would get more violent.

"Dec!" she cried as the other man lunged at her, then she lashed out with a roundhouse kick, knocking both of them down. Clear, she started to run, but the first guy tackled her and sent her face-first into the pavement.

Ben aimed his pistol and fired, hitting the bastard in the thigh. He staggered and Bryn kicked him in the chest, completing his fall, then shot forward, her eyes so wide Dec could see white all around the irises as she came flying toward them. *Nearly there, baby. Keep running.*

But one of them caught her again. The man flattened her and swept her up in front of him, using her as a shield. At this distance they couldn't shoot without risking hitting Bryn.

"Let her go," Dec growled in Arabic, frantic as the guy wrenched her to the waiting vehicle. Dec kept running, praying for any kind of a clear shot once he was within range.

"Dec!" she screamed, choking as the guy squeezed his arm across her throat and dragged her inside the back seat with him. Her eyes were terrified.

Bryn...

He aimed at the back tire, fired, but he was too far away and the bullet pinged off the fender. He ground to a halt as the black car peeled away from the curb, fishtailed around the corner. Luke skidded to a stop beside him in the truck. He and Ben leapt inside. Dec's stomach twisted as they tailed the kidnappers. He didn't know how he'd bear it if they didn't get her out.

The car didn't have its lights on. It didn't have plates. If they didn't stay close enough to maintain a visual, they'd lose them. The car wove through traffic, running lights and dodging the crowds of people leaving the local market.

Dec's heart sank. She'd dropped the phone fighting with her attackers. They didn't have a GPS chip to track her with. "Don't you lose her," he said to Luke.

Luke sent them flying around the corner, hit the

gas, searching for the car. "Where the fuck did they go?" He stomped on the brake to avoid hitting a group of pedestrians and laid on the horn to hurry them along.

The blood pounded in Dec's ears. He couldn't see the vehicle either. The muscles in his arms tensed. "Ben?"

"Can't see shit out there," he muttered.

Oh my God...

Swearing, Luke blasted the horn again, but it didn't do any good. They waited agonizing seconds for the crowd to clear enough to let them through, and when they did, the car was long gone. They drove around for a while longer, but the effort was futile.

They'd lost her.

Dec stared out the windshield, his chest hollow. The interior of the vehicle was silent as a tomb. Inside his head, he was screaming.

Luke suddenly yanked the wheel and sent them in a one-eighty, sped back down the street. "We gotta find Fahdi. That's the only way we'll find out where they've taken her."

Dec swallowed the lump in his throat. "How?"

"Transmitter. We'll follow its signal." His jaw clenched. He was pissed off at himself, as he should be. Bryn was going to die because he'd ordered her taken to Fahdi's house.

And because Dec had left her there.

****

Bryn thrashed against her captor's hold, tried to bite his hand as he wrapped her wrists with duct tape behind her. He swore and cuffed her across the cheek. Her head snapped sideways, the sting making her eyes water. He'd sat on her to bind her ankles, and now he jammed a knee in the small of her back and hog-tied her limbs together.

She screamed in outrage, but he slapped a piece of tape across her mouth, leaving her to suck air through her flaring nostrils.

She bucked and twisted like a landed fish, but all it did was exhaust her. She kept thinking of the cellar she'd been thrown into. She couldn't stand the thought of going through that again, and this time she'd be alone. But maybe they weren't going to hold her prisoner. Maybe they were just going to kill her.

Terror gripped her. Her body shook. Was Dec still behind them? Was he still coming after her?

The erratic motion of the car eased. She couldn't see out the window. Where were they? The vehicle slowed. Maybe no one was chasing after them anymore.

Had they lost Dec? Her heart thudded. She'd dropped her phone. If Dec lost sight of her, then he didn't have a way to find her. Despair almost choked her.

They drove for a long time. Neither of the men looked at or said anything to her. What were they going to do to her? Torture her? Kill her? Why? For whom?

Fahdi. He must have sent them after her. How else would they have found her? He'd planted the bomb that killed Ali. Was he linked to Tehrazzi? Maybe he'd been offered a reward to bring him to her. It would explain why she was still alive.

Tears gathered and rolled down her cheek, off her nose as she lay on her side on the back seat. Dec had been so close to saving her. The torment in his eyes when he knew he couldn't get to her, haunted her. He'd blame himself for whatever happened to her. He hadn't wanted to leave her at Fahdi's.

She wished they'd had more time together. At least they had the memory of the night of the air strike to hold onto. She wished she'd told him she loved him. Now he'd never know.

The car sped through the darkness, picking up speed. The pavement smoothed out as they accelerated. They were on a highway. She cranked her head up to try and catch a glimpse of a road sign.

Time crawled past but she kept at it until the muscles in her neck screamed from the strain. Finally they passed under a streetlight and she made out the sign.

Basra.

A silent sob shook her. They were headed south away from Baghdad.

Dec and the others would never find her now.

Then the car slowed and finally stopped. The driver's side window hummed as it lowered. Footsteps approached.

Her heart leapt. A checkpoint. Soldiers would inspect the vehicle. She reared up, flailing, screaming through her gag to get their attention. The passenger reached back and swatted her across the side of the head.

"Quiet," he snarled.

She kept on hollering, desperately trying to make eye contact with the Iraqi soldier as he came to the driver's side. He met her gaze, and she went utterly still at the lack of reaction in his face. He looked at the driver, spoke with him, checked the papers he handed him.

Why wasn't he helping her? What wasn't he doing anything?

Then he handed the papers back and waved them through.

Rigid with disbelief, Bryn watched the window go back up as the car started moving. No. *No!*

She tried to understand what had just happened. Had her captors paid him to let them through? The soldier had given her as much

287

attention as a bag of groceries.

Had to be one of Tehrazzi's men.

Shit, were they taking her to Tehrazzi? Her blood turned to ice.

The car picked up speed, the engine whirring smoothly as they sped into the darkness.

Holding back her tears so her captors wouldn't hear her, she dropped her head against the upholstery and squeezed her eyes shut. She thought of all the ways there were to kill someone.

Please God, when it happens, let it be quick.

****

Luke was in a cold rage as they drove into the desert, following the transmitter's signal with the GPS. They'd hopped a helo to Mosul, then grabbed a truck to take them the rest of the way to Fahdi. Looked like the bastard was trying to make a run for the Iranian border.

It took a lot for Luke to get worked up like this, but Fahdi's treachery had pushed him from pissed off to lethal. He wanted answers, from both him *and* Sam. And he wanted them yesterday.

Most of all, he wanted Bryn back, safe. The guilt was eating him up. If she died, it was completely his fault.

Beside him in the passenger seat, Dec sat staring at the pictures of Sam with Fahdi and his wife from the dossier Davis had compiled for Luke. He'd given it to Dec to try and take his mind off what might be happening to Bryn, after saying whoever had taken Bryn wouldn't kill her because Tehrazzi—and he was certain that's who was behind Fahdi's actions—would want her himself. Probably didn't help worth a damn, but it was the best he could do.

"We still don't know for sure Sam's involved,"

Luke offered, more to Ben than Dec, since he'd seemed most troubled about Sam's possible role in all this. All that was eclipsed by their worry for Bryn now anyway. Ben was halfway through a roll of Tums already. Dec looked sick to his stomach.

Christ, where had he gone wrong? He'd never made so many mistakes, and never with his crew. Fahdi he'd never completely trusted because of his role as informant, but Sam... He'd trusted her, as had Rhys and Ben. Hell, they all had.

Her being AWOL on top of everything else made him damned uneasy. He'd bet his right nut she had to have known what Fahdi was up to. She did all the transmitters and GPS chips, after all. How deep was she into this? Had whoever had broken into her place been pumping her for information all along?

She'd seemed so sincere when she'd come to him only this morning with her theory about Fahdi. Either she was innocent and merely behaving suspiciously, or she was one hell of an actress and in it up to her pretty neck. He'd dealt with a few of both examples over the years.

Ben sighed. "It doesn't compute. Even if she was in with Fahdi, she would never have endangered Bryn."

"Unless she had to," Luke put in. "Maybe they've threatened her."

"Or someone she cares about," Dec added.

"Most likely her cousin," Luke said. "Rhys spent time with both of them in Paris and said they're real close. He mentioned something about a photo of the pair of them at Sam's place this morning."

Ben wiped a hand over his goatee. "Christ. I never saw this coming. You?"

Luke balled his fists. "I had a hunch Fahdi was trying to protect his family by playing both sides of the fence. Didn't know he'd jumped clean over it."

A tense silence passed.

Ben finally cleared his throat. "This whole CIA shit is whacked, man. In a military op, everything's black and white. Since I came on with you, there's been nothing but gray."

"It's an acquired taste," he said dryly.

"When this is over I'm gonna stick to private security."

"Want a job?"

"What do you mean?"

"After we get Bryn back and I nail Tehrazzi and his cell, I'm gonna start my own company. Bryn's offered to rent me her father's place for headquarters. I want solid guys I can trust. You interested?"

Ben's brow creased. "Maybe."

"What is it with you and Tehrazzi, anyway?" Dec grumbled. "Is he the guy who's going to propel you to fame and fortune at the end of your career, or is it personal?"

Luke didn't give a shit about fame or fortune. "Personal. Very."

"Wanna enlighten us? I think we could use the distraction right about now."

Luke sighed. No shit. "Tehrazzi and I go way back. Over twenty years."

"How's that?"

"A little war between the Russians and the Afghans. The U.S. thought it was a hell of an idea to get in there and help defeat the Communists, and I was sent to train some mujahedin."

Dec's shot him a disbelieving look. "You trained Tehrazzi?"

"Yep. Created him and a few other monsters. Even had a hand in making America's former public enemy number one."

"No way, bin Laden?"

"I don't do anything half-assed. Even my fuck-ups." Which were few, but catastrophic. Some of he world's most dangerous terrorists. Abandoning his wife and kid. Sending his son's best friend to her death...

No. She'll be okay until she gets to Tehrazzi. They still had some time to find her and get her out.

"Christ," Dec said. "What a mess."

"Yep. So I've made it my personal mission to clean this one up before I die."

Ben raised a brow. "You gonna stick at it that long?"

"Long as it takes." Along the way he'd given up everything that mattered to him. He didn't give a shit if he died, so long as he made everything right first. The chance for redemption was all that kept him going.

Chapter Twenty

Day 12, Iraqi Desert outside Basra

Bryn tried to stop trembling in the cave dug into the hillside. Her kidnappers had blindfolded her before carrying her in and dumping her here hours ago. She'd managed to wriggle around enough to get the blindfold off, but her face was scraped up from her efforts.

At least she could see now. Even though it was pitch dark, she felt a little less helpless to know she'd be able to see them when they came for her.

She'd lain on her side all night, her hands and feet bound behind her. They'd long since gone numb. She'd dropped off into an exhausted doze, and woken to the sound of her own cries, muffled behind the tape. She'd dreamed Dec had come for her. He'd ripped the tape away and pulled her into his strong arms. Told her he loved her.

Tears threatened. No way he could know where she was.

She'd come full circle now. A prisoner again, left to wither away in the darkness. Only this time she was alone, didn't even have her father's presence to comfort her.

Calm down. Breathe. Panicking won't help. Keep your head clear.

Her breaths evened. She focused on her memories of Dec to keep her composure.

Men moved around outside in the darkness. Soldiers? She could hear them talking, but couldn't understand more than a few words and phrases. She didn't know where she was, other than somewhere close to Basra. She had no idea how many of them there were.

Not that it mattered. She was trussed up and powerless, waiting to find out who wanted her here and what they would do to her. She was terrified it was Tehrazzi.

The flap covering the entrance pushed open. She sucked in a breath when a tall man appeared, carrying a flashlight. He set in on the ground. The white beam pointed to the ceiling, illuminating his face. Her heart stuttered.

Farouk Tehrazzi.

His green eyes glittered down at her, fanatical in their glee. He strode up to her, his feet crunching on the sand. He bent and reached out a hand. She cringed, ducking her head away, but he merely ripped the tape from her mouth. She gasped at the quick sting.

"Luke Hutchinson. Where is he?"

The sharp question threw her. "What?"

He nudged her with the toe of his boot. "You heard me. Tell me where he is."

"I-I don't know."

His smile was cruel. "You don't think I can force it out of you?"

She remembered the pictures of Qamar and husband's headless bodies. The gaping hole blasted through Masood's chest. Oh, God...

"I know you're working with him. Where is he?"

"I don't know."

He hit her in the belly with his boot. Not too hard, but letting her know he was running out of patience. "Where?"

"I—your men kidnapped me off the damn street! How am I supposed to know where he is?" It surprised her she could get the words out of her tight throat.

293

His stare never wavered. "Still in Baghdad, then. Does he know where I am?"

"I don't know." She would not cry. She wouldn't give him the satisfaction.

"He will want you back."

Yes, but how would he ever find her? They had no way to track her.

Tehrazzi continued to stare at her, his face thoughtful. It was almost worse that he was a handsome man. It made the blackened soul inside that much more heinous. She trembled at the thought of how he would kill her. Would he do it himself? Or would he leave it for his bodyguard? She didn't want to die screaming and thrashing. Her heart pounded so hard it felt like it might explode.

"Perhaps you will be of use to me yet. Perhaps I should not kill you until you have served your purpose."

In an instant, she knew what he was saying. He wanted to use her to get to Luke. And through Luke, Dec. And the twins.

She'd be damned if she'd help him. He'd taken enough from her already without taking her soul for aiding in the death of people she cared about. Loved.

The fear began to fade. A rush of anger swept it away. *You spineless coward. Terrorizing me while I'm tied up and helpless. Because you're secretly afraid of me. Why don't you untie me and fight me like a man?*

She drilled him with a contemptuous glare. "I won't help you."

He sneered. "You don't have a choice."

Oh yes, she did. She could choose to die rather than submit. She swallowed. Did she have the strength to go through with it? Would she break before she died? "What have I ever done to you?"

"You escaped me."

"Why did you kidnap me?"

"You were not my intended target. Your father was."

"You killed him." Her voice shook.

"Your father was responsible for the death of thousands."

The rage kept building. This one man had caused so much pain and suffering. How could God let that happen? "I thought Islam forbade the harming of innocents."

His mouth tightened, went white around the edges. "Do not presume to lecture me on my religion. Arrogant infidel whore."

"What do you want from me?" She almost screamed it at him. "Money?"

"Money," he spat. "I have more money than you could ever dream of."

"Then what—weapons? Power?"

"Justice."

Justice? Is that what his twisted mind thought he was meting out every time he killed someone? Or sold explosives so a suicide bomber could blow up a crowd of innocent women and children in a marketplace? *You piece of shit.*

"Justice for all the Muslims that have suffered and died at the hands of men like your father and Hutchinson. Allah will wipe them and all the unbelievers from the face of the earth."

He was insane. "You sick freak—"

His eyes flared. "Do not *dare* speak to me like that."

"I hate you," she spat. "When you burn in hell after you die, I hope all you see is my father's face *and* mine."

His expression tightened. His hand twitched, went to the scabbard on his belt. Bryn's gaze locked on the hilt of the knife. Her belly quivered. If she kept pushing him, would he lose control and kill her right here? Would it be better than waiting? Would it be quicker, less painful if he did it while he was enraged?

Sweat beaded her chilled body. Faced with the reality of such a hideous death, she cringed. She didn't know if she had the courage to go through with it.

"You wish to die?"

I want to live!

His hand curled around the hilt of the knife. A hiss filled the silence as it left its scabbard. The blade gleamed silver in the stark beam from the flashlight. One side of his mouth kicked up. The promise of death was in his eyes. She tensed. Terror flooded her.

"Sir?"

She jerked her gaze to the opening at the man's voice.

Tehrazzi paused, but she could still feel his gaze burning her. "What?" he snarled.

Sucking in short bursts of air, Bryn listened as they spoke in Arabic. Something about weapons. Soldiers. When the other man left, Tehrazzi kept staring at her. His jaw muscles worked. His fingers flexed on the knife.

He wanted to kill her. It was all over his face. But then he sheathed the blade. She sagged, breath exploding out of her aching lungs. Her muscles quivered.

"You have been given a short reprieve. You can lay there and think about how my knife will feel on your flesh until I come back to finish this."

He snatched up the flashlight and stormed out.

****

Iraqi Desert outside Tikrit

Through the grimy window, Luke watched

Fahdi pull the pickup to a stop in front of the dilapidated hut, then moved into the shadows and sat in the wooden chair he'd set in the corner.

Fahdi's family was safe, halfway to Jordan by now to stay with his wife's relatives. But Fahdi wasn't safe. Not by a long shot.

Luke wasn't stupid. Bryn's capture was going to give Fahdi enough money to support his family for years to come once they crossed the border to start a new life in Iran. Bastard.

The truck door opened, then slammed shut a moment later. Fahdi had stopped in Tikrit to strip off his old clothes, shoes and watch and toss them in the garbage, probably paranoid someone had planted tracking devices on him, like Tehrazzi had before. Too bad the dumb bastard hadn't thought to take off all his jewelry.

Apparently thinking he'd outsmart everyone by switching vehicles, Fahdi had dumped the last one in Tikrit and stolen the truck from a construction site.

Luke's hand tightened on the grip of his pistol. Too bad Fahdi was probably going to live through the coming interrogation.

Through that tiny window from his seated position, Luke watched him pull a penlight from his pocket to check the door of his temporary home, seeking anything suspicious. Apparently finding everything as it should be, he unlocked it and pushed it open.

It swung with a creak, and he stood still in the darkness, listening while the musty air moved around the room. With a relieved sigh, he stepped inside and secured the door before flipping on the only light.

"Fahdi."

Stifling a shriek, he whirled around and stumbled backward. "Jesus and Allah..."

Luke sat in the chair in the corner with a cold expression on his face, Sig-Sauer in his right hand. The safety was off, and a round was chambered. "Fancy meeting you here."

"H-how did you—"

Luke rose from the chair, and Fahdi cowered against the door.

But when Luke came close enough, he merely lifted his free hand and tapped the pendant hanging from the chain around Fahdi's neck. With his index finger, he flipped it over. "Surprise."

Fahdi glanced down at it, eyes widening when he saw the tiny micro-transmitter attached to the back of it.

"B-but how—" The breath hissed out of his lungs. "Miss Sam? She did this?"

As Luke stared holes into Fahdi's face, his informant had his answer. "I suspected you all along."

Fahdi opened his mouth to babble an explanation, but Luke caught his wrist and yanked it up hard, stopping just short of snapping the bones. Fahdi whimpered and rose onto his toes to alleviate the pressure. "By the way, Ali sends his regards," Luke drawled, dropping a chunk of metal onto Fahdi's palm.

Fahdi flinched and looked down at the dial of Ali's watch, singed and blackened from the explosion that had killed him. From the bomb Fahdi had planted. Bits of charred skin still clung to the back of it.

Fahdi jerked his hand away like the dial was still burning hot, tossing it to the floor. He looked like he wanted to throw up. His eyes bugged out like golf balls.

"So," Luke said, shifting the pistol in his grip. Not that he needed it. He could kill Fahdi in any number of ways with his bare hands, and right now he was resisting the impulse to do just that. "Where's Bryn? Not to mention Tehrazzi and your pal Sam."

Fahdi gulped.

"You gonna tell me what I want to know? Or should I leave you for Tehrazzi to interrogate so you can explain why I'm still alive?"

A bead of sweat trickled down his temple. He nodded frantically. "I-I'll tell you..."

Luke pinned him with a merciless gaze. "Then get the fuck to it before I change my mind."

****

Day 12, Baghdad
Late night

Ben rolled his head on his neck to ease the tension in his shoulders and tightened his grip on the steering wheel. He pulled out of the airfield, the helo he'd taken back to Baghdad parked on the tarmac in the rearview mirror.

He'd drawn the short straw and flown back with Fahdi to turn him over to the CIA for further questioning. The asshole was on his way to a secure facility right now. Too bad the U.S. didn't sanction torture.

At least they knew Bryn was in a camp outside Basra. Luke and Dec were already down there with Rhys to rendezvous with a SEAL team and plan her extraction. If they got real lucky, they might get Tehrazzi in the bargain.

Ben was going straight to the TOC to find out if there was any information on the op yet. It still rankled that he hadn't been able to go along, but they needed someone from the team to monitor the op from the TOC. He'd have loved to be going after Bryn. His guts burned with apprehension about what they might have done to her.

He believed Luke that she would be kept alive for Tehrazzi. He clung to the hope they weren't too late.

His phone beeped from his belt, announcing he'd just received a text message. Probably Rhys. Keeping his eyes on the road, he pulled it out, waiting until he slowed at an intersection to glance at the display. When he saw Sam's number, he skidded to a stop.

What the...

How did Sam know to contact him? He and Davis were the only ones not on the op, and he'd only just arrived back in Baghdad. Who had told her? Where the hell was she?

He read the message.

Intel leakd. Op cmpmisd. Abort.

The blood froze in his veins. "Fuck!"

Breath sawing in and out, he punched in the number for the TOC and floored the Suburban. Mother of God, what had Sam done?

When someone came on the line, he ran right over top of them, demanding to speak with the officer in charge. As the general's voice came through, he blurted, "This is Ben Sinclair—sir, the op has been compromised, recommend emergency action to abort mission. Repeat, abort mission."

Racing through the back streets of Baghdad, he prayed he wasn't too late.

****

Day 13, outside Basra

Tehrazzi finished his prayer and rose in the darkness. Overhead the stars shone like a thousand lanterns in the ebony sky. The wind was cool against his face. In a few hours, the air would warm and the sun would crest over the hills near the Iranian border.

He'd calmed himself sufficiently now to deal with Daoud's daughter. He wasn't sure yet if he would kill her. She may still be of use to him. He would prefer not taint his soul with the blood of an innocent woman. He would rather leave that to his bodyguard, Assoud. But if he must, he would do it himself, and pray that Allah would understand.

He hedged. She might be the key to his teacher.

He approached the blanket serving as a flap on the cave dug into the hillside, swept it back and switched on the flashlight. She lifted her head, squinted in the bright light, but not before he saw the stab of fear in her eyes. It lasted only an instant.

She masked her unease, replaced it with a disdainful expression that made it seem she was looking down her nose at him even though she was tied up and lying on the ground.

A part of him truly admired her bravery. He'd known many men who hadn't shown a fraction of that courage when faced with death.

He waited, staring into her eyes as the tension in her grew. She was wondering if he would kill her now, yet she knew there was nothing she could do to stop him. Though she met his gaze, her breaths were choppy. Her shoulders spasmed.

He drew his hand toward his knife, taking pleasure in the way her eyes tracked the motion. He curled his fingers around the cold hilt. Squeezed. Held the position. Her gaze flew up to his. She managed a glare.

He almost smiled. Such valor, wasted in a woman's body. What should he do with her?

His muscles jerked as his phone went off. Keeping his grip on the knife, he answered, listened as his bodyguard reported in. Assoud detailed the information they'd gotten from the other American woman working for his teacher. He went rigid. He hung up and stared into Daoud's daughter's black eyes. Black as the desert night, black as death.

His death.

The Americans were planning a surprise attack. His teacher, the man who had created him, the only man he'd ever truly feared, had come at last.

A wave of fear crashed over him. Took him under, deep inside his subconscious where all his doubts and suspicions slept. It almost suffocated him.

His teacher would kill him. He must flee. Terror stole his breath, tightened all his muscles until they twitched. The Americans would order an air strike, and blow away the hillside to get him.

They'd almost done it the night Ghaliya had saved him.

His heart beat a frantic rhythm beneath his ribs. He'd never escape their aircraft from here.

His wild gaze refocused on his prisoner, a debilitating weakness taking over. How would he escape? He had to move, now, before it was too late. He'd have to leave his prisoner behind—

His prisoner.

He stilled. His mind cleared.

Daoud's daughter. Of course.

The paralyzing fear ebbed. It fell away until calm settled over his racing heart. His heartbeat slowed, his breathing evened. The sweat dried on his clammy skin.

Allah had sent her to him for this reason. He knew it to the marrow of his bones. She was the answer. His teacher would not risk killing her, not even to get to him. She was too close with his family. Nothing mattered more to his teacher than his wife and son. Killing Daoud's daughter would hurt them deeply.

No, his teacher would not sacrifice her life to kill him. While she was here, he would be safe.

Ironically, she was his only protection now. He had to keep the Americans from getting her.

He would escape. Take her along to prevent them from shooting him. God had protected him from his teacher before. Why spare his life unless he was meant to live, to serve His higher purpose?

Yes, he would use her to escape. Mind free, he left her staring after him with wide eyes to arrange safe transport.

****

Day 13, Desert outside Basra

A few hours before dawn, Dec crouched in position at the head of his SEAL team, muscles tense as he waited for the green light. They'd inserted by helo, fast-roping into a shallow canyon three klicks from their target near Basra and proceeded on foot to maintain surprise and silence.

Luke hunkered beside him, scanning through his NVGs, while Rhys was behind with the rest of the team, maintaining the GPS and satellite links with Ben back at the TOC in Baghdad.

Tehrazzi was reportedly in these hills, over the ridge in a cave where the Air Force had launched a series of DJAMs earlier to destroy a hidden weapons cache. Current intelligence said Tehrazzi felt safe there, that because of the recent air strikes the biggest danger was over.

It worked to their advantage, because Tehrazzi sure as hell shouldn't be expecting a team of SEALs to come storming into his camp, on a mission to destroy the cell before Tehrazzi and his followers could reach the Iranian border. That's what the top brass wanted.

Dec had a different focus. The most important part of the mission: extract the principal. Again.

All night he'd been tormented with fears for Bryn's safety, but now he had to keep his mind on his task. His men's lives depended on him maintaining his focus. At Luke's signal, they started forward, keeping low as they picked their way over the rough ground, dropping to their bellies at the top of the ridge.

Luke indicated he saw three armed guards at the perimeter and Dec relayed the message to the team, murmured it into his mic for HQ. He called everyone into position and gave directions using hand signals: circle around to the east and come in from behind, surrounding the camp.

Looking into his men's camouflaged, serious faces, his adrenaline pumped hot, his muscles gathering for the burst of speed. At Luke's command he took off at a run, passing him as he led his teammates down the slope.

He landed on the balls of his feet to muffle the sound, his boots hitting the sand with quiet thuds. His quads and hamstrings hummed with power as he sprinted down a rise and into a wash, throwing himself flat and put his riflescope to his eye. As the others fell in beside him, his eyes scanned the horizon for any new threats.

When everyone came back with an all clear, Dec pushed up and moved them to a protected position behind a group of boulders less than two hundred yards from their target. From here, the scent of smoke from the campfires reached them. Low voices carried on the air. Estimates put fifteen to thirty men down there.

"LT, sentry at ten o'clock high."

Dec's head swung around and up to his left. Sure enough, a figure stood poised on the rim of a cliff.

"Four o'clock high."

Shit.

"One o'clock low."

Christ. He didn't like the feel of this at all. They were being surrounded. And if they fired now, they'd give away their position before they made their attack. He glanced back at Luke, whose jaw flexed.

"Rhys," he whispered into the radio, loud as he dared, never taking his eyes off the man on the cliff to his left, "request CAS." Close air support was key here.

"Roger that." Rhys called in the request over the radio to the aircraft in the area.

They'd have to haul ass to gain better cover, and then the Air Force or Navy could pick the sentries off. The trick was getting the timing just right so that Dec and the others were already moving when the jets or gunships rolled in to lay down covering fire.

Distant shouts shattered the silence, echoing through the warm air. They'd been spotted.

No way the enemy should have seen them yet. Jesus, had they walked into an ambush?

"Time's up," Luke muttered as more of Tehrazzi's men scrambled into position above them, hovering like vultures. "Get over there and cover all exit routes. Make sure that bastard doesn't slip away again."

"Go, go!" Dec commanded, tearing out into the open, sprinting for the camp.

A thump reverberated through his chest. Acting on instinct, he hit the deck and covered his head as the mortar round exploded to his right. The blast rattled his ears as he staggered to his feet and took off again. Another blast, closer this time, two more in rapid succession.

In the bright flashes he saw his teammates hunkered down and spread out behind him, Tehrazzi's followers rushing toward them with RPGs and rifles. Dec raised his M4 and squeezed off a few

305

rounds, dropping two of them, arms flinging upwards as they fell. Bullets zinged past, tracers glowing red in the darkness. He flattened himself as deep as he could into the cool sand, fighting to stay in control, his mind racing.

Please let Bryn still be alive in there.

Another mortar round exploded close beside him, the impact enough to knock the breath out of him. He struggled up onto his elbows and fired again. When would their air support get here?

Luke dropped down beside him, yelling in his ear. "Gun ships are six minutes out."

"Keep moving," he shouted back, sweeping an arc of fire in front of them. If they could eliminate enough of the enemy to free Bryn, the air support could take care of everything else. Heart bursting, he leapt up and raced onward, picking off men as they came into view.

More and more streamed out of the cave. Shit, their intel had been way off the mark. If Dec and his team made the attack now, they'd take heavy casualties.

He fired off another round and looked out at the camp, thinking of Bryn as he gauged the distance. Too much open ground to cross. He swept his gaze over his men, lying flat as they picked off the enemy, then back to the camp.

He felt like he was being torn in two. He wanted to go now, rescue her, but he had others' safety to think of. He was responsible for the lives of his men. There were seven of them. One of her.

A curl of smoke from a campfire across the ridge rose into the air. Bryn was right there, might still be alive. If she was, she'd be terrified. Alone. Cold. Was she praying for him to find her? A picture of her formed, curled tight in a ball, rocking herself, eyes puffy from crying.

He thought his heart would break. *I'm here,*

baby. Please hold on.

Rounds whizzed past, thudding into the sand around them. He shot off another controlled burst. They had to move back. Going forward now was suicide.

His stomach knotted. The decision had already been made for him. He didn't have a choice. He was an officer. His first responsibility was to his team. Much as it killed him, he had to take his heart out of the equation. Had to take his men to safety. When the air support cleared off some of the enemy, they could make another attempt.

"Fall back," he shouted, heart heavy as a rock in his aching chest. He led his team to the relative safety of the cliffs, the spurt of adrenaline propelling him over the last stretch of open ground. The team closed ranks in a semi-circle, firing up at the cliff and around their horizon. Rhys moved in beside him, shouted down at him. "Air support inbound."

"When?"

"Two minutes."

"Relay the coordinates."

Rhys crouched behind the protective wall the team made for him and whipped out a grid map, yelling rapid instructions over the radio. An RPG round shrieked overhead and impacted higher up the cliff, slamming into the rock face. Chunks of debris rained down on them like deadly hail.

Dec rolled to his knees, shaken and disoriented. As the ringing in his ears dissipated, he caught the high-pitched roar of the cavalry overhead. Fighting to stay upright, he kept firing, hearing Rhys on the radio.

"Thirty seconds to target, danger close." He flashed Dec a grim look.

They were too close to the target and could never make it out of range within thirty seconds.

Thirty seconds, and Bryn was still in there...

Dec's heart tripped. "Move out! Go, go!"

He grabbed the man nearest him and tore over the open ground, spewing rounds for covering fire. When he glanced back, all his teammates were hauling ass, but the roar of a jet engine pierced the din.

A streak of light split the air. A missile, off course, hurtling toward them.

"Take cover!" he bellowed, diving onto his front.

The warhead roared through the sky. Impacted too close. A massive shockwave blew outward. The earth rolled beneath his feet. Pitched him upward.

His vision dimmed. He hurtled through the air, crushing pain ripping through his chest as darkness took him.

****

The sudden gunfire outside, popping noises, like fireworks, made Bryn's breath catch. Her heart lurched. A battle. With Americans? Dec might be out there. Was a team trying to rescue her?

Shouts reached her as men ran past the dugout, barking orders. They scrambled down the slope. She struggled to her side, lay there with her muscles tensed.

She'd prayed for a rescue, begged Dec to come for her. But what if he was out there right now, and something happened to him? She loved him. She probably wasn't going to make it out of this shelter. She didn't want Dec to die for her. She at least wanted him to make it back home.

Voices. Outside the opening. She recognized Tehrazzi's. Her belly tightened. Was he coming back to kill her?

He appeared through the blanket flap. His eyes met hers as he approached, pulling a knife from his belt.

She shrank back, stomach clenching at the wickedly sharp blade he wielded. *Oh God, this is it. I'm going to die.*

Smothering a scream as he stalked over, she squeezed her eyes shut, turned her head away as though it would shield her from what he was about to do to her. She braced herself for the first terrible burn of the blade in her skin.

He grabbed her shoulder and flipped her onto her stomach. A scream of denial and fear stuck in her throat.

But he didn't stab her. He seized her foot and sawed through the tape. He let go, and her legs and arms fell apart. Her legs hit the ground with a thud. She jerked her gaze up, staring at him warily while she got to her knees.

His green gaze touched hers for a moment before he bent and grabbed her wrists. She ducked her head and flinched as he sliced her hands free. They dropped to her sides, leaden as the blood rushed back. She sucked in a breath at the hot sting.

"Get up."

Eyes wide, she gaped at him. Was he going to free her feet as well?

He slid his knife back in its scabbard at his waist.

Her breath trembled in and out. She eyed him warily.

"You may thank Allah for sparing you. He has let you live so that you may help me escape."

The hell she would. Her eyes narrowed. Her fingers flexed, the burn fading. Strength flowed into her muscles along with the blood. A terrible rage invaded her. This man had taken everything from her. Her father. Her freedom. Her chance with Dec. Maybe her life, when he was finished with her.

No more.

The words echoed in her skull. She would not go

without a fight. She would show him just how strong she was. He would pay for what he'd done to her. In blood and bruises wrought by her own hands.

He produced a roll of duct tape, advanced toward her.

She stared holes into his face. "I don't think so."

He stilled a moment, as though she'd surprised him. Then he grinned. "Give me your hands."

She trembled with fury. "Come get them."

His jaw tensed, irritation snapping in his eyes. He reached for her.

Bryn shot her hand around his wrist, wrenched it up and back and threw him over her hip. He hit the ground with a grunt and swiveled about to glare at her. She hopped back, her linked ankles making it hard to keep her balance, but she managed, keeping her hands up, her body squared.

Come on, you bastard. Fight me.

Tehrazzi climbed to his feet and brushed at his robes, giving her a look of contempt. "You would not like me to lose my temper."

"Fuck you." She was out of her head with anger. "You want me? Untie my feet and fight me like a man."

For a moment she thought he might, his expression was so enraged. But then he seemed to gather himself and the hot glow left his eyes. He picked up the tape and then drew his knife.

Her skin shriveled.

"Easy way, or hard way, Miss Daoud. Your choice."

When he tried to grab her again, she lashed out at the wrist of his knife hand with a cry, knocked it out of his grip. A euphoric haze swamped her. A hysterical laugh brimmed. She wasn't powerless. She was strong. She threw a punch at his head.

He ducked back, her knuckles grazing his beard. But the punch had her falling forward, and her feet couldn't keep up with the momentum. Her knees hit the ground, and in a heartbeat he was on her, straddling her hips and wrenching her head up with a muscular arm wrapped around her neck. She screeched in outrage, twisting up to bash him with her skull, trying to get air.

He nailed her between the shoulders with the hilt of his knife. Her arms went numb, fell away from his. He released her throat.

"Bastard," she hissed, tears stinging because she knew it was over. He had her wrists taped up before she could move her arms, and hefted her onto his shoulder.

She tried to plow an elbow into his face but he dodged it and whacked her in the head hard enough to make the cave spin. Before her head cleared he had her outside and...

Slung her over the back of a horse.

She reared up just as he leapt on behind her. Facedown with her arms pinned beneath her, she was helpless to fight his powerful grip. He jammed one elbow into her spine to hold her still and drove his heels into the horse's sides, sending them rocketing forward over the sand.

****

Luke struggled up on his knees in the aftermath of the explosion. His head rang like a bell inside his helmet. Jesus, he'd almost been killed by friendly fire.

He fumbled to get the NVGs back in place. Glancing around, he shook his head to clear his blurry vision and saw Rhys pound over to the two bodies lying in the sand. Luke staggered over. McCabe lay unconscious as Rhys checked his vitals.

"Got a pulse," he said. "And he's still breathing, but not well."

Luke was already calling for a Medevac. Shots peppered the ground around them. He checked the other SEAL. Still alive, but his chances of surviving the shrapnel wounds to his belly were slim. He and Rhys dragged the SEALs behind some rocks.

"Stay with them until the medics arrive," he told Rhys, and rose to head back to the rest of the team. His knees buckled but he caught himself, gritted his teeth and rushed to help the others.

They were still firing, holding their own when he got to them. "Dec's down," he shouted to them. "Hold your positions until the air support clears the ridge." He flattened himself on the ground when another round detonated close by. He felt the rush of hot air as the debris flew past his head. Raising his rifle, he picked off a figure running at them.

In the distance, something caught his eye. He glimpsed a figure on top of the ridge. Heart racing, he zoomed in with his NVGs and tightened the focus. His breath caught. Bryn and Tehrazzi. On horseback.

She was still alive.

Pulled to them like a magnet, he shoved to his feet.

"Sir!"

He spared a glance at the young SEAL beside him. His eyes were wide.

"I'm going after him—the rest of you stay here," he shouted over the gunfire. "Medevac's inbound. Lay down covering fire for me—"

"But sir—"

"Covering fire. Now," he snapped, fighting off waves of dizziness.

The kid relayed the order, and the SEALs started sweeping the area with short bursts. Luke sprinted across the open desert, heading for the ridge. He couldn't call for air support now. Not while Tehrazzi had Bryn with him. Luke was going to have to pick him off with his rifle.

Bullets sliced through the air. Mortars whistled overhead. He kept running. His chest burned. His thighs ached. He reached the edge of the slope, scrambled up it with his rifle flung across his back. His fingers dug into the earth. He clawed his way up to the top, lay panting on his belly as he scanned the desolate ridge for Tehrazzi, weapon up. The ground tilted. He shook his head sharply.

Stay tight. You've almost got him.

The world righted itself.

No sign of them. They'd disappeared over the ridge. Panic rose. He forced it away and dropped his eyes to the ground.

There in the distance. Hoof prints.

No way could he catch up on foot, and the Air Force had its hands full. If he had to wait for another helo to pick him up, he might lose the path. He tore back toward the camp, ignoring the nausea that boiled up each time his head jarred when his feet hit the ground. Firing and hitting a sentry, he raked his gaze over the site. A motorbike. There by the dugout.

He raced over and grabbed it, fired it up. The engine sputtered and caught, roared to life. At a tingle between his shoulder blades he glanced up, saw the rifle swinging toward him. Luke fired, hitting the guy in the chest.

Twisting the throttle, he slung around and took off to pick up the trail. Finding the place where his footprints began, he tracked the hoof prints over the rise. He followed them down the bank and across the wadi.

Something made him stop. The bike idled beneath him.

This route led down to the river basin. Why would Tehrazzi come this way?

You trained him. He thinks like you. What would

313

you do?

He'd be hauling ass to the Iranian border. Which was in the opposite direction.

He blinked to clear his vision, stared at the hoof prints, precious seconds ticking past. Now that he studied them more closely, they were odd looking. Too clearly defined. Horseshoes? He frowned. Tehrazzi didn't shoe his horses. Why would he need to have his horse shod? Unless...

Shit. Had the bastard nailed the shoes on backward, to lead anyone following him in the opposite direction?

Like he'd just done. He could almost hear Tehrazzi's delighted laughter whispering in the wind.

His head pounded sickeningly. "Christ I hate you," he breathed, and sped back the way he'd come, following the tracks toward the border.

****

The scream of a jet broke through the gunfire as a fighter streaked overhead. Behind her, Tehrazzi cursed and spurred the horse to run faster. The animal put its head down and lengthened its strides, eating up the ground. A terrific explosion rocked the air. The concussion forced the air out of her lungs, thudded deep in her chest.

The horse stumbled as the shockwave rippled through the earth, but kept its footing, galloping away from the cloud of dust rising above where the camp had been only seconds before.

She would have been in there if Tehrazzi hadn't needed her for cover. She would already be dead. Maybe that would have been a kinder way to go than what he had planned for her.

Bryn's mind raced as she flew across the desert in Tehrazzi's unbreakable grip. He'd gotten away.

He wouldn't need her anymore. If she wanted even a chance of surviving, she had to come up with a way to escape before he stopped the horse.

The wind whistled past her, making her eyes water. The pounding of hooves was loud in the quiet. Tehrazzi stared straight ahead, taking them farther away from the camp. Where was he going? Didn't matter. She had to get away.

Her eyes surveyed the terrain. Some gullies. A few drop-offs. Mostly rolling landscape. She could jump. If she did, would he stop and come back for her? Or would he keep going? Maybe she could get his gun, or the knife she'd seen at his waist. She might be able to get a shot at him. Would she be able to pull the trigger? Stab him?

Yes.

The realization shocked her. She hated him enough to kill him. If that was her only chance to get away, she would do it.

But he was quick. Well trained, better than she was. She'd only get one chance with this. If she failed, he'd kill her for sure.

****

Dec came to. Someone was lifting him roughly. Pain tore through his chest. *Can't breathe.* He tried to push away.

"It's okay, man." Rhys's face peered down at him. He slung him over his shoulder. "Take it easy. Helo's waiting."

Dec tried to suck in air. Couldn't.

No air. Choking.

His vision turned gray around the edges. Rhys's voice, urgent. Rotor blades whirring. More hands on him. Pressing down where the pain hurt the worst. His body jerked.

Bryn. Was she alive? Had someone gotten her

out?

"Don't," he gasped, struggling. "Can't leave—"
They had to get Bryn out.

"Hold him down."

No! "Bryn... Is she—?"

"Easy, Lieutenant."

Someone put a mask on his face. *Still can't breathe.* He clawed at the hands holding the mask down, striving to escape his own body. *Pain's so bad. Can't stand it.*

"Can you sedate him?"

"Soon as I get this line in him."

The rotors sped up. The floor tilted.

Bryn... Can't leave her... He loved her. Didn't want to go on breathing if she was dead.

Ping. Ping. Pop. Small arms fire hit the chopper.

Rat-a-tat-tat, rat-a-tat-tat. Machine gun returning fire.

Can't. Fucking. Breathe.

Bang!

The rotors whined. The aircraft tilted sharply and then dropped.

The hands holding him clenched tight. "Shit!"

"Brace yourselves! We're going down!"

Can't breathe. Helo crashing. Going to die.

He pushed the thought away, then pictured Bryn's face...igniting a desperate will to live.

****

The whap of rotors sounded. Luke glanced over his shoulder, watched the helo climb. One of theirs. The Medevac he'd called for McCabe. He floored the bike, slowly gaining on the horse.

You're not getting away this time, you bastard.

Something exploded.

Luke's head whipped up. Jesus. A round had hit the helo. He saw the sparks from its tail rotor.

Heard the disruption in the engine, the whine as it lost altitude. "Shit," he whispered, heart pounding as it plummeted.

The ground shook when it hit. Relief flooded him when no fireball exploded. Maybe the aircraft was still intact. Maybe the guys had survived. *Goddamn.* Nothing more he could do for them, he was too far away. The others on the ground would have to order air support and another extract.

He had Tehrazzi in his sights. He wasn't stopping now. Couldn't. Everything hinged on him capturing the bastard. If he couldn't do that, he'd kill him. Or die trying.

He glued his eyes to the back of the horse. He was close enough to tell the color now. Deep brown. The engine screamed as he opened up the throttle, the wheels spinning in the dusty ground. Tehrazzi was right in front of him. His heart slammed. He'd waited six years for this. He was going to end this *now*.

****

The horse was tiring. Its nostrils flared wide as it tried to pull in more air, its sides heaving with the strain of carrying them at a full gallop for so long. They were slowing. If Bryn was going to jump, she was going to have to do it soon, before the animal stopped.

She flexed her fingers, getting the blood flowing through them so she could grab for the pistol in his belt. She'd already planned out the movement.

She was going to brace her bound feet against the horse, shove up with every bit of strength she had and throw her head up into his face. At the same time, she'd have to grab the gun with her bound hands and smash her elbow into him as she threw herself off the horse somehow. She'd worry about that when the time came. For now, she had to pick her moment.

She braced herself, body tensing in anticipation. The horse slowed a little more.

A hitch. That's all she needed—something to throw them a little off balance.

Her heart pounded. She might die doing this, either during or after, when Tehrazzi caught her. For a moment she tipped her head back to gaze up at the lightening sky. The last stars were fading into the sea of indigo. She closed her eyes, took a deep breath.

I love you, Dec. Wherever you are.

The whine of an engine had her eyes snapping open. Tehrazzi twisted in the saddle. Her gaze went past him. A man was chasing them on a motorbike, gaining on them. Elation roared through her. Was it Dec? Hope flooded her.

Tehrazzi barked out a curse and swiveled back around, bending low over the horse's neck, pinning her harder between him and the animal. She fought not to shove at him.

Stay still. Don't tip him off you're going to try anything.

But then Tehrazzi tore the pistol from his waistband and aimed it behind him. He fired. The man on the bike ducked, swerved, but kept coming. Closer now. She saw his face.

"Luke!" she screamed, rearing up despite herself.

Tehrazzi shoved her down, kept firing.

Get him, Luke, shoot the bastard!

The horse stumbled, dropped its head. Tehrazzi let her go and grabbed at its mane to hold his seat.

Now!

She smashed him in the ribs as hard as she could with her elbow and twisted to one side, shoving with her feet. She tipped over the side, head bouncing off the horse's shoulder, and hit the ground so hard she almost blacked out. She rolled with the momentum, tried to dig her feet into the ground to slow herself, but she flipped over and skidded down a bank. Below her, the hill dropped away in a sheer cliff.

Crying out, she grabbed desperately at the rocks, but her bound wrists made it impossible to get a good grip. Her shoulder slammed into a boulder, and she screamed at the pain rocketing up her arm. Her numb fingers scrabbled over the bank as she dropped, and then caught a ledge of rock.

Shaking and gasping as her feet hit something hard, she pushed with all her might to stop her descent. The muscles in her arms screamed from holding her up. Her gaze strayed to the empty void beneath her.

Drawing a terrified breath, she screamed Luke's name.

****

Luke swore as Bryn tumbled off the horse and rolled out of sight. Tehrazzi kept running that damn horse, firing random shots at him.

"*Luke!*"

He heard the raw terror in her voice as she screamed his name from somewhere down the hill. Shit. He was within range of Tehrazzi now. He could pick him off with his rifle if the ground stayed level and the horse didn't drop out of view.

Not good enough. He had to get closer.

"*Help me!*"

He gritted his teeth at the panic in her voice. She must be in trouble.

Can't stop. He had to get Tehrazzi first. He reached back and drew his rifle around. His fingers tightened on the stock. His heart thundered in his ringing ears.

"Oh God, I'm *slipping!*" A hair-raising scream followed.

Christ. He had to help her. He'd pull her up, then get Tehrazzi.

He raced up to where her skid marks ran over the side and dumped the bike. Then his gaze locked on the spot between Tehrazzi's shoulder blades before he disappeared into a gulley.

Dammit, I should have taken the shot.

"*Luke!*"

"Hold on," he shouted, sliding in the dirt to her position. She was hanging by her fingernails on the side of the cliff.

Shit. It was going to take him minutes he didn't have to climb down and pull her out. But if she lost her grip, she'd fall to her death on the rocks below. For an instant, he hesitated.

Tehrazzi was more important. Getting him would save countless lives. It would absolve so many of Luke's sins.

Redemption. Just over the next rise.

But Bryn is Rayne's best friend. Emily loves her. If you let her die...

Bryn stared back at him with terrified obsidian eyes. "Luke, help me! I can't hold on—"

If he didn't save her, he'd never be able to look his son in the eye again.

You know what you have to do.

Yeah, he did.

"I'm coming," he said, and started hiking down. Her taped hands were white from clinging to the ledge, her mouth trembling. "Just a little more, Bryn. Hold on. Almost there."

His head swam as he slipped, and fell back against the bank. Tehrazzi was gaining distance on him with every second. The Iranian border was close. Luke had to get him before he reached it. If he got Bryn out quick enough, he still might be able to catch up with him. He'd order a helo to pick them up, find Tehrazzi from the air. He could pick him off that way.

Hurry.

Holding onto a boulder with one hand, he reached down with the other and seized her bound wrists, hauled up with all his might. Black spots swam in front of his eyes. His knees wobbled. "Push," he snarled, straining up.

She shoved with her feet and scrambled up, gaining purchase on a more secure spot. He pulled steadily upward, keeping his weight leaning uphill to counterbalance them, and dug his heels into the ground for more power.

Through the muffled rattle of gunfire from the battle at the camp, the faint throb of rotors reached him. The sound was coming from the other direction. He froze for an instant. Fuck, if Tehrazzi had gotten a ride—

Get Bryn on solid ground first. Then you can go after him.

He almost howled with frustration. Lips compressed with irritation, Luke inched them back up the side of the hill, dragged her over the edge. She collapsed on her belly with a sob.

The sounds of the distant battle had stopped. The camp and Tehrazzi's followers had been destroyed.

On his knees staring up at the pre-dawn sky, his disbelieving gaze fell on the helo, moving away, dropping into a canyon. Russian. Probably left over from the Afghan war. The war in which he'd made Tehrazzi into the monster he was.

His hands squeezed into fists so tight his knuckles ached.

The helo disappeared from view, no doubt on its way to pick up Tehrazzi.

He eyed the motorbike, lying on its side in the sand. No way would he get within rifle range in time on that thing. He wanted to bellow with rage.

"Fuck," he growled instead and ripped out his knife, slicing through the tape on Bryn's hands and feet. She flinched and fell as she tried to stand. He shot out a hand to steady her.

As the whir of rotors suddenly became clearer, he glanced up. Backlit by the first golden rays of dawn as the sun peaked over the hills, the Russian-made Hind-D rose into the clear sky and banked away, carrying Tehrazzi out of reach, into Iranian airspace where he could never follow.

****

Bryn threw herself into Luke's arms, uncaring that he was so focused on the helicopter. Tehrazzi had escaped, but she was alive, thanks to Luke. A sob shot free. She squeezed her eyes shut and clenched fistfuls of his jacket.

He pressed her face against his chest. "You're okay now. You're okay."

Her muscles trembled. She took a breath and let go. He started to get up, but winced and went back down on his knees. "Y-you're hurt," she said.

"Banged my head is all." He shook it as though trying to clear it and blinked a few times.

She was still shaking all over, but managed to stand and help him up. The way he wove on his feet alarmed her. What if Tehrazzi came back to strafe them from the helicopter? "W-we should move."

"Yeah." He fiddled in his pocket, pulled out his earpiece, called someone to arrange for pickup and let out a tired sigh. He lowered his head a moment, rubbed his eyes. He swayed a bit, didn't protest when she put an arm around his waist.

He paused a moment, listening, his eyes on the

sand bathed in the orange glow of the rising sun. "Copy that." His eyes swung to hers. "Chopper's on its way."

She couldn't wait to get the hell out of there. They started walking, both of them unsteady on their feet. "Where's Dec?" she finally asked.

Luke hesitated.

Her heart slammed against her ribs like a sledgehammer. Oh God, not Dec. Not Dec. Her legs were stiff and awkward. "What's happened?" she demanded, her knees wobbling. "What's—"

"He's been wounded. They extracted him, but the chopper went down."

Her world caved in. "What?" The beat of another inbound helicopter broke the silence.

"He's being transferred to the hospital right now."

The words penetrated. Wounded, he'd said. Still alive, then. Her legs gave out.

The rotors whirred, louder and louder, kicking the sand into a whirling cloud that beat against her. She bit down on her lip. How bad was he? The aircraft settled on the ground, and she and Luke climbed in.

She clutched the seat with sweaty hands as it lifted off and soared them through the air. Across from her, Luke dropped his head back against the bulkhead and closed his eyes. He'd just lost Tehrazzi. She might have cared more if she wasn't so terrified for Dec.

They flew toward a city, passed over a river and over the houses and buildings. When the helo descended she saw the H on the helipad. The hospital. Was Dec here? She jumped out and followed Luke inside, through the corridors and down the stairs.

He stopped a nurse and conversed with her in Arabic. He took Bryn's arm. "In here."

He ushered her to the emergency ward just as the door burst open. The paramedics rushed the first patient in. Another stretcher followed, the man strapped to a backboard, his head bound with crimson-stained bandages.

Oh God.

Rhys appeared, pushing a stretcher, a bag of IV fluid held in his teeth. A medic straddled the patient's torso, holding an oxygen mask over his face. Blood soaked the right side of the stretcher and dripped onto the floor. The patient had dark hair, and a crescent-shaped scar on the back of his left hand.

"Dec!"

Nobody stopped her as she raced over to him.

"Dec—" Her voice cracked. The smell of his blood hung in the air as she put a hand against his pale cheek. He was conscious, but not alert, his eyelashes fluttering when she spoke. She could hardly see, the tears were falling so fast. "Dec, can you hear me?" She stroked the sweat-matted hair off his forehead.

His lashes fluttered again and his eyes opened, focusing on her. He moaned, his limbs thrashing weakly.

"Take this," Rhys ordered, shoving the IV bag into her hand, "but get the hell back when I tell you to."

"We need to sedate him to get the chest tube in," the medic said, still holding the mask in place.

Dec struggled beneath the man holding him down, hoarse cries of agony tearing from him.

"I'm here, Dec," she whispered, barely intelligible. He was in this state because of her. "I'm right here and I love you. I *love* you, you hear me? Don't let go. You're no quitter, Dec, you don't know how to quit, remember?" She prayed he could hear her.

They pushed through a set of double doors and

someone grabbed the bag from her. Strong hands pulled her back.

"No!"

"Bryn," Rhys warned, "let go of him. Now."

She struggled uselessly. "Get your hands off—"

He shook her hard, whipped her around to face him. "He needs surgery. Right now, and you can't be in here."

"Move back please, miss, and let us do our job," the medic ordered.

Helpless, she obeyed, her eyes never leaving Dec. His whole body shook, the muscles in his legs and arms straining as the medic exposed the blood-soaked dressings covering the right side of his chest. His head wrenched to the side and his face contorted beneath the oxygen mask. He jerked like he'd been electrocuted.

His howl of inhuman agony seared her soul.

"Dec," she sobbed, screaming inside.

"Let's go." Rhys picked her up by the waist and hauled her out of there. He set her in a chair and she went into his arms without a word. "Hang in there," he murmured against the top of her head, and kept talking, explaining what had happened.

She fell apart, too lost in her grief to make out more than Dec had a collapsed lung and had lost a lot of blood. They had to insert a tube to drain the lung and re-inflate it to help him breathe better. Whatever hit him shattered some of his ribs—that's what punctured his lung, and why he was bleeding so much.

She shut her eyes, praying harder than she'd prayed for anything in her life. *Please God, let him make it.*

Chapter Twenty-One

Day 13, Somewhere in Iran

Rays of sunlight slanted through the curtains behind Tehrazzi as he finished his morning prayers. The room was already stifling, the ceiling fan doing little but moving the hot air around. Perspiration beaded his face and throat, trickled down his back and sides as he knelt in place. His muscles cramped from staying in the same position for so long.

He was ready.

Rising on stiff legs, he padded over to the table and took up the white robes he had selected for his sacred purpose. He donned them slowly, frowning at the way his fingers trembled. How could he be afraid?

After all this time, surely he was not afraid of death. He'd escaped his teacher again. First at the club in Damascus, then the night of the air strike near Najaf, and today. Once again, Allah had chosen to spare his life. Such a gift deserved repaying that debt. To do His work, he must be calm, utterly uninhibited by the bonds of mortal fear. He was a soldier for his people, and for Allah.

Smoothing the flowing garment over his strangely chilled body, he strode to the video camera resting on its tripod and checked it was working properly. After pressing record he seated himself in front of the green martyr's flag he'd hung.

Staring at the blinking red light, his eyes felt uncomfortably dry, his skin too tight. Clenching his hands in his lap, he released a slow exhalation and looked directly into the dark, round lens.

"My name is Farouk Ahmed Tehrazzi," he began in Arabic, his voice soft and clear. As he spoke, the weight in his chest lifted, as if someone had reached inside and filled his lungs with sweet, clean air. His heart beat in a steady rhythm.

"I am a soldier of Islam, a crusader against the invading American infidels and all who sully the name of Islam. The time has come for me to announce my intention to continue the jihad against our enemies. But now I commit myself to the higher purpose Allah has called me to. I am ready to sacrifice this life in the name of holy war, and will embrace the glories of the afterlife without hesitation. Allah willing, we will rid the earth of the American people and their allies. I pray that my sacrifice will please Him, and that He will reward our struggle here on earth." Keeping calm, he added, "I speak to those who have taught me." He got up and switched off the camera.

Hands steady, he removed the recording from the machine, wrapped it in a piece of red cloth and placed it in the envelope he had prepared. Then he sealed it, his tongue lingering on the unpleasant adhesive.

When he emerged, the three men seated in the next room gaped at him, the gravity of the white robes registering. One by one, they bowed reverently, then cheered.

Ignoring their praise, he passed one of them the envelope. "See that this is delivered today."

"Yes, of course."

Turning away, Tehrazzi wished he could witness his teacher's reaction to the message. He would know exactly what it meant.

The game was not over yet. The only way to finish it was for one, or both of them, to die.

****

Day 13, Basra hospital
Morning

Battling the wave of dizziness that had him all but planting his ass on the floor, Luke forced his legs to take him to the chair next to the window. The staff had insisted he stay here for tests because his symptoms had worsened over the past few hours.

By the time he got to the window he wanted to puke up the lime Jell-O they'd forced down him and only kept it in his gut through sheer willpower. When his knees grew too wobbly to support his weight, he allowed himself to sink into the chair. Breathing through his nose to dispel the nausea, he groped on the table for his cell phone.

The staff hadn't taken kindly to him making phone calls between his MRI and CT scan. Still, he'd managed to make sure the CIA got Bryn out of Iraq while McCabe was in recovery. Not a mean feat while dealing with a severe concussion. Now all he had to do was find out where in the hell Tehrazzi was so he could finish this thing and be done with it. He'd been so goddamn close today.

He still couldn't remember everything that had happened out there. He had blank spots about events before the friendly fire incident. The idea that he might have suffered permanent brain damage and memory loss scared him worse than dying.

Dialing Ben, he saw he'd missed a call during the night. Squinting to counteract his blurred vision, he brought up the call display. The number seemed vaguely familiar to him. He struggled to figure it out, hating how slow his brain was working. After a few minutes he still had no idea who had called him, so he punched the call back button and brought the phone to his ear.

Three rings went by. Four. Then someone answered. "Hello?"

He went rigid in his chair as the gentle voice hit him like a body blow. No matter how messed up his squash was, he would never forget that voice. "Em," he croaked.

"Luke?" Her voice turned sharp. "You sound awful—are you hurt?"

"I..." Hearing her on the other end of the phone hurt him more than the knives stabbing in his skull.

"What's happened? Are you okay?"

"I'm fine," he lied. "Little banged up is all."

"God, Luke you must be more than banged up if you called me."

Yeah. He'd lost his mind. Literally.

"What can I do? Do you need me to fly over there?"

Oh, sweet Jesus, he wanted that. Wanted it so bad he broke out in a sweat at the thought of seeing her. His stomach spasmed. The muscles under his jaw tightened, the salivary glands going into overdrive. He gagged. Oh, shit, he hated throwing up. He fought it back, took a deep breath. Then another. "No, Em, I'm...I'm—" *Going to puke.*

He dropped the phone in his lap and yanked a plastic pitcher from the table just as his stomach heaved up his pathetic breakfast in wrenching spasms. His head almost split open from the pain and for a moment his vision went dark. When he could see again his cheek was resting on the windowsill. His body trembled as he tried to sit up.

"Luke! Luke? Are you there?"

Ah, shit, had she heard him? Fumbling in the folds of his hospital gown, he found the phone again. "I'm okay." His voice sounded like grinding gears.

Her voice fragmented into tears. "Oh, God—"

"Don't cry." His stomach twisted in misery.

329

Saliva pooled in his mouth. God, he was going to hurl again. "Gotta go, Em. I love you."

He pitched the phone on the floor and doubled over as a wave of sickness overcame him. This time he blacked out. When he came to, a nurse was leaning over him, her face a mask of concern as she and someone else lifted him into bed as if he was a child.

Lying there against the hard pillow, he tried to remember what had just happened. He'd been talking on the phone, hadn't he? Oh God, yeah, he'd been talking to Emily. He'd thrown up, and then—

His eyes closed on a hard sigh. Shit, he'd just told her he loved her, hadn't he?

Calling himself fifty kinds of stupid, he gathered himself, relieved when he opened his eyes the third time and the room wasn't spinning. Encouraged, he fumbled for the remote control on the bed and inched his upper body higher.

Halfway to a seated position a blinding pain sliced through his skull and he stopped, panting and sweating, refusing to lie back down. He'd survived severe injuries before. He'd get over this one, too.

He'd never been this bad before, though.

Fuck. He hated being laid up like a pansy over a goddamn concussion. Especially when Tehrazzi was out there somewhere, still breathing.

At a knock on the door, he forced his fuzzy eyes open and saw Ben.

"Hey," Ben said, stopping at the foot of his bed, chewing on his gum. "You gonna make it or what?"

Luke grunted, wished he didn't have to talk at all. "I'm too mean to die."

A grudging smile broke over the hard face. "You'll live to be a hundred then."

No thanks. So long as he took Tehrazzi with him, he'd gladly go now, become a nameless star on the wall at headquarters back in Langley. "Any news?"

"Nope. So far as anyone can tell he's still in Iran."

Yeah, where they couldn't get to him. Dammit! They'd been so close. "What about the others?"

Ben shoved his hands into his pockets. "Two dead, one other wounded besides you and Dec. They've stabilized him. Might send him stateside. Bryn's on her way there now."

Luke grunted. "Glad they're okay." He noted the antsy way Ben kept shifting his weight, thought he might know the reason. "How's Rhys?"

"Good. He's good. It's uh...it's Sam I'm worried about."

Sam? Who the hell was Sam?

He couldn't remember, drew an absolute blank.

Clammy sweat gathered on his brow as he fought the rising panic. Jesus, he couldn't remember who Sam was. He broke eye contact with Ben.

Christ, *did* he have brain damage?

"Yeah, so since you're laid up here, do you want me and Rhys to look into it? Figured you'd want someone on it ASAP, since she could be involved in all of this."

She. So Sam was a woman? He still couldn't picture her. Couldn't remember anything about her or why Ben thought she might be involved. What the hell else was missing?

"And if she isn't, then she's up to her pretty little ass in alligators right now."

Stay tight. He doesn't need to know anything's wrong with you.

Luke met the pale green stare and forced himself to appear calm even though he was losing it. "Get on it right away."

When he was alone, he fell back against the pillow. Squeezing his eyes shut, he rubbed a shaking hand over his face. Christ. What the hell was

331

happening to him?

Chapter Twenty-Two

Day 20, Lincoln City, Oregon

Bryn watched the waves pound the shore from the top of her back steps. Chin on her up-drawn knees, she stared out across the restless ocean to the purple horizon beyond it. She closed her eyes and breathed deeply of the damp, salty air, letting the rhythmic crash of the tide carry her away. The cold breeze whipped through her hair in a cleansing rush.

She'd been home for two days now. When Rhys had torn her out of the hospital and handed her over to her CIA security detail, they'd taken her straight to the airport and put her on a plane back to the States. She'd spent three days being debriefed and assessed at CIA headquarters in Langley to see if they could cobble together anything they'd missed using her information about Tehrazzi. After that ordeal, they'd finally allowed her a day to visit her mother and stepfather before flying home to Oregon.

She was exhausted. She'd hardly slept since coming home, barely eaten other than the meals her CIA-appointed bodyguard shoved in front of her. Her body went through the mechanical process of living, but she didn't feel alive.

She didn't know much more than when she'd left Iraq, but at least she'd found out Dec was stable and being transferred somewhere. She'd begged them for more, but they wouldn't tell her where he'd been sent. Luke's head injury had landed him in the same Basra hospital Dec had been in, where he was undergoing all sorts of tests. Rumor was he wasn't happy about it.

The twins were with Davis in Baghdad following up on Sam's disappearance. Fahdi was locked up in prison there. His betrayal still stung. He'd killed Ali, sent those men to grab her, put her though hell in Tehrazzi's camp. Dec had almost died because of him. Some of his teammates had.

And Tehrazzi...he was out there somewhere, maybe Iran or Afghanistan. That's why she had round the clock security. The CIA didn't consider her safe in her own home while he was still at large. In the morning, they were moving her to a "more secure location." Wherever that was. She didn't think she'd feel safe anywhere while he was loose.

Her thoughts went back to Dec. She wished he could stay with her instead of her current bodyguard, but he was recuperating and she didn't have a clue where he was. What did stable mean, anyhow? That he was breathing on his own? That he wasn't in imminent danger of dying?

Every time she thought of him writhing on that gurney with that agonized expression, she felt sick. She'd been helpless to ease his pain and distress. She didn't even know if he'd been aware of her standing beside him. He'd suffered because of her. Had almost died trying to get her out.

She blew out a breath to ease the ache in her chest. She'd tried to get word to him, to tell him she loved him and would jump on the first plane out if he wanted to see her. But she hadn't heard a word in the last week. Had he even received the message? What if he thought she'd up and abandoned him while he was in the hospital?

No. He was smarter than that. He had to know she'd have stayed if she could have. And with the amount of debriefing she'd gone through, his would be even more intensive. Maybe that's why he hadn't been able to contact her yet.

If and when he did, they had lots to sort out. For starters, they needed to find out if they had what it took to make a relationship work. Their time together had been spent in a daze of adrenaline and heightened emotion.

What would they be like together back in the real world where they weren't in life threatening situations every day? On the plus side, they did have common interests. She trusted him implicitly. Felt safe with him. She knew he would look after her, no matter what. He was dependable and solid.

She thought of how considerate and tender he'd been with her, of how protective he was. He'd be an incredible father someday.

But if he recovered to the extent he could remain on active duty, could she handle it? She didn't want to repeat the mistakes Luke and Emily had made.

How the hell could she go through life knowing that if she lost the man she loved, she'd shrivel up and die? How did people cope with a love that strong? And how could she suffer this kind of worry if he returned to the job? She remembered her sharp words to Spencer about his wife, that she should have stuck by him.

Bryn felt that way more than ever, but now she had experienced what it would be like to never know where Dec was, or if he was all right. She'd had a firsthand taste of what it was like for him in the field. Could she take a lifetime of worry every time he went to work?

If she wanted him, she'd have to. And look what she'd already survived. She was strong enough to handle it, and she wanted a future with him enough to go through all that. Having him was worth the risk of losing him.

Her eyes flew open as her front door opened and

shut. Must be her bodyguard, coming to say her ten minutes outside were up.

Pushing to her feet, she opened the old-fashioned screen door. Stepping inside out of the wind, she let it slap closed behind her. She glanced around for him.

"I sent him out for a while."

She whirled around and froze.

Golden eyes stared back at her from the kitchen doorway, a pair of dimples appearing in that lean face as he smiled.

****

Dec's heart thudded in his chest as her hands flew to her mouth, tears springing into her eyes.

"Dec."

"Hey, beautiful."

She raced over and grabbed him, crying. He groaned and held her tight, ignoring the stab of pain in his side. Her tears wet his shirt as she clung to him, burying her face in his chest. Damn it felt incredible to hold her again.

Dec pressed his face against her silky hair and breathed her in. He could hardly believe she was safe in his arms.

God, the guilt still almost smothered him. He never should have left her at Fahdi's. He'd known it, but left her alone anyway. And then he'd failed to get her out of Tehrazzi's camp. He'd been so afraid she'd blame him for all she'd suffered that hellish night.

He'd never let her down again.

Bryn raised wet eyes to his. "I can't believe it." She ran her gaze over him and laid a hand on his injured right side. "Are you okay?"

She looked amazing. "A little sore, but yeah. It looks worse than it feels."

"Oh, God, I'm so glad you're okay. Every time I

thought of you almost dying because of me—"

He laid his fingers over her lips. "If I had to, I'd do it all a hundred times over." He'd do it all again, in a heartbeat. Nothing he wouldn't do to keep her safe.

Her teary smile turned his heart over. "They wouldn't tell me anything. I tried to get a message to you but..."

"It's okay, baby. I would've contacted you sooner, but they just cleared me from debriefing this morning. I'm sorry you were so worried."

She sighed and turned her cheek into his palm. "What are you doing here, anyway?"

He stroked her hair. "I came to get you."

"Get me?" Her face fell. "But they're taking me to a safe house tomorrow—"

"Yeah. My place, in Montana." He wanted time alone with her, so he could reinforce the bond between them. He didn't know what the future held for them, or if he would return to his team when he was fully recovered. Maybe he'd do private contracting. Maybe even with Luke. He hadn't made any final decisions yet.

All he knew was, he wanted her. If she couldn't handle him going back to the Teams and he had to choose between the two, she'd win hands down.

More tears sparkled in her eyes. "Really?"

He kissed her, couldn't resist any longer. "Yeah. That okay with you?"

"God, yes." She pressed her lips to his and slid her fingers into his hair.

He caught her face and pulled back. "There's something else I wanted to tell you."

She blinked. "What?"

He gazed deep into her eyes. Almost choked up. "I love you too."

She smiled. "You heard me."

"Yes." Her voice had penetrated the fog of pain.

That's why he'd held on. To be with her. "But tell me again."

"I love you," she said without hesitation.

His heart swelled, his lungs expanding until they pulled at his sore ribs. He kissed her, slid his tongue past her lips when she opened, his whole body taut with need. Bryn flattened herself against him, taking him deeper as her hands coasted over him, under his shirt.

He peeled it over his head, winced as his healing ribs protested. She gasped at the bruises and scars marring his skin.

"I'm fine," he said. "Really."

She touched a fingertip to the puncture wound where they'd put the chest tube in and bent to kiss it gently, then the surgical scar where they'd gone in to remove splinters of his ribs from his lung and chest wall.

He closed his eyes. Her lips caressed every mark as though trying to heal him. He took her face in his hands, lowering his head to kiss her. Hard. She responded with a moan and maneuvered them down the hall without breaking the kiss. She pulled him into the bedroom and they pulled off their clothes.

He settled her against the pillows. "You're so beautiful," he whispered, nudging her thighs apart and covering her with his body. He shuddered at the feel of her, firm, yet unbelievably soft.

Bryn murmured in pleasure and enveloped him with her limbs. The touch of her mouth on his lit him up like a match strike. Her hands buried deep in his hair, fingers tightening on the strands with a delicious pull. "Come inside me."

"Not yet." He'd spent the past six days thinking about this moment. Being with her now was a precious gift, one he wasn't going to waste, no matter how sore he was. Tonight he was going to savor her the way he should have the first time. The way he would have if things had been different for them. This time he was going to go so slowly, to show her how much he loved her.

He covered her face with reverent kisses, down her throat, lingering at the spots that made her gasp.

Smoothing his cheek over the slope of one breast, he enjoyed the incredible texture of her skin. Then he took the sensitive tip into his mouth and sucked until she thrashed. Her fingers wound into his hair as her spine curled, lifting toward him. He made love to her breasts until he had her whimpering.

He felt every shift of her body, noticed every change in her breathing when he found a place that gave her pleasure. The feel of her, all sexy, sleek muscles beneath velvety soft skin, made him rock hard. She moved like liquid beneath him, smooth and flowing in her response. She was relaxed, trusting him. He liked that best of all.

His hands led his mouth to the flat expanse of her belly, drawn to the jewels dangling from her navel. She hissed out a breath when he nuzzled her abs.

"Dec," she whispered.

He rested his cheek against her, his hands coasting up her thighs, stopping short of where they both wanted them.

A tremor rippled through her. "Hurry."

He shook his head, battling the need to devour her. As his fingers trailed lightly over the folds between her legs, she let out an incredible moan.

"Dec—"

"Shh. Let me please you. Slowly this time."

She shuddered in his grasp, fingers digging into his biceps. "I..."

He leaned down and kissed her there, loving her desperate cry, the way she strained upward. Holding her hips, he lapped at her softest flesh.

"*Declan.*"

God, that low, sexy moan she made in the back of her throat. He could do this all day. She was so soft. So sensitive. So desperate for him.

She lifted her head to gaze down at him, eyes glazed. "Please," she begged, trembling.

Yes. Anything she wanted from him. He sucked her clit with exquisite gentleness, shuddering at her strangled groan. More. He needed more. Dec couldn't get enough of her. He wanted this to last so they'd both remember it forever.

Her hips jacked up off the bed, her hands gripping his head as she cried out hoarsely. "Now, quick…"

He took the condom from her, smoothed it on and drove into her. She cried out. He gasped at the feel of her body enveloping him. God, he needed her. "I love you."

Braced on one arm, he slid his free hand down to caress between her thighs as he pumped his hips. Steady, sure. He watched her face. She made a mewling sound and torqued her head back, her lips parting in ecstasy as she came.

She was the most gorgeous thing he'd ever seen.

Dec pressed his face against her hair and let himself go, savoring how tightly she held him. The orgasm pulsed through him, endless and powerful. Finally he dropped his head onto the pillow beside hers, tried to get his breath back.

His ribs were killing him, but he didn't care. He lay in her arms, enjoying the feel of her hands caressing his back. He'd never been so happy in his life. Never felt so at peace. When he raised his head, her eyes were brimming with amusement.

He couldn't help but smile. "What?"

"Just because I let you seduce me right now doesn't mean I've forgotten your promise."

"What promise?"

She tapped his chest with her forefinger. "You owe me a date, buddy. A steak, I believe it was. And a movie and a walk on the beach. I don't care which order we do them in."

He grinned. "Then what?"

"Then I'm going to wait on you hand and foot. I'll fluff your pillows, spoon feed you, massage all your sore spots...and maybe some that aren't."

He grimaced as his chest vibrated. "Don't make me laugh," he gasped, his ribs searing, already hurting from making love to her.

"Okay, no laughing. But smiling's okay, right? I bet I could put a great big smile on your face...if I danced for you."

Christ. That might kill him. "Bryn," he warned, trying not to laugh. "Stop."

She kissed him. "Just trying to give you some incentive to finish healing."

He curved his hand around the back of her neck and gazed straight into her eyes. "Only incentive I need is you."

Her eyes misted over. "You've already got me. For as long as you want."

"Yeah? I won't let you go, then."

She laughed, leaned up to kiss him. "Dec, you couldn't get rid of me if you tried."

—The End—

A word about the author...

New York Times and USA Today Bestselling author Kaylea Cross writes edge-of-your-seat military romantic suspense. Her work has won many awards and has been nominated for both the Daphne du Maurier and the National Readers' Choice Awards. A Registered Massage Therapist by trade, Kaylea is also an avid gardener, artist, Civil War buff, Special Ops aficionado, belly dance enthusiast and former nationally-carded softball pitcher. She lives in Vancouver, BC with her husband and sons.

Visit Kaylea at www.kayleacross.com

Newsletter: http://kayleacross.com/v2/contact/